Other titles by Isla Dewar:

IZZY'S

Izzy's War

Isla Dewar

EBURY
PRESS

1 3 5 7 9 10 8 6 4 2

Published in 2010 by Ebury Press, an imprint of Ebury Publishing

A Random House Group Company

Copyright © Isla Dewar 2010

Isla Dewar has asserted his right to be identified as the author of this work
under the Copyright, Designs and Patents Act 1988.

The Random House Group Limited Reg. No. 954009

Addresses for companies within the Random House Group can be found at
www.randomhouse.co.uk

A CIP catalogue record for this book is available from the British Library

The Random House Group Limited makes every effort to ensure that the
papers used in our books are made from trees that have been legally sourced
from well-managed and credibly certified forests. Our paper procurement
policy can be found on www.randomhouse.co.uk

Printed and bound in Great Britain by Clays Ltd, St Ives PLC

ISBN 9780091938123

To buy books by your favourite authors and register for offers visit
www.rbooks.co.uk

To Sri with love and thanks for loving Nick

Chapter One
Three Women Cycling to Work

There was rapture in Izzy's life. It came when she was flying, when she had such a view – God's view, her father called it. Well, he would. She thought she could write a book about the things she'd seen from above: herds of deer, hundreds of them rippling across hilltops. She saw houses, gardens; washing flapping on the line; people small as matchstick men, moving through streets and stopping, sometimes, to look up at her hovering above them, and point. Once, she'd seen a couple entangled in their own not-as-private-as-they-thought rapture on a sun-soaked moor. She saw the shape and glide of rivers, was shoulder to shoulder with mountains. It took her breath away. She was addicted to the air. Removed from earthly worries and demands, she was truly happy.

It had been her friend Elspeth's idea to learn to fly. Such a fashionable thing to do, 'Women are taking to the sky,' she'd said. 'They are the new adventurers. Flying to Australia, across the Sahara, looking for a new kind of romance.' Elspeth had taken lessons, Izzy watched. Then, unable to resist, had taken it up, too. She had never been ambitious. Had no desire to become a new adventurer, cruising the heavens was joyful enough.

In time, Elspeth had moved on to new pursuits. She abandoned flying when she became obsessed with her new accordion.

She dreamed of forming an all-woman accordion band that toured the country playing wild, stomping music. But then, Hitler invaded Poland and ambitions were abandoned, everything changed.

Izzy's felt that rapture, though it was a lesser joy, every morning when she cycled with Julia and Claire to work. Pushing through the morning contemplating the possibilities of the day ahead. Where she might fly to, and in what?

It was always the same, the rattle of bikes and the hum of tyres, hissing today over the glistening November frost, thick over everything, a stiff sparkle. A lone crow in the field beyond the hedge hopped over hardened ground. Above, a scattering of seagulls silently cruised the still air. Right now, apart from them, the sky was empty.

The bus had passed five minutes ago. Everyone on-board banged on the window, waved and mocked the three cycling. They were late. When were they not?

It was a problem, three women sharing a cramped cottage with one tiny bathroom. Mornings were a flurry. Downstairs, in the kitchen, the kettle would be coming to the boil, quietly steaming and singing, the wireless would be on. Upstairs, Julia and Claire, in their silk dressing gowns, getting ready to face the day, jostled in and out of the bathroom, bumped into one another and did polite sidestepping dances in the narrow hallway.

Izzy always made porridge first thing, standing by the stove wrapped in a voluminous thick flannel tartan robe, tied firmly round her waist with a bright red cord. It was an embarrassing garment, she knew, but comfortable and comforting. A gift from her mother and, indeed, exactly the sort of thing her mother would deem an ideal and useful thing to own. Izzy couldn't deny its warmth, and often, on the winter nights when three thin blankets did little to stave off the cold, she slept in it.

They were all used to having space. Claire and Julia had grown up in large country mansions, Izzy a manse. They were also, all of them, used to working alone. They couldn't share a kitchen. They clattered, banged, spilled tea and burned toast. And bumped into one another. Izzy was always surprised when the others refused a share of her porridge.

Claire and Julia would sit at the table, eating charred toast, drinking weak tea. Neither of them could cook. Izzy would eat leaning against the sink, saying this was the way to eat porridge. 'It's to be taken standing up.' When the weather report came on they'd fall silent and listen. Weather was important to them.

While Julia put on a fresh layer of lipstick, Izzy would run upstairs, wash in tepid water, run her fingers through her hair – a thick black curly mass – and put on her uniform. Then they'd bustle out into the day, leaving damp towels lying on the bathroom floor, beds unmade and the kitchen in chaos. At nine o'clock Mrs Brent would come in and clean it all up.

Today had been worse than usual because the Pole had been there. Jacob, one of Julia's waifs – she'd met him the night before – had sat silently, watching. His only comment was a surprised, 'You fly?' when Izzy had pulled back the curtain, pressed her head against the window and said that it was a good flying day. She had nodded, and he'd nodded back. And smiled. This had surprised Izzy. Often, when she told people, especially male people, what she did, they didn't believe her.

Still, Jacob's presence, his bulk, his stillness, the quiet way he drank his tea, made the three feel uncomfortable. They were glad to get away.

'It's been lovely to meet you,' Julia had said. 'Please shut the door behind you when you leave.'

They had collected their bikes from the side of the cottage and cycled off. Only Izzy turned to wave goodbye.

Julia cycled up front, her usual place, face into the breeze, shouting about the temperature. 'Bloody, bloody cold. I hate it.' She sat upright in her saddle, her face flushed with chill. Her coat flapped at her thighs, revealing fleeting flashes of scarlet lining.

This lining was not, strictly speaking, part of the Air Auxiliary uniform. It was her own little flamboyance. She never could resist a little bit of scarlet silk.

When she'd first joined the ferry fleet, Julia had loved the thought of being in uniform, especially one that was blue with gold bars. She'd been so tickled, she'd had one specially made up for her by her father's Savile Row tailor. The resulting outfit was not quite the chic ensemble she'd hoped for.

The gentlemen who'd measured her had never measured a woman before and the business with the measuring tape and where it had to go had made their cheeks redden. They'd coughed a lot. They had left some distance between the tape and Julia's body when measuring any sensitive area. Their recordings of Julia's bust size and inside leg length were wildly inaccurate.

The result of all this was that Julia's jacket was lumpily generous from shoulder to waist and baggy at her rear. She was always hitching up her trousers. She worried about them falling down. In fact, it bothered her a lot that if ever she got into difficulties when flying and had to bail out, her trousers might slip past her knees as she parachuted to the ground. And if she landed badly, and died, she'd be found in a tangled heap, trousers round her ankles and flappy silk knickers made from old parachutes in full view.

Pedalling along now, her breath steamed short bursts of vapour before her as she spoke. And really her complaint about the cold was half-hearted. This morning, she was happy.

Izzy envied her. She wanted to be Julia – crisp bobbed hair and scarlet lips. Julia didn't walk through life, she bounced; she always drew a crowd. Evenings, she never stayed in.

Last night she'd eaten at Bertram's, a small, dingy place in Blackpool. No, it wasn't a place. It was a joint, a dive. She loved it. It had been busy, smoky, noisy, filled with the clamour of swaggering voices. In the corner a wind-up gramophone played Billie Holiday records that some GIs at the next table had brought with them. Billie crooned silkily about the glorious and exciting things a little moonlight could do. Oooh, it was wonderful.

Julia had been with Charles, her number-one boyfriend – she called them her beaux – and the only young man she knew who wasn't in the RAF. He'd joined the Royal Artillery – mostly, Julia thought, to annoy his family. His father had flown in the First World War, and now both his brothers were pilots.

Charles had brought along Jacob, a morose Pole he'd met on the train. Charles was always taking strangers under his wing. The Pole, however, hardly spoke, but tapped his fingers on the side of his whisky glass in time to the music.

Charles and Julia had laughed, smoked, drunk too much, swapped favourite stories, toasted absent friends and tried not to mention the awfulness of the ragout they'd ordered.

Julia said she'd heard that the food there had always been pretty bad. 'So in a way, it's comforting to find something that hasn't been changed by the war.'

Charles said that was one way to look at it.

Julia told him not to think about it. 'Just eat it. One just can't think about what might be in things these days, darling. I've even heard of people eating guinea pigs. Yuck.' She made a face.

She had a habit of calling people darling. It was a word she liked, also it pleased her to note that it irritated the Pole. She'd started to dislike him.

Charles asked where Julia had been last night when he had phoned.

'You know better than to ask me that,' said Julia. 'But I was stuck out. Still, got back this afternoon. And here I am, darling.'

They never spoke in detail about where she'd been. Careless talk cost lives, everybody knew that – posters in the railway stations, messages on milk bottle tops.

Julia had often been 'stuck out'. She hated the frustration of finding herself caught at some distant airfield flunk-hole as fog deepened, impenetrable, dense, yellow. Often, she'd sat drinking thick stewed tea, watching the sky darken as delays kept her grounded, knowing she could not beat the sunset and she wouldn't have time to fly home before dark descended. There would be a blackout. From above you would hardly know there were houses, streets, pubs, cinemas and factories in the world below.

When she first started flying, it had been to take Tiger Moths and Puss Moths that had been requisitioned at the start of the war, but were now taking up valuable hangar space, north to Scotland. It had been winter and all the planes had open cockpits. She had never known cold like it. She'd worn several layers of jumpers under her flying suit, and a jacket under the flying jacket plus a couple of thick woollen scarves, and still the chill had bitten into her. Often, numb, rigid with cold, she'd hardly been able to move. Ground engineers had lifted her out of the cockpit. She'd felt her face frozen into a stiff macabre grin, a mix of shocked horror at the extreme chill she'd just experienced and relief that it was over.

The journey, technically, took just over four hours. But often the weather had closed in and she'd had to land to wait for it to clear. So, sometimes it took four days to fly from Southampton to Perth.

She had slept in strange small hotels, dormitories, in the huts of WAAF night operations officers whose beds were empty when they were on duty. These beds, only recently vacated, were often still warm. Once that would have appalled her, now it was a comfort.

She remembered nights spent on the train rumbling home to London. Hours and hours sitting on her hard parachute bag in a packed and noisy swarming corridor when there were no available seats, trying to sleep, jostled by loud bantering soldiers and airmen, none of them particularly sober, who smoked, sang and shoved past her.

Later, the ATA had sleeping cars set aside at the back of night trains. Then, she had been hauled from a deep and swaying sleep by gunfire or bombs as they chuntered through the Midlands. She'd leave the train at King's Cross, have breakfast, take another train back to Hatfield, where she was based, then start the whole gruelling trip over again, exposed to the elements in another frail and rickety Puss Moth.

Thinking about it now, humming through this icy but glorious morning, she wondered how she'd done all that without collapsing into an exhausted coma.

But, really, when she thought about it, how hellish it had been, she knew she wouldn't have missed any of it for the world.

She loved this life she was leading. Though now she was posted at Skimpton, it was mostly short flights, sometimes three or four a day. And it was usually Spitfires and Blenheims she flew. But once she was in the air, the decisions she made were hers alone. She was living, now, in the moment, no plans for the future. And, for the first time in her life, the money in her pocket was money she'd earned.

She sang as she rode along, joining Billie Holiday in her celebration of moonlight.

While Charles was her number-one beau, Jeffrey was number two. Her reserve lover, she thought. Though she hadn't seen Jeffrey in months, since he'd been posted to North Africa.

'Why two?' Izzy once asked. 'That's not very nice, two lovers. One of them is going to get hurt.'

'Both of them might get hurt,' Julia told her. 'They offset each other. Charles is rather moody but gorgeous to look at. Jeffrey is not so gorgeous, but he's fun. So I have a handsome lover and a fun lover. I have everything I want in a man from two men. And that stops me falling in love with either of them.'

'What's wrong with falling in love?' Izzy wanted to know. She had always thought falling in love was what every woman wanted to do. It was what life was about. Well, that was the message in all the songs she knew.

'Oh, darling,' said Julia. 'You don't want to go and fall in love. It will be the end of you. You fall in love, next thing you get married and once you're married your mother and his mother and probably the man himself will start wanting you to have children. So you have a baby. All you'll talk about is baby this and baby that and baby has its first tooth and baby smiled. And that's that. You'll never fly again. Oh no, darling, you must never let yourself fall in love. Just a little lust to keep you smiling is plenty.'

Last night she'd been angry at Charles for bringing the Pole with him. 'He's a gooseberry,' she'd hissed. 'I wanted to have you to myself.' She'd wanted to snuggle and kiss.

He'd told her not to be selfish. 'That man has been through hell, absolute hell. His wife is still in Poland. He has no idea what has happened to her. It's your duty to be kind to him. Besides, he's a stranger here. Knows nobody. And, he's starting work at your base. Be nice to him.'

Julia had hung her head, ashamed. 'I'll try.'

After the club, they had walked, arms linked, along the pier. Julia sang that Billie Holiday song, and broke her step from time to time with a little skip. Jacob had come with them. Though he didn't link arms, he walked behind, hands in his pockets. Julia thought he lumbered after them, like a huge stray dog. She still didn't like him, but now she felt guilty about it.

Thing was, she thought she'd seen him take the tip Charles had left for their waitress. It had been such a swift movement of hand from table to pocket, she wasn't sure. Jacob had been so quietly still, standing looking at the dance floor, that Julia had decided she'd been mistaken, and didn't mention it.

In fact, Jacob had become so attached, he'd come back to the cottage with her and Charles. He'd slept in the spare room. 'Make yourself comfortable, old chap,' Charles had said. Jacob had thanked him, 'It's kind of you.' He'd nodded to Julia. 'Tomorrow I report to your base. They'll sort me out with somewhere to stay.'

Julia had smiled, relieved.

Upstairs in bed, in Julia's small bedroom with the sloping roof, Charles had told her she was too judgemental. He pulled her on top of him. 'I like to see you making love to me.' He held her face. 'A good face,' he said. 'Verging on beautiful. But I don't see a lot

9

of kindness in it. You have to learn to be kind. There's a war on, we must all be nice to one another.'

He'd run his hands over her breasts. Kissed them. Julia had reached over and switched off the light. She was more comfortable with intimacies in the dark.

Afterwards, just before she slept, he'd told her he'd be gone when she woke up. 'Got to get back to camp.' But he'd be back soon. His regiment was going abroad, he'd have a week's leave before he sailed.

He leaned back, hands linked behind his head. He started to expound on the absurdity of war, the things he'd seen at Dunkirk, men queuing to be hauled onto a ship, drowning as they waited. He moved on to talk about his socialist principles, his admiration for George Orwell, theories he'd come across while studying history and politics at Cambridge. He stopped when he heard Julia snoring.

Claire always cycled in the middle of the group. Izzy was always last. She was a slow starter, but, in time, she'd gather strength and come from behind to take the lead and be first to arrive at the base.

In the mornings, Claire complained about the others complaining. She wished they would shut up. This time of day was precious, a time when she could think about her husband and her children. She'd shut her eyes as she pedalled along, trying to precisely conjure up their faces.

It had been over a year since she'd seen her husband Richard. He'd been shot down over France and was now a POW in Stalag Luft 1. Nell and Oliver, her children, had been sent to live in South Africa with her brother-in-law, Joe, at the start of the Blitz.

There had been tantrums when Claire told Nell and Oliver where they were going, and further tears and tantrums when she'd seen them off at Southampton docks. Two tear-stained children dressed in their Sunday best, standing beside their luggage, lips trembling and looking in disbelief at their mother. How could she banish them like this? And why was she packing them off to a distant land with only their Nanny Green to look after them on the trip? Why wasn't she coming too?

Claire had suggested she go to South Africa. But Richard had been adamant. 'I don't think so, old girl. We need you here.' He had joined up when war was declared, and was now a squadron leader in the air force. He had wanted Claire at home when he was on leave.

The childrens' first letters home had been filled with the longing of two small people out of their depths in a strange land. Slowly, slowly, the mood of the letters changed. There were hints about the good life out there – swimming every day, riding their uncle's horses. In time, there was no more hinting. Neither Nell nor Oliver remembered the holidays in Cornwall, picnics in the garden, walks with Willy, the retriever, on Hampstead Heath. Their memories of London were of rain and dirty yellow fog. Now, they didn't want to come back. The sun shone, they'd made new friends. Uncle Joe had given each of them a pony.

A pony, Claire thought, how could Joe do that? He knows Ollie won't want to leave it. And how it belittled the knitted red socks and leather football she'd sent him.

Even Nanny Green had decided not to return to Britain. She was, as Claire put it, on the wrong side of forty and was to stay with the children for six weeks to ensure they were settled. She'd written to Claire telling her she'd made up her mind to stay put.

She'd met a man, a delightful widower in his fifties, and, well, there was romance in the air.

God, even Willy the dog was happy. He'd been sent to stay outside Edinburgh with Claire's sister, Virginia, and her husband, George. Bounding around chasing rabbits, Virginia had told her.

Initially, Claire had believed that the war would end, and life would return to how it had been before it started. Now, she doubted that was going to happen. A family of strangers would reunite in that house in Hampstead. The two children wouldn't want to be there. She and her husband would be different people. She had a dreadful feeling they wouldn't fall into one another's arms. They wouldn't know what to say or do. It was going to be awful. She doubted they'd make it.

At night she studied the most recent photographs of Nell and Ollie that Joe had taken with his Box Brownie. She ran her fingers over their faces, pained at the changes she hadn't been around to witness. She wondered if they remembered what she looked like. She wrote letters to Richard, not knowing if he got them. His letters to her were heavily censored with thick black lines.

Thing was, at work, she was having the time of her life. She was enjoying this war, and that wasn't right, was it? She loved flying. She felt useful, fulfilled. This was new to her.

Richard had no idea what his wife was up to. Claire didn't worry about him as she cycled to work. She saved that slice of fretting till she was alone in her room at night, lying in the dark listening to the sounds beyond her window – bombers on their way down the coast, the river that was yards from their front door pushing against the shore, a heron calling a long desperate cry. She knew how it felt.

She was tired and lonely. She felt she'd spent the last year flying and running. There was an urgency about the job. If she wasn't in the air, following the curves and lines of railways and roads below, she was running across windy airfields, delivery chit in hand. Once it was signed, she was off, running again, to a new plane or to the taxi plane that would take her to another airfield, and then, she'd be running once more. Factories were churning out planes faster than they could be delivered.

Nights, she would write letters to Richard and to the children, fill in her logbook or sit by the fire working on the quilt she was making and listening to the wireless. If she was alone in the cottage, she'd look at the empty chair across from her and wish there was someone sitting there she could talk to about the jokes on *I.T.M.A.* Sometimes, she'd go into the hall and stare at the phone, willing it to ring. It would be Richard, escaped from the camp, back in the country and on his way to see her. In bed, she longed for him. She wanted him lying beside her, holding her hand as they spoke, low voices in the dark, about their plans for the future. She wanted someone to hold her. She wanted long deep kisses. 'Face it,' she told herself, 'you miss sex.'

She considered that and revised her longing: 'I miss a hand in mine under the sheets at bedtime.' She missed a body next to her, someone to spoon into in that quiet moment before sleep came. Though, she had to admit sex was everywhere these days. She supposed people were far from home. They'd fetched up in places they'd never heard of, mixing with all sorts of people they might never have met if the war hadn't started. They were scared, lonely and homesick, though some, far from disapproving mothers or spouses, were tasting a bit of freedom they'd never imagined possible. Everyone was grabbing any pleasure that was on offer. And now she thought about it, sex was just about the only thing that wasn't on ration. Still, it wasn't really sex she missed. 'I miss the closeness of another being. Hearing someone next to me breathe. Sharing thoughts, worries and little bits of gossip.' Intimacy, she thought. Yes, that's it, I miss intimacy.

Izzy, coming along behind, also had family worries. Two weeks ago she'd received a letter from her father. He said he hoped that living away from home hadn't turned her head, made her abandon her morals. He told her that she'd been given a good Christian upbringing and he trusted she wasn't doing anything that would disgrace her family.

'Jeepers,' Izzy had said. A word she'd picked up from Dolores, one of the Americans at the base, and a word she liked, used as often as she could. She knew what this warning meant. Her father had read 'The Letter'.

Allan had been killed in North Africa. Before the war he'd been a history teacher in Perth and Izzy's boyfriend. Their affair had turned physical after he'd been called up. Fearing he might die in some foreign country, alone and still a virgin, he'd turned to Izzy. She'd said there was nothing she could do about the alone-in-a-foreign-country bit, but she could help relieve him of his virginity.

After his death his things had been sent to his mother, who'd found The Letter and, not knowing Izzy's present address, had sent it on to the manse at Fortham, where she'd been brought up. He father had obviously opened and read it. 'Sorry, didn't notice this was for you, opened it by mistake,' said his curt note that accompanied it when he sent it on.

'Jeepers,' Izzy said again.

'Darling Izzy,' The Letter read, 'I think of you all the time. I love to think of you naked, coming to me from across the room, slipping into my bed, lying with me. I ache to feel you touch me again. Memories of your body are with me always out here.'

'Jeepers,' Izzy had said once more.

She had written to Allan's mother, thanking her for sending on The Letter, and telling her what a wonderful person he was, that she'd miss him. She would remember him always.

Nights, she would lie in bed thinking of him. She could hardly believe he was dead. She'd shut her eyes and try to conjure up his face. When she couldn't, she'd take out the few photos of him she had and examine them. She wept for him.

They'd been better at being friends than they were at being lovers. They'd both been shy and inexperienced. There hadn't been time before he left to learn to be relaxed with one another. Still, Allan might have died alone in a foreign country – and that was awful – but at least he hadn't died a virgin. Izzy was glad she'd done what she had done. There hadn't been anyone since those few stolen nights with Allan.

But now her father knew she was a wanton woman. She'd given herself to a man without first going through the holy vows of marriage. He would be furious. 'Sex outside the sanctity of marriage is a sin,' he'd told her often. It pained her that she must be a disappointment to him when he was the man she adored.

She didn't want to lie to him, but lie to him she did. Not exactly lies, she thought, just a little fiddling with the truth. I keep things back to stop him worrying. One thing she'd kept from her father, the big thing, was her job. Oh, he knew she was in the ATA, but he didn't know she flew. She'd given him the impression she was an assistant operations officer. It made life easier.

She loved her father dearly. She'd love him more if he didn't have such fixed ideas about a woman's place in the world. 'Flying's a man's job,' he'd said. 'Women don't have the brains for it.' Then seeing Izzy's horrified expression, he'd added, 'Don't get me wrong. I'm not saying women are stupid, far from it. There are some pretty clever women in the world. But flying takes logic, quick thinking, making calculations. Women run on their emotions, and thank heaven for that. The world needs their shrewd nurturing natures, their unquestioning love, their beautiful soft hearts.'

He'd given sermons on the role of women in society. 'We should fight for their right to femininity. A woman who dresses as a man is to be reviled. Women are like flowers in winter – a primrose, a daffodil in the snow, bending with the terrible travails of weather, never breaking and always beautiful. Women are wonderful and mysterious beings, strong in heart and mind, but fragile and gentle in their ways. They should not undertake the labours of men, they should not wear slacks and try to look like men.'

Obviously, Izzy hadn't mentioned to him that she was a pilot and, therefore, dressed in pilot's clothes. There would have been an argument. Arguing with her father, and winning, was impossible. This was why she lied to him. She'd been doing it since she was eleven.

It had started with her faith. She'd started to doubt there was a God and couldn't bring herself to discuss this with her father since his belief was his reason for living. She fancied he'd mock her.

Later she lied about where she'd been and what she'd been doing. 'Just out,' she'd say, 'talking to my friends.' She'd been kissing Rory McGhee and sharing a secret cigarette. How were her piano lessons going? 'Oh, very well.' She and Elspeth, her teacher and new best friend, would lie in Elspeth's garden on good days, on the sofa in her sitting room on not-so-good days and sigh about life's endless possibilities.

In Izzy's eyes, her father was a wonderful man. He adored her. He'd sweep her off her feet and dance her down the hall in the manse. He'd buy her chocolate and toys. He'd sit her on his knee when she was small, put his bearlike arm round her and read her stories – *Treasure Island* and *Kidnapped*. She adored him back. She lied because she could not suffer to be the cause of his displeasure.

She'd written to Elspeth, who was working in a forest north of Inverness, and told her about The Letter. 'I worry,' she wrote, 'because he might come to hate me. I am no longer lying to him about little things. I'm lying about my whole life.'

Thinking of Elspeth relieved her from the ticking-off from her conscience when she imagined her father's horrified face – the pulled-in lips, the heaving eyebrows – when he'd read Allan's letter. Even here, even now, hundreds of miles away from him, she could hear the thunderous silence of his disapproval.

She imagined Elspeth singing as she chopped down trees, Elspeth whistling as she strode the forest tracks, axe slung over her shoulder. Elspeth – a lumberjill, who'd have thought it?

After fondly thinking of her friend, Izzy started to contemplate her day ahead. In less than an hour she'd be flying. If the weather holds, she thought.

Right now, Edith, the ops officer, would be on the phone finding out about conditions at the airfields the pilots were expected to deliver to that day. She'd be working out who was to fly what and where and who was to be today's duty pilot, flying the taxi plane picking everyone up and bringing them back so they could do it all again the following day.

The CO would be in his office, dealing with matters of the day. Irene, the nurse, would be in the sick bay, getting ready for any physical examinations and any pilots who might be sent to her with flu or to be assessed after some sort of trauma.

Nigel, the met man, would be in touch with the central met office checking on any fronts coming in, making up his charts. It seemed to Izzy that Nigel, Edith, Nurse Irene and the CO had proper jobs with a desk, a pen, someone nearby clattering at a typewriter and a phone always ringing. The people who did these jobs looked strained and a little bit flustered.

She, on the other hand, flew aeroplanes. The pleasure this brought her made her doubt she should get paid. It was a sin to take money for doing something that thrilled her. She'd get her comeuppance for this, she was sure. Life should be filled with onerous duties, guilt and shame. It was not to be enjoyed.

In the upper reaches of her thinking, she was sure this wasn't true. But guilt was deeply rooted in the murky fathoms of her psyche. She had breathed it in on her childhood Sundays, sitting in the front pew of her father's church, listening to his searing hellfire sermons.

She remembered hearing that the Lord was watching her, knew her and all her thoughts and that she would pay for her sins. Her father, Reverend Hamish Macleod, used the word 'vengeance' a lot. She would sit next to her mother – a diffident woman in a dark-blue, fur-collared coat and skull-hugging red hat – vowing to avoid such sins as pride, envy, greed and lust. She would, according to her father, pay threefold for indulging in such things. Gluttons, fools and proud people were all doomed.

Izzy drank it all in. She'd look down at her shiny patent leather Sunday shoes, fiddle with the velvet buttons on her green Sunday coat and silently promise to be good, kind and meek. The subliminal message, the constant undertow in her father's ardent preaching, was that she would pay dearly for enjoying herself.

Life, at the moment, was very thrilling. Oh, how she would pay.

After her weekly verbal scouring, she'd return with her family to the manse for the routine Sunday lunch of roast beef, potatoes and carrots. By now, her father would have resumed being his usual affable self. Every week, he'd step into the pulpit and rant hellfire and damnation, then step back out again, greet his parishioners at the church door, shake hands, joke, ask after the sick and elderly, and go home for a hearty meal with his family. He was loved.

Away from the pulpit, Hamish enjoyed spending his free time tinkering with his MG sports car. Often, on Saturday afternoons, he'd take Izzy for a run, roof down, through the Perthshire countryside where they lived. They would thunder and rattle through Crieff towards Loch Tay, wind sweeping their hair from their faces, yelling their sparse conversation above the din of rushing air and roaring engine.

So, her father had given Izzy a conscience that she kept in prime condition, and a passion for speed and wind. He was her hero.

When she'd read about the ATA in *The Aeroplane* magazine, she'd applied, thinking she wouldn't be accepted. But she was invited for a test flight at White Waltham near Maidenhead. She'd flown round the airbase following the orders her instructor, seated in the rear cockpit, hollered down a Gosport tube. To her, and her family's, amazement, she'd passed.

Her mother had been horrified. 'But you can't go flying aeroplanes all over the country, you'll die,' her mother said.

'I'll just be on the ground planning the routes and making sure everyone gets home at night. Same sort of thing I did for Betty Stokes Flying Show.'

'Don't mention Betty Stokes Flying Show to me. I don't want to hear that name again. You, a well brought up minister's daughter, joining a show like that. It's a disgrace.'

I suppose I am a disgrace, Izzy thought. But she rattled along smiling. She'd told her parents she was a back-room girl at Betty Stokes Flying Show, making tea, selling souvenirs. But she'd been flying. Happy days, she thought. Flying over towns and villages, a long red and yellow banner trailing behind her Tiger Moth – ARRIVING TOMORROW, BETTY STOKES ALL-GIRL FLYING SHOW. People below would stop and point, and she'd heave a batch of leaflets over the side, watch them flutter down. God, she'd loved doing that. It would have been better, though, if she'd been paid.

'You'll be miles from home,' her mother had said. 'And what about the other girls? How will you get on with them? They'll be rich, and you're not.'

Izzy hadn't answered this. But, in time, she'd found this to be true. It wasn't wealth that bothered her. She'd never dreamed of being rich. In fact, she wasn't bothered when her new colleagues spoke about their huge homes. She didn't want a vast mansion. Who would clean it? She wasn't comfortable with the notion of servants. Certainly, she did have Mrs Brent cleaning the cottage she shared with Julia and Claire. But Mrs Brent wasn't really a servant. She was an opinionated tour-de-force who had a way with dusters. The thing was, Izzy knew that if she had servants, she'd be on their side. She imagined herself getting up in the middle of the night to wash dishes and sweep floors so they wouldn't have to do it. In her mind, she was sure that if she hadn't learned to fly, she'd probably have ended up as someone's maid.

No, it was the self-assurance of her fellow pilots that worried her. She was mixing with women who had ostentatious accents, loud voices and oozed confidence. They made her feel emotionally dowdy. Failure never occurred to these women. Izzy was sure none of them had ever experienced such a thing as doubt. They surged through their lives busy being right about everything. She, on the other hand, tiptoed. She entered rooms quietly. She thought she was just . . . just Izzy. I'm only me, she thought, nobody much. She went through life looking over her shoulder, expecting to be discovered for what she was – just Izzy who did not belong among these poised women.

'I thought that was what you're meant to do, follow your dreams,' she'd once said to her father.

Her father had placed his folded hands on the table, 'Following your dreams is one thing, making rash decisions is another.' He'd looked across at his wife. 'I fear that we have somehow produced a child that is prone to rash decisions. You must promise us, Izzy, that when you're far from us, you'll behave in the same way you do when you are near us. You'll not forget your faith, and you'll be true to your upbringing.'

Now, puffing as she skimmed along, Izzy shook her head, dismissing this. Memories, she thought, mustn't linger in the past.

Her bike rattled more than the other two, and was too big for her. She had to stretch to reach the pedals. It was heavy and black, and had belonged to a local policeman. He'd sold it to her for two shillings and sixpence.

'I think he saw you coming,' Julia had said when she saw it. 'You got rather ripped orff, I'm afraid, darling.'

Thinking that soon she might join the sky, Izzy cycled faster and caught up with Claire, who shot her a scathing look. 'Don't chat. You'll interrupt my worrying.'

That was it, Izzy thought. Claire just said she didn't want to chat out loud. Izzy would just have thought it. Claire said what she wanted – peace to worry – and didn't give a fig what anyone felt about that.

Izzy said, 'Sorry.' She cycled past to catch up with Julia. 'We're bound to get up today.'

'Absolutely,' said Julia.

Izzy allowed herself to feel the rapture that came when contemplating flight, and the guilt and fear that always went with it. 'Do you think this is wrong?' she said. 'To be enjoying this war? People are dying and I'm having the time of my life.'

Julia said she knew, but what could you do? 'If they weren't paying me to ferry planes, I'd do it for nothing. It's such bloody fun. Anyway, it isn't all good. There's always the chance we could get bumped orff.'

She always put an 'r' in her 'off's.

At first, Izzy had been troubled by Julia's attitude to death. It seemed flippant. But, as time passed and colleagues had been killed, she'd seen this as a way to deal with it. Considering her own mortality and the likelihood of an accident in foul weather or in a mechanically faulty plane, she decided she'd rather not die, just get bumped off. It was jollier.

Izzy said, 'Don't you worry about what you'll do when the war ends?'

'Depends on how it ends. But we're sure to win this thing. After the Blitz and Dunkirk, it's in the way of things that we should win. It's our turn. Besides, we're in the right, we didn't start it.'

Izzy said she didn't think that not starting a war necessarily meant you'd win it.

'Of course it does,' said Julia. 'Greedy, arrogant little dictators never win in the end, they always get what's coming to them.'

This struck a chord with Izzy. Of course Hitler was doomed, vengeance was coming his way. It was a pity, she thought, that he'd never attended that little hillside church outside Perth and heard one of Hamish Macleod's scathing Sunday sermons, he'd never have dared to invade Poland after that.

They were both a little breathless, faces pink with effort.

Izzy asked, 'Who was that man this morning?'

Julia shrugged. 'Don't really know. Some Polish chap Charles met on the train and invited along. He thought he looked a little lost. He'll be gone when we get back, Mrs Brent will see him orff.'

They grinned. Mrs Brent was a force to be reckoned with.

By now, they were almost at the base. Skimming along beside the long wire fence towards the gate, they could hear it and smell it – the rumble of engines, the shouts of ground engineers, the heavy leaden reek of petrol.

Nerves shifted and heaved through Izzy's stomach.

'Aren't you scared?' Elspeth had asked her once. 'I mean, don't people die doing what you do?"

'Yes, they do get bumped off, sometimes,' Izzy had agreed. And was she scared? 'Sometimes, a little.'

Elspeth had looked at her sceptically, eyebrows raised. She didn't believe her.

Izzy had looked down at her feet. There wasn't a day when she didn't know fear.

The other pilots felt it, too. Though nobody spoke about it. For, really, it didn't diminish the rapture she felt.

Chapter Two
Elspeth Moon

Elspeth breathed on her fingers. They were stiff, so cold they ached – a constant dull throb. It was a bright clear November day, but bitter. She reckoned the temperature was below zero. Still, it wasn't raining, or snowing – there was always something to be glad about.

Above her two buzzards, floating on wind thermals so high they were distant specks, claimed their patch of the sky. Elspeth stopped to watch them and felt a brief pang of envy. If she'd stuck at her flying lessons, as Izzy had, that's where she might be – up there looking down on all of this, miles and miles of forest stretching all shades of green and brown up the hillside. It would be especially wonderful today for it was clear. Usually the hilltops and the mountains beyond were draped in mist.

Learning to fly had been one of her many grand ideas. Amy Johnson was her heroine. She'd taken lessons at Scone airfield and being in the air had thrilled her. 'I could get my own plane and fly to America,' she'd said. On the bus going home, after her first flight, Elspeth had expounded to Izzy on the joys of being in the air. 'It's definitely as good as sex.' Izzy had looked at her dumbly. At the time, she'd known nothing about sex.

A year after the war started, Elspeth, having abandoned flying for another notion – she was prone to flitting from notion to notion – had joined the Women's Timber Corps, become a lumberjill. The things she knew now amazed her. Me, she thought, doing all this. Well, goodness.

She'd learned about forests and how to cut them down. She knew how to operate a cross-cut saw and fell trees so that they did not fall back into the forest when they groaned and crashed to the ground. She could swing a six-pound axe and strip the trees of their branches. It was hard, hard work. No, not work, she thought, it's graft and sweat and tears. But she was fitter than she'd ever been, not an ounce of fat on her. Her body was trim, muscled. She was proud of this.

At night, in her army cot under her two regulation scratchy grey blankets, she'd run her hands over her new perfect sinewy thighs and think that this experience had at least done *some* good.

At first, she'd ached all over. Everything hurt – muscles and bones. The cold and winter damp seeped into her. But mostly the pain she felt was the cruel complaining of long dormant muscles being stirred, suddenly and mercilessly, into everyday action. She groaned in the morning getting out of bed and would creakily, painfully, pull on her workman's dungarees. She'd hobble over the duckboards outside to the lavatories, legs, feet, arms groaning with her as she moved. At breakfast, in the wooden dining hut, it hurt to lift her porridge spoon to her lips. It hurt to sit, hurt to stand. But then, she told herself, that's what happens when you start to use your body and not your mind. The body screams in protest.

Till now, she thought, I taught music. I sat listening to reluctant children thumping out begrudging scales for hours each day. Now, I know what work, real work, is. I have learned about life. Real life. And I have endured.

But now she would go. She'd applied to join the Red Cross. She would leave this forest, north of Inverness, miles and miles from anywhere. A wilderness, she thought. Nothing like the polite woods back home where she and her good friend Izzy used to stroll, and sometimes sit drinking tea from a Thermos flask, listening to Mahler on the wind-up gramophone she'd lug along.

Soon, she would take the train south, back to her cottage. She would spend a week there, have hot baths and sleep between soft clean cotton sheets. Bliss.

As she worked, she thought about the letter from Izzy. In it, Izzy had told her about The Letter. Izzy was worried that now her father would know that she had slept with a man.

Elspeth would reply tonight telling Izzy she was a big girl now and could do as she liked with her own life. She would say it was time for Izzy to tell her father about her job, her boyfriends, her loss of faith – everything. 'It'll come out one day,' she said to herself. 'Can't keep on lying.' Sometimes she despaired of Izzy. She thought that at times Izzy seemed to be almost crazed with doubts and fears. 'You've got to stop keeping your true self a secret,' Elspeth planned to tell her.

Right now, Elspeth was breathing in the scents of peaty wind coming down from the hills, pine and freshly cut wood. She was watching buzzards and somewhere, not far away, an Italian POW was singing something from *Rigoletto*.

'So,' she suddenly said to Lorna who was standing nearby, 'what are you doing for Christmas?'

'Well,' said Lorna. 'I had thought I might spend a relaxing day, opening presents, sitting by the fire listening to the wireless, eating too much. Then, I thought, no I'll go into the forest and chop down some trees. I'll get bleedin' cold, I'll smell the shit from these horses trotting up and down pulling logs, I'll get sore and cut by pine needles and shouted at by that Duncan Bowman. That will be a grand way to celebrate Jesus' birthday.'

'I think I may join you. I will forgo the meal at a posh hotel served by flunkies wearing white gloves, the long-stemmed glasses of chilled champagne, the glistening golden turkey stuffed with crumbling apricots and chestnuts, the gleaming nubby Brussels sprouts, roast potatoes – crisp on the outside, melting soft within – the hot, rich gravy, the creamy bread sauce, cheeky little chipolata sausages, all of that. I will come up here into the bitter winter chill and chop down trees.'

They had been told earlier that morning that, no, they would not be getting Christmas day off, they would be working as usual. There was a war on, and there was no time for Christmas.

'Bleedin' hell, is that how you used to spend Christmas before you came here?' asked Lorna. 'You're too posh for me. We used to get a little present, something shiny, a sixpence and an apple. Then, if my dad was working, we'd have a chicken, but he usually wasn't, so it was sausages.'

This shamed Elspeth. The hotel and the white-gloved flunkies were imagined, but champagne and glistening turkeys had always been part of her Christmases at home. Until this moment, it hadn't crossed her mind that some people's celebrations were not very lavish. Indeed, they were frugal. 'I like sausages,' she said. 'Turkey can be dry, sausages are always good.'

Lorna said she knew that, 'But, tell me again. Not about coming up here, about the meal, only missing out the Brussels sprouts.'

'No,' said Elspeth. 'It's wonderful up here.'

'It's bloody freezin',' said Lorna.

'It's fresh,' said Elspeth. 'Good healthy weather.' She stopped breathing on her fingers and shoved her hands into her armpits, her warmest available part. 'A moment like this is as near to perfection as a person could get. We are in the depth of a forest, far from anywhere, surrounded by nature and a tenor is singing. Marvellous.' Well, she thought, I would think it marvellous. I always love a place or a person with all my heart just before I leave them.

Lorna said something like 'harrumph' and the boss shouted, 'Moon!'

She looked across at him. Duncan Bowman was standing, arms on hips, scowling. He waved at her to stop her prattling and get on with her work. Elspeth gave him a swift salute.

Duncan never did speak much. Well, not to the women, anyway. He didn't like them. Not here, working in his forest, felling his trees. It was their voices, the way they sang as they worked, their jokes, the high-pitched laughter, that irritated him. Like an itch he could do nothing about.

He'd worked for the Forestry for nigh on forty years now. 'Man and boy,' he said, 'started when I was fourteen.' He used to think he'd seen everything. Then the war started, his co-workers had joined up and been replaced by women, and he knew he hadn't.

He'd grown used to working with men. He respected men, you couldn't respect a woman, well, not at work, you couldn't. He could see they could do the job as well as any man. Except that they looked strange swinging an axe, or working the saw. Their problem was, he concluded, that they just weren't manly. He felt he couldn't be the man he really was when women were around. He couldn't spit, or swear. He just didn't want them here, talking about their boyfriends, lipstick and how they fancied Gregory

Peck, and, sometimes, bursting into tears because they were cold or their blisters burst.

'We don't cry!' he shouted. 'Foresters don't cry. Stop it.'

Once, that Elspeth one had said it was a shame to see lovely trees chopped down in their prime.

God, the stupidity of the woman. 'These aren't trees any more. They are telegraph poles, pit props, ships' masts, road blocks.' He'd shoved his face close to hers. 'They are crosses for dead soldiers.' That had shut her up. She'd even blushed. 'Ach,' he said. 'Better get used to them. All the good men gone. There's a war on. What can you do?'

Now, Elspeth, head down and working her way up the tree trunk, removing branches, pine needles thick against her fingers, breathing in the strong scent of resin, said, 'The way he yells your last name does have an unsettling effect on the digestive system. I get butterflies. I think I might fart.'

Then, hoping he didn't think her salute impudent, she took up her axe and continued snedding. 'There was a time when I didn't even know what bloody snedding was. I was happy then.'

'Thought you was happy now. You just said this was marvellous.'

'It was a happy moment: the buzzards, the smells, the tenor singing. I wasn't including the snedding.'

Lorna, bending over the tree, hacking at branches, said, 'If you'd kept yer bloody mouth shut when we were training, you'd be doin' something else.'

Elspeth knew this to be true. Her big ambition had been to work with the horses that dragged the felled logs to the clearing by the road to be loaded onto trucks. But her lip had led to this dreadful job.

When she joined the Land Army, she'd asked to be sent to work for the Timber Corps as a lumberjill. She had a notion of herself in a plaid shirt. But, on arrival at the training camp, she'd been issued with a uniform – riding breeches, green pullover, beige shirt, green tie, melton coat, green beret with a badge with a tree on it, long woollen socks and stout leather boots – that didn't include anything plaid at all. Still, she thought it wonderful. She imagined herself striding through the village back home wearing this outfit, and being admired by one and all. 'I'm a lumberjill,' she'd say. And people would think her splendid.

She was also given dungarees and wellington boots. This is what she wore, day in day out.

On her first day of training, after a dire and sleepless night on an army cot in a row of army cots, in an unheated hut along with twenty other trainees, she was handed a six-pound axe that she could hardly lift.

'Are these the only axes you have?' she'd asked. 'These are surely for men. Don't you have ladies' axes?'

Her instructor hadn't bothered to answer, and had set off up the forest track. The girls, welly boots scraping and squelching in the mud, bent under the weight of the axes that they had struggled to sling over their shoulders, had followed. They exchanged horrified glances. They all knew now that this had been a Big Mistake.

He only led them a few yards to a truck that would take them to the part of the forest where their training was to begin. It lasted four gruelling weeks. At the end of every day they'd had to walk back to their base, six or seven miles. Elspeth not only had stiff and groaning muscles, she had blisters on her feet and hands.

She'd learned how to chop down trees, how to use a cross-cut saw, how to measure timber for pit props, how to load logs onto a truck and snedding.

Snedding was her downfall. It was the word. She'd never heard it before. So when instructor had said, 'Today, yer going to learn the snedding,' she'd sniggered. 'Sounds like something naughty. Oooh, we went into the woods and did a little snedding.' She'd wiggled her hips as she said it. And the other girls had joined in the sniggering.

'You.' The instructor pointed at her – a rigid derogatory finger. 'You can help me demonstrate.' He was standing beside a felled tree and was about to show the girls how to cut off its branches, where to stand, how to stand, how to work from the base up and how to stop the emerging log from rolling on top of you. He wasn't happy about working with women. Didn't think they had the strength for man's work.

Elspeth's remark enraged him. He handed her an axe and a billhook, told her to work her way through the branches, stand on the opposite side of the trunk from where she was cutting.

'Perhaps,' Elspeth had said, 'this is not for me. I'm thinking about my hands. I'm a musician, you see.' She held them out for him to admire their softness.

He hadn't answered verbally. He'd just looked at her. A look that said he thought her as disgusting as something he might find on the sole of his boot.

Her training behind her, and now working here in the forest beyond Inverness, she was still snedding. In rain, wind, snow, sleet and hail, she snedded. It was a punishment.

Now when she looked down at her hands, she hardly recognised them. They were rough, chapped, blistered with a ring of grime embedded under the nails. These are not my hands, she thought. These are not a musician's hands.

She had brought her accordion with her. In the evenings the girls would gather round the wood-burning stove that heated their hut, and was kept stoked red-hot. They'd come from all over the country. They were shop girls, factory workers, typists, a couple of librarians. Bonded by their suffering – cold, aching bones and homesickness – they'd laugh, tell jokes and silly stories and sing. Most evenings, Elspeth would play. The tunes that filled the room were mostly songs of the day – 'We'll Meet Again', 'Don't Sit Under the Apple Tree', 'Bless 'Em All' – but sometimes she'd drift into traditional melodies – 'The Skye Boat Song', 'Marie's Wedding' – and the girls would hum along, swaying, drifting into their memories.

Years ago, a lifetime ago, Elspeth had worked in Selfridges. She'd loved that job. It had opened up whole new lifestyles to her. At home, her mother and father mostly talked about how busy the Tube had been on her father's journey home, what the man in the grocer's had said about the price of ham and what was in the news today. But at work break times the girls would chatter about lipstick, boyfriends, embarrassing things they'd done or said, their brothers and sisters. Their conversations overlapped, they interrupted one another. They giggled a lot. It had taken Elspeth a while to relax and join in. But when she did, there was no stopping her. She felt she belonged with these women.

She felt the same here with her fellow lumberjills. She was one of them. However, her background was far more privileged than any of the others. Lorna, her new best friend, was from Glasgow. She'd lived in a two-roomed flat with her mother and father and four sisters. Elspeth knew that times had been harsh for the family. But when Lorna spoke about life back home, she made it seem fun, rowdy, crowded fun. And, despite herself, Elspeth envied her that.

When Lorna had seen the hut she was to share with the other girls, she'd smiled. 'Cosy,' she'd said. She'd spread her arms enjoying the space between the beds. 'So much room. And a locker of my own. And a whole bed to myself for the first time in my life. Always had to share with my sister.' Elspeth had grinned at her. Oh, but the pang she felt at the comfortable life she'd led.

When night fell thick, black, there would be scuttlings. Not the swift fervid movements of forest animals – deer, rabbits, mice, foxes – but lovers – girls from the hut, and Newfoundlanders over to help in the war effort, working with the girls, living in log cabins nearby – slipping from their huts to meet and sneak into the trees.

They called their kissing and cuddling 'canoodling'. Elspeth abstained from this. The consequences of canoodling where dire, she thought. She didn't want to get sent in disgrace from the camp, pregnant. This had already happened. And would, she was sure, happen time and time again. She would play her accordion, she would work through pain and exhaustion, but love would never touch her.

Now, leaning towards Lorna, she said, 'What I'd really like to do is work with the horses.' She looked enviously at Avril, who was running behind Harry, a brown Clydesdale, through the clearing to the road where the logs were stacked onto a truck. Avril jumped stumps, crashed through fern and bracken. And, whenever she heard the shout, 'TIMBER!' she scarpered.

'Up at five,' said Elspeth, 'grooming and feeding the horses.'

'Shovelling shit,' said Lorna.

Elspeth ignored this. It ruined the dream. 'Caring for them, chatting. I think they'd like me to sing to them. I'd be good with the horses.'

'Well,' said Lorna. 'The only way you'd get to work with them is to make the boss think you'd hate it more than you hate the snedding. That's what he's like – spiteful.'

'I know,' said Elspeth. 'I should learn to keep my mouth shut. I just open it and out come the most inappropriate things. No matter now. I'll be gone from here soon enough.'

Behind them, two girls were at either end of a cross-cut saw, heaving it to and fro, kneeling on the ground as they worked their way through a tree trunk singing, 'Daisy, Daisy'.

The whistle blew, a blackened billycan was boiling over a small fire, time for tea. Newfies and the Italian POWs appeared from where they'd been working further in the forest. Calls and wolf whistles.

Tyler Bute, a brawny Newfoundlander who had his eye on Elspeth, called her name. 'Hey, Ellie, looking beautiful today.' He waved.

Elspeth trilled her fingers back. Then she slipped her hand into the pocket of her dungarees and fingered a bar of chocolate – a present from Izzy.

Elspeth had written to Izzy:

Darling Izzy,

You will never believe where I am now. I am in the depth of a forest a few miles north of Inverness. I have joined the Women's Timber Corps. I'm a lumberjill. Fancy that.

Living conditions are rudimentary to say the least.

Actually, they're hellish. There is no electricity here. No plumb-ing, and the food is quite awful. Though I have to say, after a day working outdoors, I'd eat anything.

Lunch for Elspeth and the rest of the workers was tea and a sandwich. These sandwiches were not the delicate things Elspeth was used to – cucumber, peeled and finely cut and placed between two thin slices of bread – they were thick and contained cheese or grated carrot and, occasionally, beetroot. Still, she ate them with relish.

I have never known hunger like the hunger I feel these days. It gnaws at me. I think this is what life should be like. We should be aching for food when we sit down to eat. I rather fancy I used to nibble too much.

Anyway, darling Izzy, could you please do me a favour? It is October and winter is coming on. It is going to get cold, very, very cold. At the moment I am wearing my silk lingerie under my work dungarees. It reminds me that I'm a woman. But I rather fear this will not do in the months to come. Could you please send me a pair of long johns?

I have no money to send you. I get thirteen shillings a week. And they take money off for our food. Not only am I eating carrot sandwiches, I'm paying to eat them. I will pay you back when all this is over.

But right now, I work five and a half days a week out here in the middle of nowhere – a real wilderness – and rarely get near any shops. What little cash I have I use for the cinema in the village and some fish and chips on a Saturday night. Oh, I do like my Saturday nights.

If you could send me the long johns, I'd be warm, or
warmer, in the ice and snow.
    Thank you.
    All my love, your old friend,
    Elspeth

Izzy had sent three pairs of long johns. She'd used her clothes
coupons to buy them. She spent most of her time in uniform and
rarely bought anything new to wear. She'd also sent several bars of
soap, two jars of Ponds cold cream, three pairs of woolly, socks and
chocolate.

She wrote:

Don't worry about the chocolate, we often have to work all
day with no time for lunch, so Cadbury's donate these bars to
us. I often forget to eat mine. Will send more, seems like you
need it more than me.
    Lots of love,
    Izzy

Sitting with Lorna on a log to drink their tea, Elspeth broke four
squares of chocolate from her bar and gave Lorna two.

'Chocolate,' said Lorna putting one square into her mouth,
letting the melting sweetness trickle down her throat.

'I know,' said Elspeth. 'Chocolate.'

Tyler shouted, 'Hey, Ellie, you don't need chocolate, you're
sweet enough!'

Elspeth shrugged and said, 'How original.'

Lorna told her not to mock him. 'He's lovely. Full of fun.'

Two of the Italian POW sat across from them. One was the

tenor – tall, olive-skinned with a mop of dark hair that he would occasionally sweep back from his brow.

'There's a man I wouldn't mind getting to know,' said Elspeth. 'Much more my type than that Newfie.'

'You're too thin. He says we're all too thin. He likes his women plump. I'd rather have the Newfie. He's a laugh.'

Elspeth said it would be a meeting of minds. 'Me and that tenor. We could talk about music and art.'

'Minds,' scoffed Lorna. 'Who needs minds? If I had a man like that, it wouldn't be his mind I'd like to meet. I mean, you don't need a man to think. You can think when you're alone.'

Elspeth remembered well that at nineteen she, too, had been wise in the ways of men. Confident, too. She wondered what had happened to her. The older she got, the less she knew. The more experience she gained, the more she realised how ignorant she was. At this rate, by the time she reached sixty, she'd be a complete fool. Even more of a fool than she was now – and she considered herself to be an impetuous idiot who'd rushed into a stupid job because she liked the notion of striding through a forest in a plaid shirt, listening to birds singing, the air around her filled with the sweet smell of pine. No-nonsense Lorna was right. Elspeth decided she didn't need a man. She needed to get out of there.

As she sipped her tea, cupping her hands round her mug, she saw Duncan approach.

'Too late to bother with any man,' she said. 'I'll be gone from here. Think of me when you're out in the wind and snow. I'll be at home in a hot bath. I'll leave the bathroom door open so I can listen to the wireless as I soak. There's often good concerts on in the evening on the Home Service.'

Duncan overheard her last few words. 'And where are you going for your hot bath and your Home Service?'

'Home,' said Elspeth. 'I've applied to join the Red Cross in Glasgow. But I'll spend a few days at my cottage before I go there.'

Duncan snorted. 'You can get all that baths and Home Service nonsense out of your head. You're not going anywhere.'

Chapter Three

Making Friends with the Loneliness

Skimpton was a tiny place, cobbled twisting streets, small cottages and Victorian terraces spreading up from the river. Emily Brent had lived there all her life. The furthest she'd roamed was Blackpool, ten miles away. She liked living here. 'No need to travel when you've all this good air and countryside around you.'

She cycled every morning from the cottage she'd lived in since she married William fifty-five years ago to the cottage Izzy shared with Julia and Claire. She pedalled slowly, upright in the saddle, plodding through familiar streets nodding hello to everyone she met, even if she didn't know them. The village was full of strangers these days, Americans, Canadians, even Poles. 'All sorts,' she said.

She wore a crossover apron under her brown tweed coat. On her head, a small navy felt hat with a brisk, no-nonsense brim. Her thick stockings were wrinkled at the ankle. She puffed as she went. 'Not as young as I used to be.' She was in her seventh decade.

It didn't surprise her to find a huge hulk of a man standing by the sink in the cottage she'd come to clean. There was often a man or two here. Friends of Julia's, usually, she was a one for the men. Well, Emily thought, there's a war on. A little bit of hanky-panky would keep their minds off things.

'Not that I approve,' she said to William. 'But there's a war on, we all got something to lose. Better it's your virginity than your home or your life.'

She bustled in, hung her coat on the hook by the door, though the hat stayed on her head, and told Jacob he shouldn't be washing up. 'That's for me to do.'

He shrugged and said it seemed polite. After all, he'd been given a bed for the night and some breakfast.

'And where did you sleep?' asked Mrs Brent.

'The spare room.'

'Well, that's more sheets for me to change. You're not English, then?'

'Polish.'

She told him to put the kettle on and eased herself into a chair. 'There's weather coming. I can always tell. My knees are giving me gyp. Crackin' with every step.'

She sat quietly drumming her fingers on the table, then heaved herself up again. 'I can't sit here and watch you wash dishes. It's no job for a man and your hands are too big for them cups you're doing. You sit down. I'll make tea, then I'll get on with the cleaning up.'

She brought a brown teapot to the table, pulled a knitted tea cosy over it and sat back. 'Give it a minute or two, can't be doing with weak tea.' She patted the pot tenderly, old hands used to hot water, bleach and dusters, liver-spotted.

They sat watching the teapot, till Mrs Brent said, 'That'll be it now.' She poured two cups, added milk and said, 'Tell me all about yourself. I need to know.' When Jacob asked why, she said, 'I'm nosy.'

'Do I get to ask about you?'

'Nothing to tell. I was born here, lived here all my days, never been more than ten miles away from here and I'll die here. Been married to William since I was nineteen. Five children, all boys. All living hereabouts, working on the land, doing all sorts. The youngest turned forty-five last week. That's me, that's all there is to me. What about you?'

He was Jacob, thirty-two years old and married to Anna. He took a battered photograph from the pocket of his shirt. 'Anna,' he said, handing it over.

Mrs Brent studied the face in the picture. She fancied she was good at faces. This one she was looking at was thin, with high cheekbones, full lips. 'She's not so much pretty as beautiful.'

Jacob agreed.

'Like Claire and Julia, they are proper English beauties. Izzy, though, is just plain pretty.' Her voice warmed when she mentioned Izzy, her favourite of the three. 'She is a good pilot, so I hear, anyway. It probably suits her to be in the air. She's not much use here on earth.'

Jacob raised his eyebrows. 'No?'

'Oh no. She's never got the knack of mingling. Other people puzzle her.'

Jacob said, 'Ah.' He somehow couldn't bring himself to say that he hardly knew Izzy. Still, this interested him.

'She doesn't have a boyfriend. The only place she ever goes out to is the fish and chip shop. Doesn't smoke, doesn't drink. She lives for flying, that one. Loves it. Loves being up in the air, away from the world. And she loves her dad, too. That's Izzy.'

Jacob nodded. He knew enough about women like Mrs Brent to know you didn't interrupt when they were in full flow. He'd seen people like her back in his boyhood village. Women and men of indecipherable age who had accumulated huge stores of wisdom and dubious opinions, and who, he thought, died of surprise.

'See,' said Mrs Brent, 'Our Izzy's a lonely one. That's all right, I suppose. But it doesn't do if you don't make friends with your loneliness.'

Yes, Jacob thought, old, and brimming with strange notions. She'd die of surprise. He'd seen it before. One day, she'd look in the mirror and see her final face. It would be creased with time, loss, tragedy and the realisation that there was nobody left who would hold her close. Her eyes would be swimming with the shock of it, a haunted look. 'Oh my,' she'd say. 'That's me. How did that happen?' Then, soon after, she'd die. She'd be ninety-eight, or roundabout that, anyway. The doctor might say it was a heart attack, or just old age. But, really it would be the surprise that got her.

'Your Anna looks gentle. Kindly, I'd say. And clever,' she said.

'Oh yes,' said Jacob. 'She's a botanist. She worked at Krakow University, but when the Germans came she moved back to her parents' house in Lubin.'

'She'll be safe there?' Emily Brent had no idea where Lubin was. But her William would know. He was good at geography, had once got two gold stars from his teacher because he knew every capital city in the world.

Jacob shrugged. He hoped Anna was safe. He told Mrs Brent about his journey from Poland to here.

He'd been in the south when the Germans attacked and had moved with his unit, sometimes only miles ahead of the advancing troops. Standing in a potato field, he'd watched the last of their planes take off for Rumania. He'd stared after it, till it was a dot in the sky. Then he'd turned and started his long walk out of his homeland.

There it was. A few facts, and what did facts say about upheaval, misery and fear? Nothing at all. He didn't tell her he'd joined thousands of people fleeing. Refugees. A moving mass of humanity, walking, crawling along in cars, carrying bags and sacks. All of them hungry, all of them scared. There had been horses and oxen pulling carts full of tables, chairs, lamps, books and children. Families uprooted, lives and homes abandoned.

Once in Rumania, he'd stayed in an internment camp for several weeks till he and another two officers exchanged their watches and rings for a car that they'd driven to Bucharest. He thought sadly about his watch, a beautiful engraved gold pocket watch, worth more than the ancient, rusting, farting car.

'It took ten days to get there.'

Mrs Brent nodded.

'Then ten months in Bucharest trying to get a visa to travel to France. All the time no word from Anna.'

He was aware of Mrs Brent studying his face as he spoke, but carried on. 'Then we got visas and drove to France. But in Grenoble the car went phut. Phut, the engine was dead. So we walked to Paris. Then we came to London. I went to the Polish General Staff Building in Buckingham Palace Road, and they found me a job driving for the ATA. First in Prestwick, then Kirkbride, now I am here.'

He'd been lost in his story, remembering nights when they'd slept in barns, and how hungry, cold and exhausted he'd been. So, it was only now that he noticed Mrs Brent wasn't listening to him. He thought he might have lost her sometime in Bucharest.

'You speak good English,' she said.

'I taught it before the war. English teacher in Krakow.' He leaned his elbow on the table, chin cupped in his palm, and studied Mrs Brent as she studied him.

He's a handsome cove, she thought. Warm lips and brown, brown eyes. But he's a rogue. Soft, though, with it. Love will have knocked all the rascal out of him. It does that. But he's sizing me up and that's what rogues do. He'll be back to living on his wits, surviving, using all his tricks to get back to his Anna.

She asked where he was staying. Looking at his face, the lines and curves of his cheeks, the way his lips moved as he spoke, she'd decided yes, he was a rascal, but kindly. She liked kindly.

'You can stay with us. There's room.'

He told her he had to report to the airbase that afternoon, and someone there would find him a billet.

'They'll only put you with someone you don't know. But now you know me, best stay with friends.'

He agreed.

'You go right up the High Street and keep going. Only a mile outside the village. The first house you come to. You'll find it easy, you having walked here from Bucharest.'

He was right, she hadn't been listening. He smiled and told her he'd go before reporting to the base in the afternoon.

She stood at the door saying goodbye when he left. Then she walked to the end of the garden path, to the gate – a crumbling white picket thing, greening with damp – and watched him go, a battered brown leather case clutched in his hand. She could see from the way he moved, the slope of his shoulders, that he was lonely. But he carried it well, long steps, head up. Loneliness didn't bother him. It was part of his life. Mrs Brent thought he'd probably use it, almost revel in it, to survive till he got back to the woman in his picture. Yes, she thought, he'd made friends with it.

Jacob didn't go straight to Mrs Brent's cottage. Instead of turning right at the end of the lane and on up to the High Street, he turned left down a small narrow track that led to the river. The ground was still frosted hard. Puddles turned to pools of muddied ice. He stamped on them, heard the ice squeak and groan under his weight, but it didn't break. The river was wider than he'd imagined. He thought it must be three hundred yards to the other side. He thought he'd swim here come summertime. Right now, the water was pewter and murkily still, iced at the banks. The trees were stark. Leafless. A single lonely duck pottered slowly by, centre stream. Jacob thought it looked how he felt – bedraggled, isolated, cold and wondering how he got here, and where were all his friends?

Up on the road that ran parallel to the river path, he heard the milk cart. The steady clip-clop of the horse, the trundle of old wheels over cobbles and the milkwoman's cry, 'Milko.' Voices as women came out carrying their jugs to be filled from the metal milk churns on the back of the cart.

He would wait a while before he went to Mrs Brent's cottage. It was always upsetting to tell his story, and he needed some time alone before facing anyone new.

He could never properly describe how awful it had been joining that mass of refugees, and he felt that nobody he spoke to understood how exhausted and scared he'd been. So, he avoided company and, when the few people he did mix with asked how he'd got here, he kept his story as short as possible. And told it in a flat, almost monotone voice. He did not want to share his feelings – his relief at getting away, his guilt that his wife, Anna, was still back in Lubin.

He rounded a bend in the riverbank and came across a small jetty. At one time, before the war, he supposed there might have been several small boats anchored here. But now there was only one weathered rowing boat tied to a post.

On the bank, in front of the jetty was a small café – Mary's Tearoom. It looked pleasantly empty – only two other customers, a couple sitting by the window sharing a pot of tea, staring out at the river. The café backed onto the Golden Mallard Hotel, a huge building with long lawns stretching down to the water. There was an ornate summerhouse in the middle of the lawns, and he could see just beyond it a tennis court. A man in RAF uniform was walking hand in hand with a woman in a trim red suit – jacket with a nipped-in waist and shoulder pads, a neat straight skirt. She had long dark hair that swept past her shoulders. From a distance, she reminded him of Anna. The couple climbed a few steps that led onto a terrace, then disappeared through a wide set of French windows.

Watching couples, even fleeting glimpses of them, always depressed Jacob. He momentarily imagined himself and Anna walking up that lawn, disappearing into the hotel and discussing if they should have a pot of tea in the lounge or take a stroll through the village. He thought, She'd want the tea; I'd want the stroll. Or maybe he'd try to persuade her to come with him to their room where they'd make love and lie afterwards, side by side, holding hands listening to the river slipping past.

He decided to have a cup of tea in the café. It looked dingy enough to suit his mood. He took a window seat at the table next to the couple and ordered a pot of tea and a slice of ginger cake from the young waitress. The couple stood up, nodded to him, a brief acknowledgement that he was in the world. They paid at the counter, then on their way out slipped a sixpence from their change under one of the saucers still on their table. Jacob watched them walk away, back along the path and out of sight. Then, as the waitress went into the kitchen to fetch his tea and cake, he leaned over, took the sixpence and put it in his pocket.

Just after noon, Jacob arrived at Mrs Brent's cottage. She wasn't there, but William, her husband, was digging in the garden. 'Letting the frost in to kill the weeds,' he said. Then he added, 'You'll be Jacob, come to stay.'

Jacob nodded. 'Your wife has already told you.'

'Oh no, won't be seeing her till tonight. She told Grace, the milkwoman, all about you. Her man's away at war so she took over the round. Grace told Jenny at the post office. And Jenny told Ben the postman who told Roger, barman at the Duck's Foot, who told me when I popped in to deliver some eggs. It's a small place, no secrets, everybody knows all about everybody here. You'll soon get the hang of it.'

Jacob said he thought he would and thanked William for the room and board.

'Think nothing of it. There's a war on, got to do your bit.' He put an old hand, liver-spotted and muddy, on Jacob's shoulder. 'Come away in and sit down. You'll be weary after walking here all the way from Bucharest.'

Jacob didn't bother to put him right about his journey from

Poland. In fact, he rather liked that people might have misconceptions about it.

His room pleased him. It was tiny, but he found it snug. And it was sparsely furnished – a bed, a small dresser and a wardrobe, all very old and neglected. The floor was bare boards. The ceiling sloped towards a small six-paned window. He had to bow his head to look out. He had a view of the Brents' large immaculate garden – neatly turned over, awaiting spring planting – and beyond were fields, then trees, bare at the moment, so he had a shining glimpse of the river.

Jacob turned to William, who was standing in the doorway – there wasn't room for two – and told him it was perfect. And so it was. Luxury in any form troubled Jacob these days. He didn't want to be warm and comfortable when he was sure Anna wasn't. He couldn't stand the guilt.

He dumped his bag on the bed, and told William he needed to change into his uniform before he reported to the base.

'Fair enough,' said William. 'I'll leave you to it.' He turned to go down the narrow rickety stairs leading to the kitchen. Paused. Turned back. 'It'll be ten shillings a week for the room and board, and we'll be needing two pounds deposit.'

Jacob said he'd bring the money with him when he came down. He changed into his uniform, he took his papers and all his money, including the sixpence stolen from the café, and put them in his pockets. He didn't think the Brents would actually steal anything. But he was sure they'd have a sneaky rifle through his things. He'd have to find a good hiding place for his back-to-Poland fund.

In the kitchen, William took the money and put it in an old teapot on the dresser, then offered Jacob lunch. He took a platter of roast beef from the pantry. Jacob wondered how he could have got hold of such a large joint of beef. Looking round, he saw shelves of jams, chutneys, salted runner beans and pickles. There was a bowl filled with speckled eggs on the draining board and, next to the cooker, a plate of sausages. Rationing seemed to have passed these people by.

William set two roast beef sandwiches on floral plates down on the table and slammed a pot of mustard dead centre. 'There you go. Proper food. You'll be wanting a drop of beer to go with that.'

Jacob refused. He didn't want to turn up at the base with the smell of alcohol on his breath.

'Quite right,' said William. 'I'll do you some tea. And we'll be needing your ration book. Can't be feeding you without it. Not that we need it for ourselves, mind. Sons working on the land get extra cheese that they hand on to us, and Emily and me, being over seventy, get tea without coupons. Tea and cheese, what more do you need?"

Jacob reluctantly handed over his ration book.

He walked slowly to the base, and was late for his appointment with Fiona Driscoll, the adjutant at Skimpton airbase. She rapped the top of her desk with her knuckles and told Jacob that lateness just wasn't in order with the ATA. Jacob apologised and said he'd been held up, and it had been a bit further to walk to the base from the village than he'd realised.

'You should have started out earlier than you did if you weren't sure of how long it would take. We have planes to deliver, we expect punctuality.'

Jacob said it wouldn't happen again. And Fiona told him to take his hands out of his pockets when addressing an officer. 'It looks slovenly. We may not be a military organisation, but we have standards. We expect you to be turned out in uniform looking smart, shoes shined, trousers creased. But we're civilians here, so no saluting or any of that. If you don't come up to snuff or break any rules, you won't be court-martialled, you'll be fired.'

Jacob decided he didn't like her. He supposed nobody really liked her. She must be lonely. She was achingly thin. So thin, she looked as if she'd be permanently cold. She moved stiffly. She was a woman who was all bones, no fat, no muscle. Her skin was translucent, her nose slightly red. She asked if he had a reliable watch. 'You'll need one.'

He did have a watch. He'd got it in exchange for a car – a beautiful MG that had belonged to one of the pilots on the base where he'd last been posted. He'd been killed when he crashed a Hurricane into the side of a hill one foggy afternoon four months ago.

The pilot's widow had come to the base to collect her husband's belongings from his locker, and Jacob had been given the job of driving her home to the house she and her husband rented. The car, mud-splattered and forlorn, had been sitting in the drive. The widow, a small nervous woman, so burdened by grief she looked as if she might, at any moment, slump to the ground, told him she didn't know what to do with the car. She didn't drive and didn't want to see it standing unused. 'It would be painful. Besides, I'm moving to Cornwall next month and can't take it with me.' Jacob offered to take it off her hands for twenty-five pounds, saying it wasn't worth much more than that. 'Hard to sell a car these days. Petrol rationing.' Besides, he told her the car was almost five years old and had high mileage. The widow had been glad of the deal, and thanked him profusely.

Jacob had taken the car back to his base, washed and polished it. For three days, he'd driven it with joy. It thrilled him to hurtle down narrow roads, roof down, wind whipping his hair, face stiff with cold. He'd be smiling. It was the happiest he'd been since he'd left Poland. Then another pilot, visiting the base, had asked if he was interested in selling and offered Jacob fifty pounds for the car.

How Jacob had laughed. 'This car is worth at least twice that. Look at her. She shines. Leather seats, just four years old, one previous owner and such low mileage.'

After a bit of haggling, Jacob had sold the car for seventy pounds, plus the splendid gold watch the pilot sported on his wrist. A very good deal, he thought. He tossed the keys over to the car's new owner, slid the watch onto his wrist, and planned to put the money into his getting-home-to-Poland fund, except for the money he used to buy the widow of the car's original owner a bunch of pink and white roses.

When Fiona asked if he had a watch, Jacob shoved up his sleeve and tapped with pride the handsome gold timepiece on his wrist. Fiona nodded, a curt movement of her head. She liked to remain aloof. She asked if he had anywhere to stay, and seemed relieved when he told her he had a room with the Brents. Plainly, she didn't like having to billet people out. Jacob supposed she lacked the charm necessary to persuade people to take strangers into their homes.

She slapped her hands on her desk and stood up. 'Right, I'll show you round.'

It was a shining place. Gleaming green lino that squeaked beneath the soles of his shoes, polished wood – doors, tabletops in the mess – the colour of freshly shelled conkers. Fiona walked briskly, pointing as she went. 'The CO's office. He's not here today, you'll meet him soon enough. The ops room, Edith is ops officer.' He peered in, a small neat woman, telephone to her ear, smiled and flickered her fingers at him.

Fiona strode on. 'The met room – that's Nigel.' Jacob caught a swift passing glimpse of a tall, awkward man wearing a bowler hat standing marking up a huge map. Fiona didn't give him time to say hello. 'The mess,' she said. A large room, a scattering of tables and chairs, newspapers lying unread and a couple of abandoned cups on a table, but nobody around to be introduced.

Outside the air was crisp, chilled. Fiona's breath spilled in tumbled mists from her mouth as she spoke. Jacob couldn't make out anything she was saying, a plane was booming overhead, coming in to land. Fiona held on to her hat. Jacob's trousers flapped wildly. Two more planes were doing circuits overhead, awaiting their turn to land. A van from the car pool trundled past

The landing plane was so low that, looking up, Jacob could see the faces of the passengers inside. They seemed to be having a good time.

'That's the gels back,' said Fiona pointing upwards. 'The taxi dispersal area is at the end of the runway.' She pointed to the plane, now landed and skimming into the gathering late-afternoon gloom. 'You'll be expected to take the van down to pick up the pilots and bring them back here.'

Jacob nodded. This job was much the same as his last job. Only this base smelled of polish and there were women here. He thought that if he kept his distance from Fiona, he could be happy here.

She led the way to the car pool. It was a short walk away from the main building. Inside the car pool were three Humbers lined up. All were gleaming. Fiona introduced Jacob to Douglas and

Brian. 'They'll show you the ropes.' Then she handed him a slip of paper. 'You will collect the CO, the Ops Officer and myself tomorrow morning, eight-fifteen. Me first, then Edith and the CO last. You'll have to come out here to collect the car. Brian will tell you which one.'

'Fine,' he said. 'I'll be there to get you in the morning.'

Fiona gave him a small stiff smile, 'Till tomorrow morning, then.' She whirled round and strode off. A stiff military walk. Jacob shoved his hands back into his pockets and watched her go.

Brian, Jacob's new colleague, came up and stood beside him, 'She's not so bad when you get to know her.'

Jacob shook his head – he didn't think so. But then, what did he care? He had no intention of getting to know her.

It was after four, and the day was turning velvet. Gathering darkness in the trees behind the airfield was thick, granular. Jacob stood watching the end-of-the-day bustle. A plane skimmed in, wheels squealing as it hit the runway. Above a Spitfire joined the remaining circuiting plane. The whole world was throbbing noise. The van returned from the end of the runway, stopped at the door of the main building and a small crowd of women clambered out. They were all in flying suits and jackets, carrying helmets, map bags, parachutes and small overnight bags. There was a gaggle of female voices.

Brian noticed Jacob noticing the women, and said, 'Out of bounds, old chap.'

Jacob smiled. 'I expect they are.'

'All double-barrelled names. Not interested in the likes of you and me. You've got to be a squadron leader, letters after your name. You've got to be rich. Like them.'

Jacob nodded. That was probably true. He shook Brian's hand

and said he'd see him tomorrow. He had to get back to the village to find out exactly where tomorrow's passengers' houses were. He'd ask William, who was bound to know.

On his way to the gate, he saw Izzy. The girl from this morning, he remembered. She turned, spotted him and smiled. Ah, he thought, a small-town girl. City people stared awhile, then perhaps nodded – a brief acknowledgement that they recognised you. Small-town people smiled first, then worked out who you were. It was considered rude in tight communities not to say hello to everybody you met.

He guessed she wasn't as wealthy as the other two she shared the cottage with. She most likely had learned to fly because, like so many young women before the war started, she'd been in thrall with the feats of Amy Johnson.

When she saw him looking at her, Izzy's face had bloomed – the full smile. Jacob could read her every thought. There's someone familiar, smile. Who is it, though? Oh yes, it's him. Bigger smile and little friendly wave.

The other two had cut-glass accents. Izzy's voice was lower, lilting. He could hardly take his eyes off her. He was drawn to her mix of warmth, determination and vulnerability. Turning the stolen sixpence in his pocket over and over in his fingers, he thought that there were many good things about Izzy. But the best thing was that she was nothing like Anna.

Chapter Four
Custard Days

Morning, ten past nine in the canteen, which was through the ever-open door at the far end of the mess, Cook made a mental list of her chores for the day. She had a name, but everybody called her Cook. Prepare veg for soup, top up tea urn, scones. Scones first, she thought, if the solid thing produced by mixing National flour, margarine and powdered eggs could be called a scone. Fluffy and light it was not. Still, what could you do? There was a war on.

It was always noisy this time of day, sounds of the mess – chat, laughter, heavy crockery chinking, the flick and shuffle of cards. But there was an undertow to that noise, a tension as the pilots waited for Edith's call: 'The chits are up.' Then they'd scramble.

'Them pilots are a noisy lot,' said Mabel, Cook's assistant.

'It's all show,' said Cook. 'They do it so they won't hear what they're thinking.'

'And what are they thinking?'

'They're thinking today might be the day they crash into a mountain.'

'You think they're scared?' asked Mabel.

Cook said that these days everybody was scared. 'You never know what's comin' next. A bomb on your house, a telegram telling you someone's dead. Never mind, you have to keep cheery when death's about, that's what I always say.'

She heaved out a baking tray and began, hefty arm working furiously, to grease it with lard. 'Of course, they're scared, every single one of them.' Then, pointing to the bucket containing leftovers, scrapings from yesterday's plates, she said, 'Take the pigs' swill out. The farmer'll be by to pick it up soon enough.'

The pilots were in the mess drinking tea or hot orangeade, smoking, knitting, playing cards or backgammon, telling tall stories about their adventures in the air, embroidering mishaps to startle their audience, 'line shooting' they called it. In one corner a space had been cleared and several women were exercising – lying on their backs air-cycling, doing sit-ups, press-ups or just swinging their torsos about, bending, stretching. This job, they said, made you fat. All the sitting in planes, or sitting waiting for planes, all the tea and scones.

Five of the male pilots sat watching, their faces expressionless. They smoked steadily and swigged tea. Julia often remarked that she couldn't believe these men had no interest in women at all. But then they were probably hungover. 'They spend every single night in the pub.'

Izzy put her feet up on the chair next to the one she was sitting on, folded her arms and dozed. She was renowned for her sleeping abilities. 'It's a gift,' she claimed, revelling in the envy it brought her. She drifted, conversations bubbled round her.

Claire was playing backgammon with Dick Wills, one of the older pilots, who'd lost his right eye in the First World War. He had a startling growth of hair on his upper lip. Too old for the RAF, he'd joined the ATA because he couldn't resist the opportunity to get into the air and fly some damned crate again.

He claimed, with pride, to be a flirt and a bit of a bounder. He thought it rather jolly to have women pilots as colleagues, even if they were annoyingly prone to obeying the rules. 'They are made to be broken.'

'I don't like the way this game is going. I'm losing,' said Claire, throwing the dice.

'Claire, you always lose. You never take risks.'

Drifting and dozing, Izzy thought this a good thing. She never took risks, either. She thought Dick Wills awfully ancient. He was forty-nine.

Across the room, Dolores, one of three American pilots, was watching a game of bridge, and telling nobody in particular that poker was her game. 'Takes real balls to win at poker. Nerves of steel.'

Izzy yawned. She didn't know Dolores terribly well. But then, apart from Julia and Claire, she didn't know any of the other pilots. They rarely mixed socially. Flying was a solitary job.

Izzy was used to this, loneliness didn't bother her. She'd been the daughter at the manse and had spent most of her time at home alone. None of her friends would come to play at her house. This, Izzy knew, was all down to her father's eyebrows. They were fiercesome things – agile, too. Her father had many variations on the movement of eyebrows and could express endless opinions just by moving them up, down or across the way, when they met in the middle of his brow. Disapproval was his forte. Izzy wished her father were here now; he could do his eyebrow dance, left eyebrow up, right eyebrow down, a look both quizzical and mocking that would definitely have silenced Dolores.

'Played poker all the way here on the boat. Six goddam days. Jeepers, that was a trip. Awful. Below the decks most of the time.

We were in a convoy and any time I *did* go on deck I'd see there was one more boat missing. Nobody would say if it had been called away or sunk. I hated being on that boat. Still, I won a hundred dollars.'

This was why, when America joined the war, she hadn't accepted the invitation to go back there. It wasn't that she didn't want to go back, she didn't fancy the journey.

Izzy turned her head so that one ear was wedged against the back of her chair, blocking it so Dolores didn't sound quite so loud. The floor shook. The exercisers were jumping up and down, waving their arms.

Julia, sitting next to Izzy, said, 'I wish they'd stop doing that.'

Diane on the other side of the table agreed. 'Bloody annoying.'

The rhythmic clicking of Diane's knitting needles kept Izzy in a quiet state of near sleep. It reminded her of home. Her mother in a chair on one side of the fire, knitting. Her father sitting opposite reading an Agatha Christie, and the wireless on – *The Brains Trust* was a favourite.

Diane was Izzy's favourite pilot. At thirty-eight, she was the oldest among the women. She'd married at eighteen and produced a daughter a year later. That daughter had also married at eighteen and had recently given birth to a son. Diane was known as the Flying Grandmother.

Across the table Julia muttered that she was sorry, but she did not like Dolores.

'She's just loud,' said Diane. Click, click, click, knit, knit. Needles a blur.

'She's after Alfie's money.'

Dolores was billeted with Lord Alfred Myers, in a flat above the stables. But she ate in the house, and in the evening sat by the fire, drinking his wine. 'Though I'm a beer gal, really.' She and the Lord had formed a lusty friendship based on a mutual love of cards, alcohol and going very fast in anything that moved – horses, motorbikes, cars and, in her case, planes.

'More fool her,' said Diane. 'Alfie's as poor as a church mouse.'

Julia snorted. 'Gold-digger.'

Glasses propped on the top of her head as she studied the pattern on the table in front of her, Diane said, 'It's none of your business, and you know it. How's your own love life, by the way?'

'Haven't heard from Jeffrey. Charles has gone orff to officers' training. Then he's orff to Burma. We'll have a couple of days in London before he goes. I'll take a couple of days orff.'

Three 'orffs' in a row, Izzy thought. That could be a record.

'Jolly good,' said Diane. Click, click, in, over, through and off. She was making a blue matinee jacket.

Last night, when Izzy got home from work, there had been a letter from Elspeth waiting for her. Elspeth had told her it was time she faced up to her father, told him about her job, her grown-up love life and that she no longer believed in God. 'You can't keep on living a lie,' she'd written. Izzy knew that to be true. But then Elspeth had never had to deal with those eyebrows, the thunderous looks, the awful thick silences that could go on for days and days. Izzy's father was a wonderful man, kindly, hearty and fun, as long as everyone round him realised that he was right about everything.

Elspeth had also told her that she'd discovered the most terrible thing: 'I can't leave this job. I'm signed up till this damn war is over. I'm stuck.' Izzy decided to write back and tell Elspeth that she was due four days' leave. She would go north to see her, she'd cheer up her old friend.

She closed her eyes, invited sleep, and was drifting to that pleasant dreamy place she went to just before oblivion – voices, knitting, dice rattling, cards shuffling, exercisers grunting, sounds were distant, somewhere far away at the end of a tunnel – when Edith Conway, the ops officer, swung in shouting, 'Chits are up!' Scrape of chairs on polished lino, people jumping to their feet, cigarettes being stubbed out, games abandoned – everyone scrambled.

There was the usual squash of people, a seething mass of blue serge, shoving and milling about the table in the corridor where the chits were placed. Every day, Edith tried to get some order into this. Why couldn't these people just queue up, file past and pick up their chit? 'We're British,' she said. 'We're natural queuers. It's something we're good at.' Nobody paid any attention. She beetled off, elbows going, to phone the engineer-in-chief and tell him to get the planes started. In weather this cold, the engines needed ten minutes warm-up time. 'We're off,' she'd say.

Izzy read her chit: 'Pilot, I. Macleod. Date, 5/11/1943, Spitfire. Castle Bromwich to Ternhill.'

Julia, Diane and Dolores had the same delivery. Moving Spitfires from factory to storage unit. Claire would fly them back and forth in the taxi plane.

Stuffing the chit into her pocket, Izzy went to the locker room and changed into her flying suit. She checked her pockets – handling notes, comb, lipstick and lucky stone. She picked up her map bag, helmet and wondered about taking her overnight bag, then decided against it. She was sure she'd get home tonight.

'This outfit does nothing for me,' she said to Julia. However, she rather liked it. She could hide inside it. Once she'd climbed into it and fastened it up, she felt safe. There were times when, apart from her size and her mass of dark hair, nobody could tell she was a woman. Not that it really mattered any more, there weren't so many men who disapproved of women pilots as there had been when she'd started doing this. Now everyone was too caught up with the war to care.

She enjoyed the anonymity of the suit. From a distance, all pilots looked the same.

'You look gorgeous, darling,' said Julia. She linked Izzy's arm and together they collected their parachutes and went to the mapping room.

It was one of the rules that the pilots went there every morning to check that there were no new barrage balloons on their flight path. After that, there was the signals room then the met room.

'Izzy,' said Julia, 'I worry about you. You need to have fun.'

Izzy said she *did* have fun. This job was all the fun she needed.

'You should grab at life while you have it,' said Julia. 'You might get bumped orff tomorrow.'

'A comforting thought,' said Izzy. She glanced down at Julia's arm entwining hers. Another wish – she would have liked to be able to link arms with people in the easy friendly way Julia did. But she couldn't. She wasn't relaxed enough with these women to slip into easy friendships with them.

'You need to be swept orff your feet by a dark handsome man,' said Julia. 'Everyone loves to be swept orff their feet. You need a distraction.'

But Izzy shook her head. 'Never.' She didn't want anything to take the edge off the joy she felt when she was flying. And, right now, the tingle of anticipation was growing.

Julia checked today's flight path. 'There, no new balloons, no target practice, we're fine.' She grinned, scarlet lips. Sometimes Izzy thought Julia only had two emotions – enthusiastic and very enthusiastic.

After that, arms still linked, they went to check on the weather with Nigel the Met.

'Lovely day, girls,' he said. 'Clear and perfect.'

The weather maps hung round the walls and were marked with reports taken from around the country. Izzy accepted that, since there was no communication with ships, information was limited. But it annoyed her that Nigel was often wrong. And when found out, he giggled.

As they left, Izzy said that she didn't trust Nigel at all. She thought that it would be better to ask Mrs Brent how her knees were doing. 'They give her gyp when the bad weather's coming. Far more reliable than anything he does.'

Julia thought she had a point.

'I mean,' said Izzy, 'the weather is so changeable. There's so much of it. The air shifts and brings in smells and tastes. Nigel should go outside and take a sip of air and never mind his actuals from around the country and three-hourly advance forecasts.'

'You think Nigel should taste the air?'

'Absolutely,' said Izzy. 'You breathe it in, let it run over the tip of your tongue, you get the flavour of the weather.'

'And what's the flavour today?' asked Julia.

'Crispy and cold,' said Izzy.

By now they'd walked along the corridor and were outside and heading for the van that would take them to the end of the runway. Jacob was driving. He smiled to Izzy, who gave him a slight upward flicker of the lips back. It wasn't a time to be friendly.

On the drive, everyone slipped into silence, a tense almost fearful thing. Izzy had once tried to explain this to Mrs Brent. It was a little bit like the tension you felt before sitting an exam, she'd said. 'But not quite, because you are about to do something you love doing. But it also scares you.'

Mrs Brent hadn't paused in her furious scrubbing of the kitchen table. 'You'll all be making friends with your fear, that's what your doing.' Izzy had been struck at how simple and true this was. Now, sitting in the van, she put the tremors she felt in her stomach down to her making friends with her fear. This was better than thinking she was scared.

She reached into her pocket, turned her lucky stone over and over with her fingers. Julia was running her lucky pearl along the chain round her neck. Claire was plucking at the fur on her flying suit. Hating how the full suit restricted her movements, she'd taken out the lining and wore only that. She looked like a teddy bear. Diane was folding and refolding her headscarf; she hated wearing a helmet. Dolores was fiddling with her lipstick. Yes, thought Izzy, they were all making friends with their fear.

At the end of the runway, they clambered out of the van, and into the noise – thirty planes with their engines roaring – and bustle. A crosswind battered round them, whipping their voices away and pushing the windsock so it was at a right angle with the pole.

The first planes for take-off were being taxied forwards, ground engineers straddled across their tails, steadying them in the wind. It always worried Izzy that one day she'd forget someone was riding the back of her plane and she'd leave the ground with an outdoor passenger white-faced and screaming in terror. The first pilots were in their planes waiting for the green light from the tower.

Seven pilots climbed into the Anson, dumped their parachutes in the tail and settled into the canvas seats. Several of the men took out newspapers. Julia fished a manicure set from her pocket and started filing her nails. Diane knitted. This settling down to small amusements to occupy a journey always reminded Izzy of a bus trip, the things commuters did on their way to work.

They landed at the factory airfield. Izzy, Diane, Julia and Dolores jumped out, steadied themselves against the gusts of wind from the propellers and made their way, running, to the administrative block. Claire took off with the rest of her passengers. She'd meet up with the girls at Ternhill.

By one o'clock, the pilots had made two trips to Ternhill storage unit and, on the second flight back, ate their chocolate bars. They rarely bothered with lunch.

Dolores had wanted to eat at Ternhill, but the others had refused. They were uncomfortable there. The CO there still hadn't accepted the notion of women flying planes and it was only recently that they'd been allowed into the mess.

'We unnerve him,' said Julia.

'I love the food over here,' said Dolores. Then she thought about this. 'Actually, the food's pretty damn awful. But I just love the way it's served.'

Izzy said, 'Ah.'

She liked eating at factory canteens. There was camaraderie; she liked the women workers in their overalls, hair wrapped turban-style in scarves, who sang 'We'll Meet Again' and 'My Old Man Said Follow the Van' as they worked their twelve-hour shifts. The crockery was white and utilitarian. It clanked noisily. There was busy chat at every table and *Workers' Playtime* – from a factory somewhere in Britain – blared over the tannoy system.

Dolores leaned towards her and asked, 'What did you mean, ah?'

Izzy said she'd got the impression that Dolores thought everyone in this country was served by people in white gloves when they ate. And that they had breakfast in the breakfast room where breakfasty things were laid out on covered silver platters. 'That just isn't so.'

'It isn't?' said Julia. She put her hand on her heart and pretended to be shocked. 'I may need to lie down.'

Izzy grinned.

'Izzy had an idyllic childhood,' Julia said. 'She was allowed to be a tomboy. Nobody insisted she act like a lady because she was going to be presented at court someday.'

Izzy shrugged. 'I'd have hated that.'

'It was a bit boring,' said Julia. 'Parties, dresses, looking for admirers. A bit of a cattle market, I'm afraid.'

Claire said she hadn't been sent off to school because she was a girl and her father thought educating girls a waste of money. 'I was taught upstairs in what had been the nursery by a governess. I don't think I learned a thing. I passed my time waiting to be grown-up. I remember sitting on the stairs watching people arrive at my parents' parties. All the women in long evening gowns. Oh, the jewellery. Everything sparkled. Everyone laughing and having such fun as they made their way to the ballroom.'

'Ballroom?' said Izzy. 'Your house had a ballroom?'

'Oh yes,' said Claire. 'And thirty-four bedrooms. I think someone like you would call my parents obscenely rich.'

No, Izzy thought, I wouldn't. But my father might. Rich man, camel through the eye of a needle, gates of heaven and all that.

Returning to the subject of lunch – the only thing Izzy liked more than talking about food was eating it – Izzy said, 'The thing I like about mess food is the custard. It makes me homesick.'

It was always satisfying to recall puddings from her childhood. True, the custard in the mess was nothing like the sweet and silky mix of egg yolks, milk and sugar her mother made. Mess custard was bright yellow, thick, industrial and tasted slightly metallic.

She had fond memories of mealtimes at the manse. Her mother produced three hot meals a day, and only now did Izzy wonder how she did it. She stared out at passing clouds, felt the thrum of the plane's engines and drifted into memories.

Breakfast and lunch were always served in the kitchen. The family would gather at the long, sturdy pine table as Izzy's mother, Joan – Joanie to Izzy's dad – would put steaming dishes of soup, stew and vegetables in front of them. All this would, of course, be consumed with relish. But while they chewed and chatted, they would dream of pudding. There was always pudding, but it wouldn't be discussed. That was the family tradition – pudding was a surprise.

Izzy remembered how her mother would slip a steamed sponge from the bowl in which it had been cooked. Everyone would hold their breath, watching as the wonder was revealed. There it would be, perfect and golden. Beaming, her mother would carry it to the table. She'd be bursting with pride, almost as if she'd given birth to it. Which, in a way, Izzy thought, she had. Portions would be dished out. Her father would clap his hands and demand, 'Custard, woman.'

Joanie would fetch a large white jug, brimming with the pale-yellow sauce.

It was not unusual for her father to toss aside his spoon halfway through a meal and shout, 'For heaven's sake, we forgot to say thanks to God. We were all too greedy, too busy tucking in to say a few words of gratitude. Do the honours, Isabella.' It was the only time Izzy ever got her full name.

'Aw, Dad. Do I have to? You're the minister. You do it.'

'God hears enough from me everyday. He'd appreciate a few words from you.'

So Izzy would clasp her hands, close her eyes. 'Thank you for all this. This cosy kitchen and for making my mum a good cook. And mostly, God, thank you for the custard.'

'Excellent,' her father would say. 'You really got to the nub of the matter with the custard reference.'

The plane was now in circuit round the factory airfield. Claire was waiting for the green light to land.

Dolores said, 'Got to go to the little girls' room when we're down.'

It always surprised Izzy to hear someone as strapping as Dolores refer to the lavatory so coyly. She thought someone so frankly outspoken, who said 'goddam this' and 'goddam that', was just over six feet tall and roared up to work every morning on a motorbike, would just say she was going for a pee.

Diane said, 'You're smiling a secret little smile, Izzy.' She was knitting as she spoke, looking down at her needles and stopping only occasionally to peer over the top of her glasses at the pattern on her knee.

The smile was about remembering meals back home, Izzy said. 'My mother made wonderful custard.'

'Well, why would anyone want a ballroom when they could have that?' said Diane.

Izzy said, 'Indeed.' And thought that she hadn't ever wanted a ballroom, anyway; she wasn't that interested in dancing.

Dolores complained that these goddam Sidcot suits were not designed with women in mind. 'The contortions you have to go through in the bathroom.'

'Just be glad you have somewhere private where you can do your contortions. When I started in this job, there was nowhere to pee. Not a single RAF base had a women's lavatory,' said Diane. 'I well remember having to squat behind a hangar. Embarrassing and more than a bit chilly on your rear end.'

Julia said that was why she rarely drank anything while she was working, 'Not even a cup of tea. I know it has to come out the other end.'

'But there are lavatories now. We're accepted. We won the battle,' said Izzy.

'We won the plumbing battle. The powers that be, the male powers that be, have decided that we are but human. We have digestive systems. We function. I don't see that as any great triumph for women.' Diane popped her ball of wool onto the ends of her knitting needles. The plane was bumping along the runway. 'I reckon we'll get another two runs in before dark.'

It was always a moment Izzy enjoyed. She and the other pilots would walk across the airfield, a huge place – miles of hangars and workshops, a large administrative building, a tower and crowds of engineers milling. Everyone would know who they were – the Spitfire Girls. Newspapers often wrote articles about them. Though there had never been any mention of Izzy. She had never been photographed or interviewed. Still, she felt proud. She was a member of an elite group.

Careful, she thought, careful. Don't strut, don't swagger.

Pride comes before a fall. She remembered those Sunday sermons when her father would prophesy doom for the swollen-headed. If she gloated too much, she would surely take off without due care and careen into one of the giant silver barrage balloons floating high above the factory. She would be engulfed in a ball of flames, a suitable comeuppance for the overly self-important.

On their last trip of the day, they flew in single file, chasing one another. Julia always led. She made sure she was first in line to take-off. Izzy was always last. Except, of course, for Claire, who was flying the taxi Anson.

It was a converted bomber with the bomb bay fitted out with seats. It was used to ferry pilots, in the morning, to the planes that had to be moved, and then, at the end of the day, to pick them up and take them back to Skimpton.

Claire loved the Anson. It was slow, steady and reliable – a carthorse of a plane. She was amused when flying over towns and villages to see people looking up. She imagined them thinking that there went a good old British bomber on a mission, when her cargo was actually a bunch of women, knitting, laughing, playing cards, singing, sometimes, or touching up their lipstick.

Julia scudded through clouds and the others followed. When she banked to the right, they banked to the right, when she banked left, so did they. And when she zoomed down to buzz a house with a red roof, they did the same. Whoosh, one, two, three, four. They all waggled back and forth as they went, a Spitfire wave. As Izzy swept by, she saw a woman dash out of the house and jump up and down on the lawn, waving wildly. People did that when they saw Spitfires.

The speed of it, the thrill of skimming through the air, playing follow the leader so high above the ground, in a plane that was light, responsive almost as if she only had to think about what she wanted it to do, and it would do it – it fitted her, this plane, so snug, it might have been bespoke – made Izzy smile. This smile came from deep inside, she hadn't known it was coming. It was as if she'd lost control of her face. It was exhilarating.

If only being back on the ground was so joyful. But it never was. Her heart would be pumping, her cheeks pink with the thrill. She'd be smiling still, heady, and all the while her legs would have to cope with the ordinariness of walking.

Then, there were men here on the ground. In the air, she was on her own, kept busy with the business of flying and her thoughts when she had time to think them. She loved the isolation and the freedom. Mixing with people, especially male people, had always been a problem.

Izzy just didn't understand men. They were bigger, louder and more competitive than she was. Their noise in the mess often drowned any conversation she was having. They took pride in downing a pint of beer in a oner. Why? What was the point of that? They told rowdy jokes that Izzy never got. Their laughter was raucous. They bewildered her.

It wasn't that Izzy didn't like men; it was just that some of them didn't like women. When she thought about it, she realised that these men didn't dislike all women, they just disliked the women who were doing men's jobs. Still, they were the ones that bothered her.

They were never openly hostile. In fact, Izzy thought it would be easier to deal with if they were. She could be hostile back. Though how she could do that, she didn't really know. Once or twice, one of these men had stepped in front of her in the queue to get a delivery chit signed. It hadn't been a particularly aggressive act – it was more as if she weren't really there. But, she had done nothing about it. She'd shrunk back and let herself be bullied.

None of the other female pilots would let that happen to them. Dolores, for example, would tap the offender on the shoulder and say, 'I was here first, fella.'

The four had landed, and were walking into the main building to get their chits signed. Julia led the way, toting her parachute and map bag. She waved hello, a small trilling of her fingers, at a group of pilots standing nearby. Then she went over to chat – shoot the breeze, as Dolores might say.

Izzy and Diane joined her, but mostly to listen rather than add to the gossip. Dolores hung back. She always did with men. She thought her height and her long nose made her a disappointment to them. 'Hell,' she said, 'I know I'm no beauty. But when you guys over here heard some American girls were coming over, you all thought we'd be Hollywood dolls. Well, we're not. I'm damned if I'm going to apologise for not looking like Betty Grable.'

There had been a time when almost all the male pilots disliked women being around. But now they'd got used to them. 'Everyone's too busy for all that bias,' Diane said. 'Soon as the war's over, it'll be back.'

Now Izzy surveyed the group for 'The One' – the one who didn't like women. There was always one, often more. She could tell them by the way they stood – kind of rigid – and their hands would be in their pockets, helmet pushed back, jacket open. They would watch the conversation, tensed, waiting for a moment when they could say something disagreeing with whatever woman was talking. They'd be waiting their chance to scorn.

71

Julia was saying, 'No, that was it for the day. No more trips. Don't want to be up there when night descends. Not with the blackout down here. I like to see where I'm going.'

'Oh, come on,' said one of the pilots. 'There's light left. Time for one more trip.'

He was The One, Izzy thought. The man who hated women. He was tall, wiry and had a thick brownish-red moustache. He was smoking a pipe. He was Roger Wutherington, Diane would tell Izzy later. He'd fought in the First World War, and was approaching fifty. 'God,' she said, 'some of these boys would fly when even a sparrow would take the bus.'

Right now, Diana picked up her parachute and slung it over her shoulder. She smiled and said that really they should all be going. She wanted to get her delivery chit signed, then she'd get aboard the taxi Anson and go home. Her knitting was sticking out of the top of the bag she was carrying.

The man who would fly when a sparrow would rather take the bus pointed at the needles. 'Oh my Lord, knitting,' he said.

Diane stopped. 'Yes, knitting.'

'Pilots don't *knit*,' said the man.

'I do,' said Diane. 'I also arrange flowers and ride a motorbike from time to time. I bake sponges, I've given birth and I can change a tyre on my car. I also fly planes and knit. What do you do? Other than sneer, of course.' She swept by and into the building, smiling, but only slightly. Mostly, she was irked.

Izzy thought, Golly, gosh that was wonderful. She had a new hero. She wished she could say something like that. But as she'd never given birth, couldn't arrange flowers, bake a cake or knit, she couldn't. Come to think of it, she realised, she didn't even sneer all that well, either.

Chapter Five
How Many Fingers Do You Need, Anyway?

It was never silent in the hut, even in the depth of night. Logs in the stove shifted, crackled, hissed. And twenty women, each one huddled under their regulation army blankets, sighed, moaned, snored, farted – with the turnip-laden diet they ate, nobody could blame them for that – and, sometimes, screamed in their sleep. A few called on their mother.

Lying awake in the dark listening to her colleagues sleep, Elspeth really got to know them. It was true intimacy. By day they all worked in the forest, laughed, sang, complained and cursed together. Evenings, they would sit round the stove and tell stories about their families, boyfriends, they'd swap ambitions, crack jokes, banter, do one another's hair, share what few goodies they had – sweets, biscuits, cake, lipstick. Elspeth might play her red button accordion. They were planning a concert, songs and dances.

They also bickered, bitched, argued and, sometimes, fought. Elspeth, who had never before seen women throwing themselves into battle, screaming, swearing, punching, slapping, scratching, would watch, shocked and secretly thrilled. The cry would go up, 'Fight, fight, fight!' Girls would gather round the battlers yelling encouragement to their fancied winner.

Avril, the lead girl, in charge of keeping the others in order, getting the hut cleaned and stopping the girls sneaking out at night to visit the men's hut, would try to prise the battlers apart. The fights never lasted as long as the heated post-brawl discussions about who started it, why and if it was justified. Still, the odd swift passionate scuffle provided an exciting break from routine.

Elspeth remarked to Lorna that the fights seemed to happen once a month.

'Well, they would,' Lorna said. 'That's when we all got the curse coming on. Everyone's in a bad mood.'

'We all have our periods at the same time?' Elspeth asked. 'How odd.'

'It's natural, the way of things. I dunno why.' Lorna, wise in all sorts of ways, was used to communities of women. She'd been convent-educated, then worked in a chocolate factory ('You eat as much as you want for the first week, then you feel you'll never want to eat chocolate again.'). She had the knack of making Elspeth feel simultaneously sophisticated and naive.

The room where they slept was no longer sparse. Beds were now covered in eiderdowns, quilts and thick spreads sent in parcels from home. The effect was startling to the eye, such a riot of colour. Many girls had a soft toy or doll that was pulled under the blankets and cuddled in the night. Pictures of Clark Gable, James Stewart and Frank Sinatra were stuck on the walls alongside photos of puppies and kittens.

Elspeth's bed had a thick dark-blue velvet and silk covering – a present from Izzy. 'This bedspread is so you, I had to buy it,' she had written. Izzy had found it in a second-hand shop in Blackpool and paid five shillings for it. It was fraying at the edges, a little bit moth-eaten, but Elspeth loved it. Every time she looked at it she was reminded of distant happier times when she'd been a piano teacher living in a tiny cottage and, every Saturday, Izzy would bang the rusting dragonfly knocker on her front door, looking grumpy and dishevelled.

How Izzy had hated learning to play the piano. Thumping out unpractised scales, banging through tunes unrecognisable from missed notes, Izzy had been the worst pupil Elspeth ever taught.

The bedspread's fading opulence also reminded Elspeth of her days living in Chelsea when she'd posed for Gregor Fox, the artist, who rented a studio in the house she was living in. If he could see her now, he wouldn't believe his eyes. Sometimes, when she'd shared his bed, she'd worn a scarlet satin nightdress, and then again often she'd worn nothing at all. She wondered what he'd make of her curled in the foetal position wearing long johns, thick socks and, when the draught from the window above her bed got too much to bear, a green woolly hat with a red pom-pom atop. Glamour no longer matters, she thought.

Bed was Elspeth's favourite place to be. It was the only place where she got some privacy. She pulled the covers over her head, huddled down and let her thoughts and memories roll before sleep took her.

When all the girls slept, the doubts and fears that had been tucked at the back of their daytime minds took over, loomed large in their dreams. The soft, sweet rhythmic breathing was often broken by shouts, bawls and wails of lament. When, at some point during the night, Lorna called out, 'Help!' Elspeth knew exactly how she felt.

Some of this dreamtime despair was, Elspeth knew, her fault. It was she who had discovered that nobody could leave the Timber Corps, unless they were seriously ill or pregnant.

'But,' Elspeth had protested, 'I want to work with the Red Cross. I'll still be working for the war effort.' She longed to get back to the city, London preferably.

'You think,' said Duncan Bowman, 'you can just change your mind. You get fed up of one thing, so you'll do something else for a wee change. You think the government can afford to train you to do whatever it is that tickles yer fancy? You've been trained to work in the Forestry. And in the Forestry you will stay. There's no leavin'.'

They'd been in his office, a hut, really. A small paper-strewn desk, a few shelves crammed with files, boxes, bottles of ink, a stuffed snarling wild cat, crouched ready to pounce. On the wall, a calendar and large picture of a seascape, tossing waves, gulls and a small boat grappling with angry water, a lighthouse in the distance. The place smelled of wood, tobacco and paraffin.

Elspeth said, 'But . . .'

'But nothing,' said Duncan.

'It's *my* life.'

'It's not your life any more. It's the Forestry's life.'

'I'll leave just as soon as this war is won,' said Elspeth.

Duncan had leaned back in his chair, put one foot on his desk, kept the other on the floor. He was lean-faced, weathered, annoyingly placid, spoke slowly, deliberately. A thin layer of white hair barely covered his scalp, not that anyone saw his head that much – he rarely removed his cap. 'War or no war, you'll leave when the Forestry says you can.'

Elspeth had walked back to the dormitory, sat on her bed and stared ahead, dumbstruck. Lorna said she looked like she'd seen a ghost. 'What's up?'

'I can't leave,' Elspeth said. 'They won't let me. I'm stuck here, sawing down trees, eating carrot sandwiches, freezing cold.'

There had been cries of horror. 'They can't do that, can they?' said Lorna. She'd been planning to leave, too.

Avril pointed out that before Elspeth arrived, Myra McDonald had left. 'But she was pregnant and they sent her home. That would be one way you could leave.'

Elspeth hadn't graced this suggestion with a reply. A scathing glance was all it got.

Avril said, 'Bleedin' heck.' She slumped onto her bed. She had also thought about leaving. She picked up her teddy bear, her night-time companion, and cuddled him close. 'Well, we'll all leave soon as this bleedin' war's over.'

Elspeth had decided it was best not to mention she didn't think they'd be able to do that. They were all stuck here till someone somewhere high up said they could go. She'd stared down at her muddy boots, tucked her icy hands into her armpits, numb with disappointment. They would all have to wait till they were demobbed. 'Just like everyone who's signed up for the war effort.'

'Demobbed,' said Avril. 'I don't want to wait for that. I want to go home.' She wept. Hot tears spilled down her cheeks. She wiped them away with the back of her hand. Then, as she rummaged in her pocket for a handkerchief, she lost control and started to sob. Face buried in her hands. Her whole body wracked with sorrow.

Elspeth gazed over at her. How flushed with emotion Avril had become lately. Laughing wildly one moment, tears the next. Why, only the day before, she had thrilled at the sight of a small bird, a crossbill, flitting among the branches of a pine tree. 'Isn't it just exquisite.' Then, later, her eyes had welled up because her tea was too hot.

She's getting hysterical, Elspeth thought. Not coping at all. She went over to Avril, put her arm round her. 'Never mind. Look on the bright side.' For a moment she couldn't think of a bright side. 'We have a roof over our heads. A stove to keep us warm. Think of the men out there fighting, sleeping in the open, under fire. We are so lucky compared to them. It's not so bad.'

Avril hadn't been convinced. But then, neither was Elspeth.

At around five o'clock, before the first glimmer of dawn, she was dragged from sleep by Avril's coughing. It was a deep violent hack that shook her whole body. And it was relentless, causing Avril to bend double, handkerchief clutched to her mouth. She fought for breath between bouts. Elspeth propped herself up on one elbow. 'Are you all right? I think your cough's getting worse.' A hoarse whispered hiss.

'I'm fine,' said Avril. 'It's just the damp and cold get to me.' She struggled into her dungarees, pulled on her boots and stumped up the room. At the door she put on her oilskin coat, lit a lantern and, holding it aloft, went out into the chill December drizzle. The stables were half a mile down the track. Avril had horses to tend in the morning before she tended to herself.

Trudging to work, half past eight, the heels of her welly boots scraping on the rough track, the shaft of her axe digging a red weal into her shoulder, Elspeth considered her life so far.

She had loved her job at Selfridges' perfume counter. A life filled with fragrance in the best department of the best store in the world. Mornings, proud in her smart blue coat with its nipped-in waist and fur-trim collar, she'd sit on the bus pleased to be a working woman. She had been eighteen years old.

At the time, she'd been living at home in Hammersmith with her mother, a piano teacher, and father, a banker. Every evening she'd sit at the supper table and recount her adventures of the day. 'They've put a seismograph on the third floor. If we ever have an earthquake in London, or anywhere nearby, we'll be able to record it.'

Her parents had looked bored at the prospect. 'We don't get earthquakes here, dear.'

She'd seen Jessie Mathews shopping one day. 'Oh, you should have seen her hat. It was lovely.' Once she'd seen Amy Johnson. 'She was walking around the store buying things just like a real person.'

'She is a real person, dear.'

'No she's not. She's amazing. The first woman to fly to Australia. You wouldn't think you'd see someone like that walking about on her own, buying perfume. Why, I very nearly served her myself. Except Miss Hartley got there first. That's what's so wonderful about Selfridges. You see everyone there.'

Elspeth's parents despaired about her. She knew. She'd overheard them discussing her. 'The girl is musically gifted,' her mother had said. 'She could have studied at the Royal Academy. Yet she chooses to work as a shop assistant, swooning at the sight of someone famous.'

Her father had agreed. 'But one day, she'll take a tumble to herself.'

In the forest, stripping giant pine trees of branches, slow cold rain dripping down the back of her neck, Elspeth thought that now, at last, that tumble was happening.

Working down the stem of the tree, her hands, blackened and sticky with resin, throbbed with cold and needles cut into her fingers. Every so often she would put them to her mouth and blow on them. The thick, oily scent of pine lined her nostrils. An icy merciless wind cut through the trees and whipped round her, cutting through her heavy jumper and the layers of shirt and vest, biting into her face. Her back ached from bending over the tree she was working on and from the pained effort of rolling it over to get at the branches underneath. Every time she straightened up, she groaned.

Behind her a slow fire crackled, sending gusts of woody smoke clouding round her. Not far off Newfies were singing 'You Are My Sunshine', a roar of male voices. Shouts of 'Timber!' Creaking, groaning, a tree crashed to the ground. The thud of horses hooves on soft pine-needled ground, the rattle of chains and scrape of logs being towed away.

Overhead, a low drone – American bombers, ferried across to Orkney from Newfoundland, now heading south. Everyone looked up, waved, cheered, sang a swift burst of 'I'm a Yankee Doodle Dandy'.

The surge of noise almost drowned the shriek from Lorna. A deep curdling howl split the air. Everything stopped. Lorna was standing by the tree she and Elspeth had been stripping. She was bent over, gripping her hand, her face frozen in shock, mouth agape, still screaming, though the scream had died and there was nothing left in her lungs to start it anew. Then she passed out.

Fleetingly, Elspeth thought Lorna was joking. She looked comical, silently screaming and slipping out of sight below a half-stripped tree. Elspeth smirked. Good one, you nearly had me there. Then she realised that this was serious.

On the other side of the tree, Lorna lay on her side, knees curled up at her chest, left hand gripped by her right. She was stricken, face ghostly white. On the ground, not far from her face, fleshy pink, bloody and grotesque among the dark green branches, was her finger.

Elspeth ran to her, put her arms round her and shouted for someone to bring the first-aid kit. 'Quickly!'

Duncan Bowman pulled off his coat and wrapped it round Lorna. He said that the bloody first-aid box was in the bloody truck down at the road. 'I forgot to bring it up.' He heaved Lorna to her feet. Arm round her, he dragged her down the track to the road. 'Got to get her to the hospital.' Lorna's knees buckled, she sank to the ground. She wailed, 'My finger!'

Duncan lifted her off the ground. 'Never mind yer finger.' He started to run down the track jumping over rocks, long loping strides, a trail of blood dripping behind him.

Lorna kicked her legs, screamed and yelled for someone to bring her finger. 'My finger, I need my finger!'

Duncan stopped, turned and, from where he stood, hollered for *someone* to get rid of that damn thing. 'She'll no be usin' it now.' He set off again towards the truck. All the way to the road, Lorna never stopped screaming.

Everyone had gathered to watch. They stood in small groups staring after Duncan. Then they turned to consider the finger. Nobody wanted anything to do with it.

The Italian POWs moved off first. This finger had nothing to do with them. If it had been an Italian finger, then, perhaps, yes, they would deal with it. But no, it was a Scottish finger. Not their business.

The other girls looked shifty. None of them wanted to touch it. In fact, most of them were revolted at the sight of it, and felt guilty about that. They slowly moved back to where they'd been working. Someone said that it must be time for tea.

Elspeth swallowed. It was up to her, then. She was closest to it, and Lorna was her best friend. She fished a handkerchief from her pocket and gingerly bent down and placed it over the finger.

'I'll do that.' Tyler Bute had been watching. And he'd been waiting for months for an opportunity to get nearer to Elspeth. A woman who played the accordion, who could resist? 'Been working in forests all my days. Seen worse things than fingers chopped off – whole legs, arms. There was a guy, a few years back, got his head chopped off. Saw it myself. He leaned down suddenly to pick up a few coins he'd seen on the ground, didn't see the other guy who was working on a tree, whack. Lost his head.'

Elspeth went pale. She hated these stories, and the Newfies were full of them. Told them matter-of-factly. But that didn't stop the gruesome visions they conjured up in her mind.

Tyler scooped up the finger, wrapped it in the handkerchief. 'You want I should throw it away?'

'No,' said Elspeth. 'Some animal might get it.'

Tyler shrugged, that was the way of things. 'I could put it on the fire.'

'For goodness sake, no.' Elspeth was appalled. The smell of burning flesh? She didn't think so. 'We'll bury it.'

At the edge of the forest, with a view over fields and snow-capped mountains in the distance, Tyler dug a hole – two feet deep, but not very long. 'There. You want the handkerchief back?'

Elspeth shook her head. 'No. Absolutely not.'

'I'll put it in the ground. Pointing east to the sunrise.'

But Elspeth said, 'No. South. Pointing home.'

He put the finger still wrapped in the handkerchief in the hole. 'You want to say a few words?' He wouldn't. But you never knew with women. They were sentimental.

Elspeth said, 'No. What is there to say? Goodbye finger? Hope you touched happy things when you were attached?'

He smiled. 'Yes. Something like that.' He filled in the hole, stamped the loose earth firm. Put his arm round Elspeth's shoulder and led her back to where they'd been working.

It was tea time. A hot black brew was being poured into tin cups. Tyler handed one to Elspeth, then, back to the group, opened his jacket, took a half bottle of whisky from his pocket and splashed a dollop into her cup. To steady her nerves, he told her. 'You've had a shock.'

She didn't approve of this. Alcohol and axes seemed like a very bad mix at work. But she drank it anyway. Felt the heat of it burn her throat then spread through her. It made her slightly giddy. She wasn't a drinker. When he asked if she wanted some more, she put her hand over the top of her cup and shook her head.

'Horrible things happen,' he said. 'You can't get away from that fact. Life is messy.'

She supposed it was. 'What will happen to Lorna?'

'They'll stitch her up and send her back to us.'

'Just like that?'

'Just like that,' he said. 'What did you think? She'd lie in hospital being comforted by nurses?'

Elspeth nodded.

'Ah,' Tyler said. 'If you want any comfort up here, you have to make it for yourself.' He tapped the bottle in his pocket.

Then the whistle blew, and they all went back to work.

By the end of the day, Elspeth had two new blisters on her hands, her feet were cold and she ached all over. She carried Lorna's axe as well as her own, one over each shoulder. She wanted to cry, but didn't think she could. Perhaps she'd forgotten how. Behind her, on the walk back to the huts, Tyler and his friends sang 'You Are My Sunshine' again. Elspeth had a suspicion he was singing it to her, but didn't respond.

Geese flew, honking, clattering, overhead. Keening in a long skein where the treeline met the sky, Elspeth stopped to watch them. It was always a joy to see them go. From the edge of the forest came the single crack of a shotgun, and the geese squawked and panicked. One lonely bird plummeted to the ground. Elspeth saw it tumble. Time was when she would have thought, Poor goose. Now she felt only envy – some lucky bugger was getting roast goose for supper. She had noticed recently that her heart was hardening.

After supper – three slices of Spam, mashed potatoes and cabbage washed down with a mug of tea – she washed her socks in the ablutions hut and hung them to dry near the stove. After that she sat on her bed playing her accordion.

It was an old thing she'd found in a second-hand shop in Edinburgh some years ago. At the time the only instrument she could play was the piano. But accordion music interested her. It was timeless. It was the music of peasants and gypsies, the music of village halls, drumming out reels and strathspeys on dance nights. Accordions play the music of the people, Elspeth had once told Izzy.

To her delight, once she had begun to master it, and realised the range she could get from squeezing and pulling back the bellows, she had found it easily played Bach.

That was what she had intended to play tonight. But sensing the mood in the room, and remembering the singing Newfies on the walk home, she played 'You Are My Sunshine' instead. She didn't let it hurl and swing like she usually did. She moved the notes out slowly, let them glide. A sad blues tune drifted out. She followed her heart and let the song shift into something else – a refrain of her own, her sorrows released in a mournful melody.

'What's that?' asked Avril

'A lament,' said Elspeth.

'A lament for Lorna's finger,' said Avril.

Elspeth said, 'Could be.'

Outside, at the far end of the hut and out of sight, Duncan Bowman stood smoking a cigarette, listening. That woman played a grand accordion. How could he let such a person go? He'd known he'd keep her here as soon as he saw her getting off the train at Inverness when she'd first arrived. A bit of music in the evening was always good for morale.

He liked Elspeth, fought hard not to show it. So he shouted at her, kept her snedding trees when he knew she hated it. Something happened inside him whenever he saw her. A ripple, a tremor, a small flock of butterflies swarming in his stomach. What *was* that? Love? He didn't know and didn't want to entertain that notion. His wife had died ten years ago. TB had taken her, a terrible way to go. But in all of the twenty-three years he'd been with her, he'd never admitted he might have loved her. 'We get along fine,' was how he had put it.

Whatever it was he'd felt for his wife, it was nothing like the feeling he had for Elspeth. This was a schoolboyish thing – a crush, perhaps. It made him hot inside, brought a lump to his throat, made him prone to silly daydreams. Sometimes, thinking about her, he whistled. He hated it. He hated himself for not being able to control it. And, in a way, he hated Elspeth for doing it to him. Though, of course, she knew nothing about it.

He lived in the forester's cottage, a small house, set in a

clearing several miles away with his black Labrador, Mac. Tonight, he'd finished his supper – a plate of potatoes and pigeon pie handed in to him by Ian McKay, whose wife had cooked it as a small thank you for turning a blind eye to his nightly poaching activities – washed the dishes, then come up here to stand in the dark. Still, scarcely breathing, listening.

He leaned against the wall, threw his cigarette to the ground, stamped it out. He'd been hoping for Bach tonight. He liked a bit of Bach, and had thought, considering the events of the day, Elspeth might be in the mood for the *Goldberg Variations*. But no, she was playing some tune of her own making. Still, it was a fine bit of music.

He allowed himself to drift into his favourite daydream. He had married Elspeth and she shared his cottage. After supper, which she would prepare, have ready to lay on the table the moment he got in from work, they would sit by the fire, logs roasting, flames leaping up the chimney, and she would play for him. She'd be on the wooden chair by the table, foot stamping, smiling at him. He'd sit in his old armchair, fingers dancing to her tunes, a small glass of whisky on the little table beside him. That would be grand.

A thought darkened his dream. What if Elspeth did what Lorna did? She was dreamy enough to let her attention stray, look up at some passing bombers and chop off her finger. Then what would happen to the music? Accordion players needed all ten fingers, he was sure of that.

He would take her off the snedding, and let her work with the horses. It was time, Duncan decided, to get rid of Avril. He was wondering if she had TB. He'd seen it often enough – the flushed emotions, the sweating, the coughing. Others would come down with it in this damp place. And every single one of them would be half-crippled by arthritis when they got old. The wet and the cold and the kneeling on the ground and the heaving and lifting just wore your bones away. He had it himself – a cursed stiffness in his toes and fingers every morning, a throbbing, burning when rain was on its way. Pain with every step, sometimes he thought his legs would no longer hold him up. It would get him one day. He'd need sticks to walk, then a wheelchair. He'd lose his job, his house, everything, really.

The music stopped abruptly in the middle of 'Beautiful Dreamer'. Duncan didn't know why. He was sad about that, 'Beautiful Dreamer' was one of his favourite songs.

Inside, Elspeth put down her accordion. She went a greenish shade of pale. The events of the day had caught up with her. The image of the lonely finger lying on the pine branches kept creeping into her mind. Then there had been the absurd burial, the whisky-laced tea, the long walk carrying two heavy axes, the flaccid cabbage for supper. She cupped her hand over her mouth and rushed out the door, over the mud-caked duckboards to the outside lavatory, where she threw up.

Duncan, unaware of Elspeth's speedy exit, waiting for a new tune to start up, listened to the girls talking about Lorna. 'Good job it wasn't her engagement finger,' someone said. 'That would have been too bloody awful to bear.'

Avril coughed and agreed, 'Gosh, yes. I never thought of that.'

Duncan smiled wearily. He spread his hands in front of him. Stumpy things, two fingers missing from the left, one from the right. 'Ach, how many fingers d'you need, anyway?'

Chapter Six
Elspeth and Izzy

Saturday, seven o'clock, Izzy lay back on her hotel bed and sighed. She'd made it north in three hops, usually it took four. She'd left Skimpton at ten, hitching a lift to Preston in the taxi Anson. Dolores was duty pilot. From there she'd flown to Prestwick, sitting on a small metal bench in the back of a bomber. A second taxi Anson took her up to Lossiemouth on the east coast. They'd swooped in over long beaches and landed just after three in the afternoon.

After that she'd hitched a lift in a jeep to Inverness. From there she caught a bus. She'd rattled through the countryside she'd recently flown over, staring out at passing forest, hillsides, cottages cowering in huge landscapes and, from time to time, slipping into a shallow sleep. She'd wake, wonder a moment where she was – it had been a long day – then drift off again.

It was almost six when the bus pulled into Brantly, the village where Elspeth spent her sweaty Saturday nights eating fish and chips before dancing to the local band. The place was busy, narrow cobbled streets alive with uniforms, Norwegian soldiers on training exercises in the area and foresters. The pub was thronged, drinkers standing shoulder to shoulder, shoving for enough space to lift glass to lips, and the air was heavy with wafts of alcohol.

Shouts, calls and whistles from foresters revving up for their big night out as Izzy passed on her way to her hotel. She ignored them, pulled her coat round her. It was cold. There was wildness in the atmosphere.

This was the third time she'd made the trip. She thought she was getting better at it, becoming used to travelling. It wasn't something she'd done before the war. In fact, back then, a trip to town, barely twenty miles away, had been a big adventure, something to be planned in advance. It had involved filling a Thermos flask with tea, making sandwiches and taking extra clothing in case there was a change in the weather.

And here she was making her way almost from one end of the country to the other and booking into a hotel on her own. She thought her parents would be proud of her, if they knew. But they didn't because telling them would lead to questions – for example, if she could go to Brantly to visit Elspeth, why didn't she come home to visit them? Were they not a couple of hours' train journey further down the track?

Seeing them was hard. She had to watch what she said lest she let slip that she was working as a pilot and not, as she'd let them to believe, as an assistant operations officer. Keeping up her stream of untruths, easy in short phone calls and letters, was tricky when talking to them in the flesh.

This time she would visit, however. She wondered if she should have sent them a letter telling them she was coming. But no, this would be a surprise visit. They'd love that. She'd go tomorrow morning, sleep in her childhood bed, eat at the big kitchen table, hope for custard, make small talk and try not to tell too many lies before heading back to Skimpton on Tuesday. Now she had a new lie to add to her other lies. She'd have to let them think this was her first trip back to Scotland. She felt guilty about how hurt they'd be to discover she'd seen Elspeth without dropping in on them.

The hotel foyer was tricked out for Christmas, though it looked a little unenthusiastic. Dusty paper chains hung in deep loops from the ceiling, a small cluster of cards were grouped on the reception desk, a tree draped with lights and tinsel stood in the corner. And beside it had sat Elspeth.

She'd got up and spread her arms. 'At last. Where have you been?'

Izzy had smiled and said, 'Getting here.'

After she had checked in and taken her key, the pair of them had gone up to her room on the first floor speaking in library whispers. Hotel life thrilled and hushed them. It gave them a brief taste of a life they'd always thought beyond them.

Their room was large and frighteningly patterned – floral wallpaper and tartan carpet. The sparse furnishings – two single beds, both with a discreet chamber pot tucked underneath, a fat uncomfortable chair and a dresser – were a relief. Izzy had dropped her case and lain on one of the beds; Elspeth had draped her coat over the chair, taken a towel and gone to the bathroom across the hall. 'A bath,' she'd said. 'Been looking forward to this for ages.'

This was the routine they'd developed. Elspeth would take the first of several baths she would indulge in during her overnight stay; Izzy would lie spreadeagled on the bed, recovering from her journey and from the long days leading up to it. She normally worked thirteen days on, two days off. But in order to get four days off, enough time for a trip north to visit Elspeth, she had to run two stints without a break. It was tiring.

Eventually, Izzy heaved herself from the bed and changed out of her uniform. She put on a simple wool dress, folded her jacket and trousers and put them in the bottom of her case. Tomorrow, when visiting her mother and father, she'd wear her blue tweed suit. She never let them see her in uniform; the wings on her jacket would give away her secret. They'd know she was a pilot.

At eight they went down to dinner. It was too late for both of them, used to eating at six, so they were beyond hungry. For the first ten minutes, they ate in serious silence.

'Are you going to tell your folks the truth when you're home?' asked Elspeth when she'd cleared her bowl of soup. She sat back waiting for her next course, roast beef.

Izzy said she'd thought about it. 'But I don't want to ruin things. I haven't seen them for months and months. Next time, perhaps.'

Elspeth said, 'It will all come out one day, you know.'

'I know,' said Izzy. 'But I'm having fun right now. If they found out, they'd disapprove, we'd argue and fight. In the end, they'd win. They always do. I'd give up my job to please them. And I'd be miserable. Sometimes it's best to lie.'

Elspeth said she thought it strange someone should lie to their parents about the job they did. 'People usually lie about their sex lives.'

Izzy said that right now she didn't have a sex life to lie about.

Elspeth said that families were difficult. She was glad she no longer had one. 'You seem to navigate your relationship with your parents through an intricate tangle of lies.'

'Not exactly lies,' said Izzy. 'A re-routing of the truth.'

They ate their main courses quickly. The waitress appeared, cleared their plates and asked if they wanted pudding.

'Of course,' they said.

They were offered apple crumble or jam sponge. They opted for the crumble, fearing the sponge would be a concoction of National flour and dried eggs. The waitress took their plates and bustled off.

'Re-routing?' said Elspeth.

'Just pointing the truth in the most convenient direction.'

Elspeth said, 'What do you mean? A lie is a lie, isn't it?'

Izzy shrugged. 'In a way, I suppose. But take the job thing. My father doesn't want me to do a job he couldn't do. He likes to think of me as his little girl. So he'd prefer me to be a typist or a secretary, something girly. Also, he'd hate me to be doing a job that required me to wear trousers. He thinks it's really wrong for women to wear trousers. So, he knows I'm in the ATA, he just doesn't know I'm a pilot. It's convenient for us both. Of course the sex thing is just a normal lie that everyone tells.' She took a swig of water. 'Nobody tells their parents they've had sex, especially if they're not married. I wasn't going to burst into the living room waving my fists like a champion boxer and shout that I'd done it. I wasn't a virgin any more.'

The waitress put a bowl of crumble and custard in front of each of them, looked at Izzy and hurried off.

'She's got a fine bit of eavesdropping to report,' said Elspeth.

Izzy agreed. 'Of course, my big lie is God. I just can't tell my father I don't believe any more. It's against all his teachings. He'd be furious with me. I'm scared he'd banish me from his life for ever. I'd hate that.'

Izzy had been about twelve when her doubt set in. Then, it had shown itself as curiosity. She'd asked her father endless questions.

'When Adam and Eve were first put on earth, how did they know what to do?'

He'd put down his book and looked at her over the rim of his glasses. 'What do you mean?'

'How did they know how to light a fire and get something to eat?'

'He spoke to them.'

'What language did he use? Did he make Adam and Eve complete with fingers and toes and speaking English?'

'He spoke to them in their minds. He gave them instincts, thoughts. They knew what to do as naturally as breathing.'

'So how did Adam and Eve speak to each other if they only had thoughts and instincts?'

Her father had smiled at her. 'Questions, questions. I like questions, a sign of a healthy enquiring mind, but sometimes you just have to believe. Have faith, don't ask questions.'

'But the apple,' said Izzy. 'How did they know not to eat the apple? If they didn't speak, and didn't have an actual language, how did they know what an apple was?'

Her father hadn't answered. He tried to read.

'How old were they. Did they arrive on earth as grown-ups? If they were children, wouldn't they have needed a mum and dad, if only to tell them what an apple was?'

'They had God,' her father had said. 'They had everything.'

Izzy had known this was a dismissal. She went to her bedroom to finish her homework. But the questions lingered in her head. Over the next few months, she'd pestered her father with them. 'Noah? How did the animals know to come to the ark?'

'God told them.'

'How did they get there? Tigers all the way from India and lions from Africa and badgers and squirrels?'

'God guided them.'

'Did they swim over oceans and crawl over deserts?'

'Yes.'

'Suppose the hedgehogs came from here, Perthshire – did Perthshire exist then?'

'Yes, but it was called something else.' He hadn't known what.

'How would they have got to the ark? Would they have walked right down to the bottom of the country and jumped into the sea and swam to France then walked for miles and miles and miles?'

'Yes.'

'And why did God choose these hedgehogs and not another two?'

'God knows a good hedgehog when he sees one.' And he'd flapped her away.

Izzy hadn't been satisfied. Questions plagued her. She needed answers. 'How did Moses manage to carry all those tablets of stone down the mountain?'

'God gave him strength.'

Doubts had filled her mind. She chased them away with prayer. Every morning and evening she got on her knees and prayed. She prayed in break times at school, though not on her knees. She'd find a quiet corner and communicate with her Maker. Soon, she was regularly talking to God, keeping him up to date with her regular comings and goings. 'It's me again, God. I'm walking down the road on my way to school. Had porridge and a boiled egg for breakfast.' It had seemed to her that she was doing all the talking in this relationship. She supposed He must be busy. Then again, perhaps he wasn't there at all.

She then started asking for signs. 'Don't mean to be annoying, God, but could you send me a sign that you exist. If you do, I promise to dedicate my life to you.' She'd thought she might travel the land on foot preaching to people in towns and villages. No sign came. Izzy hoped for a white stag to appear in the garden, a shower of meteors, or for the sky to open and a booming voice to call, 'Izzy, why do you doubt me?' Nothing.

In time, the fervour had faded. The doubt, however, stayed. Izzy went to church on Sundays, listened in awe to her father's sermons, but didn't believe what he was saying.

There would be stories about Jonah living inside the belly of a whale, Daniel in the lions' den, the walls of Jericho tumbling down and Izzy would gaze round at the congregation in amazement. Did all these people really believe this stuff?

By the time she was fifteen, Izzy was a secret atheist. When, one day, her father had asked if she was having doubts about her faith, she told him, 'Of course not.' He'd summoned her into his study for one of his chats.

These mostly one-sided conversations took place once a month. Hamish would impress on his daughter the importance of working hard at school, being respectful to her mother and setting an example in the community. She mustn't be seen in the company of the village's rough elements. She had a responsibility to her family, and her family had a responsibility to the village. 'We must set an example,' Hamish told her. 'We must show the way. We must be kind, respectable and good-hearted.'

This little chat, however, had been about Izzy's behaviour in church. 'I can't but notice that you are not paying attention. You are looking about you, staring at the other members of the congregation.' The room smelled musty, of tobacco, papers, ink and old air. He never opened a window. In the hall outside, the grandfather clock ticked, a loud sombre beat. Her mother had rustled past the door, carrying a bunch of lilacs from the garden.

Izzy had told him that she liked watching people watching him. He was flattered. That was good, but she had to listen to his sermon. 'Partake by listening and being seen to listen. In fact, I've been wondering if you've been having doubts, if you've lost your faith.'

Izzy said, 'Of course not. I just needed to work out things for myself. I think you have to find your own faith.'

Her father said, 'Good girl.' Then he'd rummaged in his desk drawer and brought out a rumpled bag of lemon drops, offering her one. They'd sat back sucking in unison, smiling at one another. She loved him too much to let him know she didn't share the passion that drove his life – his calling. And she loved her own peace of mind too much to suffer one of his lectures.

Izzy had found her way. She knew now how to get by, how to avoid fuss and arguments. She would agree with her father and, privately, think her own thoughts, follow her own path. She'd do whatever she wanted to do without asking his permission. She'd keep her life a secret. She didn't want to upset him with her longing for adventure.

Izzy and Elspeth finished their pudding and asked for their coffee to be served in the hotel lounge. 'Oh joy,' said Elspeth, 'a comfy seat. The simple pleasures are the best.' She caught Izzy's surprised expression. 'Life is harsh in the forest.'

'But you've made new friends?' Izzy asked.

'Yes. We are united in our discomfort.'

'What about the men? Do you fancy anyone?'

Elspeth shook her head. 'There's one who has taken a shine to me – Tyler Bute. He sings to me, calls my name, makes jokes to me. It all a bit schoolboyish.'

'Is he nice?'

'He's big.'

'Fat?' asked Izzy.

'No, tall, broad. There's a lot of him and he has a huge personality. He's the one in the crowd that you notice. The main man, I suppose. If we were together, there would be him with his big voice, hearty in his plaid shirt, and me with my accordion. I think we'd be the sort of couple people avoid.'

They sipped their coffee, agreed it was ghastly.

'I can't help thinking about your mother and father,' said Elspeth. 'All the years you've been part of their life, all the time you've been with them, the things you've shared – your first words, first steps, birthdays, Christmases, holding your hand when you walked along the street, scolding you, hugging you, reading you stories, playing games, loving you and, in the end, they know nothing about you. They want you to be their little girl. They don't know who you are.'

Izzy thought that was true. 'I'm dreading the day when they find out. I hope I'm not around when it happens.'

Chapter Seven
Careful, Careful

The village hadn't changed. The war had hardly touched it. Sunday evening in December, a handful of soldiers sat on the bench in front of the hotel, a noisy cluster of sparrows hopped round the base of the fountain in the square, but really, the place was empty – barely a soul to be seen. No shops were open. Small drifts of smoke spiralled out of chimneys. The Sabbath day and silent as a churchyard; the soldiers spoke in murmurs and even the sparrows were less boisterous than usual.

Not that this meant Izzy's walk from the bus stop to the manse went unobserved. Though she didn't notice anybody noticing her, she was self-consciously aware of being spied on. By tomorrow morning, the whole village would know that the minister's daughter had come home. She knew that was the way of things in a small place. It shouldn't bother her, but it did.

Living in Skimpton was different. She was an outsider there, not part of the local community, and her comings and goings were of little interest to the people who'd lived there all their lives. They knew that when the war ended, she, and all the others who'd turned up in the village, would disappear.

'What will you do when the war's over?' Elspeth had asked last night. They'd been back in their room at the time. Elspeth had just enjoyed her second bath and had sighed at the softness of the bed and the luxury of clean sheets.

'Dunno,' said Izzy. 'Maybe I'll get a job as a commercial pilot.'

'Flying is the future,' said Elspeth. 'Everybody will want to fly everywhere.'

Izzy had said that she was sure that when the war ended nobody would want to go anywhere. 'People will go home and stay home. They'll want to feel safe. And, if anyone did want to go anywhere, they wouldn't want it to be in a plane flown by a woman. In fact, I'm sure if a bunch of people were on a plane and they saw a woman in the pilot's seat, they'd all get off. That's what they think of women.'

Elspeth said, 'Nonsense. This is a time of women. We have proven we can do anything men can do. When this war is over, there will be golden opportunities for women.'

'Golden opportunities to have babies and bake cakes,' said Izzy. 'Neither of which I want to do.'

Outside, the night had turned wild. Frenetic music poured from the village hall, the dance band strumming out a few frantic struts before winding up with a slow last waltz. The pubs had closed, drinkers who hadn't gone to the dance were milling about, shouting.

'Noisy out there,' said Izzy.

'Hectic but not frenzied, a normal Saturday night.'

Izzy asked if there would be a fight.

'There are fights all the time. The men are miles from home and they miss their families. They let off steam. They fight.'

'What do you do?'

'Make a wide berth, a very wide berth.'

Izzy had been glad she was in the hotel and not out there in the night surrounded by men who were a long way from home and letting off steam.

Now, she reached the gates of the manse, always open. She walked up the short drive to the house pondering the business of letting off steam. She decided it was a good thing to do. The male pilots did it often. Sometimes, they were still letting off steam when they came in to work – still a little drunk. Mostly, though, they were hungover. Julia let off steam. Izzy had heard her at it through the bedroom wall – a long moan of pleasure. Claire didn't. But Izzy got the impression she'd like to. It was time, Izzy decided, to let off some steam, to sow a few wild oats before the war ended and she'd be expected live a safe sensible life.

Meantime, for the next two days, she'd be the good daughter. She'd tell her parents the things they wanted to hear. She'd tell lies.

She stood in the hall and announced herself. 'Hello, it's me. I'm home.' Nothing. She'd been expecting her mother and father to appear in the doorway and gush. She had thought they would run towards her, take her in their arms, kiss her and weep with joy. She went into the kitchen. They were at the table eating supper, listening to the radio and, for a few moments, didn't notice she was there.

Her father saw her first. He stopped eating, put down his fork and said, 'What the hell are you doing here?'

Her mother turned, looked astonished and asked her why she hadn't let them know she was coming. Izzy shrugged and said she'd wanted to surprise them.

'You should always let us know you're coming,' said her mother. 'We might not have been here. We could have been away somewhere.'

'Where?' asked Izzy. This was absurd. Her parents hardly ever went anywhere. Her father went out in the evenings to meetings or to visit parishioners and her mother went to the Women's Institute, but one of them was always at home.

She took off her coat, hung it on the hook at the back of the door.

'You're wearing ordinary clothes. Where's your uniform?' her mother wanted to know. 'I've never seen you wear it.'

Izzy said she had left it behind. 'Mrs Brent is going to give it a clean.' It was in her bag. She sat at the table, and said that they didn't seem all that pleased to see her.

'Of course we're pleased to see you. It's lovely to have you here. Just a little bit of a shock. We weren't expecting you,' said her mother. She smacked her palms on the table, stood up, 'I'll get you something to eat. Really, you should let people know you're coming.'

She disappeared into the pantry, emerged with two sausages and a potato, started to bustle and complain. 'You really should tell people in advance that you're planning a visit. There's a war on, nobody knows what they'll be doing any more. They certainly don't drop in. The days of dropping in are over. Everything is rationed. You can hardly offer someone a decent cup of tea.'

She peeled the potato, chopped it and threw it into a sizzling pan. The sausages were already frying. 'This will have to do you. I'll see what I can get at the butcher's tomorrow. You . . .'

'. . . should have let you know I was coming,' said Izzy. 'I know.'

Her father smiled at her from across the table and asked how she got here.

'I flew up to Prestwick, then I got the bus. Well, several buses.'

First lie, but only a bit of a lie. She did fly to Prestwick, and she had caught a bus.

He nodded, sighed, said he had to go. 'Young Christians Bible study this evening, then I have to visit the McKinnons. They got word yesterday that their boy was killed last week.' He put his hand on Izzy's shoulder, told her it was good to see her. 'Nice of you to come all this way. I'll be back sometime after ten.' He walked slowly from the room, shoulders slumped.

Izzy heard him heave on his coat before going into his study to collect his Bible and notes for his Bible study class. Then he walked up the hall, sombre steps, and left the manse.

'He's not taking this war well,' said her mother. 'It's wearing him down. Barely a week passes without someone in the village losing someone. You just never know who's going to be next. Your father visits every bereaved family. He's seen a lot of tears.' She brought a plate of sausages and chips to the table and put it down in front of Izzy. 'Still, we don't have to worry about you. That's a comfort.'

She took off her apron, hung it on the back of the pantry door. 'He's in a spot of bother at the moment. He no longer gives the old hellfire sermons everyone used to love. He talks about compassion and forgiveness. It doesn't go down well. Last Sunday he said that we had one thing in common with the enemy. There would be tears of sorrow and loss in German homes as well as those within our own shores. Nobody liked that. Some people refused to shake his hand as they left the church. There are whisperings in the village that he's a conscientious objector.' She put her hand to her cheek. 'I must powder my nose. It's the Spitfire fund committee night tonight.' She headed for the door, stopped. 'There are scones in the tin in the pantry, tea's in the pot. Help yourself.'

She bustled out, reappeared ten minutes later, hair combed, face freshly powdered, lips tinted with a thin scraping of Scarlet Rose, the lipstick she'd worn for years. She buttoned her coat. 'Sorry, darling, but this was the only night everyone was free for the meeting. Still, no need to tell you to make yourself at home – you are home.' She paused at the door. 'I've left fresh sheets on your bed. You'll have to make it up yourself.'

She went out, walked up the hall, turned and came back again. 'And I probably won't be here when you get up in the morning. I work three days a week at the cottage hospital. They're short-staffed with the war. Nurses away at military hospitals.'

'You're a nurse?' asked Izzy.

'Don't be daft. I help out. Clean the wards, serve tea and such. Just doing my bit.' She left again shouting as she headed for the front door, 'I'd like to have been a nurse. If I had my time again, it's what I'd do.'

When she was younger, being alone in the house had been high on Izzy's list of favourite things. She'd wander the rooms, revelling in the freedom of having nobody to check on her doings. She'd turn up the wireless, rummage through the drawers in her parents' bedroom, poke about in cupboards and read the vast tome *Everything Within* that was kept discreetly hidden in the bottom of her father's wardrobe. It had advice on worming pets, cleaning windows, clearing blocked drains, making mustard poultices to relieve bronchitis, treating wasp stings, getting rid of nasty teacup rings on tables. It covered every aspect of modern life. Though none of these things interested Izzy. She limited herself to the three paragraphs offering handy hints to the newly wed couple on page 344, headed 'Sexual Intercourse, a Vital Aid to a Happy Marriage'.

When she was ten, these paragraphs had fascinated and alarmed her. If she had to do *that*, she had decided, she was definitely never going to get married. These days, she felt differently. She still wasn't keen on marriage, but sexual intercourse was no longer alarming.

This evening, she didn't find the prospect of being alone as alluring as she had when she was ten. The house was ominously cold and empty, silent, except for the serious ticking of the grandfather clock in the hall. She finished her supper, washed and dried the dishes, then found the scones in the tin with the picture of two Highland cows on the lid and took out two. She ate them with plum jam. And thought about her mother.

It hadn't ever occurred to Izzy that her mother was a person. She'd been Mum – the face behind the large lunch-time puddings, the one who wiped away tears, the ironer of clothes, the general all-round fixer of things. She was just *there*.

Sometimes she'd be singing along with the wireless, and sometimes her face would be drenched with worry. Nobody called her Joan or even Mrs Macleod. She was always the Minister's Wife. She was a woman defined by her role in the community. It came to Izzy that her mother had never been happy.

Happiness had never been an issue in the household. It was never discussed. It was just assumed that if someone was good, worked hard, prayed, obeyed the law, led a noble, upstanding life, then happiness would follow. Now, Izzy doubted this. She had met a group of women who were truly, sometimes even riotously, happy – the pilots she worked with. They all had one thing in common – no matter what anybody said, or thought, even if they disapproved, they did what they wanted to do. They were free in a way that Izzy had never thought possible.

The next day passed quietly. Izzy explored the woods where she'd played as a child. She visited favourite haunts – the huge rock by the stream, the trees she'd climbed and the ivy-covered fallen tree where she'd asked God for a sign that he existed. She sat on it, but didn't ask for any more signs. She didn't need them, she no longer believed.

It was after four when her mother and father returned home. Her father had spent the afternoon at the local school, eating lunch with the pupils, then watching their Christmas nativity play. She had gone from the cottage hospital to the village hall where she had helped make up parcels to be sent to soldiers serving abroad. They'd walked back to the manse together, moving up the street slowly, stopping to chat to people they met on the way. It was one of Hamish's favourite things to do. It was important, he said often, to be seen out and about in the community. To be a friendly presence, always ready for a bit of small talk, always interested in the folk around them. Their lives are our lives and our lives are their lives, that's the way of things. No secrets.

Joan put on her apron and set about making supper. She chased Izzy and Hamish from the kitchen. 'Can't be doing with people getting under my feet when I'm cooking.' The two sheepishly left her to it.

In the hall, Hamish put his hand on Izzy's shoulder and suggested they have a little chat. Izzy thought he was going to invite her into his study as he had done when she was a child and quiz her on her faith. But no, he suggested a stroll round the garden. 'We've dug up the flower beds, grow our own potatoes, cabbage and Brussels sprouts. Fruit in summer – strawberries, raspberries, blackcurrants. Do it all myself.'

There wasn't really much to see. It was December, the ground was frosted hard and it was getting dark. First stars appearing in the sky. 'Venus,' said her father, pointing to the heavens, 'star of the evening this time of year.' They stopped on the brick path, looked at the patch of ground that once held a dense growth of poppies, pansies and campanula, and considered the rows of Brussels sprouts. 'Fresh winter vegetables,' said Hamish. 'Healthy food straight from the earth.'

Izzy agreed.

He put his hands in his pockets, turned to her and asked if she was behaving herself.

'Of course,' she said. 'I'm too busy to do anything else.'

'It's a pity you can't be home for Christmas. It's a time for families to be together.'

'True,' said Izzy. 'But I can't get the time off. Perhaps you should write to Hitler and tell him how inconvenient this war is for everybody. We all want to be home for Christmas.'

He laughed. 'Talking of coming home, which bus did you come on?'

'The one from Perth. I got a train from Glasgow, then the bus. Why?'

'You were seen getting off the one that came from Inverness going towards Perth. Southbound.'

'Was I?' said Izzy. 'Who saw me?' She noticed her voice had slipped up an octave. She was feigning indignation. She was sounding like a liar.

'Just one of the teachers at the school,' he said. 'She lives beside the bus stop. She said she saw you. Said it must be nice to have you home.'

'Well, I don't care what she thinks she saw. I know which bus

I got off. And, by the way, it's nice to be home.'

Hamish said it was nice to have her here, no matter which bus brought her. He pointed to the area beyond the sprouts and said he was going to put peas in there next year. 'I'll be sitting on the doorstep shelling them in the sunshine. That's a happy thing to do.'

'Yes,' said Izzy. 'Are you happy? I mean, apart from when you're shelling peas in the sunshine. Generally, in your life, are you happy?'

He snorted. 'Happiness is not something I pursue. Goodness is what interests me.'

Izzy looked at him. Hands deep in his pockets, leaning back and gazing at the darkening sky, he was nodding, agreeing with himself.

'Is that why you said what you did about tears in German homes?'

'I said what I think must be true. Young men are dying and their families are in tears. I fear there will be repercussions. I've been told that one or two people have written to the head of the Church of Scotland, accusing me of being a German sympathiser.'

'And you're not,' said Izzy.

'Of course I'm not.' Then, he asked, 'Are you happy?'

'Right now, yes. Absolutely, almost deliriously so. I love my job. I love my life.'

'Careful, careful,' he said. 'I'd be very worried about that kind of happiness. It can make you careless. It could all come tumbling down around you. Don't give in to it.'

'Why not? What's wrong with being happy?'

'Nobody is happy,' he said. 'Only fools delude themselves that they are. There is contentment, I'll give you that. But it can only be reached by living a life of goodness and honesty.' He turned to her, bathed her in his graceful stare, the look he gave people when he was gifting them with his wisdom.

Izzy said, 'Well, now, honesty . . .' If it was honesty they were discussing, she could give him honesty. Now was the moment to tell him all her truths.

But then the singing started. It filled the air, voices, harmonies – choir practice at the church – 'Oh, Come All Ye Faithful'. '. . . Joyful and triumphant . . .' they sang. A soft wind brought sweet drifts of wood smoke and above them Venus shone in an indigo sky.

Enraptured, Hamish sighed, rocked on his heels and said, 'Perfect, perfect. It doesn't get better than this.' He smiled at Izzy. 'I read your letter from Allan.'

Izzy said she'd guessed that.

'I disapproved at first. Then I thought about it. All those young men dying, some of them only nineteen or twenty, not even started on their lives. Never to know what job they'd end up doing, who they'd marry. Never even having enjoyed proper intimacy.'

Izzy held her breath, she wasn't sure she liked the way this conversation was going.

'You did a good thing, Izzy,' Hamish said.

'I thought you'd hate me for doing that. I had sex with a man I wasn't married to. You've always said that was a sin,' said Izzy.

'I suspect this war has made me revise my opinions on sinning,' said Hamish. 'And I'll never hate you. Not ever.' He put his arm round her, sniffed the air. 'I smell supper.'

They walked back down the garden. Hamish kept his arm

round Izzy. 'A good thing. A very good thing. You made Allan happy. I'm proud of you.'

Izzy thought how odd it was that you were sure you knew all about someone close, then found out you didn't.

Chapter Eight

Christmas and a Brief Lesson in Line Shooting

On the days leading up to Christmas, the weather was foul. First there had been choking hail-laden gales battering in from the sea, hammering the airbase, then the fog came down. Izzy said that if ever she were to lose control and step outside to shout at the weather, it would be fog that brought on the outburst. It was stubborn weather – damp, thick, yellow, silent, shrouding everything, hiding the sky.

The pilots were grounded. Edith was exasperated, fifty planes waiting to be moved and nothing to be done about it till the air cleared. She phoned other bases to see what the weather was doing there. Foggy. She bustled to the met room to ask if there was any sign of it lifting. No. She tutted and went back to the ops room.

In the mess, pilots read the scant newspapers of the day, played cards or backgammon, drank tea, sewed. Dolores stood on her head, ankles propped against the wall. This, she claimed, was good for the brain. And she'd be needing that as soon as the fog cleared. There would be a large backlog of planes to be shifted. Julia filled in her logbook. Diane knitted.

Izzy wrote to Elspeth and to her parents. From time to time, she'd lean back, listening to the squall of voices nearby. Full, rich, rounded words surrounded her. Women saying things she couldn't. She found it impossible to call a plane a 'darling thing' or a 'sweetie'. But she envied those women whose enthusiasm didn't just pour from their lips, it oozed from their whole bodies. They keened forwards laughing as they spoke. 'Darling, that Hurricane was such a sweetheart.' Izzy knew if she said such a thing at home, there would be mockery – her father would burst out laughing. But then, perhaps he wouldn't. He was turning out to be surprising.

Sometimes, hearing someone trilling about a plane or an adventure in the sky, Izzy would wince. At such moments, Diane would often stop knitting, reach over and touch her hand. 'It's only how they talk. Doesn't mean they're not the same as you.' Often, Izzy would walk to the window, stare out, sigh and rest her forehead on the pane. 'Yes, Izzy,' Diane would say, 'banging your head on the window and sighing is a well-known way of changing the weather.'

Often, as the morning wore on, things got rowdy. There would be challenges. Who could lift a chair by one leg, hold it aloft and carry it across the room. Who could make it from one side of the mess to the other without putting their feet on the floor. When that happened, Edith would bustle to the CO's office, and tell him that the troops were getting boisterous. 'Tears before bedtime, I fear.'

Carlton Willoughby would look at his watch, then out at the weather and say, 'Send them home. No flying today.'

Edith would busy back to the mess, stick her head round the door. 'It's a washout, folks. You can all go home.'

*

On Christmas Eve, Julia left to spend time with friends in London. Claire went to her parents' house outside York, taking with her a turkey she'd bought from Mrs Brent. Izzy was working.

Christmas turned out to be a good day. The fog lifted. It was still bitterly cold with a strong wind shoving out from the sea. There was a heartiness in the air, everyone shouting, 'Merry Christmas!' Cook had baked scones, and, for those who were around at lunchtime, there was turkey. The mess was decked with boughs of holly. Long colourful paper streamers hung criss-cross from one end of the ceiling to the other. A tree from the woods behind the base had been dug up, brought in and decorated. A carol service played on the wireless.

Izzy and Diane were given Spitfires to take to Marriat Hall – a huge country house in North Yorkshire that had been taken over by the MOD as a storage unit. Its lawns, once lush, were cluttered with planes waiting to be moved on. Giant gaps had been cut in the hedges to make a runway.

'Good-oh,' said Diane. 'I love Marriat Hall. Used to go to parties there, and they had a jolly good hunt once upon a time. C'mon, Izzy, tally-ho.'

Twenty minutes later, they were in their planes ready to taxi. Dolores was first up to the runway, Harry Norton straddling the tail of her Spitfire to keep it steady in the crosswind. It was probably the excitement of being on the go after days of sitting about watching the weather that made Dolores forget Harry was there. She didn't pause at the end of the runway to allow him to jump off. Instead, she speeded up, rushed along, preparing to take to the sky.

From her vantage point in the queue, Izzy couldn't see Harry's face, only his body hanging on and his fists flailing against the side on the plane. There were half a dozen ground engineers running up the runway, shouting. Sensing something was wrong – the tail felt heavy – Dolores braked. Harry jumped off. Izzy couldn't hear what was said, but she could see it. Harry standing shaking a furious fist, foul language pouring from his lips, and Dolores peering down at him, looking slightly, but only slightly, sorry.

The flight was over frosted fields, country roads and hills. The world below seemed empty, though, now and then, Izzy saw a car wending along winding roads. People off to visit relatives, Izzy thought. Once, she saw a church and, outside, a milling group of people. This was the first time in her life she hadn't gone to church on Christmas Day.

She looked at her watch, twelve o'clock. Back home, the service would be over. The congregation would have sung 'Hark the Herald Angels Sing', her father's favourite hymn. Soon, everyone would be off home for their festive lunch – mock goose or mock turkey, whatever that was. Izzy didn't know.

And there wouldn't be many Christmas puddings. Suzie, at the local shop, had told Izzy she had five hundred registered ration customers and only two Christmas puddings for sale. Izzy didn't care. She hated Christmas pudding.

Marriat Hall was hard to find. It was tucked behind a small copse and covered with camouflage nets. But Izzy could see Diane in her cockpit give a thumbs-up. Time to land.

From her place in the sky, it was clear to Izzy that Diane was having the time of her life. She had bumped down, a small bounce, and was now whooshing over the grass airstrip through the hedges. It was a gallop.

Izzy followed, opened the canopy, checked her brake pressure, flaps down, the plane pitched a little, nose down. Still, she had to tilt her head to the side to see the ground. Then she was speeding forwards, through the hedges – grinning.

They taxied to the delivery bay. Then climbed out and went to find someone to sign their delivery chits.

Diane was pink-cheeked. 'Wasn't that splendid? Makes you long to go back up and do it all again.'

An elderly man, part of the Home Guard, signed their chits, then took them to a room at the front of the house where they could watch for the taxi plane that would pick them up and take them back to base. He brought them each a mug of tea. 'Fresh leaves for the ladies,' he said with a wink. 'Merry Christmas.'

'Look at this place,' said Diane. 'This used to be a beautiful house.' She waved her arm at the mess. 'Chipped paint, posters everywhere. When this war is over, I doubt anyone is going to be able to put everything back the way it was.' She sighed and stared out of the window. 'It's all terribly sad.' She took out her knitting, settled back and started work. 'So, what did you make of Dolores' little faux pas?'

Izzy shrugged. 'She forgot Harry was there.'

'Well, that's obvious. But what d'you think she'll make of it? What line will she shoot?'

Izzy shrugged again.

'Will she say she had an instinct something was wrong? Or will she overplay the thing and say she took off with him aboard, felt the tail heavy and came back down again and Harry might be given a dressing down for taking an unofficial flight?'

Izzy chose the unofficial flight. Diane shook her head. 'I think the instinct. Care for a wager? Two shillings?'

'OK.'

They shook on it.

'Izzy,' said Diane, 'you must learn to line shoot. I've noticed you don't do it. But it goes with the job, relieves the tension.'

'It's telling lies,' said Izzy. Though, who was she to disapprove of such a thing? She was the queen of liars.

'It's embellishing the truth. It's verbal bravado. After all, it isn't death everyone fears, it's that moment when you know you're going to die that brings you out in a sweat. When you've mucked up, made a stupid mistake and are about to get bumped off, that's what we all dread. So, when that happens and we somehow don't die, we shoot a line or two. You should try it. It makes you feel braver, relieves the tension. It's fun to swagger a little now and then. You should take it up.'

Izzy said that she'd been brought up to think telling lies and swaggering were wrong. 'Not that I haven't told the odd lie. I just can't help thinking I'll get my comeuppance for doing it.'

Diane, knitting furiously, said, 'Nonsense. Embellishing the truth and swaggering are good for the soul. I urge you to take them both up and abandon all religious nonsense that shuts you off from the juicy things in life.' She leaned forwards. 'Sin a little, Izzy, before it's too late.' She looked out of the window. 'E, F, B, C, D, A.'

'What are you talking about?' Izzy asked.

'I've got a physical coming up and I'm revising the eye chart. I have it memorised.' She tapped the side of her forehead.

'Isn't that cheating?'

'Of course it's cheating. How else am I to pass the eye test? I can't see the damn chart without my specs.' She sighed. 'Where's that bloody taxi?'

The Anson, when it finally arrived at half past two, was full.

Marriat Hall was its last stop. There were twelve other pilots on-board, all keen to get home. Dick Wills was at the helm, smoking. Lighting up was a sacking offence, so he called his cigarettes 'instant dismissals'. 'Time for another instant dismissal, folks. What about a singsong, a few carols?'

They started with 'Oh Come All Ye Faithful', and were swaying from side to side, belting out a hearty 'Ding Dong Merrily on High', 'Glo-ooo-ooo-ooo-ria . . .', pink-cheeked and giddy with song, when they landed at Skimpton. In the van taking them from the end of the runway back to the base, Dolores said, 'Did you see that guy hanging on to my tail? He didn't jump off. Something told me something was wrong. An instinct. Pilot's instinct. Born with it, I guess.'

Diane nudged Izzy. 'Two shillings.'

Dolores asked Izzy what she was up to now. 'Going home to a huge meal?'

Izzy shook her head. 'There's nobody but me at the cottage at the moment. I'll have whatever I can find and a cup of tea.'

'You could come eat with Alfie and me if you want. We're having duck.'

Izzy declined. It was rumoured that Dolores had stopped living in the flat above the garage at Hiddlington Hall and moved into Lord Alfred's bed. Not that Izzy cared about that. And she thought Julia's tales about the pair of them chasing one another up and down the mansion's long corridors, Alfie wielding a riding crop, Dolores dressed in little more than a riding jacket, hat and black stockings, were just a flight of Julia's fanciful imagination. No, it was the way Dolores said Alfie that made Izzy turn down the invitation.

'Alfie,' she'd said, deepening her voice, keeping the name in her mouth for as long as possible, as if it were the most beautiful word in the world. Tempting as a plate of roast duck was, Izzy guessed that, on this most special of nights, she'd be playing gooseberry.

Besides, she was tired. She had her evening planned out – a bath, then she'd eat, open the parcel her mother had sent, listen to the wireless and go to bed early. She was looking forward to it.

She cycled home. The evening was bitter and turning indigo, darkness falling, early stars glimmering – it looked like Christmas. At home, her mother and father would have eaten – roast chicken, if they could get it, and pudding, heavy with dried fruit her mother would have saved from her rations. They'd have opened the parcel Izzy had sent – tins of pears, salmon and condensed milk, cologne, soap, tobacco, a dressing gown and pyjamas for her father and a silk blouse for her mother.

Now, they'd be preparing to go out to the evening service. The sermon tonight would be softer than her father's usual scolding rant. They'd definitely sing 'Once in Royal David's City', another of her father's favourites. Izzy sang it as she swished along over the frosty road, watching the small flickering light beaming the way ahead. She was alone now, the bus had passed, and the car taking Edith and Fiona home. Dolores had thundered by on the motorbike, honking as she went. Izzy had rung her bell, and kept ringing it long after Dolores had disappeared. She was happy.

Once home, she followed her plan – a bath, food, then the present. Mrs Brent had, at some point in the afternoon, come to the cottage and left several slices of turkey, cold roast potatoes and a pot of gravy to be heated. Izzy thought this splendid. This was how Christmas ought to be, sitting in the kitchen wrapped in a comforting, if unflattering, dressing gown, eating and listening to the wireless. She opened the parcel from her mother, and found a hand-knitted navy jumper with a dark red collar and cuffs. It had been made from a couple of her father's old jumpers, rattled down and knitted anew. Izzy could see her mother in her chair by the fire, needles clicking as she listened to the wireless. Her father would be in the chair opposite reading. The jumper smelled of home. Izzy held it to her face, breathed it in – old damp house, wood fire, lavender polish, her mother's cologne, her father's pipe tobacco – and felt a pang of homesickness.

She'd write a thank you note to her parents immediately, while the joy of the new jumper was still with her. She fetched her notepad and pen. It was a Parker, fat and tortoiseshell with a gold nib, a present from her mother. 'No excuse not to write now you have this.' It was a beloved possession.

Someone on the wireless was singing a Christmas song. She was thanking her mother for the jersey – 'I'm wearing it now, as I write' – which wasn't true, but was what her mother would want to read. And someone was banging on the front door.

It was Jacob. He followed her into the kitchen, sat at the table. 'I heard you were alone. I thought you might like some company.'

'I'm fine,' said Izzy. 'I'm happy on my own.'

He told her that she wasn't fine, couldn't be fine. Nobody who spent Christmas on their own was fine. He'd had a wonderful time with Mrs Brent and her family.

Izzy offered him a cup of tea. 'I'll refresh the pot.'

He asked if she didn't have anything stronger. 'It's Christmas.'

'No,' said Izzy. She didn't drink much. She put the kettle on.

'I should have brought something with me,' he said.

Izzy shook her head. 'Not for me, you shouldn't.'

'It's Christmas. You need something stronger than tea.'

The kettle boiled. Izzy filled the teapot. Poured him a cup. 'Tea's fine.'

He took the cup, smiled and asked if she'd like to go to the cinema with him.

Izzy's mother had warned her about men. Though the advice had been vague – some men weren't very nice, some were only out for what they could get and, when they got that, they'd leave you high and dry. She never specified at the time what it was such men wanted.

Elspeth had been more worldly wise. It wasn't just men, she'd told Izzy, there were people who were wild inside. 'You can see it in their eyes, a certain glint. They don't set out to hurt you, but they do. They draw you in, but when you get too close, they push you away. Some people never really look you in the eye, they look over your shoulder to see if there's someone better just down the road. Some people are always strangers. Even if you've been married to them for years, they're strangers.'

Izzy looked long and hard at Jacob. She knew she was seeing someone who'd always be looking over her shoulder, checking that there wasn't someone better just down the road. He would always be a stranger. She said no.

'You won't go out with me because you are a pilot and I'm just a driver.'

'I won't go out with you because you are married.'

'I didn't say I wanted to sleep with you. I just wanted your company.'

Izzy shook her head. 'I don't go out often. Too tired.'

'I just want someone to talk to, someone like you who doesn't belong.'

She asked what he meant by that.

'You don't talk like the other women. Don't walk like them. You look at the ground, they stare straight ahead. When this war is over, they'll go back to their tea parties and their balls and their big houses. You won't. You have changed your life. It's not that you've nothing to back to. It's that you can't go back.'

This was true. Izzy knew there was no going back for her. Her mother and father wanted her to settle down. Settle down? What did that mean, exactly? Get married, have a baby, do the washing, dust the mantelpiece, darn socks. Oh no, she didn't think so. She worried about what would happen to her when the war ended. 'What about you, can you go back?'

'Going back is all I think about. It fills my life. But what to? My country in ruins. My wife, my mother, my father – are they even still alive? Who knows? And, if they are, what will they have done to stay alive? They may not be the same people. I am not the same man. Maybe one day we'll be able to sit together and talk about little things, the weather, what will we have for supper – but I think it will be a long time before the things we've seen, the pictures in our heads, fade away.' He stood up. 'I should go.'

Izzy showed him to the door. He turned, touched her cheek. 'Perhaps you could have a drink with me, or a walk by the river. We could chat. We could tell each other our stories, our lives, our plans.'

Izzy said, 'Why not? We could do that.' It seemed to her, though, that as he spoke, as he stroked her face, he was looking past her, over her shoulder into the cottage, taking it in, sizing it up.

'We'll speak again soon,' he said. And walked away down the path.

Izzy went back inside. She washed the dishes, made more tea, then sat down to finish her letter home. She put her hand out to the spot on the table where she'd left her pen. It wasn't there. She looked around, lifted her notepad, stared down at the floor. She got down on all fours, crawling about, searching. But the pen – the beloved gold-nibbed, tortoiseshell Parker – was gone.

Chapter Nine
The Flavour of the Day

A week after Christmas, Izzy had a flight into Yorkshire, and something to be moved on waiting there for her.

Diane and Julia were headed for the Cotswolds, Claire was on taxi duty and Dick Wills was off to Siberia. 'Lovely flight. Excellent views.'

'Up the coast,' said Izzy.

'No,' said Dick. 'I prefer to fly over land, even if it is mountainous.'

'That's too dangerous for me,' said Izzy. She hated going to Kirkbride, nicknamed 'Siberia' because it was so far north, in Cumbria, cold, isolated and wild. But she could see it offered Dick a chance to smoke, loop, roll and skim low between mountains.

'Darling Izzy,' said Dick. 'You must learn not to shy away from danger. Taking risks is addictive. You get into a spot of bother and your heart starts pumping, you can almost smell your blood. You sweat. You forget to breathe. Then it's over, you land. All is well. And you ache to get up there again. Taking risks again. It's a thrill, dicing with death.'

Izzy didn't agree. She never took risks. She obeyed the rules – always on the ground twenty minutes before dusk, never flew in adverse weather, kept below any clouds, checked in at the mapping room and meticulously went through her pre- and post-flight routines. She didn't think dicing with death at all thrilling.

She checked her route in the map room. Then she went to the met room to check on the weather with Nigel.

'Lovely day,' he said. 'Clear and perfect. Little bit of a front coming in late afternoonish, about five. But you'll all be safely down and headed home for tea by then.'

'And what's the flavour of the air today?' asked Julia as they climbed into the van.

'Green,' said Izzy. 'Not fresh spring green, but mouldy damp green. The air tastes of murk.'

She took off after the taxi Anson. This was her moment, it wasn't just a physical whoosh speeding along the runway, into the air, ground slipping away beneath her, it was an emotional whoosh, too – a thrill almost euphoric. This was why she stayed home nights, never got drunk, didn't date and this was why she always obeyed the rules. She didn't want anything to take the edge of this buzz, and she didn't want to get fired and lose it all.

She cruised out over the sea, a gasp of ozone, then she banked, a glimpse of water below, turned the plane inland, pulled the cockpit shut, climbed and settled on her course. There was a slight mist rising, but it was nothing. Nothing at all.

She saw the road she'd follow, a thin black ribbon winding below, after that she'd pick out the rail tracks, straight and gleaming. Sometimes, Izzy followed a road exactly, every loop and twist and turn just for the fun of it. Mostly she did it to prolong her time in the air, the joy she felt.

On days like this, when the weather was clear – no clouds – and engine and airframe sounded as they should, Izzy relaxed.

She'd watch the world below – fields, treetops – keep an eye on her instruments, daydream a little and sing a little.

Today she sang 'I Can't Give You Anything but Love, Baby' as the plane waltzed from side to side A thousand feet high, and alone, this was the only place in the world she could let her voice roll. It was too flat, too tuneless to be set free anywhere else.

'Izzy,' Elspeth had once told her, 'as your music teacher, I have to be honest. You are tone-deaf. You will never master the piano. And your singing voice is painful to the ears.'

For Izzy, this had been a relief. She had known this all along. She gave up trying to play the piano, ponderously ploughing through simple tunes she didn't like and had allowed Elspeth to instruct her in other matters – art, music, love and, mostly, life. Life, according to Elspeth Moon, was a lot more joyful and juicy than life according to Hamish Macleod, whose views on the inevitable dire comeuppance of sinners Elspeth found alarming.

This arrangement suited them both. Izzy loved to listen to stories about a life more adventurous than the one she'd led so far. Elspeth loved to talk.

After the piano lessons stopped, they had spent most Saturday afternoons listening to Elspeth's wind-up horn gramophone, which they carried out into the woods behind her cottage. They lay under the trees, looking up at sunlight sifting through branches above listening to Mahler, Mozart and Beethoven's 'Pastoral Symphony', drinking Pimm's. Elspeth had instructed Izzy on matters of love. 'It is a wonderful thing. It will make your heart float and sing, and it will bring you the most glorious and fulfilling misery you will ever know.' Izzy believed everything she was told. It had to be true. Elspeth was wise. She was four years older.

She had told Izzy about her time in Chelsea, posing nude for the artist who lived in the room along the corridor from hers. She spoke of the importance of expressing oneself through free love. 'We must abandon ourselves to the physical,' she'd said. Izzy had said, 'Goodness.' She wasn't sure about that. Her father would definitely not approve.

Once, on a stroll by the river, Elspeth had found a small blue almost heart-shaped stone, which she had given to Izzy. 'This will be lucky for you.'

'Shouldn't you keep it, if it's lucky?' said Izzy.

'Oh no. It wouldn't be lucky for me. Only for the one I give it to. Luck always comes as a gift. Also, you must pass it on. You must share your luck. You will know when the time comes to give your stone to someone new. You will recognise the moment.'

Izzy had that stone still. She kept it with her always. Had it now in the pocket of her flying suit, her lucky stone. She didn't feel safe without it.

The sprawl of York was below her. She buzzed on, following the rail tracks, till she saw what she'd been looking for – a small wood beside a river and, beyond them, an airbase. She did two circuits, checking the runway was clear, and landed.

Her next plane was a battered old thing that had seen more of the war than she had. It was NEA. – Not Essentially Airworthy – and, walking round it, taking in its failings, Izzy thought it was not *exactly* airworthy, even, not at all airworthy. She didn't know if she wanted to fly this plane. She gave it another tour. Checked her delivery chit, one Spitfire, NEA. to Cosford, where it was to be dismantled.

'It's fine for one flight,' said the ground engineer. 'It passed its daily inspection.' He stuck his hands into his pockets and looked at her hopefully.

'So is the fuel pipe OK?' Izzy asked, considering the pool of petrol on the ground.

'All fixed.'

Izzy suspected liberal use of sticky tape. She dithered. Cosford was just over an hour away, not far. Then again, taking a sip of the air, she still thought the flavour murky, a deeper damp than she'd tasted this morning. She didn't like that at all.

But, if she didn't fly this plane, someone else would. She'd be seen as chicken, afraid of a plane that wasn't airworthy. Pah! She'd be a woman. For, wasn't that what women were like – small, frail and not exactly risk-taking?

'OK,' she said. 'I'll do it.'

They were standing at the end of the runway. One or two other engineers had stopped to watch. Izzy had the feeling there were bets on if she would take the plane or not. There had been a small ripple of triumph when she'd said OK.

There was a pale watery sun in the sky, and a breeze blowing. But then, airfields, being open to the elements, there was usually some kind of breeze blowing. They were dull places to look at, Izzy thought, long runways, a tower at one end and rows of nondescript buildings. They were only enlivened by what went on inside them – flight. When a plane flew in or took off, people did what she did. They looked up.

By the time she was ready to take off in the tired old Spitfire, there was quite a crowd ready to look up and wish her luck as they waved her goodbye. If that was what they were doing; she had a notion they were mocking her.

A thick black cloud belched out of the back of the plane when she started the engine. Not a good sign, but perhaps it had been standing idle for a while. She lumbered rather than whooshed down the runway. When it reached one hundred miles per hour, she heaved the plane into the air. There would be no daydreaming, singing or idle waltzing on this trip.

The world below looked dinky. Little cars on ribbon roads, fields were chunks of muddy January land divided by hedges, a train shoved along the rail tracks trailing billows of smoke. The plane's engine chugged, the airframe sounded out of sorts, and Izzy wasn't happy at all.

She followed the main southbound railway for a while, then headed across towards Birmingham. She knew there was a front coming in from the west, but she planned to be back on the ground before it arrived.

She checked her instrument panel. She looked at her watch. She'd been in the air for ten minutes. She sniffed, rubbed her nose on the back of her glove. It was cold up here. She traced her route on her map. The road she planned to follow should be below her. She peered down. But the road, railway line, fields and trees she expected to see were gone, enveloped in mist. It had been a matter of minutes, and she hadn't seen it coming.

The mist engulfed her plane. She lost contact with the ground. She was eight hundred feet up, alone and so scared that she could hear the blood in her veins and feel fear prickle and spread inside her. She felt dread heavy in her chest and, for a few seconds, she forgot to breathe.

Chapter Ten
A Guardian Angel

At Elvington, an air base near York, Julia stared at the window. Thick rivers of rain streamed down the pane, blurring the world outside. Not that much of the world beyond the windowpane was visible, anyway. A thick mist shrouded everything, trees, bare at this time of year, appeared as ghostly shapes as did the odd figure that loomed out of the greyness, running for shelter.

She and Diane had brought Spitfires up from Brize Norton in the Cotswolds. It had been a pleasant flight. They'd skimmed along, taking turns to be the leader, giving one another the thumbs-up as they went. The weather had closed in not long after they'd landed.

Julia shoved her hands into her pockets, put her forehead on the pane. 'My day is in ruins. I have – or had – a date tonight.'

'You seem to have a date every night,' said Diane.

'No, I go out most nights. But that's with friends and that's just a matter of not staying in. Tonight was a date and it was special. Charles is back after his officer training, then he's orff to Burma in a few days. I'll miss him. We both need a spot of comfort.'

She'd had her day planned out, a tight schedule. She'd been sure she would be picked up sometime after three in the afternoon, be back at the base around four, cycle home, meet Charles, who would by then be at the cottage. Quick kiss, bath, change, out to dinner and back to bed. They had decided to eat at the hotel in the village because it was a passionate five-minute distance from there to Julia's bed, and bed interested them both more than food. 'How could Nigel not have seen this coming?'

Diane said she never really trusted weather forecasts. 'Weather is a force of nature. Bigger than us all. It seems unnatural to predict it.'

Julia said that Izzy had predicted it. 'She knew it was coming. She tasted it in the air. She's all instinct, is Izzy. She can tell the time just by looking at what she calls the colour of the day.'

Diane said, 'Goodness.' Then, she sighed and said, 'Bloody stuck out.' Then added, 'Stuck out and damp.'

'Bloody stuck out, very damp and very, very fed up,' said Julia.

Diane looked at her watch – half past three – stood up and said she'd better phone in.

Julia watched her walk out of the mess and head for the operations room. She liked Diane, there was a calm about her. But still, she'd been looking forward to an evening with Charles and everything Charles had to offer. So the company of an older woman who knitted constantly and rarely put any gin into her orange juice wasn't all that appealing. She would spend her time lamenting what she was missing, sex and juicy conversation.

Can't be helped, she thought, in times like these, things go wrong, small plans go awry. Really, she shouldn't complain about that because horrible things happened these days. People you knew died.

Julia had friends who'd died. She'd seen someone die. It had been at an airbase she'd been delivering to. Not long after she'd landed, it had been bombed. Julia, waiting for someone to come pick her up and take her back to Skimpton, was on her way to the mess. Planes had come out of the blue, strafing the ground below. Chaos. Everyone ran. She froze. People hurtled past, yelling at her to get to the shelter. A young ground engineer, Simon – she knew him, had flirted with him – swept past her and screamed at her to take cover. She started to run, yards behind him. Then he'd fallen. He'd stumbled forwards, his legs gave way and he slumped to the ground, landed with a dull thump. It was strangely unspectacular. One minute, Simon was running, the next he was dead.

She'd been struck by the expression on Simon's face. She'd stopped running and stood in the middle of all the hullabaloo – sirens, anti-aircraft fire, shouts, the thunder and rumble of planes overhead – staring at him. His expression had been of shock and huge surprise. As if he'd been thinking, This can't happen to me, I haven't . . .

Julia didn't know what Simon's regret was, what he hadn't done. But she was familiar with the thought. Other women at the base had expressed similar emotions. Careening over a runway, brakes not working, and a group of trees looming large in front of her, one of the pilots, Joy, had confessed, 'All I thought was, Damn, I've a new green frock I haven't worn.' Others who'd had scary moments owned up to thinking of such things as – Damn, I've two eggs I haven't eaten. Or, Damn, I've petrol rations I haven't used yet. Or, Damn I've got leave coming up. Perhaps, Julia decided, death was so final, so huge that the moment you met it, you couldn't really take it seriously. Whatever it was, that young face stayed in Julia's mind, she thought about Simon often.

There was a story she'd been told by her friend who drove an ambulance for the Red Cross. One night, during the Blitz, after a particularly dreadful raid, her friend had helped extricate a woman from the rubble that had once been her East End house. The woman hadn't gone to the air-raid shelter, and had, instead, taken refuge under her kitchen table. After she'd been put in the ambulance, just before she'd died, the woman had said, 'No, no, I haven't finished washing the dishes.' Julia understood. Finality, when it came, was hard to grasp. And, perhaps, when in the throes of your last moments, there was comfort in the ordinary.

Diane came back and sat opposite Julia. 'It's bloody everywhere. Mist and rain. Absolute havoc.'

'How could that happen? How could they miss all this weather coming in?'

Diane said, 'They didn't factor in the moisture already in the air when the front moved in. They think they've lost Dick Wills somewhere round Dumfries. And Izzy hasn't phoned in.'

Julia said, 'Izzy will be fine.'

'Her instinct?' asked Diane.

'That, and I think she has a guardian angel. Someone up there likes her.'

Chapter Eleven
Not Yet

Izzy went down. She straightened out at six hundred feet, but didn't break cloud. The little aeroplane sign on the artificial horizon instrument didn't seem to be working, but she was sure she was level. She checked her compass and watch, figuring out how far she had come. She dropped another hundred feet. But still she was enveloped in thick mist.

The flush of horror, sweat and fear had ebbed a little. She was rigid with nerves, but calm enough to think. She knew that, in this part of the country, airfields were only ten miles apart. Red dots on her map marked them. 'Jeepers,' Dolores often said, 'this country in one big airfield held up by goddam balloons.'

She considered bailing out, but didn't know for sure what lay beneath. The abandoned plane could tumble and crash into a small village. No, can't do that. She went down to three hundred feet, but all she could see was mist and sheeting rain. Down to one hundred feet, and still shrouded in grey. She droned on. Dropped another twenty feet. Treetops, at last she'd made contact with the world below. All she needed was a field, an area of green big enough to land in.

If she had her bearings right, there was an airfield around here, and beyond that an American hospital which ought to have a landing strip. She was hurtling far too low. She could crash into a hill at this level. Perhaps this was it. Today was her getting-bumped-orff day.

Her parents would be furious with her if she died. Well, they'd find out she'd been flying when she'd sworn she wasn't. There had been scenes, arguments when they'd discovered she'd joined the ATA. 'You're irresponsible,' her mother had said. 'Indulging yourself, flying about, not a thought about your father and me sitting at home worrying. All you want is quick thrills and fun.' True, thought Izzy. So to ease the atmosphere, to escape into the world with the minimum of fuss, she'd lied. 'I won't be flying. I'll be on the ground as an assistant operations officer. For goodness' sake, do you think they'd let the likes of me fly a Spitfire?'

Her mother had stopped, looked her up and down, taking in her daughter's smallness and untidiness. 'No, I don't suppose they would.'

Izzy had felt triumph at winning the argument and insulted her mother thought so little of her.

She thought back to her time with the flying show – what a thrill that had been. Then again, she'd had to spend nights in cold, seedy bed and breakfast places. And, she hadn't been paid.

How Betty had laughed when Izzy had asked for her wages at the end of the first week. 'Wages! Money! You're getting flying hours in your logbook, you're getting fed, a bed at night and you want paid. Oh, my girl, if it wasn't so funny, I'd cry.'

'I've been a fool,' Izzy said. Sweat streaming down her face, she hurtled through thick mist and teeming rain.

Her father had told her she had a duty to stay home, get married and produce children. 'You should be here with us, helping out in the village during these dark days.'

Buzzing through the murk, Izzy thought he was right. Once, she'd been his little princess. He'd taught her to play cards, and always let her win.

She'd let him down. She promised him now that if she got down alive, she'd quit this job. She'd never fly again. She'd go home, marry, give him grandchildren, learn to knit. She'd be his good girl again.

Peering down, she saw two long rows of Nissan huts, running alongside them – glory be – a runway. She slid open the cockpit roof, felt the weather swirl round her and headed for the ground. She came wavering in, slid over muddied water, walls of wet cascaded up the sides of the plane, into the cockpit, over her.

She stopped. She was soaked. Rain was dripping down her face, down the back of her neck. The dampness, she realised, was not just on the outside of her flying suit, but inside as well. It was sweat – thick, clammy fearful sweat. And, she was shaking. She stared ahead, panting, blowing out her cheeks. 'Oh, God. Oh, God.'

She really ought to go inside and introduce herself to the row of faces at the window, staring out in alarm at the plane. But she didn't think her legs were quite up to it yet. So she sat, stared, breathed, waited for her heart to start beating normally.

It was a moment or two before she walked weak-kneed across to the nearest of the huts, carrying her overnight bag and map bag, parachute lugged over her shoulder. She was smiling the smile of her life, the thing that happened when emotions took over and her face got out of control. It wasn't so much that she was glad to see the small crowd that had gathered to watch her arrival, she was. But more, she was overjoyed to be alive. She was exhilarated. She'd been eight hundred feet up facing the elements and she'd won. She felt momentarily invincible.

The thrill didn't last long. Inside the building she was confronted by a group of nurses and a couple of doctors, all American. 'Jeepers,' someone said as she pulled off her helmet, 'you're a woman.'

Izzy said, 'Sorry.' Apologising not for her sex, but for the puddle forming at her feet – rain dripping from her sodden clothes. Her mother would be appalled. 'I had to get down out of this weather,' Izzy explained.

'You surely did.' The man who answered was tall, hair cropped so his face looked bigger that it actually was. He had a long square jaw, dimpled in the centre and sparkling-clean rimless glasses. 'Sorry we're staring, we didn't know women flew planes till right this moment.' He offered his hand. 'Jimmy, Captain James Newman.'

'Izzy Macleod,' Izzy took the proffered hand and shook it.

The place smelled of antiseptic, well, all hospitals did. But this one didn't have the dull undersmell of boiled cabbage like the cottage hospital back home where Izzy's tonsils had been removed.

On a wireless somewhere Bing Crosby was singing 'Wrap Your Troubles in Dreams'. The walls were a mass of drawings of American life. Things Izzy was familiar with from trips to the cinema, New York taxis, drugstores, families sitting on a front porch, people in diners, a man wearing a hat sitting in a pick-up truck, elbow on the open window, baseball games. There were jukeboxes, pies cooling on window-sills, dogs, horses – too much for Izzy to take in.

'You like the decor?' the Captain asked.

Izzy nodded. 'Very much.'

'American life,' he said waving at arm at the drawings. 'It goes on through the wards. A lot of the guys who come in here add something, it helps with the homesickness.'

Izzy supposed it would.

Then he shoved his hands into the pockets of his white coat and guessed she'd like to phone in to her base, then get out of her wet things. 'You're gonna need a bed for the night. And I guess we'd better feed you.' He'd learned that all the Brits who stopped by needed feeding. 'You like pork chops?'

'Oh, yes,' said Izzy.

'Pork chops,' her father used to say, rubbing his hands, 'lovely grub.' Four fat chops would be sizzling, spitting fat in the frying pan, the kitchen would be filled with their dark rich smell, the windows steamed. Everything in the world would be bright and beautiful.

'I surely do,' she added.

He pointed to the office. 'Phone's in there. Irene, here –' pointing now to one of the nurses '– will show you the nurses' dormitory. And I'll see you at six for pork chops and ice cream.' He gave her that look that Izzy knew well – surprise, curiosity. Izzy was too excited by the prospect of pork chops to care.

She thought life wonderful. She'd faced the elements and beaten them. She'd made a pretty damn near perfect landing in foul wet weather – not an easy thing to do in a Spitfire – now, hopefully, a hot shower, then, pork chops and ice cream.

She decided she wouldn't take up knitting after all. She wouldn't go home, get married and produce grandchildren. She'd stick with this job, it was too thrilling to quit. There was a small pang of remorse, she was breaking the promise she'd made to her father in those fearful, sweat-laden moments when she'd thought she might die. But then, he didn't know, did he? Anyway, she was vindicated. She could fly. Who was he to decide what a woman could or couldn't do. What the hell did he know? One day, she might do all the things he wanted her to do. Just not yet.

Chapter Twelve
Drowning the Whistle

The snow started slowly – just a soft whisper of weather, drifting down. Elspeth hardly noticed the flakes landing on her. She was upset. She'd received a letter from Izzy. She'd written that she'd had a lovely time with her, but thought it might be three months before she got another long weekend. 'Can't tell you how busy we are.' Damn, Elspeth thought, three months without a decent bath and a night in a soft bed. Damn, blast and bugger.

Now this morning, Avril had been sent away. Elspeth didn't know where she'd gone. Duncan Bowman had taken her to the village and returned alone a couple of hours ago.

'Where's Avril?' Dorothy had asked.

'You'll find out soon enough,' Duncan said dropping the official lead-girl whistle into her hand. 'Don't go blowing that too much.'

But Dorothy did. Couldn't resist. Men got a sharp blast for whistling at women, women for chatting too much as they worked. Everyone got a double blast for lingering over their mugs of tea at break time. All this added to Elspeth's upset. She worked, shoulders tensed, waiting for the next air-splitting screech. 'Some people are not cut out to have whistles.'

She was working with Tricia, the camp's glamour girl. Her lips were painted scarlet, her hair kept, somehow, perfect, and she had the enviable knack of looking desirable in dungarees, big boots and a woolly jumper two sizes too big for her. Men fought over her. She claimed this annoyed her. Men were so childish. But the sway of her hips, the way she pushed her hair from her face and her slight pout made it plain to the rest of the girls that the brawling for her attention pleased her.

'The trouble with you is, you don't see men watching you,' said Tricia. It was a knowing statement from a young woman who considered herself to be an expert on men.

'I hadn't noticed,' said Elspeth.

'Well, you wouldn't,' said Tricia. 'Not with you being so old.'

'What do you mean by that?' Never before had Elspeth been accused of being old. She considered herself to be sophisticated and mature. In her prime, in fact.

'I mean,' said Tricia, 'that it's not really right someone your age working up here. All the other girls are much younger than you. You should be married and settled with children.'

'Should I?'

'Oh yes,' said Tricia. 'I wouldn't want to be single when I get to be as old as you. All the good men will be snatched up. Poor you. Actually,' Tricia went on, 'it's obvious to me that it's been ages since you had a boyfriend.'

This was true. It had been years since there had been a man in her life.

For a few seconds she was back on the platform at King's Cross, holding Michael Harding, her last love, whispering goodbye, promising to write, promising to return soon. She had been on her way to Scotland to care for her mother, who'd had a stroke. 'A month,' she'd said, 'at most two, then I'll be home.'

He'd said he'd wait. 'For ever, if I have to.'

They'd kissed. All round them the clatter and bustle of the station, porters, steam in clouds from shuddering engines, whistles blowing, doors slamming, people shouting and they had only been aware of each other, and their sadness.

Her bags were already on the luggage rack in her compartment, he had put them there. When the whistle blew, she'd climbed aboard, leaned out of the window for one last kiss, then held his hand as the train moved off, him walking along the platform, hanging on to her. But she'd had to let go, she'd waved as the train pulled out of the station. He'd waved back. That was the last time she'd ever seen him.

He was a wonderful man. A lawyer, steady, reliable, nothing like the artists and musicians she'd known before she met him. They had beards, wore corduroy trousers and oversized jumpers. He wore a suit. And shaved.

She'd met him at a dinner party thrown by one of her mother's friends and they'd shared a taxi home. He had asked her out to dinner the following night. After that, they'd fallen into a routine of nights at the cinema and eating out together. They were courting. He was her young man. Elspeth had found it pleasant and undemanding after two torrid affairs. At last, she'd met someone she could introduce to her mother.

Elspeth hadn't returned to London after two months in Scotland. Her mother's condition worsened. Elspeth had to feed, bathe and dress her. Evenings, she would write long letters to Michael. Mornings, she'd look out for the postman, hoping for a long letter from London. Time passed, the letters got shorter and came less often. Elspeth's mother died. But Elspeth didn't go back to London. She stayed on in her mother's cottage and started teaching the piano, getting by on a meagre income. She befriended Izzy. She began to enjoy an independent life.

When Michael's letter arrived, telling her he'd met someone else, a woman he was going to marry in two weeks, Elspeth had sat quietly at her kitchen table reading it over and over. She had sighed. But she hadn't been broken-hearted. In fact, she'd felt relieved. She was enjoying her life. Marriage did not appeal to her. She'd taken up flying, and, two weeks previously, on a trip to Edinburgh, she had fallen in love with a second-hand accordion in a shop window. On impulse, she'd bought it.

Then she had to learn to play the thing. And what man would want his new wife to sit of an evening, squeezing and heaving at an accordion, making groaning wailing noises, when they should be snuggling on the sofa together listening to the wireless? No, it was for the best. An accordion was far more challenging than a man.

Well, she thought now, that had seemed reasonable at the time. Though, living this sparse and very basic life, marriage, a comfortable home and a warm bed complete with husband seemed very appealing.

Back then, she had come to enjoy living on her own. She could eat what she wanted, when she wanted. Could linger in the bath, listen to her choice of programmes on the wireless, play her own selection of music on her gramophone. She was answerable to nobody. In shops she overheard women fretting about what to buy for supper, complaining about the amount of washing and ironing they had to do. They had socks to darn, buttons to sew on, collars to starch. All that and they had to dust, polish, bake, make jams and jellies, knit and all sorts of other domestic chores she thought tiresome. Goodness, she thought, none of these women would have time to listen to Brahms or learn the accordion. Marriage, she'd decided, was not for her. Besides, she was beginning to be regarded, in the village as an eccentric spinster. Much to her surprise, she rather liked that.

Tricia, hacking at the limbs of the tree she and Elspeth were working on, puffing with effort as she worked, expounded some more on her favourite subject. 'You've lost the knack of men,' she said. 'You don't know how to make them work. You see, you have to make men feel good. You have to encourage them, agree with them, look pretty for them. Make them feel they're the boss. And all the time you are getting them to do what you want, buy you the things you want, take you out where you want to go. Only they think it's them in charge.'

Elspeth said, 'That's what you think?'

'That's what I know,' said Tricia. 'And it's what you've forgotten, if you ever knew it in the first place. You don't even notice men, except for the Italians here, and that's only because they sing songs in Italian, which you find romantic.'

Elspeth squirmed again. This was true. Time was, she and Izzy would have long dreamy conversations about the perfect man. Elspeth's would be tall, interestingly handsome, quietly humorous, with perfect hands. 'A man's hands are so important.'

Izzy hadn't known about that. Back then, her perfect man would have been someone like her father. Elspeth sniffed, she'd always found Izzy's father authoritarian, and his sermons terrifying. Though, she was shrewd enough to know that even eccentric spinsters had to show up in church every Sunday. She also knew to keep her opinion of the local minister to herself, till one or two people had touched on the matter. It seemed that some people in the village found Hamish overly opinionated. On the subject of the perfect man Elspeth had decided, 'I don't want marriage. I only want romance.'

'*And,*' said Tricia, stopping work to make her point by waving her axe at Elspeth, 'you don't notice men noticing you. I've noticed that. You haven't seen that Duncan Bowman looking at you. I tell you, you have to watch him. He's creepy. He wouldn't send you roses or chocolates or ask you out on a date. He'd just jump out at you from behind a tree one dark night and try to have his way with you. You watch out for him.'

Elspeth turned to watch out for Duncan Bowman. But he wasn't looking at her, he was busy at one end of a cross-cut saw, one of the Newfies at the other. He was barely visible through the weather. The soft whisper of snow had turned into a deluge. It was a white-out.

At three o'clock there were two short sharp blasts on the official whistle. Dorothy shouted that they were packing it in for the day. 'Before the weather closes in.'

'It's bloody closed in already,' said Elspeth. She pulled up the collar of her waterproof coat, collected her tin mug, hefted her axe over her shoulder and started the trudge back to camp.

It snowed for the rest of the day. Elspeth found it mesmerising. She sat on her bed watching it fall. Endless, endless, she thought. The boards outside the hut were sodden, grey with slush. A row of drying socks hung above the stove.

The floor at the door was dark with damp, small icy lumps of snow here and there where people had come in stamping their boots, blowing on their fingers, bringing with them a rush of frozen air. Girls gathered round the stove, palms outstretched to the warmth and shouted, 'Shut the bleedin' door!'

Tricia stomped in, heaved off her boots and, eyes agleam with the joy of being the one to deliver shocking news, said, 'The road's blocked, the camp's cut off.'

Nobody was surprised by that, but, she had saved the worst till last. '*And*, the supply van couldn't get through. We're running out of food. Cook says we're down to two sacks of potatoes and some turnips.'

Gasps of horror – exactly the response any bringer of bad news wanted. Tricia looked triumphant. It was a good rumour.

It was a time of rumours. Small snippets of gossip grew into scandalous tales as they were passed from person to person. Elspeth always knew when a new rumour was on the go – the rumourmonger would lean into the rumour receiver, whispering, face aglow with the joy of being the bringer of shocking news.

That night the girls went to bed early. It was the only way to keep warm. They lay in the dark, listening to the nightly scrapings and scratchings at the walls of their hut.

'Rats,' said someone.

'They spread plague,' said someone else.

Voices in the dark.

'Don't be daft. It's only mice.'

A silence as they contemplated rats and mice. Then, 'I wonder what's happened to Avril.'

'Maybe she's been kidnapped.'

'Who would kidnap Avril? She's got a horsey face and a big nose. Nobody would pay the ransom.'

There were giggles.

'She'll have run away,' said a disembodied voice in the gloom. 'She'll be hunted by the police and brought back in chains.'

Elspeth shouted, 'Shut up. I'm trying to sleep!'

For a few moments the room silenced. The heavy layer of snow shifted and creaked on the roof. Then, unable to bear the quiet, Tricia started singing 'We'll Meet Again'. One by one, others joined in.

Next morning, it was still snowing. The road was even more blocked. The girls ate porridge made with water for breakfast and drank black tea. The mood was gloomy. It was Saturday, normally everyone's favourite day.

On Saturday afternoons, most of the girls in the camp cycled to the village. They would arrive in time for the matinee at the cinema – *Mrs Miniver* was showing this week.

After the cinema, they all headed for the fish and chip shop. In summer, they'd sit on the window-sill outside, newspaper-wrapped food hot in their hands. They'd blow on scorching vinegar-drenched chips to cool them before slipping them into their mouths. Winters, they'd squeeze into the wooden booths, and order mugs of tea and slices of bread and marg to soak up the salty greasy mix on their plates.

After that, it was on the village hall for the weekly dance. It started at seven and ended sometime close to midnight. It cost ninepence to get in, but that included tea and cakes. Everyone from the surrounding area went. They sweated, lurched, stamped and clapped to the gusty tunes of Frank MacMurtry's Highland Band. The girls thundered round the floor doing reels, strathspeys, jigs and the occasional waltz. It didn't do to sit anything out. No need to – there were over six men to every woman – they were all in demand. Elated, exhausted and flat broke till next pay day, they'd cycle back to camp, shrieking and giggling in the black dark, the way ahead lit thinly by their bike lights, hooded so no light was visible from above. They weaved about the road, squealing in mock fear at the barks of vixens and the hoots of owls in the forest.

'No fun for us, then,' said Tricia. 'Stuck here 'cos the road's blocked. Nothing to do and it's Saturday night.'

Elspeth said that people should always know how to make their own fun.

'So they should,' agreed Tricia.

They were sitting in the dining hut, sipping tea, looking out at the snow. It was still falling, streaming past the window.

'We should have a party,' said Elspeth. 'Everyone likes a party.'

'It's a bit spur of the moment,' said Tricia.

'Best kind,' Elspeth enthused. 'We just let it happen.'

It was, everyone agreed, just what they needed. There was no chance of anyone providing cakes, but there was tea. And there was booze. They were sure there was booze.

Out in the forest there were bottles and bottles of it – buried under damp leaves and bracken, tucked into hollows of trees. Most of the Newfies had a little alcoholic something or other hidden away, handy to swig in moments of homesickness and despair.

Only Dorothy, the new lead girl, thought the party a bad idea. 'Alcohol is forbidden. If we get found out, we'll get sent home.'

The girls silently considered this. Getting sent home for misconduct hadn't occurred to them. They looked at one another with gladdening hearts. They clapped their hands, jumped for joy and squealed with glee, 'Excellent. Let's do it.'

Dorothy dug into her pockets, searching for her whistle. She reckoned a swift blast would restore order. But after rummaging through her dungarees, she couldn't find it and decided she must have left it in her locker. She went to fetch it; a lead girl should never be without her whistle.

Tricia waited till she was gone. Grinning, she held up the

whistle. 'One Acme Thunderer. Found it lying on the floor by Dorothy's bed.'

Elspeth said that it deserved a respectful end, something that would forever dull its awful blare. She led the way to the water butt outside the ablutions hut. They gathered round as Tricia held the whistle above the icy water. In the pouring snow, they saluted, sang, 'Wish Me Luck as You Wave Me Goodbye', and watched the Acme Thunderer slip beneath the surface and sink, a shiny silvery thing, to the bottom of the barrel. Then singing 'Goodbye Whistle We Must Leave You', they marched in perfect line back to the dining hut. They were jubilant, united in mischief. 'Splendid ceremony,' said Elspeth. They all agreed.

In the afternoon, while the rest of the girls prepared the dining hut, shoving back the tables and hanging decorations, Elspeth walked down the track to invite the Newfies to the party. It was still snowing – a fresh layer covered the tangled tracks of all the comings and goings of the morning. If she looked up, all she could see were fat flakes streaming towards her.

She stepped into the forest and stood still, holding her breath. There was an exquisite silence. Here, standing on a damp carpet of brown needles, it smelled of cold, damp snow and pine. Hardly a flake slipped through the thick branches overhead. It was the first time in months that she'd been truly alone. She wandered deeper into the trees, something she and all the girls had been warned not to do. 'You can get lost in the forest,' Duncan had said. 'Trees, trees and more bloody trees is all you'll see and you won't know which way is back. You can walk round and round for days and nobody'll find you.' But the silence was alluring, not a rustle or scurry of an animal foraging for food, not a bird singing, Elspeth was tempted to walk and walk. It would be wonderful to live alone again. To be away from the babble of voices, the constant closeness of other people eating, washing, complaining, sighing, working, just getting by and the night monologues of sleeping homesick girls.

She wondered if the roads weren't blocked, and she set off on foot for home, how long it would take her, and if they would send somebody to bring her back. She fantasised a moment about life on the road, walking – the wind in her face, each stride taking her closer to her cottage, a soft bed, a fireside. It would be worth it, she thought.

A scraping noise drew her from her daydream. She walked back through the trees and saw Dorothy moving slowly along the track, eyes on the ground, shoving snow aside with her foot. Elspeth guessed she was looking for her lead girl's whistle and felt a pang of guilt. She shrugged, thought, Oh well, she can get another whistle, then carried on towards the Newfies hut.

There were several hundred of them working in different parts of the forest, but here there were eighty. Elspeth thought that if every one of them brought a bottle that would make an awful lot of drink.

Standing at the entrance of the hut, she spread her arms. 'The girls are having a party. Everyone's welcome, and anything you can contribute to the festivities would be appreciated.' Wolf whistles, stamping of feet, clapping of hands, winks and cheers – they all knew what she meant. Tyler Bute said he'd bring his gramophone and records. He had six, he said, so they wouldn't be playing the same tune over and over.

The party started at seven o'clock. Everyone had been told to bring their tin mugs, as there were no glasses. The contributions to the festivities were hidden outside the back door in case Duncan Bowman showed up.

Elspeth played her accordion as everyone arrived. The Newfies were all freshly shaved, with their hair slicked, smelling of Brylcreem, shoulders covered in a light powdering of snow. It was still tumbling down outside. All the girls were scarlet-lipped and scented.

Mary Noakes demonstrated the art of pouring sixty whiskies in forty seconds. She lined up all the tin mugs in a tight row, then ran along beside the table, a whisky bottle in each hand, pouring an exact measure into each one. Not a drop was spilled. She got a round of applause and a small fanfare on the accordion for her efforts. 'A trick I learned working in my father's pub. When the mills came out on payday, we'd have the drink lined up on the bar waiting for the workers as they came in.' She took a bow.

Elspeth played a waltz, one or two people took to the floor, others milled about chatting. But, by nine o'clock they were jumping and jiving to 'Little Brown Jug'. Every so often the throng of dancers would part and let one couple show off their moves; girls were tossed over men's shoulders, twirled, slung between legs and came up, flushed, smiling and still dancing. The air was thick with smoke, heavy with vapours of booze, alive with the chatter and shout of flirting talk. Whisky flowed. Nobody was sober.

There was sweat, there was heat. Tyler yelled it was time for some good old Newfie music. He put on his only record from home, the Kitty Vitty Minstrels, to wild cheers and stamping of feet. An accordion, a fiddle and a mandolin stomped out a jig. Tyler grabbed Elspeth and swung her round and round.

The room was stifling and someone opened the door. Outside the night shone. It had, at last, stopped snowing. A fat moon floated above the trees. The temperature was below freezing. Everything, white and still, glistened. Tyler tightened his grip on

Elspeth's waist and danced her out of the hall and across the snowy ground. She was breathless and laughing. Why, he was an astonishing dancer. Much better than me, she thought. Round and round they went.

Others followed, dancing. On the gramophone, the Kitty Vitty Minstrels shifted into a reel. The crowd swirled, then started linking arms and whirling one another, moving on to whirl the next person, round and round. Everybody was dancing with everybody. The record had come to an end, but nobody noticed. On they danced, skipping and whirling, singing, whooping and wildly drunk.

Later, Elspeth was to say that of course such alcohol-fuelled mayhem was bound to end in tears. But, oh, wasn't it fun while it lasted?

At the height of the frenzy, two men collided. One, angered, pushed the other. The second man, furious at the uncalled-for shove, punched the first. The second punched back. Others joined in. In seconds, the dance became a brawl. Everyone was shoving and punching, rolling and wrestling in the snow. Some girls joined in, slapping and kicking. Others stood on the duckboards outside the hut, screaming for everyone to calm down.

Elspeth remembered her accordion. If the fight moved inside, it could get beaten up. It was too old to suffer any brutal treatment. She went inside to fetch it. While she was there, it crossed her mind that if she put the record back on, the fighting might stop and the dancing resume. But this only made the brawl more intense. The noise of shouting, scrapping, swearing and the wild thrum of music became a cacophony. 'Oh dear, a mistake,' she said.

Skirting the mob, she took her accordion to her dormitory

hut. Whilst she was sliding it to safety under her bed, she heard several short angry blasts of a whistle. Looking out of the window, she saw Duncan Bowman standing at the edge of the brawl, cheeks tight with air, face red, furiously blowing his whistle. 'Ye bunch of bloody hooligans!' he shouted.

Everything stopped. The whole rabble turned to look at him. He was surrounded by panting, drunken, fired-up men, and took a few steps backwards. 'Ye'll clean this place up, all of you.' He stood looking at the faces around him, searching for someone.

Elspeth sidled from her hut. She should be seen. After all, this party had been her idea. She deserved her share of the blame. She stood, hands in pockets, leaning against the wall. She thought she was declaring herself – she had been part of the fracas. The whole place was silent, save for the steady dripping of water melting from the huge icicles that had formed on the eaves of the hut.

Duncan turned, saw her, said, 'Ah, there you are.' Then he smiled.

It was a fleeting thing, this smile. It seemed to take his facial muscles by surprise; it wasn't something they were used to doing. His eyes remained cool. Here was a man who saw everything objectively – huge trees, landscapes and working men. He had long left tenderness behind. His smile looked more like a facial quirk, and it chilled Elspeth to the bone.

Chapter Thirteen
Guilt and Kisses

It struck Claire that Izzy could have done with going to a proper finishing school. Eating two helpings of pork chops followed by two helpings of ice cream wasn't ladylike. 'A bit greedy, don't you think?'

'Couldn't resist,' said Izzy. 'When did I last have pork chops? Can't remember. And when am I ever going to have them again?'

'Who knows?' said Claire. 'Do you think about anything other than food?'

Izzy said she did. 'But I like eating.'

Claire said she'd noticed.

Izzy asked what Claire thought about.

'All sorts of things, my children, Richard – I worry about him in that prisoner of war camp. And other things.'

'What other things?' asked Izzy. She imagined Claire having profound philosophical thoughts, too deep to impart.

'Just things,' said Claire. Mostly, these days, she thought about sex. She missed it. She missed having someone in bed, breathing next to her. She wanted to feel skin on her skin, lips on her lips. The softness of kisses. She wanted to get lost in pleasure. She longed for these moments when she clung to someone – and in her dreams it wasn't Richard, but some faceless man who adored her – sighing and moving, intent on rapture.

This was why she had slept with Julia's boyfriend, Charles, last night. And that was why Mrs Brent, having discovered only one bed had been used, when two people – one male, one female – had been in the cottage overnight, and, showing her disapproval, had left only two sad, lonely dried-up rissoles each for supper.

'There's been hanky-panky going on in that cottage, and it's not right. Oh, I know there's not a lot to eat these days. And it's dark because of Germans flying about looking for somewhere to bomb. So it's no wonder people are going at it like rabbits. What else is there to do? But one of them at the cottage had a bit of you-know-what with another one's boyfriend. And that's plain wrong. So, it was rissoles for them,' Mrs Brent had told Mr Brent as they ate a hefty plate of sausages and mash.

So, Claire and Izzy were eating out in the fish and chip shop tonight.

It was Claire's first time there. She was impressed by Izzy's reception. People working behind the counter called her name and waved when she arrived. Izzy was a star in the fish and chip shop. She walked past the long queue and into the tiny smoky café, saying they were going through to the back. This was a small area packed with long wooden tables and benches not unlike the pews in Izzy's father's church. It was where the elite of the fish-and-chip eaters went.

A woman behind the counter, furiously shaking a wire basket of chips shouted, 'The usual?'

Izzy raised two fingers, jerked her thumb at Claire behind her and said, 'Twice.'

Claire had never been greeted like this at any restaurant. The most she ever got was if a headwaiter graced her with a watery smile and said it was nice to see her again.

Through the back, the air was thick with chatter and the hot smells of food frying. It was noisily friendly and, right now, Claire preferred that to the genteel tinkle of her usual dining haunts. Here, people ate with vigour, elbows going as they shifted hearty forkfuls of food from plate to mouth. They smoked, gossiped and swigged tea. Of course, people did all these things at the Savoy, just not simultaneously.

'You're known here,' said Claire.

'I sometimes come after supper.'

'You eat supper *and* fish and chips?'

Izzy said she got hungry. 'Food is a comfort.'

'There are other ways of finding comfort besides food,' Claire said.

Izzy said she knew that. Inside her head, she listed comforting things – her dressing gown, as long as she didn't look at herself while wearing it, lying in bed listening to rain falling outside, sitting watching the fire in the evening, Mozart's Clarinet Concerto.

Two plates were put in front of them, fish in thick crispy batter atop a layer of golden gleaming chips. Izzy reached for the vinegar and showered her food, then added a liberal sprinkling of salt from a battered aluminium shaker. She sipped tea from the heavy china cup, contemplating some serious eating. 'Food is best, though.'

Claire picked up a chip, put it in her mouth and shook her head. 'No, sex is best.'

Izzy wasn't going to comment on that. Her sex life so far had been miserable. She and Allan had been beginners and hadn't had time to polish their skills. Of course, there hadn't really been anywhere they could do that. Izzy had lived at home and rarely had the manse to herself. Allan had had a room in Perth, where his landlady kept an eye on him and did not allow lady friends to visit. So, they had camped. They had cycled out of the village on laden bikes, found a quiet spot by a river fifteen miles away and pitched their tent. In the morning, Izzy had woken to find a heavy warm weight pressing against her back. For a while, thinking it was Allan, enjoying the extra heat, she'd snoozed. But when she finally heaved herself from her sleeping bag, she'd discovered it was a sheep on the other side of the canvas. It had been pressed against her, and was also enjoying the heat. The weekend hadn't been a huge success. The fire had been smoky, the sheep intrusive and curious and there had been a lot of flies swarming round them.

For their second, and last, weekend together, they'd booked a room in a small hotel not far from Edinburgh's West End. They'd booked in as Mr and Mrs Moon, giving Elspeth's address. That had been better. Izzy had felt loved, wanted and, for the first time in her life, grown-up. They'd clung to one another. Almost as if they both knew that Allan, who was leaving in a couple of days, would not come back.

Still, after mixing with Julia and Claire, Izzy now knew her sex life had been unadventurous.

Recently, however, her eating life had been rather good. Last night's double helping of pork chops had been a highlight.

Yesterday, she had been taken through the wards – wolf whistles, whoops of approval and loud invitations from patients to join them in bed – to the nurses' quarters where she would spend the night. Nurse Irene had shown her to a vacant bed at the end of the dormitory and told her to meet the Captain in the officers' quarters at six o'clock. Meantime, she might like to have a nap. Izzy had thought this a good idea. Napping was, after flying and eating, her favourite thing to do.

'There you are,' Captain Jim had said when she entered the room. He'd stretched out his arm, welcoming her, waving her to a seat opposite his at the table. Their food would be along in a minute. 'Pork chops, but tinned, of course.'

'Lovely,' said Izzy. She thought tinned food exotic. So much more interesting and tasty than real food.

He'd watched with amused interest as she ate, and, when she'd cleared her plate, asked if she wanted some more.

'Oh, please,' Izzy had answered, then, feeling a little ashamed of her eagerness, 'well, pork chops. There aren't a lot of pork chops around these days.'

They'd spoken of their plans for when the war ended. He was going back to Montana to work in the local general hospital and breed horses. 'Appaloosas.' Izzy hadn't a clue what she was going to do.

From somewhere in the hospital came a loud surge of laughter. A wave of mirth. 'The Marx Brothers,' he said. 'We show movies for the patients twice a week. It's *A Night at the Opera* tonight.'

Izzy had said she loved the Marx Brothers. Harpo was her favourite. She started on her second plate of chops and sweetcorn. They'd brought out photos of life back home. His were of his parents' ranch in Montana. Hers were pictures of her mother and father in the garden and one of Elspeth in a straw hat sitting beside her horn gramophone.

She'd told him of her life back in Scotland, her parents, the manse, her best friend Elspeth who had encouraged her to learn to fly, and her time working for Betty Stokes All-Girl Flying Show.

And, no, she hadn't done stunts. 'Wanda the Wonder did them. Rolls and loops and zooming, twirling from high up to just a few feet from the ground.' She'd waved her arms, demonstrating twirls and loops and a plane zooming low over the pork chops.

He'd told her of his time working as an intern in New York, where he'd met his wife.

'Is your wife in Montana, too?' asked Izzy. She'd started on her second bowl of ice cream by then.

'She died,' he'd told her. 'A car crash, drove her Buick into a truck. Going too fast, she always went too fast. She'd been at a party, whooping along, singing. She just didn't see that truck coming.' And, seeing how embarrassed Izzy was at her question, he'd asked how her parents felt about her flying career.

'We don't talk about it, really.'

'And your boyfriend?'

'I don't have a boyfriend.'

Now, Izzy finished her fish and chips and leaned back as Ella, the waitress, cleared the table. Claire hadn't finished, but indicated that she wanted her plate taken away. She felt too guilty about last night's indiscretions to eat.

'Is that you done?' asked Ella.

Claire nodded.

'Your friend's a lady,' Ella told Izzy. 'Not like you – stuffing yourself. You want to get a man, something to take your mind off food before you get too fat to fit into them planes you fly.'

Remembering how she'd felt after last night's meal – she'd been Christmas-full – Izzy thought this might be good advice. She and Claire pulled on their coats and headed out into the night.

The air smelled of coal fires and cooking fat, thick aromas that made Izzy homesick. This was how the world smelled when she was making her way home to the manse for tea after visiting Elspeth. She breathed it in. 'Wonderful.'

They walked through the narrow winding cobbled streets. Dark now, windows blacked out, but there was enough of a moon to light the way back to the cottage. Izzy asked Claire what she'd done last night.

'If you must know,' said Claire. 'I slept with Charles.' There, she'd told someone. It was a relief to confess. 'Well, it had been a hellish day.'

She'd arrived back at the base at about one o'clock to have lunch as the taxi Anson was refuelled, and had sat by the window of the mess eating a cheese sandwich, watching the weather close in. Curling silky mists silently and swiftly had enveloped everything. One moment she could see the rose beds and Dolores' bike parked beyond them, then nothing but grey. She'd waited till four before going to ask Edith if the day had been declared a washout.

Edith had been in the corridor wiping Dick Wills' name off the board. 'Flew into a hill. But everyone else is fine.' They had exchanged a long look. Nobody here spoke about death; they just quietly and privately dreaded it. 'It would have been quick,' said Edith. 'And he wouldn't have wanted to be permanently injured. Not Dick.'

Claire had said she supposed not, and walked slowly back to the mess. She didn't like to ask about going home now. But, half an hour later, Edith had put her head round the door and said, 'It's a washout. Nothing more to be done today.'

It was always the same when someone died – fixed smiled, voices higher, more sing-song, a forced cheeriness. Claire wondered what was wrong with a bit of gloom. She thought being gloomy, when gloomy things happened, helped.

She had been almost out the door, dreading a grim cycle home, when Fiona, the adjutant, came bustling after her, skimming over the lino, flapping her hands, shouting, 'Boots! Boots!'

Claire had looked down at her feet. 'I am indeed wearing boots.'

'Well, take them off,' Fiona had said. 'You people are wearing your boots too much. They're only for flying not for shopping or general walking about. No boots off base is the new rule.'

Claire had sniffed, a sharp drawing in of breath, shut her eyes and said, 'Perfect end to a perfect day – I'll cycle three miles through this teeming rain and mist with nothing on my feet. Excellent idea.' She'd walked out wishing the door wasn't on a spring, so she could slam it shut.

'Boots,' said Izzy. She was panting, trotting beside Claire, who was reliving her fury and striding ahead. 'I love my boots. My feet have never been happier.'

'I know,' agreed Claire.

'Oh, Treacle,' said Izzy.

'Treacle?' Claire was baffled.

'My dad had a dog called Treacle that never did what he was told. He never came when anyone called him. He pretended he hadn't heard. Eventually, so he wouldn't lose face, my dad pretended he hadn't called him in the first place. That's what will happen with the boots. Everyone will pretend they don't know the boots rule, so Fiona will pretend she hadn't made it.'

'Very wise, Izzy,' said Claire. 'We'll just ignore the rule and it will go away. Anyway, then I had to cycle through all that weather yesterday. Rain streaming down my face – I could hardly see. I was soaked to the skin, frozen to the marrow.'

Charles had been at the cottage when Claire arrived. He'd found the spare key under a stone by the front door and let himself in. He looked disappointed to see her. He'd been hoping for Julia.

'She's stuck out,' Claire had told him. He was in his uniform – the Royal Artillery – and leaning against the wall looking idly at her as she stood shivering, dripping rain in the hall.

It always interested Claire how people looked in uniform. It seemed to make big men bigger and small men smaller. Charles was tall, broad-shouldered, prone to scowling and filled the hallway, leaving little room for her. He was drinking her whisky.

At that moment she had felt upset. It was everything – the diminishing whisky bottle, the look on Charles' face when he realised she wasn't Julia, the relaxed way he leaned on the wall when she was cold and soaked through, the wallpaper behind him – pale pink covered with a string of red roses – which she hated and, had the cottage belonged to her, would have changed. But mostly, it was the death of Dick Wills.

She was haunted by the thought of him alone several hundred feet up in the air, knowing death was near. The fear, that she never expressed, that she could be next. For the next few weeks, she would walk into the mess and Dick would not be there, and she would remember why. All that, and she would miss him.

'You can pour me a glass of that whisky before you bloody finish it,' she'd said. 'Then you can bloody light the fire and put whatever Mrs Brent left for supper to heat in the oven while I have a bath.'

Knowing that both Izzy and Julia were stuck out, and hoping that perhaps one of them wouldn't have access to a bath, Claire had treated herself. She added the six inches of water that mightn't be used to her regulation six inches.

Downstairs again, dressed in pale trousers, woollen jersey with a silk scarf at her neck, she had refilled her whisky glass. So, by the time they had sat down to eat, dry and warm at last, she was feeling mellow.

She was mellower after they'd finished their meal and were in the sitting room, on the sofa in front of the fire. He'd poured two more glasses of whisky and, by then, she was too mellow to refuse, or even to point out that he was being liberal with her whisky. He'd told her he was off to Burma in a few days and how he wasn't looking forward to it. 'I hate the heat. Always get a rash.' Then he'd asked about Richard. 'Do you hear from him at all?'

She did. 'I get the odd letter. He seems to be surviving. Or so he says. There's always a PS saying that I should tell his friend Johnny in the marines that life in the camp is quite good.' She'd sipped her drink. 'Odd, really, because I didn't know he knew anybody in the marines. So, I haven't a clue who to get in touch with.'

Charles had put down his drink and stared at her. 'You're joking, surely.'

She shook her head.

'Tell it to the marines. You know, tell it to the marines – the thing you say when you know someone is shooting you a line.'

She'd looked shocked. 'Of course. There are no marines. How could I be so stupid?' She clapped her hand over her mouth, her eyes glazed with tears. 'Here I am doing a job I love. Eating stew. A comfortable warm bed to sleep in at night. And there's him probably starving in a rat-infested hut.' She sobbed. It wasn't something she was prone to doing, and as she heaved in air, wiped her eyes with her sleeve, she dimly realised it was excess of whisky that was making her so emotional.

He'd moved along the sofa, took her in his arms, said, 'There, there. I'm sure he'll be fine,' and gently stroked her back. She'd buried her face in his neck, wept and wailed. He'd held her closer. It felt wonderful to be touched. How she'd missed physical contact. So, when he'd kissed her, she'd kissed him back.

'And after that it was easy,' she told Izzy. 'A kiss, another kiss, then another, getting closer and closer. A bit of fumbling, then we went upstairs to bed and you know . . .'

'Did it?' said Izzy.

'Yes, did it.'

By now they were at the end of the row of cottages where they lived. They could hear the river, the tumble of icy water, smell the mix of cold and chimney smoke. A heron rasped somewhere nearby.

Last night, for a while, on her ancient squeaky bed, Claire had lost herself in the pursuit of pleasure. It hadn't been two people, each intent on pleasing the other. They had both been lost in their own moment, escaping their demons. Charles, his dread of going to Burma and Claire; her guilt. Afterwards there had been no shared cigarettes, no soft spoken conversation, definitely no words of love. They'd sunk into deep drunken sleep.

Claire had woken a couple of hours later. Her mouth dry, head aching. She'd had a few seconds of wondering where she was and how she'd got there. The horror when she'd turned and seen Charles in a tumble of sheets and blankets, rumpled head on the pillow, sleeping next to her. Oh, the scolding from her conscience when she remembered what had happened.

The heron cried again. Claire and Izzy heard the whistle of its wings as it passed in the darkness overhead. 'I'm furious at myself,' said Claire. 'I've been angry all day. I was angry when I got home last night – upset about Dick Wills, drenched and furious at Charles for drinking my whisky.'

'Maybe that's why you had sex. A release from your upset about Richard and a release from your anger.'

Claire said it hadn't worked because she still felt angry.

'Well,' said Izzy, 'you probably need more sex.'

Claire put her arm round Izzy's shoulders as they walked the last few yards to their front door. 'Yes,' she agreed. 'I probably do.'

Izzy, too, was getting a talking to from her conscience. Last night, the Captain had walked her to the dormitory where she would spend the night. It had been late, but the film was still showing. Bursts of laughter drowned their chat. At the door, Izzy had thanked him for dinner and for his company. 'I had a lovely time.'

He had kissed her. Not the full Hollywood smooch she would have liked. He lightly touched her cheek with his lips. 'You're not going to fly that crate tomorrow?'

'I most certainly am,' she'd said.

'Well, phone me once you've landed. Let me know you're safe.' Then he'd said goodnight, and left her.

She touched her cheek, stroked the spot where the kiss had been placed. She had wanted a lot more than that.

Walking up the path, she cursed herself. She was not a good girl. She'd eaten too much, talked too much and lusted after a man. Three sins in a row. She'd suffer for that.

Chapter Fourteen
I Love a Bit of Brahms

Charles and Julia had finally made to London, they'd arrived the previous day, made love, gone out to a club, come back to Julia's flat, made love. Now, in the morning, they'd made love again. Afterwards, Charles had rolled over, sighed, said, 'Ah,' and drifted into sleep.

Julia got out of bed, went to the bathroom and washed. There was no hot water, but she had no intention of lighting a fire to heat the tank, as she was going back to Skimpton that evening. Shivering, she went to the kitchen to make a pot of tea. Tea and toast were the only things she prepared here.

The flat was sparsely furnished – a bed, a wardrobe and a dresser in the bedroom, a chair and a rug in the living room – and those had been a twenty-first birthday gift from her father. Visitors often asked if she was thinking of getting a sofa for the living room, or perhaps a pot or two for the kitchen – something to sit on the shelves beside her kettle, teapot and four cups. Julia would reply that she'd get round to it soon. 'I may only have four cups and a teapot. But, it is a lovely teapot.'

She had no intention of doing anything to the flat, however. She was too superstitious. She planned to live here after the war; furnishing and decorating the place before she moved in seemed to be tempting fate. If she bought a sofa, she would probably never sit on it. If she painted the walls, kitted out her kitchen, did anything, in fact, she would probably die and never get the chance to live here. She promised herself she would indulge in some interior decorating when the war was over, if she was still around to do it.

Monkeys had woken them. They always did. Nearby was an RAF training school that did not have the facilities to feed the service men, so they were marched at dawn to the canteen in Regent's Park Zoo for breakfast. The stomp of feet and loud morning voices disturbed the monkeys who shrieked, howled and jabbered in alarm, waking the neighbourhood. All the other animals had been moved. Julia didn't know why the monkeys had stayed, only that their morning din annoyed her.

The noise had reminded Charles that he'd soon be in Burma. He'd reached for Julia. He needed a little comfort.

Julia padded across the bare floorboards to the kitchen, made a pot of tea, which she brought to the bedroom and put on the floor while she poured two cups. She woke Charles, and gave him one, then stood beside the bed drinking hers. He asked if she had milk. She shook her head.

'Sugar?' He asked.

'Don't be silly,' she said. 'Of course I don't have sugar.'

He put his cup on the floor, then sat back, hands clasped behind his head, watching her dress.

'Do you have to go?'

'I don't *have* to go. I want to go. So, I'm going.'

'You always do what you want to do.'

She was pulling on her stockings, sitting on the chair across from the bed. 'Of course. Why shouldn't I? You know I can't sit still. I like to be doing.'

'I'm not asking you to sit still. I'm asking you to lie still while I do things to your body. Ravish you.'

'You ravished me already this morning, and last night after we got in, and again before we went out. That's three ravishings. How many more do you want?' She pulled on her slip, turned to the mirror to comb her hair and put on her lipstick.

'As many as I can get, I'm off to Burma. I may never have sex again.'

Julia doubted that. Charles would win women over wherever he was.

'I'm going to see Myra Hess at the National Gallery. I may not have the chance again for ages,' she said.

'You haven't even asked me to go with you.'

'Why should I? You'd hate it. You'd sigh and wriggle and look at your watch wanting the concert to be over. You'd spoil it for me.'

He knew this to be true, so didn't argue the point. Instead, he said, 'I sometimes think you are ruthless. You appear to be this party girl, dancing with everybody last night at the club, but underneath is a heart of steel. You do a man's job, flying planes because it's what you love doing and nothing will stop you.'

'I never thought I'd get the chance to fly Spitfires and get paid for it. And, yes, I love it and nothing will stop me doing it.' She put on her uniform.

'There's something hard and sexless about women like you. You should be doing womanly things – nursing, raising a family.'

Julia laughed. 'You just don't know how to handle women like me.'

He snorted. 'Nobody does.'

She buttoned her jacket, took her coat from the wardrobe. 'By the way, what did you and Claire get up to last night?'

'We talked.'

'What about?'

'Things. Her husband. Life.'

She didn't believe him. 'You didn't try to get her into bed, then?'

'I didn't *try* anything.' There had been no need to try. Claire had been perfectly willing. 'She feels bad that Richard's in that POW camp. The poor woman is swamped by guilt.'

Julia said she knew that. 'Still, a swift bout of passion might have taken her mind off things for few seconds.'

'I think I could do better than a few seconds.' Charles thumped his pillow, lay down and pulled the blankets over his head.

Putting on her forage cap, Julia said, 'There's more tea in the pot if you want it.'

'Thanks.'

She made for the door, then turned, came over to the bed and kissed his forehead, the only bit of him available beneath the bundle of bedclothes. He seized the moment, pulled her to him, turned the light peck into something more lingering on the lips and ran his hand up inside her skirt. 'Let's not argue. Stay with me.'

She pulled back. 'I'll be back around two, maybe before. You can ravish me then. But I have to catch the seven o'clock to Blackpool. Back to work tomorrow.'

He asked when the concert started.

'Twelve o'clock.'

'It's only half past ten. You've got lots of time before it starts.'

'There will be a queue. There is always a queue for everything these days – bread, sausages and Myra Hess playing at the National Gallery.' She kissed him again and left.

There was a queue. Julia joined it, thinking that if she'd taken the bus she'd have been here earlier and would have a place nearer the door. But she'd walked. It gave her time to think about last night.

They had gone to a club in the West End, sat at a table on the edge of the dance floor. She had paid for their steaks and champagne since Charles, as usual, had no money. It had cost her more than a week's wages. 'It would, these days,' she said.

'You earn more than me.'

She had shrugged.

'I don't mind,' he'd told her. 'In fact, I rather like the idea of being a kept man.'

She had asked what that meant. 'Do you intend to live with me and not work? Is this some kind of backhanded proposal?'

'Good heavens, no,' he'd said. 'I'll never propose to anybody ever. I don't fancy marriage. I don't hold with all that loving and honouring, having and holding till death do us part. Especially not in public. Vows should be made in private, in the dark, in bed preferably.'

She'd cut up her steak, pointed her fork at him and said that it was the obeying bit that she objected to.

'There you go,' he'd said. 'We'll have none of it. We'll live in sin. So much more interesting than marriage. And we'll have lots of little bastards running around with no pressure on them to be anything other than what they are.'

She'd said she wasn't convinced about the bastards bit. 'I

don't think I want children. And if I did, I wouldn't want them lumbered with that label.'

The band had started playing 'Moonlight Serenade'. Julia asked if he wanted to dance. He'd told her no. 'You know I hate dancing.' So she'd picked up her glass of champagne and gone to find someone who didn't.

The rest of her evening had been spent on the dance floor. She had no shortage of partners, plenty of her friends were in the club. She waltzed, jitterbugged and foxtrotted to the rhythm of Snakehips Jonson and his jazz band. The room glittered, trumpets soared, saxophones crooned and, in her red silk dress, she whirled round the floor, laughing, singing along to the tunes she knew and only occasionally glancing across at Charles who sat smoking, watching her. He looked distant, almost cynical, she thought. Then, a long familiar note sounded, the band started to play 'Take the "A" Train'. She had joined a conga line skipping and jigging across the floor, lacing its way through the dining tables. Such fun. For a while she'd forgotten about Charles.

They'd left shortly after two o'clock, headed towards Oxford Street, looking for a taxi. He put his arm round her, kissed the top of her head. It was the time of day he loved most – early morning, and he was doing the thing he loved most – going home. London was still thrumming mostly with servicemen on leave. It was dark. Julia wondered if she would ever see the like again – this city, lit only by the moon.

They were both a little downhearted. Charles, because he was leaving soon for a land he didn't want to visit. Julia, because it had occurred to her that she was having the time of her life, she had danced all night and tomorrow she'd take the train back to her base. She'd be flying again. Who'd have thought a war could make her so fulfilled, so utterly happy. But if this was the best of her times, what would happen when the war was won? Life would never be this good again. After this, she'd thought, it would be all downhill. There would be nothing.

When they'd eventually made it to bed and turned to one another, the love they made was slow, gentle and filled with melancholy.

She sighed, walked more quickly. Her trouble, she decided, was that she knew very little about anything except flying. She'd been educated at home by a governess. Once she'd grasped the rudiments of the three Rs, the governess had been dismissed. 'No need for a girl to learn anything,' her father said. 'All she needs is a few womanly wiles.'

It sometimes shook her to remember how ignorant she'd been. She'd known nothing about sex. Her mother assumed she'd find out one day. Probably when she married and her husband would tell her what was expected of her.

'Huh,' said Julia, striding along. 'Too much stiff upper lip.'

But then, her family had never discussed anything other than horses, dogs and who was coming to dinner and what to serve them.

Once, when her younger brother had been very ill with pneumonia, Julia had been sent away to live with her grandmother. When she returned, her brother wasn't there. 'Where's Lawrence?' Julia had asked.

'He's gorn,' her mother said stiffly.

'When's he coming back?'

'Don't be silly,' mother scolded. 'He's not coming back.'

In the end it was Ralph the butler who'd told her that

Lawrence had died. Oh, of course, the family had wept, but all the sobbing went on in secret behind closed doors. They never spoke about grief, ever.

'Well, I'm not going to have children. But if, by some mishap, I do, I'll never treat them like that. And they won't be bastards, either.'

The queue outside the National Gallery started to move forwards. The man behind her said, 'At last.'

She turned and smiled.

'I spend half my life queuing these days,' he said.

Julia agreed.

He walked with her to the Barry Rooms, where the lunchtime concerts were held. The place looked ghostly without the paintings. 'Nobody knows where they are,' Julia said. 'It's a secret.' She tripped along beside him, six steps to every one of his.

He asked Julia about her uniform.

'Well, I've heard of the Spitfire girls, of course, but I never thought I'd be lucky enough to meet one of you. You actually fly the planes?'

'Oh, yes,' Julia told him. 'Aren't these concerts wonderful? Such a bloody good use of the space. And it's absolutely darling to be able to come here and listen to music. It's as if everything stops. No bombs, no war. Only the sound of Beethoven or Brahms. It's so uplifting. I just love it.'

He grunted. It wasn't that he didn't agree. He just wasn't prone to waxing lyrical about anything. 'I'm more of a Bach man, myself. Find Brahms overly lush sometimes.'

'Oh, I love a bit of Brahms.'

He was taller than her, but then, who wasn't? Older, too, about forty, she reckoned. He was wearing a long coat, collar up, and a hat, brim down, so she couldn't really see his face. She asked what he did.

'War correspondent.'

She said, 'Ah.'

Not that she minded newspapermen. They often turned up at the base looking for a story. And women flying Spitfires was a story. She and other female pilots were photographed sitting in planes smiling, looking glamorous. Or they might be asked to be photographed running in a group, carrying their map bags and parachutes, towards a plane. Nobody minded being snapped sitting looking demure in an open cockpit, they hated the running, though. Parachutes weighed forty pounds, and photographers were never happy with their first shot and wanted them to do it over and over, till, sweaty, aching and puffed, they refused.

They chose seats near the back of the Barry Rooms and stared ahead at the gleaming Steinway on the platform, waiting for Myra Hess to come flowing out to play for them.

It never lasted long enough, Julia said afterwards. She had been rapt, sitting with hands clasped on her knee for the whole concert, hardly moving. 'But it is a tonic. Oh, I wish I'd stuck in at the piano.' Standing on the steps leading to Trafalgar Square, she demonstrated piano playing, gloved fingers twinkling through air. 'She plays so deftly, such precision, don't you think? And it's all so heartfelt.'

He nodded, agreeing. He was not a man who went in for criticism. He liked a film, a book, a song, or he didn't. Explaining or defining his position on such matters never appealed to him. He had enjoyed the concert, but hadn't spent much time looking at the pianist. Instead, he had watched Julia watching her.

He thought Julia lovely. He was taken with her energy and enthusiasm. Coming here had made today a good day after months of dreadful days. He'd recently returned from Tripoli, weakened after a bout of dysentery. Most of the voyage home had been spent lying in his cabin, too ill to care if the ship was attacked, sunk even, by an enemy submarine. Now he was working from an office in Dean Street, despondent at being desk-bound, perhaps for the rest of the war.

Still, here was Julia. She had cheered him. He asked if she'd like to join him for a cup of tea. He knew a café nearby.

'Ooh, tea, lovely,' said Julia. 'Just what the doctor ordered.'

He had his hands plunged deep in his pockets, but held out his crooked arm for her to link into. 'Come on, then.' He led her towards Soho.

It wasn't a part of London she knew. She'd imagined Soho's streets to be lined with illicit drinking dens and gambling joints, and thronging with spivs, prostitutes and other ne'er-do-wells.

The café was small, steamy and smoky. The customers were mostly people in uniform, but then there were people in uniform everywhere these days. They took a table near the back.

He shouted his order, 'Two teas, two buns, Rita!'

Rita said, 'Okey-dokey, coming up.'

'Ooh, a bun. I love buns,' said Julia. She considered the table-top, wooden decorated with teacup rings and cigarette burns, and becrumbed. 'Julia Forsythe-Jones,' she said, holding out her hand.

'Walter Cruickshank.' He took the hand and shook it. 'Do you enthuse about everything?'

'No, darling. But I do enthuse a lot. It's annoying, I know, but it keeps me sane. It blows away my worries.' She smiled. 'And in fact, I do love buns.' She paused, thought about this. 'Perhaps I like the word, more than the actual thing.'

He agreed. It was a good word. 'Bun,' he said. Enjoying how it slid off his tongue.

The waitress brought two steaming cups and two buns nestling on one plate. Julia was used to daintier service. She looked round and said she rather liked it here. 'It's got character. Quite cosy, really.'

He nodded. He liked it, too. Came here often.

A group of soldiers at a table nearby started to laugh. Julia watched them. They gulped tea, flicked their cigarettes into the ashtray, nicotined fingers. These days, she couldn't look at groups of young uniformed men without thinking about the boy she'd seen die. She'd been present at that final intimate moment in his life, and always felt she could have done more for him. She could have held his hand, though he was gone before she reached him. But still, he shouldn't have left this world so suddenly and so alone.

Some of these men laughing, bantering would die. Others would witness death. Julia hated to think of this. It saddened her, frightened her and made her feel old. She pulled apart her bun, put a small lump of it into her mouth, 'War,' she said. 'It will change us all.'

He agreed.

It was odd, Julia was to think later, that she had chatted to this man for over an hour, discovering that they had nothing in common – he had no interest in flying, didn't like horses, had never owned a pet, country life bored him, he'd travelled to places she hadn't even heard of, hated dancing and liked drinking whisky with his friends and reading – yet loving his company.

'I do like talking to my friends, but not the whisky,' she said. 'Gin for me. I just take it how it comes these days, can't get a slice of lemon for love nor money. You've never had a pet? Not even a dog? You've got to get a dog, they're lovely.'

'I'm away too much.'

'Well, your wife could take care of it.'

He shook his head. 'No wife.'

She said, 'Ah.' And thought, Oh good.

'You?'

'Oh no, darling. I'm not married, either. My mother is distraught about that. I'm past twenty-five. She thinks I should have a husband and a clutch of children by now. Luckily this war has come along and all the young men I know are orff serving somewhere. Mother has temporarily stopped nagging.'

'You sound rich,' he said. 'I bet your family is loaded.'

'Yes, as a matter of fact, they are. But I'm just a working girl these days. Not rich at all.'

Outside a slow fog was creeping down – yellow, acrid. Julia looked at it and said, 'Bugger, fog. I hate fog.'

He had, by now, removed his hat. She could see his face. An excellent face, she thought. He would be stunningly handsome, if time and life – disappointment, loneliness, too much whisky and laughter, probably – hadn't left a mark. There were wrinkles, creases, lines, also some time in his past his nose had been broken and hadn't been fixed properly. Still, she liked what she saw. She never did trust overly good-looking men.

He caught her looking at his nose, and touched it. 'Boxing,' he said.

'You box?'

'Not any more. I got old.'

'Did you win any cups or titles?'

He told her a few. 'I had my moments.'

She looked at her watch and apologised. She had to go, she had an appointment. She had agreed to be ravished one more time before Charles left for Burma, though she didn't mention any of that.

He had to go, too. 'Better get back to work.'

He walked her to Oxford Street and hailed her a taxi. 'Can I call you?'

'Oh yes, please. Lovely.' She took the pen he offered and wrote her number on the inside of his cigarette packet.

'I'll come up and see you,' he said. 'Take you to dinner.'

'Lovely, darling. I'll look forward to it.' And she climbed into the taxi, slammed the door.

He watched it trundle into the afternoon traffic, disappear into the fog. He hated privileged, rich women with their dogs and horses, who said 'orff' instead of 'off' and who called you 'darling' when they hardly knew you. Yet, he thought Julia charming. He stepped into the road, could just make out the taxi and Julia sitting in the back. He wondered if she'd turn and wave to him. Bet himself half-a-crown she wouldn't. She wasn't the type to look back, but she'd know he was watching her go. She didn't turn. I won, he thought. And felt a little sad about that.

Chapter Fifteen
The Toast

'I'm moving you to work with the horses,' Duncan told Elspeth. 'You'll be taking over from Avril. She's not coming back. She's in a sanatorium outside Edinburgh. Got the TB.'

It took a few seconds for this to sink in. Elspeth stared at him, mouth open. 'Poor Avril.'

Duncan said, 'Aye. It's not a good thing to have, TB.'

'Tuberculosis? Isn't that infectious? We could all have it.'

'Do you get sweats at night? Have you got a cough?'

Elspeth shook her head.

'Well, ye've not got the TB, then. There's a war on, and we've got quotas to fill. People are wanting their wood, there's no time for anybody else to get ill.' He told her to report to the stables next day. 'Frazer will show you the ropes.' Then he waved her away, dismissing her.

At half past five the next morning, Elspeth stumbled through the dark, struggling to keep herself awake and upright. Frazer looked her up and down and told her she'd do, even if she was a woman. 'Not my favourite kind of person. Look at you, there's not much of you.'

He was a man with a face of a thousand wrinkles. Its features – nose, eyes, lips – were lost in a maze of interlinking creases and pouches. It was weathered dark brown, though his forehead above the cap line was shockingly pale. Frazer didn't smile often, but when he did, he gave observers an unashamed sighting of his teeth – both of them.

He always wore a striped collarless shirt, long grey waistcoat and grey herringbone trousers tied tight at the ankles with string. His ancient boots were moulded into the shape of his feet and looked as if they could walk the daily paths he trod on their own. He'd spent his life working in these forests and would sometimes stand in front of a tree, stare up into its growth, forty or more feet above him, and say he remembered well when it was planted. Nobody knew how old he was, just that he was old. He limped.

As he spoke, the day outside the stables spread across the sky, red and gold. Elspeth watched, transfixed. Frazer wanted to know what she was looking at.

'The sun coming up,' she said. 'It's beautiful. I want to gaze and gaze.'

'The sun'll come up tomorrow. And it'll come up on your day off. You can look at it then.'

Behind them three other stable workers swept out the stalls. Two were Italian and spoke a constant stream of their own language, stopping now and then to gesticulate. Neither Elspeth nor Frazer understood a word, but Elspeth felt they were talking about her. A thin stream of sunlight filtered in through the door, lighting up flecks of straw and a thick dance of dust motes. The place smelled of bran mash heating on a pot-bellied stove in the far corner. It was warm here. Elspeth felt a pang of jealousy that the horses were better housed and fed than she was.

Frazer pointed to a steaming heap on the floor and handed her a shovel. 'Clear all that up. That's your first job every morning.'

Elspeth took the shovel.

'You put the muck outside on the dung heap and on Friday you fill that barrow and wheel it down to Duncan.'

'Why do I have to do that? Why can't one of them?' She pointed at the Italians.

'Because you're the wee-est, and you're the last one here. It's always the job of the last to join the stables.'

She was about to complain that trundling horse manure for several miles was not part of her contract, but she was butted in the back and swept off to one side.

'It knows,' said Frazer.

She turned to glare at the horse that had shunted her aside. 'It knows what?'

'It knows you know nothing about horses.'

'It's right,' said Elspeth.

'Of course it's right. Horses are always right. And when you're done with the shit you can groom Harry. She's your horse, now. Used to be Avril's'

Harry was a Clydesdale, and seemed immense – seventeen hands. It turned to look at Elspeth, showing the whites of its eyes. She stepped back. Frazer pushed her forwards. 'Don't let her see you're afraid. She'll take advantage. And watch your feet. If she stands on yer toe, you'll know all about it.'

Elspeth asked if that's what happened to him. 'I've noticed you limp.'

'Yes. Broke my foot.'

'Goodness. Didn't the doctor set it properly, then?'

'Doctor? What doctor. I couldn't afford a doctor. Just kept my boot on, that's the best way to fix a foot.'

Elspeth stepped nearer to the horse, looked her in the eyes.

'That's the way. You'll do fine. Better than that Avril. She was a bit scatty. Though, it's a pity she died.'

'Avril isn't dead.'

'No. But she's got TB. She's as good as dead.' Frazer pointed to the floor, jerked his head towards the door. 'Get on with your work.'

Elspeth, bent double, heaving a shovel-load of dung out through the stable door, pointed out that she'd never groomed a horse in her life.

Frazer said he could see that. 'City girl. No use to man nor beast. I'll get you a box.'

Thinking that perhaps there was something she should have brought with her and hadn't, Elspeth said she'd nothing to put in a box.

'It's to stand on. How else is a wee thing like you going to reach up to a horse the size of Harry.'

Days faded into more days. Elspeth got used to her new routine – up before dawn, walking to the stables, lighting her way with a tilley lamp, shovelling shit before breakfast. By April, the world was softer, warmer, greener, birds sang and Elspeth was working well at her new job. She loved her horse, spoke to her, sang to her, asked Frazer why she'd been given a boy's name.

'Don't like girly things,' he told her.

Sweeping Harry's flank with a handful of straw, Elspeth said, 'Ah. So is Frazer your first name or your last?'

Frazer said, 'Yes.'

'Well, which?' Elspeth asked.

'Both.'

'You're Frazer Frazer?'

'Yes, but I only use one of them. Don't need them both.' He was leaning at end of the stall watching Elspeth work. 'It was my mother did it to me. She always wanted a boy called Frazer, so when I was born that's what she called me even though my last name already was Frazer. See women, daft, all of them.'

'Oh, you know that's not true,' said Elspeth. She started humming a Mozart aria from *The Marriage of Figaro*. 'So, when I'm talking to you, am I calling you by your first name or your last?'

'Depends,' said Frazer. 'If you keep asking me bloody stupid questions, it's my last. If you sing that song again, it can be my first.' He gave her a swift happy sight of his two teeth.

Elspeth smiled back. 'You like Mozart, then?'

'Seems like I do. Who'd have thought it?' Then, in case she got too familiar, he said, 'Don't forget it's Friday. You take the dung to Duncan.'

The days were longer now. The girls worked till five in the afternoon, sleeves rolled up, arms showing the first blush of sunburn. Evenings, they strolled by the river that ran through a small meadow at the edge of the forest, yelling encouragement at the Newfies who stood on the bridge hollering and hallooing, beating their chests before diving into the water ten feet below.

'Showing off,' Elspeth said. 'I'm not impressed.'

'I am,' said Lorna. 'Some of these men have lovely bodies. I like a man with a lovely body.' She sighed. 'Not that any of them would look at me. Who wants a deformed woman?'

Lorna had returned to the camp a few days after losing her finger. Unfit for work, she'd spent two weeks hanging about with very little to do, waiting for her hand to heal. Now she was back in the forest, Duncan had moved her to the roadside, measuring timber for pit props, saying she wasn't to be trusted with an axe.

'That's one good thing to come out of all this. No more snedding.'

'Exactly,' said Elspeth. 'Look on the bright side. Besides you're not deformed. There's just a little bit less of you.'

'Still,' said Lorna. She looked over at Tyler Bute. He yelled at Elspeth to look at him and, wearing only a pair of underpants, launched himself off the bridge, clutching his knees as he hurtled downwards, hoping for a spectacular splash. He landed. A spray of water drenched the people on the banks.

'Fool,' said Elspeth. 'What gets into men? They think because they can leap off a bridge you are going to sleep with them?'

'Yes,' said Lorna. 'It's optimistic. I like it. At least someone jumps into the water for you. Who is going to do that for a woman with one finger missing?'

'Don't be silly,' said Elspeth. 'You've got a lovely body.' She nudged Lorna's boobs. 'You think a man's going to be interested in your fingers when you've got them?'

They wandered on, watched a trout jump, silvering out of the water, catching flies.

'At least our snedding days are over,' said Lorna.

'Thank God,' said Elspeth. They sighed. Elspeth sang a snedding song, 'I'll never sned again. Unless I sned for you-oo-oo.' Lorna linked arms and joined in.

On Friday, as always, Elspeth joined Lorna for lunch. The horse came with her, grazing on the trackside grass, and, from time to time, nudging Elspeth for the carrot she knew Elspeth had in her pocket. 'Steal them from the cookhouse,' she said. 'I'm hoping to diminish supplies so they have to get something else to put in our sandwiches.'

'Actually,' said Lorna, 'I'm getting quite partial to carrot sandwiches.'

'I'm not,' said Elspeth. 'When this war is over, I'm never going to eat carrots again.'

'They're good for you,' said Lorna.

'So are cheese and eggs and smoked salmon and lots of other things that can go in sandwiches.'

Lorna agreed. Though, she'd never eaten smoked salmon in her life. They sat on a log, swigging their tea, looking about them, enjoying the day. From somewhere far off, a cuckoo called. Nearby, birds chirruped in the trees, high above a buzzard cried.

'I think I'm going to quite like working out here in the summer,' Elspeth said.

She loved working with her horse. She ran along beside it, pulling logs from the clearing where they were felled to the trackside where they were measured and loaded onto a lorry. Her only worry was that the horse knew the job so well, she felt she was hardly needed. It knew where to go each morning, and contentedly trotted back and forth all day. This job, after months of snedding, was bliss.

'I've got a date tonight,' said Lorna.

'Really, who with?'

'Freddie Tait.'

'A Newfie,' said Elspeth. 'I love a Newfie, a bonnie bonnie Newfie,' she sang.

Lorna smiled.

'Where are you going? Dinner at the Savoy, then dancing at a club, and you in your best evening dress?' asked Elspeth.

'We'll probably walk in the woods. Maybe explore some old track we don't use at the moment. I thought I might wear my dungarees, though I'll roll them up. Show a bit of leg.'

'That'll do the trick. Men can't resist a woman in rolled-up dungarees. You might get a cuddle.'

'I like a cuddle,' said Lorna.

'So do I,' said Elspeth.

'You could come if you want,' Lorna offered.

'What? And play gooseberry. I don't think so. Besides it's Friday. And, as you know,' she jumped up, spread her arms and shouted, 'FRIDAY NIGHT IS DUNG NIGHT.'

Lorna asked what Duncan did with all that horse manure.

'Who knows?' said Elspeth. 'Every time I take a new load down to his cottage, the old load is gone.'

After supper, Elspeth loaded the barrow – old, wooden, chipped green paint – with the usual mix of dung and straw and set off for Duncan's cottage. It was a downhill journey, and the load heavy. The barrow was slightly out of control. It wobbled. But, the air was warm, balmy. Birds sang – a blackbird, a thrush, somewhere. There were rustlings, stirrings in the forest either side of the road. Deer, Elspeth thought, but they wouldn't emerge till after dark. She sang her trundling song, 'My Old Man Said Follow the Van'.

Duncan wasn't home when she arrived. She emptied the barrow at the usual spot, looking round from time to time. The silence here unnerved her. The breeze shifting in the trees and the wood pigeons calling somehow made it louder. She had the feeling someone was watching her. Relieved to be finished, she started back to the stables. A short way up the road, Tyler was waiting for her. 'Come to help,' he said.

'You'd have been more welcome if you'd helped when the barrow was full.'

'True,' he said. 'But I can help now. Get in, I'll wheel you home.'

'I'm not getting in that. It's been full of dung. It stinks.'

He had to admit that was true. He disappeared into the forest and came back with several branches of larch which he laid inside the barrow. 'There,' he said. 'Soft and sweet-smelling. Now get in.'

Elspeth was tired, and a ride up the hill to the stables was too tempting to resist. She climbed in. The larch was fresh, but there was still a distinct smell of horse dung. As Tyler wheeled the barrow, she lay back and watched the clouds and treetops passing above. 'I like this.'

He ran, tipping the barrow forwards, then zigzagged back and forth across the road. Elspeth squealed.

'Do you like picnics?' he asked.

'I love picnics.'

'After this, we'll have a proper Newfoundland picnic.'

They left the barrow at the stables. Tyler led her to a small track, the haunt of deer and rabbits, just beyond where the horses were kept. 'Come.'

The woods were deep and dense. The only sounds were the odd snapping of twigs underfoot. The smell of pine was thick in the air. Elspeth asked if he knew where he was going. 'We could get lost in here.'

'I was born and raised in forests, worked in them all my life. I never lose my way.'

They emerged at a clearing, with the river running through it. There was an area of lush grass, marked by the tramplings of deer headed to the water to drink. The river, which rushed and gurgled further down, was deep and still here. 'Good for fish,' said Tyler. 'And swimming.'

'You swim here?'

'Sometimes, but not tonight. Tonight, we'll eat.' He pointed to four small trout lying in a pan on by the bank. 'Caught them before I came to get you.'

'Isn't that poaching? You could get jail for that.'

'Only if you tell.'

She shrugged. She wouldn't tell. She wanted to eat a freshly fried fish.

'And before you ask,' Tyler said, 'the pan is mine. Bought it in the village.'

Elspeth nodded, then sat on the grass, leaned back and looked around. 'This is a beautiful spot. How did you find it?'

'I told you, I know trees and rivers. I followed the deer trails.'

'How clever,' said Elspeth.

He made a ring of stones in the sandy gravel by the river's edge, and built a fire in the middle of it. 'Dry wood,' he said, 'the secret of life. Brought it with me.' He took the fish from the pan, carried them to the water's edge, gutted them and washed them in the river. 'Now we wait till the flames die down. Then we cook. Then we eat.'

She asked how he came to be working in these forests.

'I heard about it on the radio. They needed foresters over here, and I thought it would be a good chance to see a bit of the world and earn some money. Two dollars a day.'

'Two dollars a day,' said Elspeth. 'That's a lot more than me.'

He shrugged. 'I'm a trained forester. Why did you come here?'

'Wanted to do something for the war effort. So I joined the

Forestry Commission. I liked the uniform and rather fancied being called a lumberjill. I had no idea how hard the work would be. Didn't think it through. Then, I never think anything through.'

'Do you regret it?'

'When it rains. When it's cold. It's not so bad now the weather has turned. When this war's over, I'm going to have a long deep hot bath, stay in it for hours and hours. I'll eat oranges and listen to Mozart.'

They sat and watched the fire. Something moved in the trees behind them. 'What's that?' asked Elspeth.

'A deer,' Tyler told her. 'Waiting for us to go away so he can come drink.' He put the pan on the embers.

'It didn't sound like a deer,' said Elspeth. 'It sounded more clumsy. A twig snapping, trees moving.'

'It was a deer.'

A trout jumped out of the river, catching flies that danced on the surface. 'The one that got away,' said Elspeth.

'You only take what you need. Leave the rest for another day.'

The air filled with the smell of wood smoke and frying trout. Using the fat blade of his knife, Tyler flipped them over. 'When I get home, I'll work in the forest. And on my days off, I'll do this. Cook fish by the river. Don't think I'll ever leave the place again. There, all done.' He came to sit on the grass beside her, put the pan between them. 'You'll have to use your fingers.'

She tried to break off a piece of pink flesh. Pulled back, blew on her fingers. 'Hot.'

He took up a small sliver, blew on it and put it in her mouth. 'How's that.'

'Lovely. No plates, no forks. But this is perfect.'

'Just a little water to cook the fish, catch the juices, stop it sticking to the pan.'

She took another piece and then another. Behind them, a small wind shifted through the trees, somewhere far away a fox barked. Trout jumped. Birds sang their last songs of the day. They sat close, sharing their food, licking their fingers.

'Pity we don't have any wine,' said Elspeth. 'Chilled Chablis would be wonderful with this.'

'No, I don't have wine. But I do have –' he brought a flat quarter-bottle from his hip pocket '– whisky. A mug for you, I'll use the bottle.'

'Excellent,' said Elspeth.

He poured a measure into his tin mug, gave it to Elspeth. As she lifted it to her lips, he put his hand over the top. 'A toast. Can't drink without a toast.'

'Cheers,' she said tilting her mug at him. She drank.

'Cheers? Cheers? That's not a toast.'

'Well, bottoms up, down the hatch, whatever.' She drank again. Drained the mug.

He poured her another measure.

'Now a toast from me, a Newfie toast.' He raised the bottle. 'I bows towards you –' he bowed '– I nods according –' he nodded '– I catches your eye and I smiles.'

Elspeth smiled back. They drank. The heat of the fire, the food, the soft evening and the whisky made Elspeth feel giddy. She wiped her fingers on her dungarees. 'Now I'll smell of fish and dung.'

He leaned in close, put his lips on her neck, breathed her in. 'You smell of fish and dung and water and pine and of being a woman. You smell of being alive.' He kissed her.

She forgot her vow never to get involved with a man while working here and kissed him back. Oh, it was good. To be touched, to feel arms round her, stroking her back, fingers through her hair, a body pressed to hers, lips on her lips, his tongue gently in her mouth. She pressed herself against him. Couldn't get close enough.

'Wait, wait,' she said. She unclasped the top of her dungarees, slipped out of her working shirt and held out her arms to him. He threw his shirt across the grass, took her to him.

It was late, the sun sending out last flares of light, a defiant glow before it slipped below the horizon. An owl called, a long eerie note. As Tyler pulled her down onto the grass on top of him, Elspeth opened her eyes. She saw a shape amongst the trees high on the hill on the other side of the river, and a piercing glint, final shafts of sunlight reflected in glass. Binoculars, Elspeth thought. But she was too far gone, filled with lust, too eager to make love here in this lush green place and, certainly, too heady with whisky, to care. But, definitely, someone was watching them.

Chapter Sixteen
Pork Chops to the Rescue

Today was a happy day. Izzy had flown into Yorkshire, delivered a Spitfire, flirted over a cup of tea and sandwich with some Canadian airmen, then been driven ten miles to another base for another Spitfire, which was to be taken to Lichfield, then an Oxford to be taken to Skimpton to be moved on tomorrow. The weather was idyllic, the sky a brazen blue and hardly a whisper of wind. Izzy hummed 'Whistle While You Work', admired the view and felt blessed.

She checked her watch. She was an hour ahead of schedule, and decided to take a detour past the American hospital, scene of her pork-chop orgy. She still felt embarrassed about that.

She had written to Captain Jimmy, thanking him for his hospitality and inviting him to visit her. He'd accepted and, a fortnight ago, they'd spent the day together in Skimpton. He'd arrived shortly before noon. They'd eaten lunch in the Golden Mallard Hotel. This time, sharing a meal, Izzy had been careful about her eating habits and had politely consumed a modest portion of turbot. Though she cursed herself for being too enthusiastic about the pudding – trifle.

Afterwards, they'd hired a boat and rowed up the river. Izzy sat at the back, trailing her fingers in the water, wondering, since this was fun, why she'd never thought to do it before. He spoke about his plans for after the war – the house he was going to build not far from his parents' home, the horses he was going to breed. He was going to keep his life simple, enjoy each day as it came. Izzy, as always, was vague about her plans, mostly, because she didn't have any.

Back at the cottage, they'd kissed. Standing at the foot of the stairs, clinging to one another, she'd noticed how expertly he'd run his hand down her back, teased his tongue into her mouth, run his hand back up her back and over her breast, and thought that he was a lot better at this than she was.

He'd led her upstairs, asked which room was hers. Inside the bedroom he'd pulled her onto the bed beside him, started to undress her. She didn't object. He certainly knew what he was doing, when they were done and he was leaning out of the bed to get a pack of Lucky Strike from his trouser pocket, she said, 'Gosh.' So that was what all the fuss was about. And *that's* what Elspeth meant when she'd said all those years ago that flying was almost as good as sex. 'Gosh,' she said again. She was sweaty, blissful, relaxed, smiling and thought she might like to do it again. There was time. It was only four o'clock, Claire and Julia wouldn't be home for ages.

The front door had opened. Izzy froze. Someone walked down the hall and into the kitchen. 'Mrs Brent,' said Izzy. 'Oh, God.'

Jimmy said, 'What's the problem?'

'I don't want her to come upstairs and find me in bed with a man.'

'Why not? You're a big girl. You're only doing what big girls do.'

'But we're doing this and we're not married.'

'Oh, Izzy. Grow up.'

They'd heard Mrs Brent walk back down the hall and out the door. Izzy sighed, relieved.

'Izzy,' said Jimmy, 'You were only fucking. Everybody is doing it. We are living in hard times, fucking helps. Mrs Brent will know that.'

Izzy had turned to face him, shocked. 'You swore.'

'Yes. Haven't you heard that word before?'

She had, often. The language in the mess was nearly always polite, but out and about on the base, where the engineers worked, in the garages, on the runway, the air regularly turned blue. Naughty words flew.

'You want to relax a little,' said Jimmy. 'Go on, say "fuck". It helps in all sorts of situations. In times like these you got to fuck and you got to swear now and then. Say it.'

'Fuck.' The word whispered, squeaked out of her and sounded harmless. She'd taken the sting out of it. Still, she'd looked round, checking nobody was about. She imagined her father bellowing, 'Isabella, WHAT did you say?' She blushed.

He'd told her she'd have to do better than that. 'Say it like you mean it.' He pulled her on top of him. 'If you can't say it, do you want to do it?'

Like the good girl she was, she said, 'Yes, please.'

He'd left early. He had work the next day. Besides, he told her, the headlights on the motorbike he'd borrowed to get there had a grille over them, and a hood so the beam couldn't be seen from above. He didn't fancy travelling roads he hardly knew when the way ahead was barely lit. He'd kissed her. Told her to keep practising the naughty words. 'You might need them one day.'

In her letter to Elspeth telling her about her day, she'd said that she couldn't help but think that swearing was rude. 'But I had a wonderful time.' She hadn't mentioned the sex. She thought that doing it was excellent, but talking about it, especially in a letter that some stranger might read, was rude.

Elspeth had written back, telling her about a wonderful picnic she'd had. 'Cooked trout straight from the river, drank whisky, had a kiss, too. Actually, a little bit more than just a kiss.' Well, Elspeth was one for exploring her passions. Izzy thought she should be more honest and in her next letter might confess that she was exploring her passions, too.

Izzy circled the hospital, hoping to see someone below who might wave. But there was nobody. She decided to land. She'd go say hello to Jimmy. She bumped along the grass airstrip. She jumped from the plane and ran inside, asked the first nurse she came across if the Captain Newman was about.

He was in the mess, finishing lunch. 'Hi, Pork Chops. What're you doin' here?'

'Just passing, thought I'd drop in. Don't call me that.'

'OK, Pork Chops, I'll try not to call you Pork Chops.'

'Thank you.'

He asked what she'd been up to that day.

She dumped her gloves and helmet on the table, sat down opposite him and said, 'Delivering planes. Actually, it's against the rules to make social calls when I'm working.'

He said he was flattered she'd risked instant dismissal to come see him. 'Have you had lunch? There may be some pork chops on the go?'

'Please don't mention that. I wouldn't mind some Coca-Cola.'

He fetched a bottle, flipped off the top and handed it to her. She asked what he'd been up to.

'The usual. Patching young men up, taking lumps of shrapnel out of them, shipping them home or sending them to the burns unit. The meat wagon came in at four this morning, then again at six and again at eight. The wards are filling up.'

Izzy didn't know what to say. She took a swig of her drink. 'You must see some truly horrible things.'

He said, 'I surely do.' Then, changing the subject, since seeing horrible things was enough, he didn't want to talk about them, he asked, 'What are you doin' Saturday night?'

'Why?'

'There's a dance on. We've got a swing band coming.'

'I've got two days' leave coming up.' She was, in fact, due four days' leave, and had planned to visit Elspeth, but this was too good to resist. She'd see Elspeth next month. Elspeth would understand. Izzy was only hoping for some simple pleasure.

'Well come, then.'

'I will.'

He said he was sorry, he had to get back.

'I should go, too.'

As he walked her back to the door, they met Nurse Irene who'd shown Izzy round on the mist-laden day she'd first arrived there, soaked, sweaty and surprised to be alive.

'Hi, Pork Chops.' Nurse Irene was pleased to see her.

'You've been telling people about me,' said Izzy.

Jimmy told her she was a legend. 'You'll always be Pork Chops round here.'

*

It was late afternoon, after five, when Izzy got back to base. She dropped off her signed delivery chits to the operations room, and was on her way to drop off her parachute when Edith came storming after her. Nobody could storm a corridor like Edith. She surged forwards as if the very air she had to push through was an annoyance. For a second Izzy thought she'd been found out. Edith knew about the social call she'd made that afternoon. Or, perhaps, it was her boots. Izzy, along with everyone else, had ignored the boot rule.

But Edith was shouting, 'Pee one, Izzy. Pee one!'

Izzy turned and waited for Edith to catch up with her.

'Priority One Spit for Sealand,' said Edith. 'Just came on the books.'

Izzy sighed. She'd been looking forward to going home. Her plan for the evening was to write a couple of letters. One to Elspeth and one to her mother and father, enclosing, as she always did, a pound – a weekly contribution to their savings. Hamish and Joan Macleod dreamed of retiring to a cottage by the sea. Izzy's money had doubled their nest egg. In two years' time, they reckoned they'd have enough for a four-roomed, whitewashed home with a garden, a picket fence and a view over the water.

'Can't someone else do it?' asked Izzy. 'What about her?' She pointed at Claire, who'd just come out of the locker room.

Claire waved. 'Not me,' she said. 'I'm seeing a friend tonight.'

'You don't have any friends,' said Izzy.

Claire said of course she had friends, and ducked back into the locker room.

Izzy took the chit. 'P1, W,' it said. Priority One, Wait. She would have to wait by the plane at all times till it was delivered.

Edith smiled and said she'd send a driver to pick her up. 'It isn't that far.'

'Still, pee one,' said Izzy. She went to the locker room and took out a new set of maps. She didn't really need them – Sealand was on the coast, south of Blackpool, and she'd often flown there, knew the way – but she'd already broken the rules once today, and didn't want to push her luck by breaking them again. Rules dictated she carry relevant maps with her, always.

After that, she visited the met room. Nigel told her there was a front coming in, but she should be back on the ground before it arrived. 'Quite a downpour,' he said. 'The farmers should be happy, though.'

Izzy said, 'As long as somebody is.' She no longer trusted Nigel.

The flight didn't take long; Izzy followed a route along the coast. It was more spectacular. After landing, and getting her delivery chit signed, she waited for the driver. By now, the day had changed. Standing outside one of the huge hangars, she could breathe in a fresh chill and dampness. The downpour was coming. By the time her driver arrived, it was raining.

Izzy threw her parachute in the back, climbed in and said, 'You took your time.'

'Sorry.' It was Jacob. There was a faint scent of beer in the car.

Izzy guessed he'd stopped for a pint on the way. 'You're not meant to drink on the job,' she said. 'You could get sacked for that.'

He said sorry, again. 'It was hot. I was thirsty.'

'You kept me waiting.'

'I didn't know you'd be ready to go back so soon. Often I have to wait for pilots.'

'It'll be after ten before we get back,' said Izzy. She slumped in her seat, closed her eyes. The car bumped along, wipers squeaked against the windscreen, Izzy yawned. She fancied she might sleep.

The sky blackened. Jacob put on the car lights, not that it did much good. Just a thin wavering light filled with sparks of hammering rain.

'So how did someone like you learn to fly?' asked Jacob.

'Someone like me?' said Izzy. She suspected this might be insulting, though he probably hadn't meant it to be. He was just blunt. 'My friend Elspeth had the notion she wanted to be like Amy Johnson. So she took lessons.'

Elspeth had grabbed her arm, 'Izzy,' she'd said, eyes agleam. 'I am going to learn to fly. That's the thing to do. Explore new possibilities, new boundaries. Flying will open up new opportunities for me.'

'I went with her,' Izzy told Jacob. 'Only I got fed up watching and wanted to learn, too. So I did. Elspeth got caught up with new passions, she always does. I carried on and got my pilot's licence.'

'Didn't flying lessons cost a lot of money?'

'Oh, it wasn't too expensive. I used the money my grandmother left me.'

That sounded so simple. It gave away nothing about the guilt Izzy had felt at using the inheritance that had been set aside for her wedding. Izzy had thought she'd rather learn to fly than get married.

Then again, saying in a flat tone that she'd used her grandmother's legacy to pay for flying lessons revealed nothing about her father's fury when he found out about it. Oh, the rage in the manse when the depleted bank account came to light. The thunder of fist on table, the doors slammed, the shouts – Izzy remembered it all. 'You did WHAT?'

'Learned to fly. Like Amy Johnson,' Izzy had said.

Thump of fist on table. 'AMY JOHNSON. I'll Amy Johnson you. You bloody fool, girl. That money was for your wedding.'

'What wedding? I don't even have a boyfriend. I don't think I ever want to get married.'

He'd told her not to be stupid. 'All girls want to get married. It's what they do.' Then considering what she'd done with her money, he'd said, 'Flying? What possessed you? It's not feminine. What man would want a woman who flies planes? You don't understand men. They don't want to be with a woman who can do things they can't. You are unmarriable.'

This had been the first time Izzy stood up to her father. Usually, his rages would send her rushing from the room in floods of tears. This time there was more to his rage than fury. Pain, she thought.

But, Izzy had found something she loved to do, and had no intention of giving up. 'If a man didn't want me because I can fly a plane and he can't, then he wouldn't be worth knowing,' she'd said. 'And there are plenty of things married women do that their husbands can't. Cook. Sew. Knit. Bake. It seems to me that men like women who do the things they don't want to do.'

Hamish had told her she was being childish. 'A woman's place is in the home. A man's place in the world is to shelter and protect her. And there's many a man doing work he hates just to provide for a wife and children.'

The argument had developed into a staring match that neither of them won. In the end, her father had blustered from the kitchen saying he'd work to do, a living to earn, bread to be put on the table. But the matter of flying and the amount it had cost was still a rift between them.

Now, travelling along, head against the car window, feeling the thrum and rumble of the road on her cheek, Izzy remembered that fight with her father. It had been a turning point. There had been a moment, a slight glitch in the staring contest, just before he'd stormed from the room, when his shoulders had slumped and his glare had turned from rage to pain. Izzy had ceased to be his darling, his lovely girl, his pal and had become something else. Izzy couldn't work out what. A woman he could no longer control? A rival? She didn't know.

Rain drummed on the roof of the car. Huge and sudden pools of water gathered at the roadside, sheets of spray every time the wheels spun through them. 'You're going too fast,' said Izzy.

'No, I'm not,' said Jacob. 'I know what I'm doing.' He wanted to get back before the pub closed.

Izzy yawned again. Too tired to argue, she shut her eyes and drifted off.

Stillness woke her. The car had stopped. They had pulled off the road and were parked beside the gate of a field. She didn't have to ask why. Rain was hammering on the roof of the car and the road had turned into a river.

'Couldn't see where I was going,' Jacob said. 'We'll have to wait till the rain eases.' He told her she'd been snoring.

'I have not,' said Izzy.

'Snoring and mumbling,' he said.

'What was I mumbling about?'

He shrugged and said he didn't know. 'It didn't make sense.'

They sat in silence. The windows steamed. Rain seethed down.

Finally, to ease the disturbing intimacy, Izzy said, 'Do men resent women who do things they can't?'

'What sort of things?' said Jacob. 'Giving birth?'

'No,' said Izzy. 'Things that they might want to do themselves, but can't.'

'Like flying?' said Jacob.

'Perhaps,' said Izzy.

He told her he had no desire to fly and didn't resent the women who did. 'I prefer to find my pleasure here on the ground.' He slid his arm along the back of Izzy's seat, leaned in to her, face close to hers.

'You're not going to kiss me, are you?' said Izzy.

He told her he was thinking about it.

'Well don't,' she told him. 'It's against the rules.' She didn't know if this were true. Nobody had mentioned the kissing of drivers when explaining the rules to her.

He withdrew. Said he didn't think kissing was against the rules, but if she didn't want to, he wouldn't force himself on her.

The rain stopped. He wiped the steamed windscreen with a cloth, started the car and said it was time to get home. As they pulled out into the road he said, 'Be careful, Izzy.'

'What do you mean by that?'

'There's an innocence about you. You doubt yourself, but you don't doubt other people. You think their opinions and way of life are probably better than yours. You're wrong, of course. In time, you'll find that out. And I suspect you haven't been kissed very much. Be careful, Izzy, you could get hurt.'

Izzy snorted. 'Don't be so absurd.'

They pulled out on to the road, started towards Skimpton. Izzy still thought he was driving too fast, but kept her mouth shut.

It was almost eleven o'clock when they reached the village. They were rounding the steep bend at the top of the hill that led into the square. He looked over at her, watched her stretch, then rub a small hole in the steamed window to peer out. 'You're still going too fast,' she said.

'No, I'm not. I'm driving. You sit still and allow yourself to be a passenger.'

The bend was steeper than Jacob remembered, the road wet, slippy. The car veered out of control and skimmed, sliding down the hill. Jacob hauled at the wheel, working to straighten the car's course.

The pub was closed, but locals always lingered late. Eddie Hicks, mechanic at the local garage, stumbled out. He was still carrying, and swigging from, a jam jar half full of beer. He never looked when crossing the road. Why should he? There was never anything coming.

He never saw the car that hit him. He slammed the jam jar on the bonnet as he disappeared under it.

'You bloody idiot.' Izzy opened the car door and clambered out, before it stopped. 'I said you were going too fast.'

'I took my eyes off the road. I was looking at you,' said Jacob.

Izzy didn't hear. She ran back to the body splayed out behind them. She knelt down. 'Eddie Hicks,' she said. She didn't know him well, but they'd sometimes exchanged a few words in the queue at the fish and chip shop. He didn't move.

A small sliver of a moon slid out from among the clouds. Izzy put her ear close to Eddie's mouth. Was he breathing? She couldn't hear anything. She didn't think so.

She didn't know what to do. Her knowledge of first aid was scant. She remembered something about pressing down on the injured person's chest. Was that not something to do with saving the life of a drowning man? Perhaps not. She drew back her fist, and punched Eddie, not in the chest as she intended, but in the stomach.

Eddie gasped, wheezed and sat up, eyes bulging. 'What the hell?'

And from the pavement came a voice: 'Izzy? Izzy Macleod, what are you doing?'

Edith, the ops officer, uniform fiercely ironed, was standing watching, rigid with disapproval.

'He was lying here,' said Izzy. 'I thought he was dead.'

'You bloody punched me,' said Eddie. 'That was bloody sore.' He looked round. 'What am I doing here? I was dreaming I was in bed.'

Izzy's knees were soaked. Her hair frizzed; dampness always did that. She turned to look for Jacob. He would help her explain. But the road was empty. He'd gone.

Chapter Seventeen
Winning's Important

Charles had always been in Julia's life. Their parents were old friends. Once, at a weekend party at Charles' family's country house, he'd told Julia about sex. She'd been fifteen at the time, and innocent.

They'd just finished a game of tennis and were lying on the grass outside the court. Sounds of a new game drifted across to them – a ball being whacked back and forth. On the terrace, Julia's mother and Charles' mother were having tea. Every so often, their laughter would bounce through the afternoon. Julia was glistening hot. Charles had dark patches of sweat on his shirt. 'I won,' said Julia.

'You always win,' Charles admitted.

It wasn't because he let her. She was good at everything she took on, and, winning mattered more to her than it did to him. He stroked her cheek with a daisy. 'You're growing up.' He was four years older than her. He leaned over and kissed her. She rubbed her dampened cheek. Not that she hadn't liked the kiss. It was a reaction to the small thrill that rippled up from between her legs to her stomach. She hadn't felt anything like it before. But it was, she thought, really rather nice. Much, much better than the thrill she felt on Christmas morning.

'You don't like being kissed?' he asked.

'I'm beginning to like it. I used to hate it. Of course, it all depends on who's kissing me.'

'What about when I do it?' He leaned over and kissed her again. 'I'm waiting for you to grow up so I can make love to you.'

She asked what he meant by that.

'I want to be your lover.'

She looked blank. And he said, 'Sex. I want us to have sex.' He watched her face as she wrestled with this. 'You have no idea what I'm talking about, do you?'

'Not really,' she said. Well, she was aware there was something about men and women nobody was telling her. And the word 'sex' wasn't new to her; she just didn't know exactly what it meant.

He rolled back on the grass, covering his face with his hands, 'Oh God, oh God. You are such an ignorant virgin.'

Offended, she got up to flounce off. He grabbed her arm, pulled her back down beside him and whispered in her ear. He told her everything, no detail spared. She was shocked. 'I don't believe you.'

'Oh, it's true,' he said. 'That's what grown-ups do.'

'Well, I'm not ever going to do that. Ever, ever, ever.' And off she flounced. She strutted and huffed across the lawn and up the steps of the terrace, past the tea-drinking women.

'Flouncing again, Julia,' said her mother. 'What's wrong this time? Didn't you win at tennis?'

'Of course I won,' said Julia. 'I always win. Winning's important. It's just Charles. I hate him.'

A few years later, Charles became her first lover. She decided that sex was fine. Indeed, more than fine, it was rather splendid.

She thought she might marry one day. But not now, not yet.

She made sure she always had two lovers, and joked about this. 'I like things in twos. I never have one gin, always two.' Or, 'Two lovers keep me awake, on my toes.' Though she rarely said that since Claire had remarked that it was more likely they kept her on her back. But really, it was a safeguard against needing one man too much, or ever feeling lonely, or getting her heart broken. However, one of her two lovers was always Charles.

When Julia had got home from the Myra Hess concert, she'd slammed the front door and clattered down the hall shouting, 'Yoo-hoo, darling, I'm back and ready to be ravished!'

Silence. Bastard's still in bed, sleeping, she thought. But the bed had been empty, blankets tossed aside. Charles' uniform, which had been draped over the end, was gone. 'He's buggered orff,' said Julia out loud. Still, she'd searched the flat. Peeped into the tiny spare room, the bathroom, living room and kitchen. 'He has absolutely gone. Damn.' She'd been in the mood for a bit of ravishing.

Back in the bedroom, she'd found a note on the dresser:

I hate this flat without you in it. It's cold, empty, no wireless and no food. I'm starved. Gone to Cornwall to eat lots and say goodbye to Ma and Pa. See you when I get back from Burma. Probably won't write, I'm useless at keeping in touch. But you keep well, and think of me.

C x

Julia had reread the letter several times before slipping it into her pocket. She made the bed, washed the cups and teapot, pulled the blackout curtains, then locked up the flat and headed for the station.

She'd thought about Charles on the journey back to Skimpton, sitting on the rattling train, chugging through the dark. Then, on the country bus that trundled slowly, slowly along narrow roads and was dim inside because the interior lights were taped over, Julia cursed herself. She shouldn't have gone to the lunch-time concert, she certainly shouldn't have agreed to have tea and a bun with a stranger. She wished she and Charles hadn't bickered before she left. There's no time to bicker these days. And, she should have told him she loved him. She thought, because in a way, I do. And if something happened to him out there, he would never know.

But by April, when the world turned balmy, she was in love with someone new.

A few days after she'd got back from London, Walter Cruickshank phoned. He was coming up her way in a couple of days, and could he take her to dinner?

'Ooh, dinner,' said Julia. 'Lovely, darling, I'll look forward to it.'

They ate roast beef at the Golden Mallard, and afterwards walked over the long lawns to the river. She took his arm. He asked why she called everyone darling.

'Bad habit, and, to tell the truth, I'm not awfully good at remembering names.'

'Mine's Walter, call me that. If you call me darling, I'll think you've forgotten that I'm Walter, and don't care.'

'All right, darling.'

They walked on, arms linked. He said, 'We must do this again some time soon.'

She said, 'I'd like that.'

The following week, they'd dined again at the hotel, walked by the river and chatted. He told her he thought she was a toff.

'Probably,' she said. 'But, so what? I'm not going to apologise for being born into a wealthy family. I think you've got a chip on your shoulder.'

'Yes, but it's a good chip. It has served me well. I'm proud of my chip.'

He picked up a stone and skimmed it across the water. He watched it bounce to the other side of the river. 'So, the flying thing, how did that happen?'

'My father gave me lessons for my twenty-first birthday.' She paused. 'And an aeroplane to go with it.' Then she asked what he had got for his twenty-first.

'A suitcase.'

'A hint that it was time to leave home.'

'Exactly,' he said. 'Did wonders to nourish the chip, though.' He skimmed another stone. 'Perhaps that's why you got a plane. Your parents thought it time for you to fly out of the nest.'

She thought that might be true. 'They were certainly keen to marry me orff. They kept introducing me to eligible young men.'

'But you didn't get any offers?'

'Of course I got offers. I just didn't accept any of them. All the men I knew wanted a wife who'd produce a clutch of children while they went orff to have fun being soldiers or working in the city.' She sighed. 'Didn't think it was for me.'

He agreed, he didn't think it was for her, either.

The next time they met, he hadn't told her he was coming.

She'd had a busy day. She'd taken a Spitfire into Yorkshire, been driven twelve miles to another airbase, picked up a damaged

Spitfire, taken it to a repairs unit and then brought an Oxford back to Skimpton to be moved on the next day. The weather had been chasing her all day, giant black clouds gathering behind her – the downpour arrived not long after she'd landed. She'd waited till it was over, then cycled home, deliberately splashing through puddles.

It reminded her of when she'd been a child and had ridden her bike top speed down a hill in the family's country home. She'd whizzed along, hair flying up, urging herself to pedal faster, harder, till she realised, to her horror, she couldn't stop. She'd crashed into the lake at the bottom of the hill, sending up a shrieking squall of ducks. Puffing out her cheeks, relieved at being alive and unhurt, she'd hauled her bike out of the water, and wheeled it back to the top of the hill. That had been wonderful. What speed, such a thrill. Taking risks was such a hoot. She'd do it again.

She took her feet off the pedals at the top of the hill that led down to the cottage, and freewheeled, rattling over cobbles, bouncing in the saddle and careened into the lane.

Walter was leaning on his car, hands in his pockets, waiting for her. A tremor ran through her stomach, her face creased into a broad grin. She waved. And she didn't like herself at all. She hated when her body did that – acted on its own, without waiting for instructions from her. She liked to be in control of her emotions.

'What are you doing here?' She hoped he hadn't noticed how delighted she was.

'Came to see you,' he said. 'Thought you might like to go out to dinner.' He followed her as she wheeled her bike up the path. She told him she was tired. 'But, thanks.'

Inside, she went straight to the kitchen and put the casserole

Mrs Brent had left into the oven to heat up. 'You can set the table,' she told Walter, flapping her hand towards the cutlery drawer. 'For two, Izzy and Claire are away tonight.'

He asked where.

'A dance.'

'When will they be back?' He was hopeful it would be late.

'Tomorrow.'

He said, 'Ah.' This was better than late.

She went upstairs to change out of her uniform, 'There might be some whisky in the living room if you want it.'

He did. He poured a glass, emptied it, poured another and emptied that. Then he went outside to fetch the bottle he had in the car. He kept it on the table as they ate, topping up his glass from time to time.

'Do you always drink whisky with meals?'

He shrugged. 'No. I prefer beer with food. Whisky afterwards.'

'I think perhaps you drink too much.'

He thought about this – long nights in bars, the bottle he kept in the desk at work, the first thing he did in the evening when he got home was pour a drink. And that was after several in the pub. He tried to think of a single war correspondent who didn't drink too much. But couldn't.

'Goes with the territory,' he said. 'Like saying "orff" instead of "off".'

She told him saying 'orff' wasn't bad for her liver.

He said that having a plummy accent might do some damage to her health sometime.

'Are we bickering?' she asked.

'I do believe we are. I think we should wash up and go to the pub before it develops into a full-blown argument.'

She glared at him. For a moment, he thought she didn't want to go to the pub. But realised it was the washing-up part she didn't approve of.

'You don't wash up?' he asked.

'I leave it for Mrs Brent.'

He said he couldn't do that. 'It's my old army training. Can't leave a mess.' He tossed a dish towel at her. 'I'll wash. You dry.'

Painstakingly wiping a plate, she said, 'I didn't know you were in the army.'

'Gordon Highlanders.'

She moved on to a second plate. 'Did you wear a kilt?'

'Of course.'

'I love men in kilts.'

'Most ladies do.'

He finished washing the dishes, took the dish towel from Julia and started to dry them. 'You're taking too long. I want to get to the pub before closing time.'

'So, when were you in the army?'

'When I was eighteen. I was at the Somme.' Wiping a bowl, he remarked, 'The rhubarb crumble was excellent, by the way.'

'Mrs Brent does a good pudding.'

He folded the dish towel, draped it over the edge of the draining board, put on his jacket and said, 'Let's go.'

The Duck's Foot was Saturday-night humming, heaving with people drinking, talking, singing. Beer was being served at full throttle. The old wooden bar was already filmed and sticky with froth. The small space between the top of the drinkers' heads and the beamed ceiling was thickly wreathed with smoke.

Walter pointed to the only vacant table and instructed Julia to grab a seat in the snug, while he shoved and shouldered his way to the bar through the mass of uniforms – Americans and Canadians billeted in the village. He had to shout his order, 'A pint and a half pint for the lady,' so the barman would know to serve it in a stemmed glass. He held the glasses aloft as he jostled back to his seat.

'I don't drink beer,' said Julia.

He told her she did now. 'Unless you'd prefer a port and lemon. They're out of gin.'

She shook her head and sipped her drink. 'It's quite nice.' Then, she asked, 'Were you scared?'

'No, I've ordered drinks before. And it's been a long, long time since I've been asked if I'm old enough.'

'I mean at the Somme. You were just a boy.'

'No, I wasn't scared. I was absolutely bloody terrified. Couldn't breathe for fear. Legs like jelly, thought I wouldn't be able to walk.'

'Walk? I'd have run.'

He took a long swig. 'Orders were to walk. Fifty yards a minute.'

At first there had been artillery fire. It had gone on so long, so loud it stopped sounding like a series of bangs. It became orchestrated. 'An orchestrated bombardment.' Yet, the silence that had surrounded him was intense, and the fear-filled staccato breathing of the soldier next to him had made him want to scream. When the whistle went he'd climbed the ladder and started to walk across no man's land.

'Actually, I don't know if I could have run,' he said. 'I was carrying two hundred rounds of ammunition, two sandbags, two grenades, two gas helmets –' he counted on his fingers '– wire cutters, an entrenching tool and extra rations. Oh, and we had a tin triangle tied to our backpacks, so those watching from behind the lines could mark our progress from the reflected glint in the sun.'

'Probably running would have been difficult,' said Julia.

He nodded. 'Anyway, there we were walking into gunfire. Couple of officers linked arms and looked as if they were out for a Sunday stroll in the park. It was sunny, nice day for a walk. They got shot. Every so often we'd flatten ourselves to the ground. And, every time I got up again, I'd see fewer and fewer men in the line. We were sitting ducks out there. I was in Berlin a few years ago, nineteen thirty-five, met a couple of Germans who were at the Somme. They said if we'd run, we'd have made it to the trenches and probably beaten them.'

He finished his drink. Pointed his empty glass at her and asked if she wanted another.

She shook her head. 'I have to work tomorrow.' She watched him shove through the throng, and lean on the bar trying to attract the landlord's attention. He was chatting to a man and a woman. Locals, Julia thought. Locals always hogged the area near the bar. She leaned forwards and saw that Walter was chatting to the Brents. Mrs Brent waved. Julia trilled her fingers in reply. Someone, in the depth of the room, Julia couldn't tell who, started to sing 'April Showers'. Others joined in.

Walter returned, put his drink on the table and asked if she liked a sing-song.

'Sometimes we have one in the taxi Anson coming home. That's fun.'

The singers moved seamlessly into 'The Old Bull and Bush'.

'Where was I?' asked Walter.

'The Somme, you were walking across no man's land on a sunny day.'

'Right,' he said. 'That was it, really. I reached the trenches but didn't get through. I never got to use my knuckleduster.'

'You had a knuckleduster? Was that part of your kit?'

'No. Lots of us had them, or chains, in case of hand-to-hand combat. We were a rough lot. Kids from the streets, mostly. But my kilt got caught in the barbed wire. I didn't make it any further.'

'What happened?'

The singing was getting louder, merrier and 'It's a Long Way to Tipperary' was being belted out with gusto.

'Got caught in the wire. Panicked. Got caught up even more. Could hardly move. Got shot.'

It had felt like someone had run at him and whacked him in the leg with an iron bar. And the world melted. He'd screamed. Not that anyone would have heard, everyone was screaming.

'Anyway, I lay there by the barbed wire for hours. Then the stretcher-bearers found me, took me back behind the lines. Few weeks later, I was sent home.'

The singers, most of the pub by now, were roaring 'Roll Out the Barrel'.

'I hate that song,' he said. He downed the last of his beer. 'Do you want to go?'

'Yes, it's getting rowdy in here.'

They waved to the Brents as they left. Outside, they linked arms and started down the hill to the cottage.

'I usually like rowdy pubs,' he said. 'But I'm not in the mood tonight. I was hoping to have a game of darts. I'd have let you win.'

'No need to let me,' said Julia. 'I'd have won, anyway. I always win.'

'It's important to you?'

'Very,' she said.

They walked on, the roar of singing following them. She said, 'You got shot in the leg and you don't limp.'

'I do,' he said. 'But only when it rains.'

He asked who Charles was.

'How do you know about him?'

'The couple at the bar, the Brents, asked if I was one of your new boyfriends now Charles was away.'

'Charles is a friend. I've known him all my life. Our parents were friends. He's gone to Burma.'

'He's your lover?'

She nodded.

He said, 'What did they mean "one of"? One of your new boyfriends – you have others?'

She shook her head. 'No. Not at the moment. I usually have two. Right now it's Charles and Jeffrey. Except Jeffrey's away, too, North Africa, haven't seen him in months.'

'Two? Why stop at two. Why not three or four? Why not write to the Coldstream Guards?'

She slipped her arm from his, turned to face him. 'That's a horrible thing to say.'

He shrugged. 'I know.'

They carried on down the hill, side by side, but not touching.

'In my heyday I had four,' he said.

'Not all at the same time, I hope. The bed would have been very crowded.'

'That would have been too tiring. I went a bit wild after I got back from France. Drinking, fighting, womanising. I was at university at the time. Studying English.'

He'd had nightmares, though they didn't only come when he

was sleeping. Vivid pictures of what he'd been through – walking across no man's land on a sunny day, getting caught in the barbed wire, faces of men as they fell – would flash in his mind. At such times, and he never had any warning of when these memories would arrive, he'd press himself against a wall, or hold on to the bar in the pub where he was drinking, sweating and shaking.

'In the end my mother sat me down at the kitchen table with a cup of tea. She told me I was going to die anyway.'

'What did she mean by that?' asked Julia.

'She meant, really, that life went on. Things I'd seen happened and I'd have to learn to live with them, knowing that terrible things happen, would always happen. Meantime, it didn't matter how many women I had, I'd still have to deal with getting hurt, having my heart broken. I was still going to suffer grief and loneliness at some time or other. I was going to die anyway.'

The night filled with a shrill, out-of-tune rendition of 'A Nightingale Sang in Berkeley Square'.

'Mrs Brent,' said Julia. 'She does that every Saturday night.' She stuck her hands in her pockets and looked pained. 'I've heard about it. But this is the first time I've actually heard it.'

'You have to take your hat off to someone who is truly awful at something, but believes in herself so much she is prepared to do it in public week after week.'

'Takes courage,' agreed Julia.

They were briefly united in mutual admiration of the awfulness of Mrs Brent's singing.

'Anyway, death,' said Walter. 'You're still going to die. That's what my mother told me when she found out I was seeing four women and drinking myself stupid. I was in pain and I was angry. I had to shut myself off. Couldn't suffer any more.' He put his arm round her shoulders and led her down the hill. 'Got to get away from that singing.'

She asked if he was afraid of death.

'Oh, yes. Scared stiff. Not of being dead, but of being aware of death happening.'

'Me, too,' said Julia. 'I'm also terrified of being burned. Being horribly scarred. But that's not why I have two lovers. There's no profound reason, I do it because I can.'

At three o'clock in the morning, he woke. He sat up in bed, rubbed the ache in his leg. It was going to rain. He could hear Julia breathing next to him and reached out to touch her, to run his fingers down her back. He kissed her naked shoulder. When this war is over, he thought, people will go home, lock their doors, pull their curtains, sit by their firesides, pretending that all this sex never happened. And he wondered, If she always has two lovers, and I'm one, who would be the other? He hated him already.

Chapter Eighteen
The Dance

Captain Jimmy phoned to check Izzy was coming to the dance. A hop, he called it. 'There will be a band, and all the people from the village down the road come along with food, just what you love most, Pork Chops.'

'Don't call me that,' Izzy said. 'I hate that name.'

'I know,' he said. 'That's why I do it. Love to make you mad.'

'So it seems.'

He phoned often. But with calls limited to six minutes, conversations were brief. Izzy would just be beginning to remember things she wanted to say when they'd be cut off. Julia thought this was a good thing. 'These short calls always leave you longing to be in touch again. They're awfully good for your love life.'

On Saturday, Claire and Izzy caught the train for York at Blackpool. Izzy eyed the net luggage rack; if Claire hadn't been with her, she'd have climbed up and settled down for a nap. She found it a relaxing way to travel.

She would have slept, anyway – train travel always made her nod off – but Claire wanted to chat. She asked Izzy what she thought of the new man who'd been brought in to replace Dick Wills.

Izzy shrugged. 'He seems nice.'

'Yes,' said Claire, 'he does.' She was taken with him.

Edith had brought him into the mess, clapped her hands to get full attention from everybody. 'This is Simon Masters, our new pilot.' Then she'd left.

Simon had strolled over to the table Claire and Dick had used when they'd played backgammon, and sat down. He'd nodded and said hello to people around him and started to read *The Times*. Since he was sitting at the scene of many enjoyable games, most of which she'd lost, Claire had leaned over and asked if he played backgammon.

'As a matter of fact, I do,' he'd said. 'Though not awfully well, I'm a beginner.'

Good, Claire had thought. I may just beat him. Winning a game would be something new.

Next day had been a washout, so Claire and Simon had played backgammon quietly for three hours, waiting for Edith to tell everyone to go home. They'd chatted, laughed a little, gently mocked one another's moves. When, finally, just after one o'clock, Edith had come into the mess and said there would be no flying today, Simon had pushed back his chair, yawned and stretched. He thought he'd have lunch at the Golden Mallard where he was staying till he could find a cottage to rent, and would she join him? Claire had said that would be lovely.

At a table overlooking the gardens, they'd eaten and talked about how things had been for each of them before the war. He'd been a vet in Cumbria.

'You saw a lot of sheep.'

'And cows and horses, dogs, cats, everything. My partner runs the practice now I'm doing this.'

'I was a housewife, I suppose. I hosted a lot of dinner parties and tea parties. A bit boring now I think about it.'

He'd patted her hand and said she was never that. The hand pat had a strange effect on Claire. Something happened. A tremor trilled through her. She looked at him, moved her hand away. But she thought he had felt it, too.

He said he was dreading the end of the war. 'Everything has changed. My wife runs the home, tells the children what to do, pays the bills. I feel at a loss when I'm there. Not needed any more.' He ran his fingers through his hair, 'Fact is, I prefer working, flying, to being at home.' He was ashamed of that.

Claire agreed. 'One day all my family and I will be home. I sometimes think we'll hardly recognise one another. None of us will be the person we were before the war. After the big reunion we'll have to start getting to know each other again. I fear there will be rows, silences and, from the children, tantrums. I'm not the same. I'm not sure I can just stop flying and go back to socialising again.'

He'd taken her hand, squeezed it. This time she did not try to take it away, instead she kept it there. 'I'm dreading it,' she said.

A week later, Simon had moved into a small cottage across the river from the one Claire shared with Julia and Izzy. 'Two rooms,' he told her. 'A matchbox, really.' He invited her to view it.

She thought it cute. The bedroom was at the front and had a view of the river, the living room was tiny – a sofa, an armchair and a pine dresser. It took three steps to get from one side to the other, not in a straight line. That wasn't possible, the furniture had to be avoided. The kitchen and bathroom were in an add-on extension made of corrugated iron. 'It'll do,' he said. 'Home for the meantime.'

He'd poured them both a glass of whisky, and they drank, standing too close because the room was so small. Kissing was inevitable. Neither of them initiated it. They'd just moved into one another's arms.

At ten o'clock she pushed aside the blankets of his bed. 'I have to go.'

'Stay,' he said. 'I want you here beside me all night. I want to you to be the first thing I see when I wake.'

She shook her head. 'This has to be our secret. Everyone at the base knows my husband is a POW; there would be rumblings of disapproval. Someone might write and tell him.'

He supposed that to be true. 'But you will come again.'

She stopped pulling on her stockings, leaned over and kissed him. 'Just try and stop me.'

Now, sitting on the train, Claire was regretting this trip. She didn't want to go her parents' home, hated it there. She longed to be with Simon, in his cottage, in his bed. She thought she might be in love. And this was new to her.

Claire's father, Derek, picked them up at York. 'Brought the Morris. The Bentley bloody guzzles petrol,' he said, crushing Izzy's hand. 'Good to meet you.'

The house was thirty minutes' drive from the station, at the end of a wide, rolling drive, swathes of lawn on either side. Izzy had been expecting a big house, a mansion, even. This was a palace. Vast, ornate, turreted – wide steps led up to the front door, statues poised at the foot of them, more statues set into carefully clipped niches in hedging that surrounded the courtyard. A thousand windows, Izzy thought. Her mother would weep for whoever had to clean them.

Derek apologised. 'Rack and ruin,' he said. 'The place is falling apart. No staff, they've all been called up.' He sighed. 'The rose garden, croquet lawn and tennis courts are all turned over to vegetables. And we dine at the ungodly hour of six o'clock. I have to be on duty at seven.' He was captain of the Home Guard.

Inside the house was bleak, forbidding – oak panelling, an oak staircase, portraits in ornate gold frames, busts on plinths. Izzy hated it. The only things that made the grandeur bearable were the pile of muddy boots by the door and the two old black Labradors panting quietly beside it.

The room she would be staying in was on the first floor, overlooking what had once been the tennis courts, and was now rows and rows of potatoes, cabbages, onions and peas. The room was huge, draughty. In winter, it would be icy. There was a four-poster bed, a dresser and a wardrobe, on one wall a vast oil painting of a hunting scene. By the time she got there, someone had already brought her bag up and unpacked it. Izzy was horrified. Some unknown person had seen her absurd packing. The tangle of clothes she'd hurriedly shoved into her bag. They'd hung things up and put her knickers and bra neatly folded into a drawer. If she'd known this was going to happen, she'd have brought her best underwear.

Price, the butler, had shown her to her room. He told her that should she need to freshen up, the lavatory was at the end of the hall. Izzy put her head round the door. It was an awfully long corridor. She thought these people must have sturdy digestive systems having to hike so far to the loo. She went to the window. A small woman with thick trousers tucked into wellington boots and a patterned silk headscarf was fervently hoeing a row of onions. She looked up, saw Izzy and waved. 'Jolly good.'

It was the heartiness, the brusque confidence of these people that made Izzy uneasy. She felt a deeper shyness than her usual reticence. Here, there would be small social rituals she knew nothing about – the correct way to take tea in the afternoon, the proper time to appear for breakfast, an array of cutlery to master at dinner. Should she have tipped the butler? She didn't know. She was bound to make a gaffe or three.

Downstairs, Claire offered to show Izzy round. 'We'll avoid the gardens in case we run into Ma. She'd rope us in to do some digging.'

Izzy thought she might have already had a wave from Ma.

The stables and garage, once whitewashed, were now covered with camouflage netting. Behind them was a huge, run-down barn. Claire said, 'Come and look at this. You'll love it.' Inside was a yellow Tiger Moth just visible under a tarpaulin.

'You have a plane,' said Izzy.

Claire nodded.

'Is that how you learned to fly? In your own plane?'

Claire nodded. 'It's Pa's. We used to fly up to our house in Scotland every year for the grouse shoot. He used to fly it everywhere, even when he was just dropping in on friends.'

She had been thirteen when her father first arrived home with his new acquisition. She'd been sitting on the steps outside, reading a book when he'd come buzzing overhead, calling, 'Hello, below!' She had looked round, looking up hadn't occurred to her. 'Ahoy, the ground.' At that point she'd raised her eyes skywards. Her father was skimming past, wearing flying jacket and leather helmet, waving and pointing to the drive. 'Coming in to land.' After that, he'd flown whenever he could, and had to be dissuaded from taking the plane to the village five miles away to collect his copy of *The Times*.

The flights to Scotland had usually taken three or four hours. While the rest of the family travelled by train, taking with them the dogs, the cat, all of Claire's mother's wardrobe and most of Claire's – a pile of trunks that took up most of the guard's van – she and her father would take the plane and arrive red of face, stiff with cold and exhilarated. They always celebrated their safe journey with a large whisky. To this day Claire always associated her first hours in their Scottish house with being drunk. 'Happy days,' said Claire. She looked at her watch. 'Oh goody, time for tea.'

Tea, at this time of year, was served on the veranda outside the drawing room. Claire's parents were already there. Margaret, her mother, had removed the boots but not the headscarf. Derek had changed into his uniform. They waved, though Izzy and Claire were only yards away. Izzy waved back, and doubted herself. Perhaps one shouldn't do that. It seemed absurdly familiar, since she hardly knew them.

Margaret said, 'Jolly good.' Patted a seat next to her and told Claire to sit down and give her all the news. 'How's Richard, any news?'

'He's bearing up,' said Claire. 'I get letters, but they're heavily censored.'

'He'll be terribly upset to be stuck away in that camp,' said Derek. 'He's missing all the fun.'

Claire agreed. 'He does seem a bit down. Ah, tea at last.'

A maid, carrying a tray, appeared. She laid out a teapot, a pot of hot water, milk, a small bowl of sugar, cups, saucers and a plate of scones, nodded and went away.

'Susan,' said Margaret, 'along with cook and Price, are all the staff we have left. Of course, we have a couple of land gels from the village to help with the gardens. We're selling quite a bit to the American base these days. And Bernie helps in the stable, but he's over seventy now.' She sighed. 'Things just aren't the same.'

'Bloody chap from the government came and had a look round. Said we didn't need a chauffeur or a pastry chef, or anybody, come to that. Off they all went to the army or whatever. Damned chaps at the top have decided we can't get a decent slice of fruit cake.'

Margaret poured the tea, handed out the cups. 'Can't get anything these days. Were just about down to the last case of claret. And you can't make a proper martini for love nor money. This war is so inconvenient.' She turned to Izzy. 'And what is it you do?'

'The same as Claire. I fly.'

'But before that?'

'I flew with a flying circus.'

'Ah. You're a Macleod, I believe.'

'Yes.'

Margaret turned to Derek. 'Do we know any Macleods in Scotland?'

He shook his head. 'No.'

She turned back to Izzy. 'And who exactly is your father?'

'He's a minister. The parish is a village not far from Perth.'

'Church of Scotland, then?'

Izzy said, 'Yes.'

Margaret said, 'Ah. A bit dour. We prefer something with a bit of show. I think our chaps have brighter robes.' She smiled and said she had a delivery of potatoes for the base tomorrow morning.

'This war will be the end of us,' said Derek. He swigged his tea and helped himself to a scone.

'Oh, I don't think it'll be the end of us,' said Izzy. 'We'll win. I'm sure of that.'

Derek said he didn't doubt for one moment that they would give the Hun a sound thrashing. 'But I meant it will be the end of us. Our kind of people. The aristocracy, the landed gentry, the privileged landowners or whatever these socialist types call us.' He glared at her. 'You're not one, are you? A bloody red.'

Izzy blushed, said, of course she wasn't. And hated herself, because, of course, she was. Elspeth had been passionate about the iniquities of upper-class privilege, and she believed everything Elspeth told her. 'But you're quite posh, yourself,' Izzy had said.

'That's only by birth, not by belief. I have forsaken my posh beginnings and now consider myself to be working class.'

'We are the backbone of this country, and we're doomed,' said Derek. 'When all this is over, the staff won't come back. They'll all be taking factory jobs. Life in service will have no appeal. No, we are a dying species. And these damned scones are like rubber.'

'I'm afraid that's true,' said Margaret. 'Can't help the scones. It's the flour and the powdered egg.' Then before her husband could embark on a political rant, she shot Derek a silencing glare and said, 'The broad beans are doing awfully well this year. More tea, Izzy?'

Derek sighed and sat back, rummaged about his mouth with his tongue to looking for stray bits of scone, and stared out over his tattered daisy-infested lawns.

Izzy said, 'Yes, please.' She held out her cup to be refilled, and vowed to say as little as possible for the rest of her stay.

She was still holding her tongue halfway through the dance. Captain Jimmy had collected her and Claire. In fact, Izzy didn't much like dances. She preferred to watch the action rather than join in. Still, it was an enjoyable show. A noisy spangled affair – young girls from the village nearby tricked out in their best summer frocks, airmen in pressed uniforms and shiny shoes, older folks sitting waiting for the slow numbers to be played, all this jitterbugging and jiving wasn't for them. A long table against the far wall was heavy with cakes, buns, sandwiches, all contributed by the villagers, and Coca-Cola, the American contribution.

And the band played, roaring out songs of the day. The dance floor was a mass of swirling legs, girls being tossed in the air, slung between their partner's legs – a vibrant show of stocking tops and knickers.

Izzy wasn't up for any of that, but she did enjoy jiving. Here was a dance she could do. Waltzing and other dances bemused her. She'd find herself face-to-face with someone she barely knew, forced to chat but unable to think of anything to say. She'd be gripped tightly and whirled about. She'd drift off into a daydream, forget her partner was leading and stand on his toes. But jiving was just jumping about to music, and she loved it. Every now and then a pair of jiving masters took the centre of the floor and performed acrobatic dancing feats. Izzy and Jimmy stood back and cheered them on.

Towards the end of the evening, after they'd been dancing for a couple of hours, he asked if she wanted to step outside. 'Cool off a little.' The band was blasting 'Boogie Woogie Bugle Boy'. He had to shout.

Izzy nodded.

They squeezed their way to the door, past airmen in wheelchairs, on crutches, bandaged, almost immobile, who couldn't make it to the dance floor. Jimmy knew all their names.

The night was soft. Under a slip of a moon, couples

smooched. He took Izzy's hand and led her across the grass. 'You're awfully quiet. Don't you like dancing?'

She told him she just wasn't very good at it.

'Doesn't matter if you're no good at it, you're meant to have fun.'

She said she liked jiving. 'It's fun.'

He pulled her to him. 'I think you're happier in the air than you are on the ground. In fact, I think being on the ground scares you.'

'Don't be silly.'

'I think you're happy up there.' He pointed to the sky. 'You can just sit up there and be you.'

'I fly because I can,' said Izzy. 'It's something I can do. It's mine. It's the only thing I stood up to my father about. I'm not very good at anything else.'

'Rubbish,' he said. He put his lips to her ear, whispered, 'Fucking, you're good at that.'

She tried to ignore this. 'I wasn't all that clever at school. I can't sing. I never mastered the piano. Can't cook. I'm not very good at dances. When I stayed at home, and there was a dance at the village hall, my dad was always there. He'd give the heaving eyebrow to all the boys who asked me up, and he always had the last dance with me and took me home. I never got the chance to be naughty.'

Music from the dance drifted across to them. He held her close, did a little slow shuffle dance with her. 'But you are here and your father is hundreds of miles away in Scotland, you should grab the chance to be naughty. Naughtiness is good. Lifts the spirits.'

He was all confidence. Cocksure, Izzy's father would have said. He wouldn't approve of, or even like, Jimmy. This made him very appealing to her. How did people get to be like him? How did a person get the knack of jazzing through life, rushing from moment to moment, arms spread, expecting only happiness? Why did she feel she slouched, head bent, expecting rejection, apologies always on the tip of her tongue? And what did it take to join the confident people who did whatever they wanted to do? Damn it, Izzy thought, I want to be like them. She wanted to feel the joy she felt when flying down here on the ground.

She blamed her father. He'd taught her to be humble. 'Conceit will get you nowhere,' he'd told her. But Jimmy wasn't conceited. He was confident. And so were the ostentatiously voiced women she worked with. And there was nothing wrong with that. 'The meek will inherit the earth,' Hamish often said. Izzy was beginning to doubt that. She rather agreed with Elspeth, who'd declared that if ever the earth was up for inheriting, the meek would get trampled in the rush. She had never mentioned this to Hamish.

Recently, she'd been worried about him. His sermon about there being tears in German homes, too, hadn't gone down well. He'd been sure that the rumblings about his being a German sympathiser would go away, but they hadn't. In fact, Izzy's mother had written in her last letter that they'd got worse.

Jimmy stroked Izzy's face. 'Next time you come, I'll book us a B and B,' he said.

'You mean a dirty weekend?' Izzy brightened at the thought.

'If you want to put it like that, yes.'

'I'd love to.'

He kissed her. 'There, it's a deal.'

They were well into their second kiss when Claire found them. 'I've been searching everywhere.' She said she wanted to go home. 'I've had enough of jiving and Coca-Cola.'

On the drive back to her parents' house, Claire said she needed to catch an earlier train than they'd originally planned. 'I've things I have to do.' She wanted to see Simon.

Izzy said, 'OK.' She told Jimmy she'd get another two days off in thirteen days' time. 'Thirteen days on, two days off.'

Jimmy said he could come over and see her before that. He had a bit of time off coming up. 'OK, Pork Chops?'

'Pork Chops?' said Claire.

'My nickname,' said Izzy.

'She deserves it,' said Jimmy. 'She can out-eat me. She sure has a capacity for pork chops.'

Claire snorted. Izzy thought, Damn. Now Claire would tell everybody at the base and they'd all call her that. She didn't think Pork Chops a suitable name for a woman about to jazz through life, rushing, arms spread, towards happiness.

Chapter Nineteen
The Orange

'Moon.' Duncan Bowman stood at the door of his hut, hands on hips, cap shoved back. 'I'll see you in my office.'

It was after six. All the girls were in the dining shed; Elspeth could hear the clatter of dishes and the waves of chatter and laughter and longed to join them. She was hungry.

She was always late for meals. She had to feed and water her horse before she fed herself. She had rinsed her hands in the water trough and was drying them by wiping them on her dungarees as she walked. The ground, once a quagmire, was baked hard. It hadn't rained for weeks.

'Won't take a minute,' Duncan said. He noticed her long sad glance towards the dining hut.

'It's lovely and cool in here,' she said. Her skin stung from a day in the sun. She sat on the dubiously shaky wooden chair across from his desk.

'You're doing fine with the horse,' said Duncan.

She nodded, a little disappointed to find he was pleased with her. Her hopes of getting sacked were fading.

'So,' Duncan went on, 'I'm going to increase your quota. Sixty logs.'

'A day?' said Elspeth. 'I have to take sixty logs a day to be loaded on the lorry?'

'That's what I said.'

'That means I have to run back and forwards one hundred and twenty times a day.'

'You're young and fit. There are quotas to meet and there's a war on. Though, from the way you young lasses behave, nobody would know it.'

She said nothing. Shifted in her seat, a little guilty at this remark.

'There's goings-on in the woods.'

'Well,' said Elspeth. 'People have to amuse themselves somehow. There's not a lot to do out here.'

'And there's miles and miles of forest to get up to what you're calling not a lot to do.'

Elspeth sniffed and studied her fingers.

'It needs to stop. I'm not having any of you girls getting in the family way. I'd need to send them home and there might be no replacements. I'm putting you in charge of that.'

'In charge of stopping girls getting pregnant? You want me to give contraceptive advice?'

'Don't be stupid.'

'Do I get a whistle?' asked Elspeth. 'I can walk about blasting at people I see getting into mischief.'

He ignored this. 'You need you arrange some entertainment. Play your accordion. Do something to stop people wandering off and . . . you know . . . getting up to things they shouldn't be getting up to.' He waved her away. 'That's it. New quota and arrange something to take people's minds off –' he searched for a word '– things.'

She rose, said she'd see what she could do.

As she was leaving, he said, 'Oh, and I've got something for you.' He opened a drawer in his desk, peered inside.

Please don't let it be a whistle, Elspeth prayed.

Duncan brought out an envelope and an orange, slapped them on the desk. 'There. A letter for you. And that, it's an orange.'

Elspeth, never one to hide her feelings, swooned. 'An orange. An actual orange. I haven't had one for years. Where did you get it?'

'I get things from time to time.'

'But an orange,' said Elspeth. 'They're awfully good for you. Are you sure you don't want it for yourself?'

'Can't be doing with fruit,' said Duncan. 'It's not proper food.' He waved her out, a long sweep of his arm, gesturing towards the door. 'Away you go and have your tea. And remember, sixty logs tomorrow.'

Elspeth slid into her seat beside Lorna at the table. 'Guess what.'

'What?' said Lorna.

Elspeth started to eat her Spam, potatoes and carrots. 'I'm starved.'

'Just as well, or you wouldn't eat this stuff,' said Lorna.

'Actually, I'm getting a taste for Spam. I quite like it.'

Lorna said, 'Good. Now, what am I to guess?'

Elspeth turned to her, eyes agleam. 'Guess what Duncan Bowman gave me. You never will.'

'A kick in the bum,' said Lorna.

'No.' Elspeth shook her head, looked solemn. She took a slice of bread, folded it over, put a slice of Spam in the middle and bit into the sandwich, eyes shut. 'So starved.'

'A puppy,' said Lorna.

Elspeth shook her head. 'Don't be silly.'

'An engagement ring, a kiss, a bottle of gin, a bunch of red roses, a whistle, a quick look at his . . .'

'Stop,' said Elspeth. 'You're getting rude.' She leaned over, whispered in Lorna's ear. 'An orange.'

'Really, a real one?'

Elspeth nodded, a furiously eager bobbing of her head. 'An actual orange.' She gripped Lorna's arm. 'We'll sneak away and eat it after supper.'

Tricia, sitting across from them, suspicious at their fervent whispering, asked what was going on.

'Nothing.' Elspeth's voice went up an octave. She never could tell a lie.

'It's Duncan,' said Lorna. 'He's given Elspeth –' She stopped, leaned down to rub her ankle where Elspeth had just kicked it.

'He's given me a new quota,' said Elspeth. 'And he wants me to organise a concert or some sort of entertainment.'

'Why?' said Tricia.

'To stop you all slipping into the woods and having hanky-panky.'

The girls round the table, who'd been listening, gave a loud whoop. 'Oooh, hanky-panky.'

Elspeth put a firm palm on the table. 'It has got to stop. We'll have a concert to take your mind off it.'

Somebody said she'd rather slip into the woods for a bit of slap and tickle than go to a boring concert.

Elspeth protested, 'It won't be boring. It will be a merry evening of music, songs, jokes and skits. Can anybody do anything?'

Lorna said she could flare her nostrils, and gave a

demonstration. Elspeth shook her head. 'I don't think people at the back will see that. Or people at the front, actually.'

Tricia said she could play the *William Tell* overture on her head. Her boast was met by calls to prove it, and she did. She tapped on the top of her skull, and by moving her jaw, opening and closing her mouth, she made a wide-ranging variety of notes. 'Took me ages to learn a tune,' she said. 'Got a real headache at times.'

Girls round the table drummed on their heads while opening and shutting their mouths.

'How did you discover you could do that?' Elspeth asked.

'Holidays at the seaside. We rented a caravan and it always rained. We'd be stuck inside with nothing to do. It was really boring. My sister could play "Land of Hope and Glory". She's dead now. A bomb fell on her house.'

The tune-makers stopped, everyone sighed.

Lorna said she was sick of this war. Everybody she knew had a relative or friend who'd died. 'Too many people are dying. Just think, right now somebody is dying.'

Communal gloom – everyone round the table, except Elspeth, had lost somebody. Thinking about brothers, lovers, fathers, cousins and friends was kept for private moments in bed with the blankets pulled over their heads when nobody would see them cry.

Elspeth's black moments came when she thought that probably some of her old friends had died, but she didn't know for sure, she'd lost touch with them all. Her blackest moment was when she realised she had nobody to lose. Everybody she had ever loved was gone from her. Except Izzy, of course. Fingers crossed for Izzy.

She took Lorna's arm. 'C'mon, let's go for a walk before we get all maudlin.'

They strolled up to the stables, then took the steep path that led down to the spot where Elspeth and Tyler had picnicked. The ring of stones where he had built the fire was still there. And the grass was flattened slightly in the place beneath the trees where they had lain many times since, making love.

Lorna looked round. 'Lovely spot. How did you find it?'

'Tyler,' said Elspeth.

It was still warm. The river widened here, gathered into a pool that was glassily still. Nothing moved.

'Is this where you and him get together?'

Elspeth nodded.

'You'll have to be careful. You don't want to get in the family way.'

'I won't,' said Elspeth. 'I take precautions.'

'You do? Golly.' Lorna thought Elspeth the most sophisticated person she'd ever met.

'I have a cap. Don't you?'

Lorna shook her head. 'No. How would I get one? I'm not married.'

'I just went to the doctor and told him I was going to get married and didn't want a baby yet. Of course that was some time ago. Before I came here. Long, long before I came here.' She'd only brought it with her because she thought her cottage might be requisitioned (it would be empty, after all), then some stranger might find it. A Dutch cap was not the sort of thing a single woman was meant to own.

'I just don't let Freddie go all the way. I don't want to get pregnant. Sent home in disgrace. God, my mother's face if I had to tell her I was expecting.' Lorna put her hand to her mouth, imagining the horror of her mother's expression. 'She'd go off her head. She'd fold her arms and glare at me and tell me I'd let her down. That's how she brought us up, by feeding us boiled cabbage and potatoes and glaring at us if we were bad. Actually, that's why I like it here. I'm miles and miles away from my mother. And the war, and everything.'

'I like the smell,' said Elspeth. 'And Harry the horse. And the companionship.' But other than that, she felt stuck. Far away beyond this forest, all sorts of things were going on, and she was missing it. She sank her hands into her pockets, felt the letter Duncan Bowman had given her. She'd read it tonight.

She brought out the orange. She held in her cupped hands, breathed in its scent, handed it to Lorna. 'Smell that.'

Lorna took it, turned it over and over. 'It's perfect. Not all old and wrinkled and dried up.' She held it to her nose. 'Orangey. I'd forgotten that smell.'

Elspeth slowly peeled it, split it in two and gave half to Lorna. They ate in silence, wiping with relish the stray streams of sticky juice that ran down their chins. It was a moment too precious for talk. They tenderly took segments to suck, eyes shut, as they drifted through memories of oranges past. Christmas oranges stuck in the toe of the stocking at the foot of the bed, a bowl of oranges on the dresser in the best room, an orange hurriedly eaten in the school playground, sticky hands wiped on gymslipped bum as the bell rang.

'This is the best orange I've ever had,' said Lorna. She stroked her lips with the back of her hand. 'I'll remember this for the rest of my life.'

'Me, too.' Elspeth got up, walked to the bank to rinse her

fingers in the river. Squatting, hands wrist deep in the water, she was tempted to jump in. It was that time of year when, this far north, twilight lingers late. It never quite got dark. The air was soft, still warm and there wasn't a ripple of a breeze. 'Oh, to hell with it, I'm going in.'

Quickly, before the impulse gave way to common sense, she pulled off her clothes, tossed them into a heap beside her. Then, she sat on the bank and eased herself into the river. Shrieking, gasping as the sudden chill hit her chest, she waded into the deep holding her arms aloft. 'Bloody hell, it's freezing.'

When she was finally out of her depth, she took off swimming. Head held above the surface, she moved out to the middle of the pool, turned and called on Lorna to join her. 'It's lovely.'

Lorna was shocked. 'I can't come in. I haven't got a swimming costume.'

'Neither have I,' shouted Elspeth.

Their voices, shrill in the quiet of the forest, ricocheted round the small clearing, rose up, seemed to bounce off the trees and sounded a lot louder than they actually were.

'I know!' Lorna shouted back. 'You're naked.'

'There's nothing wrong with naked,' said Elspeth. 'Skinny-dipping in the evening in a cool clear pool is a splendid thing to do.' She could see Lorna was tempted.

'I can't get naked,' said Lorna. 'Nobody's ever seen me without my clothes.'

'What? Nobody?' Elspeth laughed.

'Nobody,' said Lorna.

'You've got nothing I haven't got. Come on.'

The river was clear, tinged peaty brown. Looking down, Elspeth could see her legs treading water, small sparks and bubbles

236

rising round them, green moss-covered rocks. She swam to the far side and beckoned Lorna to take the plunge. 'Scaredy cat. I dare you.'

Lorna never could resist a challenge. Besides, Elspeth looked serene and really rather beautiful swimming back and forth. What fun, Lorna thought. She took off her clothes slowly, folding each thing, leaving them in a polite pile. She kept her knickers on. She was a good girl, after all. She minced to the bank, tiny steps, arms crossed over her breasts. She was shy.

At the water's edge, she paused, wondering how best to get into the water. The gentle slide in from the bank, or the abandoned leap into centre stream? The leap won. She launched herself, screaming, from the bank, sending a deluge of water into the air as she landed. The screaming resumed once she surfaced. 'It's freezing.'

Elspeth swam round her. 'You'll get used to it.'

Lorna gasped, sucked in air, flailed about and asked if there would be any fish about.

'Not since you arrived,' said Elspeth. 'They'll have scarpered, thinking a whale's come to get them.'

They moved in circles round one another, from time to time one would skim the surface with her arm sending a shower sparkling over the other. They lay on their backs, kicking up a cascade with their feet. Elspeth dived, sped along the bottom of the river, watching waving plants. She pushed her way back up, burst through the surface, heaving air into her lungs and shoved her hair out of her eyes. She looked round at the thickly treed slopes and saw a movement among the branches about halfway up.

'Sometimes, when I come here, I get the feeling someone's watching,' she said.

Lorna looked round. 'There's nobody.' Then, she called out, 'Hello, hello, is there anybody there? Are you spying on us?' Her yell went ringing up through the trees. 'Nope, nobody there.'

Elspeth thought it time to go. 'Best get back before it gets dark.'

They headed for the bank.

'You know what we haven't got?' asked Elspeth.

'No.'

'A towel.'

They dried themselves roughly with their dungarees. Dressed, wriggling damp bodies into damp clothes, and headed back to the hut.

Elspeth took her toilet bag across to the ablutions hut. She brushed her teeth, noting that her tin of Gibb's toothpaste was running out, washed her face, then carefully rubbed Pond's cream onto her cheeks. She changed into her pyjamas – men's striped pyjamas, they were warm – and walked back over the duckboards.

She hung a tilley lamp beside her bed and turned the letter Duncan had given her over in her hands. It seemed to be from Avril, but the writing on the envelope wasn't hers. She opened it.

My dear Elspeth,

I hope you don't mind my calling you by your first name when we haven't met. But Avril spoke of you so often, I feel I know you.

I'm afraid I have very bad news. Avril, my lovely daughter, died last week. We buried her yesterday. As you probably know, she had TB and was very ill by the time we lost her. There was hardly anything of her when she finally went. She was so pale and thin, it broke my heart to see her.

We visited her most days at the sanatorium, but, of course, we were not allowed near her. She was on one side of a glass screen, my husband and myself on the other. It is a cruel life, I sometimes think. I would so have loved to hold Avril in my arms before she died. How dreadful it is not to be able to comfort the sick. Especially when the one who is sick is someone you love.

Anyway, I won't detain you any longer, dear Elspeth. I just wanted to let you know about Avril. And to tell you how much she liked you and enjoyed your company up there in the wilds. I don't know why, but she claimed that her days in the forest were the happiest of her life. I often think of you girls working in the forest, doing your bit for the war. I hope that from time to time you will spare a kindly thought for our dear Avril.

Yours sincerely,
Morag Osborne

Elspeth put down the letter. 'Avril's dead.'

Cries of, 'No,' and 'She can't be.'

'When did she die?' asked Lorna.

Elspeth told her last week. 'Her mother wrote this letter the day after the funeral.'

Lorna took the letter, read it and handed it to Tricia, who, in turn, handed it to Dorothy. Slowly it was passed round till everyone had seen it.

The atmosphere turned black. Minutes before, the girls had been quietly pottering, preparing for bed. Now, they stared at one another in gloomy disbelief.

'Only weeks ago she was running with the logs,' said someone.

'She was only nineteen, maybe twenty,' said Lorna. 'That's too young to die. I hate death. Why do people have to die?'

Elspeth didn't know the answer to that.

Tricia said they should have a memorial service. 'Tomorrow morning, before we go to work. Someone should say a few words about Avril and we'll sing a song.'

'Duncan Bowman wouldn't like that,' said Lorna.

'To hell with him,' said Elspeth.

'He might dock our pay.' Lorna worried about this.

'If he does,' said Elspeth, 'we'll go on strike.'

'Yes.' A ripple of rebellion shifted round the room. 'Strike.'

'We have a right to mourn one of our fellow lumberjills.'

In the end, though, their dreams of rebellion came to nothing.

After breakfast, the girls had ignored the call to climb on the trailer that would take them into the forest. They gathered in a circle and listened as Elspeth spoke of Avril. 'A good and true friend. An honour to have known her . . .'

They nudged one another, watching in quiet amazement as Duncan joined them. They sneaked shy peaks at him as he took off his cap. How odd he looked without it, they thought.

'Let's have a minute's silence,' Elspeth said. 'We'll have a quiet word with God, as we remember her.' She wasn't sure about God. She wasn't sure about praying. But she thought the other girls might want a moment's communion, and a chance to convey good thoughts about their old friend to whomever might be up there would be comforting. They sang a thin wavering rendition of 'Swing Low Sweet Chariot'. Only Elspeth knew all the words. After that she bowed her head and said, 'Thank you for bringing Avril into our lives. She was a wonderful lead girl, may her whistle never be silent. May she forever be at peace. Amen.'

The girls gathered their axes and trudged down the track to the trailer, Elspeth behind them. Duncan caught her arm. The cap was back in place.

'That was a grand thing to do,' he said. 'A bit of a service for the dead, helps us all.' He smiled.

It was the same stiff upwards movement of the lips he'd given her when he'd turned up to stop the party – a begrudging shifting of rarely used muscles. Elspeth's stomach turned over. She had a niggling notion that this man's approval was not something she wanted.

But she smiled back, picked up her axe and joined Lorna on the back of the trailer.

'I'm a terrible person,' said Lorna. 'I didn't think about Avril at all when we had that silence. I didn't pray or anything. All I thought was how funny Duncan Bowman looked without his cap. Sort of naked and vulnerable. I wondered if he kept it on in bed.'

'Me, too,' said Elspeth.

She vowed that the state of Duncan's head at night, cap on or cap off, was something she would never discover.

Chapter Twenty

You Owe Me

It was a time of rumours. Hamish knew that. There were spies everywhere. In the village, strangers were treated with suspicion. Gracie Fields was a traitor. She'd been accused of taking her money out of the country and fleeing to Canada when her husband, an Italian, should have been interned. Hamish loved Gracie Fields and doubted this was true. There was a rumour that the Germans had built a decoy airfield entirely out of wood and the Allies had sent a plane over to drop a wooden bomb on it. Hamish was convinced this couldn't be true. Why bother? Why let them know that we know their airfield is a decoy? He shoved his hands into his pockets and sighed. Rumours and sex during wartime – he supposed it took people's minds off their worries.

He knew, for sure, that the rumours about him weren't true. He was not, as the village gossips said, a German sympathiser. He had simply said that German mothers would be weeping as British mothers were also weeping. But there had been an intake of breath across the congregation when his words came out. Perhaps he'd said it too passionately. All he'd meant was that war was ruinous. The innocent suffered. He was sure that there must be Germans who disagreed with Hitler.

But it had been taken the wrong way. On their way out of

church that Sunday, one or two people had refused to shake his hand. In the days that followed, whispers had spread. He was not just a German sympathiser, he was a conscientious objector. He was not a man to be trusted.

Now, when he walked through the village, there were some who turned away from him. They refused to say hello. Some people stared at him in astonishment. It broke his heart. He'd been told the Kirk Session was meeting soon to discuss his position. He feared they might ask him to resign. He could hardly believe it.

After all this time, all his work, this had happened. Twenty-six years he'd been here, building up his parish, helping people with their troubles, welcoming them into his home, offering tea and advice. At first, Joan had hated it. The manse was cold. It was the biggest house she'd lived in. She was a city girl, missed streets, traffic and shops.

They'd both come from poor backgrounds. He'd been the first in his family to go to university. He'd studied theology at Edinburgh. Lived in one room, read his books at night wearing a coat and gloves, it had been so cold. He'd met Joan at the church he'd attended where she was a Sunday school teacher. At the time she'd been living with her parents and three sisters in a two-roomed flat. When they'd moved here, thinking that if they had children, the country air would be good for them, Joan had wandered the manse saying they didn't need so much space, so many rooms. They should take in orphans or homeless people, she'd said. But they hadn't.

At first locals had been wary. They didn't immediately warm to strangers from the city. But as time passed, Hamish's sermons moved from being quiet lectures on loving your neighbour to passionate rants about paying for your sins. This, he learned, was what was wanted. Parishioners liked to have an hour or so of feeling awful about themselves once a week before they went back to their normal comings and goings.

Then Izzy had come along and Hamish's life got sunny. God, he loved the girl. Watched her grow into a tomboy. He played with her, danced with her, read her stories. Now she was gone from him. She lived her own life, did what she wanted. Sometimes, he wondered if she thought about him at all.

He wondered what she would think of all this. She might be shocked. She might sympathise with him. Whatever, she'd make up her own mind. That was how she was.

He'd decided he hardly knew his daughter. She'd been so shy, so unsure of herself. But she was changing. He'd noticed a new confidence in her when she last visited. She'd gained a certain poise.

She was a stranger in the village where she now lived. He had an uneasy feeling that she hadn't been telling the truth about what she did. Izzy is flying these planes, he thought. Awkward in company though she is, she's wilful, stubborn. She wouldn't want to tell pilots where to fly. She'd want to be up there doing it herself. Oh my, he thought, the little minx, she's just like me. She goes her own way, does exactly what she wants to do, no matter what anyone says. What did the people in Skimpton make of these young women who flew Spitfires and of his Izzy in her blue uniform?

In Skimpton, Izzy was a star. People doffed their hats, smiled, said 'Good morning', 'Hello' and 'Isn't it a lovely day?' She had broken a social barrier and was no longer one of them lady pilots, an outsider. These days, everyone called her Izzy and seemed delighted to find her walking down the same street as they were. She was a heroine. The lady pilot who'd saved the life of Eddie Hicks.

This shamed her. She'd done nothing except punch a man she'd thought was dying in the stomach. She didn't deserve her glory.

'You just left me there,' she said to Jacob. 'I was kneeling in the road and I turned round and you were gone.'

Jacob shrugged. 'What was I meant to do?'

'Stay around,' said Izzy.

Late afternoon, they were in the car pool. Izzy had finished her day's work and was about to go home. Jacob was polishing the Humber, but he didn't stop to look at her. He just kept slowly, deliberately buffing the bonnet. Sleeves rolled up, sweat patches at his armpits; it was hot.

'You want me to get the sack, then?' he asked. He kept his back to her, still working up a sheen on the car.

'No,' said Izzy. 'Of course I don't.'

'I was driving too fast, took my eyes off the road and knocked a man down. It's my fault. I didn't want to get the sack, so I drove away.'

'You should get the sack for driving away.'

He admitted that. 'But you're not going to tell, are you?' He turned, leaned on the car, hands in his pockets and smiled at her.

No, she wasn't going to tell.

'I parked round the corner and walked back to check everything was all right.'

He had been standing in the darkness, collar up, observing as

Izzy leaned over the body lying on the road. He'd been anxious at first, shoulders tense, as he'd peered into the gloom. All he could see were shapes. He thought he'd killed a man. To his horror, he'd seen Izzy punch the corpse. God, he'd thought, what is she doing? That's not what you do with a dying man. He'd wanted to scream at her to stop.

To his amazement, the dead man had sat up, gasped for air and complained loudly about the blow to his stomach. Jacob had laughed. Hand over mouth, stifling giggles. He'd seen Edith, the ops officer, come along and stand at the kerbside, demanding to know what exactly Izzy was up to, 'punching an injured man'.

Izzy had said she thought that was what you did to people who'd passed out. Edith shrilly said, 'I don't think that's at all right, my dear. But it seems to have done the trick.' They'd helped the poor breathless man to his feet and, propping him up between them, helped him home.

Jacob had slipped back to the car, examined it carefully by torchlight, and found nothing – not a scratch. He realised that whoever he'd hit couldn't have been badly hurt. His victim must have slid to the ground and lain in a drunken coma between the wheels as the car cruised over him.

'You should thank me,' he said to Izzy. 'You've been declared a heroine.' He spread his palms, unable to believe the absurdity of it. 'There was a glowing report about your quick-thinking actions on the noticeboard. "A shining example", it said.'

Izzy blushed. Edith had posted a report about 'one of our brave pilot's quick-thinking action' on the notice-board just below the official report on Dick Wills' death and the order that boots were not to be worn while conducting personal business. Izzy cringed every time she saw it. She'd scurry past it, eyes down.

'People in the village look up to you,' Jacob said. 'They're saying you saved a man's life.'

Izzy said, 'You know I did no such thing.'

'Mrs Brent made you a batch of scones and gave you half a dozen of her best brown eggs.'

Izzy couldn't argue with that. It was true.

'I bet all sorts of good things are coming your way,' said Jacob.

Izzy shrugged, she didn't want him to know the benefits her new reputation as a heroine had brought.

Eddie Hicks, the man whose life she was supposed to have saved, was a popular man. He'd been called up at the start of the war, but had been sent home when the army doctor had discovered his heart murmur. His wife, Susie, worked for her father at the local general store – a low-ceilinged shop that sold everything from paraffin to cabbages. Now, whenever Izzy went in to buy her weekly two-ounce allowance of oatmeal for her porridge, she was greeted with a smile, a wink and an extra scoopful. Her money was always accepted, but sometimes her ration book was waved away. 'We'll not be needing that.'

For a while this had puzzled Izzy, till Mrs Brent had told her there were ways to get round rationing. 'But, there are always ways to get round things that don't suit you.' It seemed that Susie spent one evening a week cutting up newspapers into ration-shaped squares. These she slipped in among the regular coupons that she sent to the Ministry of Food. She reckoned it would be impossible to check the millions and millions of coupons that must be sent in every week, and so it was unlikely anybody would look at hers. All her favourite people in the village got the smile-and-wink treatment.

'You owe me,' said Jacob. 'You should be grateful to me.'

Izzy said she owed him nothing.

'Of course you owe me,' said Jacob. 'You are reaping the rewards of the accident. I was driving the car. It was really my accident. You should share your good fortune. You owe me. One day I will come to you and expect you to return the favour.'

Izzy was shocked, unsure of herself, swamped with self-doubt. Could he be right? Surely, she owed him nothing. 'Cheek,' she said. 'You ran away.'

'I ran away and let you take all the glory. Now, you owe me. If you don't see the logic in that, it's only because you are a woman. Men know the rules. You return favours.'

'You have done me no favours,' said Izzy.

Jacob shouted, 'Yes I have. You know I have!' A plane roared overhead, the garage trembled. The thunder of engines drowned Jacob's voice. He made himself understood nonetheless. He pointed at her. 'You owe –' he pointed at himself '– me.'

Chapter Twenty-one
Earthbound and Loveless

'Look at you,' said Elspeth. 'You're glowing. And you're quite smug. Are you having an affair?'

'Is it that obvious?' said Izzy.

'Only to me. I know how apologetic you usually look. Is it your American friend?'

Izzy nodded.

'God,' said Elspeth. 'You're glowing more just remembering him.'

Izzy looked away, trying to hide her face. She felt it was glowing out of control.

'You're in love,' said Elspeth. 'About time, too. Your social life so far has been a disgrace.'

'I love my job. I didn't want a social life,' said Izzy. 'This affair just happened. It crept up on me when I wasn't looking.'

Elspeth said that was how it was with love. She was sitting on the hotel bed wrapped in a towel after her first bath of the weekend. 'What I resent is you abandoning me for your boyfriend. Women do that. They get all wrapped up in love, give themselves over to their boyfriends and forget about their friends.'

'I haven't forgotten you. It's hard to get away when you only get two days off in every thirteen.'

'How do you manage to see Jimmy?'

Izzy said that if she wasn't working, and he was, she'd go to see him. 'I stay at a bed and breakfast. Then if I'm working and he isn't, he stays at the cottage. I see him when I get home.'

Elspeth stood up, dropped the towel and started to dress. Izzy looked away. Naked bodies embarrassed her. Elspeth had been living, washing, sleeping in intensely close quarters to other women for so long she no longer had any inhibitions about being seen without her clothes. Well, that was her summertime routine. When winter rolled round, she behaved differently. It was cold. She even went to bed pretty much fully clothed, then undressed under the blankets.

'I didn't know it would be like this,' said Izzy. 'That I could find myself thinking about someone all of the time. Looking at the phone, willing it to ring. Hoping for a letter. Remembering things we'd done together. Planning what I'm going to say to him. I find myself sighing all the time. It's driving me crazy.'

'Does he feel the same?' asked Elspeth.

Izzy shrugged. She didn't know. 'We don't talk about how we feel. Mostly we just . . . you know. There isn't a lot of time for chat.'

Elspeth said, 'Careful, Izzy.'

'What do you mean by that?'

'I don't want you to get hurt.'

'I am going to get hurt. It's inevitable. If I break with him now, I'll get hurt. If I leave it till the war ends and he goes back to America, I'll get hurt. So there's no point in telling me to be careful.'

This was the third time she'd been told to be careful and she didn't like it at all. All she wanted to do was fly and make love, what was wrong with that? One day the war would end, Jimmy would go home, she'd be out of a job, earthbound and loveless. Meantime she planned to enjoy herself and to hell with being careful. 'Let's go eat dinner,' she said.

They didn't talk much as they ate. Izzy was thinking about Jimmy. Elspeth was watching her and regretting the rough life she was living. She missed simple private things – making toast when she fancied a slice, lying alone in bed reading, soaking in a bath. She ate, washed, worked and slept in the company of other women. Sometimes, she just wanted to be alone. She ached. She thought she smelled of horses and pine resin. She cursed herself for getting ecstatic about an orange. How pathetic, she thought.

Izzy's affair was being conducted in the softness of a bedroom. Hers was an outdoor fling. She made love in the forest or lying on the grass by the river. Pleasant enough, but wouldn't it be lovely to slip into bed with a lover? Oh, the comfort of it. Izzy and her love ate at the local hotel. She ate trout with her fingers straight from a frying pan – though, it was tasty. It struck Elspeth that for the first time in their long friendship, she was jealous of Izzy. She hated herself for that, but couldn't help it.

After dinner, they went for a walk. The place was busy as usual – thronging pub and the air vibrating with the thrum and skirl of the dance band in the village hall. Elspeth asked if Izzy wanted to go in. 'A quick whirl round the floor, a waltz and a jive might be fun.'

Izzy shook her head. 'I don't really like dances. I can't dance. And it's too noisy in there.'

Elspeth shrugged and said, 'Whatever. Just thought it would be a laugh.'

They strolled down to the river and sat on a bench beside the water. It was nine o'clock, still light, swallows skimmed overhead. Izzy watched them.

'You wish you were up there, don't you?' said Elspeth.

'I'm happy when I'm flying,' said Izzy. 'I feel anything is possible when I'm up there. I sing to myself and I sound fine, not out of tune at all. I do believe that if I took a piano up there, I could play it.'

Elspeth snorted. 'Izzy, tone-deaf is tone-deaf, here on the ground or one mile up in the sky.'

Izzy said she supposed so, but somehow things seemed more possible when she was up among the clouds. 'I owe you so much,' she said. 'You're the one who got me flying in the first place.'

'You owe me nothing,' said Elspeth. 'Even if you did, you've paid me back many times over with all the stuff you send me. How do you get all that, anyway? Don't you need coupons?'

Last week Izzy had sent Elspeth a tin of pears, a bag of sweets and a jar of cold cream. 'Well,' said Izzy, 'I don't always need coupons.' She was still riding high in local esteem and her ration book had been waved away. All that, and she was still Edith the ops officer's darling. Edith had arranged for Izzy to hitch a lift on a plane going from Preston all the way to Lossiemouth. Tomorrow, she'd been promised a ride from Lossiemouth to Prestwick and, from there, a flight to Preston. Edith had arranged for the taxi Anson to bring her back to Skimpton. Izzy was wondering if she didn't owe Jacob after all. He had, indeed, helped to make her a heroine.

She was about to confess to Elspeth, tell her why her coupons weren't always taken by the local shop, but was distracted by rustlings in the bushes behind them. There were sounds of passion in progress.

Izzy sighed. 'I'm glad I don't have to sneak off into the undergrowth to satisfy my lust. I like my love in bed in comfort under the blankets.'

This was the wrong thing to say to Elspeth. 'Some of us don't have that option. You may find it coarse, but love under the stars can be wonderful.' She got up and started back to the hotel. It was time for a second bath.

They didn't speak much for the rest of Izzy's visit. When, in the morning, they were standing at the bus stop waiting for the bus to take Izzy back to Inverness, Izzy asked Elspeth if she was speaking to her. 'You seem distant.'

'Of course I'm speaking to you. It's just your remark about outdoor love touched a nerve. For some of us outdoors is the only place for love. I don't have access to a private bed. I sleep in a dormitory with a lot of other women. If I had a man in my bed, they'd notice the squeaks of bedsprings and the grunts and moans of passion.'

Izzy apologised. 'I didn't think.'

Elspeth said, 'I know.' She was contemplating her day. Cycle back to the camp, sweep out hut, wash socks and underwear in the ablutions hut, eat disgusting food. Izzy would fly home, where Mrs Brent did her laundry, she'd have a proper bath, eat a decent meal, sit on a comfortable sofa, sleep in a decent soft bed. There's no denying it, Elspeth thought, I'm really jealous.

On the flight south, Izzy sat behind the pilot. She looked down at the forest, miles and miles of treetops, miles and miles of green. Elspeth was down there somewhere. It occurred to Izzy that it should be the other way round. Elspeth should be up here, and she, who had succeeded at nothing before this, should be trudging the forest paths, axe over her shoulder, aching from all the physical labour, eating carrot sandwiches. It's all I'm really good for, she thought.

Ten minutes later, she saw a small cluster of houses below, smoke drifting from chimneys, roofs glinting in the sunlight. 'That's the village where I grew up,' said Izzy.

'Want to go down and say hello?' asked the pilot. He circled, swooped low.

'Look,' said Izzy. 'There's the manse where I lived. And, that's my dad.'

They cruised lower. Buzzed over the garden. Izzy's father, busy planting peas, stood up, put his palm in the small of his back to ease the pain of bending into the ground. The plane whooshed overhead, thundered, the roar deafening. He shook his fist at it. Izzy giggled.

As they cruised away, climbing back into the clouds, she looked back. She saw her mother emerge from the back door, shade her eyes with her hand and gaze after them.

'They'll be wondering what that was about,' said the pilot. 'You'll have to let them know it was you.'

'Yes,' said Izzy. But she knew she couldn't do that.

Chapter Twenty-two
The Bathing Belle

People adopted a certain nonchalant walk when they emerged from the woods after lovemaking. Elspeth had noticed this. The men would stroll, hands in pockets. Sometimes they'd whistle. They'd look down at their boots, kick stones, assume an air of casual indifference. The women would twirl a sprig of heather in their fingers, gaze down at it as if it was a specimen of dramatic interest. They'd look about them, smiling slightly, feigning innocence. Though their cheeks would be flushed and their eyes still glazed with pleasure.

Elspeth did this herself when she and Tyler returned to the camp after one of their bouts of passion. The pair of them tried to look as if they'd just enjoyed a healthy evening ramble and an interesting debate on the joys of nature.

At first the pair had always gone to their spot, the shady green dell by the river where evening deer came to drink. Recently, Tyler had suggested they find other places to pursue their rapture. 'I hate routine. I hate going to the same place all the time. Let's explore. We'll have secret spots. Then when we leave we'll have made love under so many trees, the whole forest will be ours and full of our passion.'

It sounded so romantic, Elspeth agreed. Once, he led her out of the forest and to the top of a hill. The view was stunning, treetops, and, in the distance, the rooftops of a village twelve miles away. It had been windy, so they'd found shelter behind a boulder. The sex wasn't spectacular, as the long hike had tired them both. Other times, they'd lie under trees thirty or forty years tall. Elspeth loved this. She loved taking her clothes off out there, the soft air on her skin. She loved his lips on her neck, she loved his kisses. And she loved the feel of him on her and the blissful intensity of moving towards a moment of ecstasy.

She'd open her eyes and see above her a lacework of treetops, small birds chittering in among the branches, shafts of sunlight streaming down – the forest as a cathedral. Why, she thought, this is almost holy.

Tyler would turn to her, stroke her cheek. 'We're getting quite good at this.' Elspeth said it only took practice. While she was practising, she forgot to be jealous of Izzy and Izzy's comforts. This was fun.

The good side of all this was that the original secret spot, that had once been their spot, now belonged to Elspeth alone. It was where she went swimming on the evenings she didn't go thrill-seeking with Tyler.

The days were hot now. As she ran back and forth-slapping Harry on her rump, jumping over tree stumps and bracken, Elspeth would comfort herself with thoughts of water. Soon, she would go down to the river. She'd take off her boots and socks, feel the grass between her toes. Then she'd strip. She'd spread her arms into the evening, let the air spread over her whole body. She'd slip into the river, waiting for that moment when its chill would hit her chest and make her gasp. She'd swim slowly up and down, push herself below the surface, skim along, hair streaming behind her, then burst up into the sunlight, shaking her head, sending sparks of water scattering round her. This thought kept her going as she sweated and puffed, and worked at her new sixty-logs-a-day quota.

Tonight was especially good. A parcel had arrived from Izzy. It had contained three tins of condensed milk, a tin of pears, two bars of soap, two bars of chocolate and a copy of *Woman's Own*. Lorna had seized the magazine and settled on her bed to read it. 'It's good to know there's still a world out there.'

The letter from Izzy had said that one day she'd tell Elspeth the full silly story of how she managed to get these treats without using up any ration coupons. 'Just enjoy everything.'

Elspeth put the box under her bed beside her accordion, took a bar of chocolate and her towel and headed for the river. Chocolate and a swim, this was as close to heaven as she was going to get, until the war ended and she could escape this place.

When she arrived, she put her towel and chocolate on a tree stump. Then she peeled off her boots and shoes. She stood up to unfasten the straps of her dungarees, and looked round. Trees were swaying, a breeze gusting. There were soft whisperings, leaves moving against leaves. She thought there were deer about, waiting for her to leave so they could come to the river. 'Me first,' she called. 'Then you can have your drink.'

She took off her clothes. Before she got into the water, she broke the chocolate bar in two, and took one half into the river with her. She stepped from the bank, waded out to midstream, holding the chocolate high above her head. She swam on her back, kicking up a fountain as she went. Chocolate melting in her mouth. She flipped over and struck out for the riverbed, trailed her hand over stones, looked for fish, though she never saw any. Then she pushed herself upwards and broke the surface, shaking her head, heaving in air.

The wolf whistle was long, deep and wild. It split the air. Elspeth crossed her arms over her breasts, looked round. Nobody. 'Tyler?' she called.

There were whisperings, the sound of many people trying to silence one person, an almighty 'Ssshh . . .' Elspeth waded back to the bank, hurrying was hard. Another whistle. Then many, many people whistling, a cacophony of shouts, cheers, applause and deeply appreciative whistles. Elspeth clambered onto the grass and scuttled to her towel, which she wrapped round herself.

When she looked up, forty or fifty Newfies emerged from hiding places behind trees. They were all yelling, clapping, and shouting her name, many had brought bottles of beer to swig as they enjoyed the show. 'Elspeth, Elspeth. Give's a kiss, Elspeth.'

Elspeth shouted, 'Bastards! Bloody bastards! Filthy scum!'

Which only made her audience cheer harder.

'Come up here, Elspeth. I've got something to show ya,' someone hollered.

'Bugger off, all of you.' She yanked her knickers over her damp body, wriggled into her shirt and dungarees, shoved on her boots, stuck her socks into her pocket, picked up her towel and chocolate bar and stumped back up the path. 'Bastards, bastards!' she shouted. 'You can't let a woman have some fun, can you?'

Tyler was waiting at the stables. Elspeth steamed up to him and slapped his face. 'Arse,' she said. 'You knew, didn't you?'

He nodded. Rubbing the stinging cheek. 'It was just a spot of fun.'

'That's why you didn't want to go there. You knew they'd be watching. But you let me put on a show.'

'They're men. They don't get to see a woman these days.'

'Well, that's the last time they'll see me. Did you organise this?'

He shook his head. 'I just found out about it. You were safe, though. I said they could look but they couldn't touch.'

'You won't be touching, either. Not now.'

'Aaw, Elspeth, don't be like that.'

She started to walk away.

'C'mon, Elspeth. It was just a bit of fun. There's not a lot to do round here.'

She turned and said that it hadn't been fun for her. 'I've been humiliated.'

He shrugged. He was proud of Elspeth. She was clever, witty, could play the accordion and the physical work in the forest had made her body lean and strong. He'd enjoyed other men lusting over her. He'd been showing her off.

She told him he was an oaf. She never wanted to see him again. This, she knew, would be hard, considering they were both working in the same part of the forest, and he was living in a hut several yards up the track from hers. Still, she could always turn her back. She walked away, head in the air, reminding herself to look dignified.

'Don't be like this,' Tyler said.

Elspeth shouted, 'Huh!'

'Marry me,' Tyler said.

'Never.'

'Marry me and they'll let you out of here.'

Elspeth stopped, turned to face Tyler. 'How do you know that?'

'Everyone knows that. If you marry, you can leave.'

She asked if he was sure.

He thought so.

Elspeth walked away again. Behind her Tyler was shouting, 'Marry me. Come live with me in Newfoundland. I love you.'

Back in the hut, Elspeth ate the rest of her chocolate. Marriage hadn't occurred to her. Well, it wouldn't. She hadn't, till now, anyone to marry. Why not marry Tyler? she thought. He was kind, he was fun and the most enthusiastic lover she'd ever had.

She contemplated opening a tin of condensed milk. But no, she'd take it to work tomorrow, put a dollop into the thick black tea she drank at breaktimes.

Newfoundland, she thought, would probably be cold, wet, pounded with all kinds of weather. But it would be an adventure. And she was always up for that.

She didn't want to marry anybody, really. But she did want out of here, and now she'd found an escape. She was so excited, she almost forgot about her horde of peeping Toms.

Chapter Twenty-three
Wanda the Wonder

'Eezzy.'

The voice was familiar. She turned. At first she didn't recognise the face behind the voice. It was the moustache that threw her. When she'd known him, Wanda the Wonder had been clean-shaven. Naturally.

'Remember me?' he said.

'Wanda!' Izzy threw her arms wide. 'This is wonderful.'

A friend, a familiar face among the sea of strange faces she saw every day. The joy of it.

He took her to him, kissed her, first on the right cheek, then on the left, and lifted her from the ground, twirled her round. 'Look at you, a lady pilot.'

'I know, and look at you flying with the Free French.'

'I'm plain old Jean-Louis now. Wanda has gone for ever, I'm afraid.'

'Pity,' said Izzy. 'I liked old Wanda.'

She was in Yorkshire again, at Elvington, the Free French airbase. As she'd been approaching the runway, she'd seen a group of men lounging in the grass, smoking, idly watching planes land. She knew what they were up to – betting on the landing skills of pilots, betting on who would bounce on hitting the ground. She'd vowed to do a perfect three-point landing, and had.

'You lost me two shillings,' said Jean-Louis. 'When I saw it was a lady pilot, I put money on the bounce. If I'd known it was you . . .'

'You'd have bet ten shillings.'

'True. I remember Izzy the bouncer of Betty Stokes Flying Show.'

'I've improved,' said Izzy. 'Hardly ever bounce. My bosses don't like it.' She thought a moment. 'Still if I'd known you were betting on me, I'd have bounced. We could have split the winnings.'

They walked together towards the office where Izzy would get her delivery chit signed. She linked her arm in his. 'How is Betty these days?'

'She died,' he told her. 'In the Blitz. She tried to join your lot, the ATA, but they wouldn't have her. Told her she was too old. She was fifty-eight. But a woman of passion, and a good pilot.'

Izzy said she knew that. 'She was also a bit of a bitch.'

In the ops office, busy at the moment, planning the night's raid over Germany, they found an officer who signed the chit. After that, they went to the mess for a cup of tea. It was four o'clock, the evening meals started at five, still there were buns to eat with their tea.

'I miss coffee,' said Jean-Louis.

'You can still get coffee,' said Izzy.

He shook his head. 'That's not coffee.'

They found a seat at the far end of the room.

'Betty went back to London to stay with her mother,' Jean-Louis said. 'One night, when the bombing started, she didn't go to the shelter. She and her mother crawled under the kitchen table. The house took a direct hit.'

'That's awful,' said Izzy. 'Betty was a one-off. Does anybody here know you used to be Wanda the Wonder?'

He held his finger to his lips. 'Not a word.'

Unable to find a woman who could perform the feats she needed for her flying circus, Betty Stokes had hired Jean-Louis, given him a long blonde wig and told him to walk daintily. After performing his death-defying routine – loops, rolls, a long twirling, speedy plunge to the ground from eight hundred feet up, pulling level at crowd height, skimming upside down only feet from the ground – he would climb from his plane, arms aloft, beaming, curtsying, before mincing, tiny steps, one hand on his hip, to the tent where he'd whip off his wig and refresh himself with a cup of tea heavily laced with cognac, and a cigar.

Betty had often criticised the walk and the way he'd blow kisses at the crowd. 'No woman walks like that. Only Rita Hayworth blows kisses. Stop it.'

But Jean-Louis claimed that the trouble with women was that they didn't know how to be women. 'They should all wear big hats and lacy things. They should show off what they've got.' He did a demonstration wiggle across the tent. Betty had said, 'Pah.' Izzy had giggled.

Not that Jean-Louis had any doubts about his sexuality. He slept in Betty's bed, and told everyone that if they thought she was bad-tempered, they should see what she was like when she didn't have him to keep her sweet. He'd also bedded both the girls who stood, hair streaming behind them, on the wings of the plane Betty flew at the start of the show, the daring wing-walkers.

But Izzy had resisted his charms. 'Oh, Izzy, I can take you to the heights of ecstasy. The reason I make a good woman is I know women, I know their secret places, I know how to make them smile.'

Izzy was sure he did. 'Just not this woman,' she'd said. The man was very attractive. But his skill at impersonating a woman put Izzy off. Besides, at the time, she was still trying to be her father's good daughter. She only had to think about being naughty and images of his heaving eyebrows and pursed lips floated into her mind.

'You always resisted me,' he said.

'I know. And you so irresistible. Like a teapot, you told me.'

He took her hand. 'Small with a bit spout. That's me. We can always make up for lost time.'

Izzy didn't think so.

He smiled. 'What a time that was, touring the country with Betty and two old planes.'

'Yes,' said Izzy, she got quite misty-eyed remembering. 'God, all that tatty bunting and those tents – all rips and holes. And those poor girls standing on the wings, waving. Betty told them to dance. I used to have to wrap them in blankets soon as they got into the tent. Goosebumps bigger than watermelons.'

'Yes, and Brigit fell off. Broke her arm and leg and two ribs. She was lucky at that.'

'I know,' said Izzy. 'And that cracked recording of the "Toreador Song" that she played when you were doing the stunts, remember that? And the little wooden planes she sold as souvenirs that broke as soon as you touched them. And the places we used to stay. I think she deliberately hunted out the worse bed and breakfast in town.'

'Bedbugs, lumpy porridge, one bathroom two floors down from our rooms, no baths after eight o'clock, creaky beds.'

'Did you ever get paid?' asked Izzy.

He shook his head. 'And I had to provide services above and beyond the call of duty. Betty was a passionate woman.'

'Happy days,' sighed Izzy.

He raised his mug of tea to that. 'Happy days.'

They drifted into silent memories.

Izzy said, 'That's the thing about happiness, you don't know it when you've got it. It's only when it's gone, when you look back, that you realise you'd been having a good time.'

He nodded. 'Never mind. This war will be over one day. Then I'll go home.'

'To France?'

'To France. I'll sit in the sun, a pavement café. Gitanes, a glass of wine and a good omelette. You?'

She shrugged. 'I don't know. I'm saving as much money as I can, so I'll have something to live on while I look around. Don't know where I'll go or what I'll do. I've got used to this, this war, this way of living.'

Thirteen days on, two days off, life had become a blur, filled with weather reports, maps, the slam of locker doors, roads, railways, rivers, woods and towns viewed from above, windswept airfields and chits and chatter and bad food. And, all the while, she felt that if she wasn't flying, she was running. And if she wasn't doing that, she was sleeping. At RAF bases faces, once strange, had become familiar. In her private life, precious loved faces were becoming distant.

She hadn't seen her mother since spring. And she had promised Elspeth she'd visit once a month if she could, but that hadn't happened. She spent most of her free time with Jimmy. She wrote to Elspeth apologising, saying how hard it was to get away. 'Time,' she wrote, 'is just hurtling past.'

Meantime, Izzy had bought a motorbike. She'd spotted it in the cluttered forecourt of Eddie Hicks' garage and decided it was just the thing for her. It was old, noisy, had canvas grips on the handlebars and wasn't happy travelling at more than thirty miles per hour, but it was cheap, and didn't use as much petrol as a car. Apart from the bike, it was the first vehicle she had owned. So she loved it. Claire had said, 'What were you thinking, buying that? I think you've been done.' Julia called it 'The Beast' on account of the clunking roar it made as it trudged along. But Izzy didn't care. On her days off it took her out of Skimpton and into the arms of Captain Jimmy.

Izzy was in love. This surprised her. It had come upon her slowly, this love. She had no former knowledge of this condition, it had never happened to her before. So she had always thought that being in love would be like floating on a silken cloud arms spread open to the breeze, heart filled with song. A person in love would be in a constant state of happiness.

Nobody had told her about the anxiety, the sighing, the loneliness when they were apart. There ought to be lessons in love at school, she thought. Someone should prepare you for this. They could get rid of maths and hockey and replace them with basic instructions on how to deal with matters of the heart.

She worried a lot. She longed for the phone to ring, she watched for the postman hoping for a letter from him. They exchanged letters once or twice a week, but only recently had she put 'Love, Izzy' and a kiss at the bottom of hers. He just put his name, Jim. And he still called her Pork Chops.

On his days off, he drove over to see her in his new MG. 'Got to have a Brit car when I'm over here.' On her days off, she steamed over to see him on The Beast.

Still believing she'd saved his life (though she'd told him often this was not true), Eddie supplied her with his behind-the-counter, black-market, secret, touch-the-side-of-the-nose, don't-tell-a-soul, unrationed petrol. It was the last dribblings, sneaked into a can at the end of every fill-up. Only a special few got this privileged fuel.

Izzy drained the last of her tea, shrugged, and asked Jean-Louis, 'Do you ever get scared?'

'All the time.' He thought everybody got scared. 'I cope,' he said. 'I've got used to being afraid. Wouldn't feel right if I wasn't.'

Izzy said, 'I'm really scared of the war ending. What will I do? I can't go back to my old life, not now.' She put her hand over Jean-Louis'. 'Different planes, different places, different faces everyday. Sometimes I feel like a stranger in my own life.'

'You'll be fine.'

She looked at her watch. 'I should go. The taxi's coming for me.'

They saw it coming in to land as they walked towards the runway. Izzy turned, kissed him. 'It's been lovely to see you. An old familiar face.'

He told her to take care. 'And when this is over, you come see me in France. We'll raise a glass to Betty Stokes.'

As Izzy walked towards the Anson, he shouted, 'Hey, Eezzy! Ordinary steps, that's no way to walk. Do it like Wanda.'

In flying suit, helmet and boots, Izzy minced, wiggled hand on hip. It was slow going, she preferred her ordinary walk. The girls on the plane whistled and clapped. 'It's Mae West.'

Claire, sitting reading *The Times* asked what all that was about.

'Just being silly, met an old friend,' said Izzy. 'He used to be Wanda the Wonder.'

'Wanda the Wonder was a man?' said Claire.

'Yes.'

'Did anybody ever guess?'

The plane rushed along the runway, heaved into the air. The ground, and Jean-Louis, slipped away.

Izzy said, 'No, nobody ever guessed.' She waved to the figure below, now a speck, waving wildly. 'Isn't it odd the people you meet, get close to, then lose. I travelled the country with that man, stayed in the same boarding houses, made him cups of tea, shared jokes and, perhaps, I'll never see him again.'

Chapter Twenty-four
An Evening's Extravaganza

Elspeth wrote:

Dearest Izzy,

Life up here goes on. It's hot here. I never knew I could sweat so much. Trees are falling, and we have cleared a great deal of the forest. Stumps everywhere. I have learned to fish, Tyler taught me. Caught a trout and ate it right away. Had whisky and condensed milk for afters – it's nicer than it sounds.

Last Friday night we held a concert. It went very well – at first.

The rehearsals hadn't gone well at all. Mostly, because the girls hadn't wanted to be distracted from their love lives, the warm weather and long, light evenings were ideal for flirtatious excursions into the forest. Still, Elspeth believed she had discovered some talent.

Lorna admitted that as well as being able to flare her nostrils, she could tap dance. Tricia could do a passable imitation of Marlene Dietrich and Dorothy had briefly gone to ballet classes when she was seven. Costumes were a problem, since the girls only had dungarees, boots and their official uniforms with them. There were no lights. But, Elspeth thought, it will be light on the night. This time of year, it hardly got dark.

There was no curtain and the only music would be from the wind-up gramophone and Tyler's six records. But she could always accompany acts on her accordion. It will be fine, she told herself. 'Forest Frolics', she would call it – 'An Evening's Extravaganza with the Dungareed Darlings'. She always did like a bit of alliteration.

On the morning of the grand concert, Elspeth asked Frazer if he was coming.

'I am. But I'm a wee bit hurt you didn't ask me to do a turn.'

Elspeth said she hadn't known he was talented.

'Well, I am. I do bird calls.'

'What sort of birds?'

'Any sort of bird. It goes down a fair treat at parties and the like.'

'Well,' said Elspeth, 'come along tonight. Do some bird calls, why not? You could do requests. You know, someone will call out a bird – a raven or a corncrake – and you could do it.'

'Ye've just mentioned two birds I can't do. But, never mind. I'll be there. All dressed up and all.'

Elspeth said, 'Excellent.' Then she worried.

'The thing is,' she said to Lorna at lunchtime. 'It's got to be saucy. I mean, there has been so little rehearsal, the only way we can keep the audience entertained is by being naughty.'

They had to shout. Four bombers were thundering overhead, roaring south.

'Something's up,' said Elspeth. 'That's the third lot today.'

'I know,' said Lorna. 'Really noisy. He could do rude bird

calls. Like the noises birds make when they're mating. All frenzied.'

'I don't think he'd be willing to do that. No, some of the girls will have to stand behind him, cupping their hands to their ears, sexily looking up into pretend trees.' Elspeth sighed. It was a worry putting on a concert.

She was even more worried at seven o'clock that night when her audience started to throng into the open space between the dormitory hut and the dining hut where the concert was to be held. Word had spread. Men had come from other camps. Instead of the fifty or so Newfies Elspeth expected, there were over two hundred men waiting for the show to go on. Not many of them were sober.

Earlier in the evening, Tyler and one or two others had made something of a platform by putting two strips of duckboard over a long pile of logs. It wasn't much, but it raised the performers enough for people at the back to see what was going on. A couple of chairs were placed at the side to ease the entertainers' climb onto the stage.

Elspeth started proceedings by welcoming the audience and asking them to please keep down the noise and give the girls lots of appreciation for their efforts. 'Let's get on with the show.' She played polkas for the first ten minutes because the girls, preparing themselves in the cookhouse, were scrambling about, tripping over one another, putting on lipstick and arguing. But, at last, Lorna stuck her head round the door, stuck up her thumb and nodded. Time for the cancan.

A row of high-kicking girls would always meet with wild cheers and whistles even if they were wearing dungarees instead of multi-frilled skirts and petticoats. The noise was so loud, it drowned

271

Elspeth's frantic rendition of Offenbach's 'Galop'. Still, there were cartwheels, screams, legs were shown and, at the end, the row of dancers turned their backs on the audience and wiggled their bums. It got a standing ovation.

Next up was Tricia's Dietrich impersonation. She sang 'Boys in the Back Room', looking sultry, one hand on her hip, the other thumbing over her shoulder, indicating where the back room with the boys was. The audience stamped their feet in time to the song. At the end, she winked. Another ovation and calls for an encore. Adrenalin was flowing. Elspeth was getting high. Time for her comedy turn.

Tyler and Lorna's beau, Freddie Tait, heaved a log onto the stage. Elspeth, dressed in dungarees, boots and a sou'wester hat, draped with sprigs of heather and as much jewellery as she'd been able to gather from the girls in the dormitory – beads, bracelets, brooches – came on stage. She had made two huge hands out of cardboard and attached them using elastic bands to her own hands. She carried an axe. Slowly snedding the log, she sang 'A Lovely Way to Spend an Evening'. Trilling an octave higher than her normal voice, clutching her bosom as she delivered her heart-aching melody, she gazed at the audience in gentle rapture and whacked off branches. It took a while for the onlookers to realise that every time she raised her hand, a cardboard finger was missing. 'Thees ees a lurvely way . . .' she sang. She whacked a branch, lifted her hand to her breast, one finger missing. She sang with verve and passion till all ten fingers were gone, waved her stumpy hands, bowed and walked off the stage. Everyone cheered, and Elspeth wondered if this hadn't been a bit tasteless. Heartless, she thought, but then out here – cold, homesick, hungry – every-one was a bit callous. There was nothing like sleeping in an army cot covered by two scratchy blankets, living on a diet of spam, cabbage and carrot sandwiches to harden the heart. She'd come down in life; Izzy had gone up. Much as she loved the girls she worked with, loved their openness, she couldn't help wishing she were somewhere else. Her envy of Izzy got deeper and deeper.

Lorna came on next. She tap-danced 'It Don't Mean a Thing If it Ain't Got that Swing' with a chorus in the background singing 'Doo wop de doo wop de doo de oooh!' Dorothy, in bare feet, danced 'Dance of the Sugar Plum Fairy'.

The trouble started with the bird calls.

Frazer's dinner suit, threadbare at the shoulders, fraying at the cuffs, got a roar of approval along with cries of, 'Penguin, penguin.' He stepped from the chair to the platform, feeling like a true trouper, a seasoned entertainer accompanied by his trusty assistant, Lorna.

'Let me take you on a stroll through the woods. Let's meet a few of our feathered friends.' He looked up, pointed, turned to the audience. 'What do I spy? Why it's our gardener's friend, the thrush.' He cupped his hands over his mouth, whistled and trilled. Lorna put her hand behind her ear, leaned forwards, lifting one leg behind her and did a good job of looking entranced.

The crowd clapped, and one or two added their own bird whistles. Frazer took that as a sign of his audience's appreciation of his talent.

'And who is that sitting on a branch watching us with his bright beady eye? None other than a cheeky little robin.' More whistling and trilling that made the robin sound not dissimilar to the thrush. Lorna pointed upwards and mouthed a thrilled 'Oooh'. By the time he'd spotted the goldfinch and that shy little stranger, the crossbill, the audience was joining in – whistles, chirrups and somebody was doing a rooster. There were calls for impersonations of budgies, sparrows and ducks. A voice from the depth of the rows of men watching shouted, 'Get off!'

Several people turned to the get-off shouter and told him to shut up.

'Who are you telling to shut up?' the get-off shouter shouted.

'You,' said someone behind him, giving him a shove.

The shove was met by a punch. And the punch was met by a punch back. A scuffle started.

Elspeth had seen it all before. She signalled Lorna to get Frazer off the stage.

But Frazer, ignoring the fight, spread his arms wide, gazed up in rapture. 'Who is that soaring above me? None other than the king of the sky – the golden eagle.'

Everybody who heard it thought it a startling impersonation of an eagle. A thrilling high-pitched call. Frazer bowed and stepped down from the stage. 'That went well.'

The fight was spreading. Elspeth decided to go straight into the grand finale. No time for the planned sing-song. Get the girls up there dancing and wiggling and pouting.

She hustled the girls out of the cookhouse. 'Quick, quick, get on and dance.' Dorothy hopped across to the stage, pulling on her boots. The others shoved and jostled behind her. Elspeth did a swift chord on her accordion, the girls linked into a line and off they went – high-kicking, squealing, jiggling.

They weren't co-ordinated. Tricia lost her balance and the line started to tip over. Then, in a burst of enthusiasm, Dorothy kicked too hard. Her boot flew off and hit somebody in the face. Squealing, she jumped down and crawled into the ruckus to retrieve it.

Elspeth yelled for the fighting to stop. Waving her arms, she shouted, 'Enough, enough. That's the end of our show. The extravaganza is over. Thank you and goodnight.'

It was agreed afterwards that playing the National Anthem was a brainwave. Elspeth struck the first chord, and began to sing, 'God Save our Gracious King . . .' The effect was stunning. Everything stopped. The audience stilled, stood rigid. Dorothy appeared from the depths of the crowd, still on all fours, boot stuffed down the front of her dungarees. She stood to attention till the anthem was finished, then scarpered.

Elspeth stopped playing and told everyone to behave themselves and go back to their huts in an orderly fashion. Much to her surprise, they did. Grumbling and shuffling, they headed into the night.

Bats were flickering through the gloaming when Elspeth made her own way back to her hut. She had helped clear up and served tea to all the performers. Duncan Bowman was waiting for her outside the cookhouse.

'Good concert. Too many dancing girls, though. You reminded these men of what they're missing.'

'They always fight,' said Elspeth.

'Well, they would. It's what they do when they're frustrated. Women cry, men fight.'

Elspeth supposed this was true.

'Anyway,' said Duncan. 'It's Friday and you forgot the dung. I'll be expecting it first thing in the morning.' And he stomped away.

'. . . and that was that,' Elspeth wrote, 'next morning I trundled the dung to Duncan's cottage. I didn't mind, the sun was shining, birds were singing and for a little while I had the world to myself. Is that all it takes to make me happy, these days? I have become accustomed to this life, I fear. And I am not the person I used to be.'

She put down her pen, folded the letter, stuffed it into an envelope. This is my life, Izzy, she thought. It can be rapturous. I love the scent of the morning, the soft warmth of the horse's mouth when she takes a carrot from my hand. I love the feel of her by my side as we run back and forth taking logs to the roadside. I love my new friends. Sometimes, at work, everyone bursts out singing. That is wonderful. There are jokes and there's laughter. But, sometimes, Izzy, life is hell. Mud under my fingernails, mud everywhere. Rain, sleet, snow and, sometimes, I'm so very cold. There are rough men, fights and I have to shovel up an awful lot of horseshit. You don't seem to know this, but you have everything – an exciting job, a decent place to live and someone to love.

The last time you visited, you seemed dreamy. You were distant, thinking of your love. You are lost to me. I am jealous of the man you love. I'm jealous of you. And I'm ashamed of myself. But I can't help it.

Chapter Twenty-five
Three Women in Love and One Woman Who Isn't

'Jeffrey's dead,' said Julia.

For a moment, Walter thought, Who?

'His plane burst into flames not long after take-off. Leaking fuel pipe.' She was sitting on the bed reading a letter from Jeffrey's mother.

Ah, Jeffrey, Walter remembered, one of the other lovers. A rival. In the months he'd been seeing Julia, he'd put them out of his head. He said he was sorry to hear that.

'His mother found my name in his address book when his things were sent home. She's writing to everyone.'

Walter was lying on the bed next to her. In Julia's flat there wasn't much else to do. There still was no furniture.

'Dead,' said Julia. 'Just like that. He was only twenty-four, and such fun. A life wiped out. He won't see the end of this war, come home, marry, have kids.' She put her hands up to her face. There were tears. 'I was awfully fond of him.'

Walter listened as Julia talked about Jeffrey. He was beautiful. 'Not, you know, in looks. But the whole person was beautiful. He was such fun, bubbling with energy. Now he's gone. A life snuffed out.'

Walter said he'd make a cup of tea. He heaved himself up, and went through to the kitchen. Julia followed, leaned on the sink watching as he filled the kettle. He pulled the blackout curtains, switched on the lights, poured two cups and listened. Julia was full of tales about Jeffrey. The fun they'd had, racing cars down the long drive at his parents' estate, playing poker all night, the masked ball they'd attended where he had only revealed himself after he'd kissed her. 'Oh,' she said. 'It's all gone. Life will never be like that again.'

He sipped his tea, said nothing. Life had never been like that for him. He stroked his chin and said, 'Awfully fond? I hope you're not awfully fond of me.'

'Why?'

'Because awfully fond is not enough. Not for me, anyway.'

She didn't say anything.

'I want passion. Love. Longing. I think about you all the time. I'd like to think you thought about me, too.'

'I do.'

'Not in an awfully fond, tepid sort of way, I hope. I hate that. It's as if I'm not good enough to love.'

He went through to the living room. 'Look at this flat. Empty. I don't believe you can't afford some furniture.'

She followed him through. 'I can afford furniture. Not that there's a lot around to buy these days. I just . . .'

'You just don't want to buy it because that would be a waste when you might die.'

'Yes.'

'You don't want to let yourself love somebody when you might die.'

'Yes.'

'Well, Julia, I've got news for you. You *are* going to die. We all are at sometime or other. So we live the best we can while we're alive. So why don't you get a table and a sofa and fall in love with me and marry me?'

She said, 'I don't want to stop flying.'

'What has that got to do with anything?'

'I don't want to leave my job. I love my job.'

'I love *my* job,' he said. 'I'm not asking you to leave your job. I'm asking you to marry me. Fly and marry me. Fly and have my baby. Fly and learn to cook a meal. Fly and . . .' He ran out of steam. He waved his arms in the air, searching for words. 'Live.'

Julia said, 'All right.'

'All right, what?'

'All right, I'll marry you. I'm not awfully fond of you at all.'

He stared at her. 'Damn it, woman, say it.'

'I love you. I think about you all the time. I want to marry you. But, right after the honeymoon, I'm going back to work, flying.'

Love had never occurred to Claire. If she sang a love song, it was because she liked the tune. The emotions expressed meant nothing to her.

Of course, she loved her children. That had startled her. She marvelled at their small faces, laughed when they laughed and wasn't truly happy when they were away from her. She would have liked them to be safe at home, under the same roof as she was. These days her bitterest regret was that she had never told them how much she adored them. Should've mentioned it, she thought. If anything happens to me, if I die, they'll never know.

But now she knew what all the songs and poems were about. She had a love. It amazed her that one face among all the faces she saw every day could now mean so much to her. She'd kiss his eyes, his cheeks, the side of his mouth – where the smile started – wondering how one set of features could become beloved.

Several times a week, Claire would tell Izzy and Julia she was going for a walk, or to meet someone for a drink, and set off in the direction of the Golden Mallard. Then she'd double back, cross the bridge, heels clicking on the wooden boards, and hurry to the cottage, to Simon and his double bed.

They'd have a glass of whisky, kiss, then make their way to the bedroom. Sometimes they skipped the whisky. Sometimes, Claire would come to him, a coat over her underwear and, once inside the door, would let it slip to the floor as she took him to her. She'd arrived ready for love.

At half past ten, Claire would get up, dress and go back to her cottage. She was sure nobody knew about this. But Diane did. And so did Mrs Brent, who also cleaned for Simon. She recognised the scent on the pillows, and the lipstick traces on the glass Claire used. More than that, Mr Brent had spotted her slipping up the path to Simon's front door, and reported his interesting sighting to his wife.

'It's this war,' she said. 'Everybody's gone crazy. They can't control themselves. Hanky-panky, slap and tickle, a bit of the other is all they think about. And when it's over, they'll pretend it didn't happen.'

Still, Claire believed her affair was a secret. But it wouldn't have made any difference if she'd known it wasn't. She was smitten. Too smitten for guilt. They had a new unspoken rule. They no longer discussed their families. Talk of distant husbands, wives and children killed the passion.

Every time she and Simon got together there was an urgency

between them. They couldn't wait to get their clothes off, to hold one another, to kiss, feel the pleasure of skin on skin. Now Claire had one more reason for not wanting the war to end – she'd be parted from her love.

Izzy's romance was relaxed, an easy-going affair, a mix of sex and long rambling conversations. Voices spilling into the dark. He spoke about Montana, winters so cold that the icy air burned your lungs and you thought your very breath would freeze and hang for a second, a crystalline lump, before it crashed to the ground. Huge skies, mountains bluing into more mountains. The ranch was so vast that his father used a small plane to fly over it, looking for stray cattle. He told her of ranch hands with calloused hands and leathery faces who turned up, worked for a year or a few months, then moved on. Others had been with them all their lives, lived in houses his father had helped them build.

He talked longingly about his mother's kitchen, her food – meatloaves, burgers, cookies and milk laid out for him when he came home from school. He had a horse, Jericho. He could ride for days and still be on his father's land. His homesickness was infectious. It made Izzy pine for a country she'd never been to.

She told him about her father – his red-hot sermons, his sweet tooth, his love of driving fast, the disobedient dog, Treacle, the endless stream of people who brought him their problems, the comfort he gave them. She didn't tell him that she was beginning to find her father rigid in his opinions, and she didn't say she no longer sharing his religion. She didn't mention that her father didn't know she was a pilot. Instead she spoke about the village that smelled in the evenings of cooking fat and coal fires. Everyone knew her name. 'Sometimes my face aches from all the smiling and saying hello that I have to do.'

Her mother made thick Scotch broth and glistening apple dumplings swathed in custard. In autumn the family picked brambles that were made into sweet jelly, which she spread on freshly baked bread. Eating this left her with a sticky purple coating on her lips and cheeks.

She was going home for her annual fortnight's leave. 'I'll have to. They'd never forgive me if I didn't.'

He asked if he could come along. 'I'd like to meet your folks. And I've never been to Scotland. I'd like to taste haggis.'

'OK. That'd be wonderful. I could show you around. I suppose my mother could get hold of a haggis. I don't know what the haggis situation is like what with rationing and all.' Then, after a long pause, she said, 'They don't know about us. I mean, you know, that we sleep together. We'd have separate rooms. They don't approve of sex outside marriage.'

He said he just bet they didn't, pulled her to him and kissed her neck, ready for some more pleasure that would make her mother and father tut and scowl and wag their fingers.

On her days off, she visited him. She felt guilty about this because she'd promised Elspeth she'd save up her leave and travel north to be with her. But love and lust got the better of her.

She would rattle for miles over neglected, bumpy roads on her motorbike and arrive stiff, cold and aching, arms throbbing from the vibrations of the struggling engine and from holding the handlebars for an hour or so. Her face would be red and numb from the rush of wind.

When he visited her, he'd use his car. He'd be relaxed as he walked up the path to the cottage, she'd run to him and he would lift her up, swing her round and kiss her before he put her down again. He was over six foot tall; she wasn't much over five foot. He still called her Pork Chops, but she had stopped caring about that. In fact, he said it so affectionately, she had come to like it.

When Izzy went to him, she stayed at a small bed and breakfast not far from his base. He didn't think it proper for her to sleep in his bed there, and he liked his comforts. 'I don't want to hang about condom alley.'

This was the passage between the Nissan huts where soldiers and airmen, patients at the hospital, courted local girls on dance nights. Evidence of their passion was littered on the ground for all to see on Sunday mornings.

'This country is too cold for love in the open air,' Jim told Izzy.

So, they'd found Mrs Barton's small and comfortable guesthouse. She called them her Lady Pilot and her American Doctor, and was rather proud of them. If she disapproved of their not being married, she never mentioned it. She said, 'That's the way of things, these days. People rushing at life, afraid it might end soon.'

Once, when Izzy was sitting in the tiny dining room eating breakfast – toast, tea and porridge – Mrs Barton asked Izzy if she and Jim were thinking of tying the knot. Izzy said she didn't know, they hadn't discussed it. But secretly, she'd thought about it. She wanted to marry Jim. She loved his long lean body, his cropped hair that softly tickled the flat of her palm when she touched it, the deep cleft in his chin. She loved him, she was sure. But she never mentioned it. He hadn't told her he loved her. Izzy thought if she told him, she'd break the spell. Better to keep it to herself, lest he thought her pushy or silly and left her. She wasn't one to take risks in the air, why take one here on the ground?

Elspeth forgave Tyler. What else could she do? He was always there.

'I'm wooing you,' he said.

'Well, stop it,' she said. 'It's annoying.'

He followed her everywhere, shovelled dung for her, brought her flowers he'd picked. In the end her heart melted; they became lovers again. On walks through the forest he told her about the lives of trees. 'They're the same top and bottom. Their roots spread out under the ground in the exact same way their branches spread into the air.' She said she hadn't known that.

She thought him handsome, funny, generous, big-hearted, really rather wonderful. But when he asked her to marry him – and he did most days – she'd say, 'The war will end; everything will change. Maybe we'll change. Let's just enjoy this time together. Marriage can wait.' She didn't want to admit that she was temted by the offer.

'But I love you,' he'd say. 'Don't you love me?'

'Let's not talk about love,' she'd say. 'It complicates things. Let's make love and grab a little happiness instead.'

Love? She was too busy hoping the war would end and planning what she'd do when that happened to think about love. Love made a person do silly things, think silly thoughts and make silly decisions. She wanted nothing to do with it.

Chapter Twenty-six
Cream Cakes
and Carpets

Lorna was in love. She poured out her heart to Elspeth when they were on their way to Lady McKenzie's house. 'I love him awful. He's the nicest, kindest, handsomest man in the world, don't you think?'

No, Elspeth didn't think. Freddie Tait was small, with crooked teeth, wiry sandy hair, a drooping lower lip and small eyes. But Elspeth supposed love was blind, anyone could be beautiful in the eyes of their beloved.

It was three o'clock in the afternoon. Duncan had reluctantly let four of the girls away from work early to have tea with Lady McKenzie. 'To let these gels know how grateful we are for their valiant effort in doing difficult work in difficult times,' she had said. 'How many of them do you have?'

'Over forty,' Duncan had said.

There had been a black silence as Lady McKenzie took this in. 'Too many. Send me four. I'll do four, that's enough when it comes to sandwiches and a few cakes. Pick me four of your best gels.'

Naturally, Duncan had chosen Elspeth, who'd picked Lorna. He'd had to select Dorothy, as she was lead girl, and Tricia had managed to push herself forwards, smiling, daring him not to choose her.

The four had washed in cold water, changed out of their dungarees and into their uniforms and were now making their way to Lady McKenzie's large country house.

Dorothy and Tricia surged ahead. This was grand, time off work and chance to see inside the enormous house they passed on their way to the village for their weekly treat of the cinema, fish and chips and a hot, sweaty stomp of a dance in the local hall. Plus, there might be tea with actual milk and sugar. There might be cakes.

'This is the best thing that's happened to me in two years since I came here,' said Tricia.

'Me, too,' said Dorothy. 'Pathetic, isn't it?'

They pedalled furiously. Then Dorothy said, 'We better slow up. We don't want to arrive looking too eager and dripping with sweat.' She turned and, with a sweep of her arm, urged the two lagging behind talking about love to hurry up.

Elspeth shouted that they were coming, then turned to Lorna. 'Are you going to get married, then?'

'Oh, yes. Soon as the war's over. I'm going to Newfoundland. We'll live in his cottage overlooking the sea and we'll have four babies, two of each kind and I'll make bake apple pie, whatever that is.'

'Sounds like you've got it all worked out,' said Elspeth.

'We have.'

The road was lined on either side with trees. Six or seven bombers thundered overhead. In the distance a skein of geese clanked and keened, heading south. 'Soon they'll be gone,' said Elspeth. 'They just carry on like always, arriving for winter, leaving when spring comes. Do you suppose they know there's a war on?'

'No,' said Lorna. 'They just do what they do.'

Elspeth remembered a time when she just did what she did. She'd been a piano teacher, she hadn't made much money, but she'd been happy – happy enough, anyway. Certainly, there hadn't been anybody blowing whistles telling her when to stop work and when to start again. And she'd been warm. The winter had been cruel; she thought the cold had entered her soul. She felt chilled inside, a thick ache in the joints of her fingers, her elbows and her knees. Mornings, there was pain thudding within her, and it took a slow walk to the ablutions hut to ease it. She knew she would suffer for the rest of her life for these years working in the forest, the days spent running back and forth leading the horse, the time chopping branches and twigs from felled trees, hours and hours outside in snow, rain and wind.

'I hate Hitler for what he's done to my knees,' she said.

Lorna said she that if he hadn't started this stupid war, she'd still have ten fingers.

They turned into the drive and rattled towards the house, legs splayed out because it was downhill and they didn't have to pedal.

Tricia and Dorothy were already at the door, their bikes lying on the ground beside a gleaming Bentley.

'Crikey,' said Lorna. 'Posh car.' She peered into it. 'All polished on the inside, too.'

Lorna banged the giant knocker. They stood in a neat row, waiting, listening to footsteps coming nearer and nearer from a long way off. They giggled.

A maid opened the door, welcomed them in and led them down the hall into a large drawing room. 'Lady McKenzie will be with you soon,' she said and left.

There was a lot to look at in the room – portraits on the wall, a scattering of chairs, a long well-plumped sofa, a huge polished dresser, ornaments, a fire crackling in the grate.

Once, Elspeth would have been at home with all this opulence. But she'd been removed from it for such a long time, she, like the other girls, was overwhelmed. She was unnerved by the luxury. She realised she'd become a Forestry girl, comfortable only in the company of other Forestry girls and used to cold-water washes, communal dining and dormitory sleeping. She'd forgotten what it was like to be civilised. She joined the others in looking down.

'Carpets,' she said. 'God, carpets. I'd forgotten about them.'

They'd been walking on wooden floors and duckboards for so long, the luxury of something soft underfoot had slipped from their minds. Lorna leaned down and stroked it. 'Gosh, it's lovely. I could lie down and sleep on it.'

Elspeth dug her fingers into the pile. 'Axminster or Wilton, or maybe something posher. And there are rugs on top of carpet.'

The carpet was deep blue, the rugs, probably Persian, were an elaborate mix of pinks, reds and browns. Tricia knelt down and put her cheek on one of them. 'Lovely. I'm going to have something like this as soon as I get away from the Forestry. I'll have carpets everywhere, up the walls and everywhere.'

They didn't hear Lady McKenzie enter the room. They didn't see her stand behind them looking bemused as they fondled her carpets. 'Good afternoon, gels. Isn't this lovely, a tea party?'

The four, abashed, turned and agreed, 'Yes, lovely. Thank you for inviting us.'

Nobody mentioned the carpets.

Lady McKenzie said, 'Well, sit.' She waved them towards the sofa, while she opted for one of the chairs by the fire. 'Tea will be with us in a moment.' She beamed round at them. 'So, what is it you do?'

'Work in the forest,' said Lorna. 'Chopping down trees and such like.'

The beam did not falter. 'Yes, but before you did that, what did you do?'

Lorna said she'd worked in a chocolate factory, Dorothy said she'd been training to be a teacher but had got married. 'And they don't let you teach if you're married, so I left. Then my husband got killed at Dunkirk, so I joined up to do this. I needed to get away, couldn't bear to be alone in the house and see his things all round me.'

The other girls stared at her. They hadn't known that.

Lady McKenzie said that was tragic. 'Such a waste of life, this war.' She turned to Elspeth. 'And, you?'

'I was a piano teacher, private pupils.'

Lady McKenzie clapped her hands. 'Splendid. You must come and give us a recital. I'll arrange it with Mr Bowman.'

Elspeth protested that she hadn't played in some time. 'I haven't been near a piano since I came up here. I'm rusty.'

'Nonsense, it will be delightful. We need all the entertainment we can get during these dark times.'

Tea arrived. Two maids, one with a tray bearing a teapot, hot-water pot, cups, saucers, milk jug and sugar bowl; the other maid with a platter of sandwiches and a laden cake stand.

Lady McKenzie offered to be mother, and pour the tea. Tricia said that she'd worked in Woolworths but was hoping to be a dancer, since nobody had asked her.

'How lovely,' said Lady McKenzie. 'Milk? Sugar? Anyone?'

They all nodded. Tea with milk and sugar, what a treat.

They ate fish-paste sandwiches, scones and jam and were allotted a cream cake each. The conversation was stiff, banal. The heat of the fire, the comfortable seat and the food had an effect on the girls. Their eyelids drooped, they yawned. Sleep was taking them. At half past four Lady McKenzie stood up, said it had been a wonderful afternoon and they must do it again sometime and the girls were ushered out.

Cycling back to camp, Tricia said she felt nauseous. 'Carrot sandwiches have ruined my stomach. I can't be doing with cream cakes, now. They're too rich, it's not fair.'

Lorna stopped, dug into her pockets and drew out two scones. 'Stole them for Freddie.'

They were dripping jam, sticky and had a fair amount of lint clinging to them.

'He'll be delighted,' said Elspeth, looking at them in horror.

'Just whipped them on the way out. Nobody was looking,' said Lorna.

Elspeth said, 'Good ploy. You might have pinched one of the ornaments, they looked antique. Worth a bit.'

Lorna shook her head. 'She'd have noticed.'

'I think she'll also notice the missing scones,' said Elspeth. 'I don't think anything gets past her.'

Lorna said, 'Crikey.' She climbed back on her bike and pedalled furiously, looking back in case Lady McKenzie was thundering after her in her Bentley. 'She'll be coming for me, tooting her horn, shouting, "Scone thief". Maybe she's phoned the police.'

'You'll be in the dock pleading guilty, and you'll get six months in jail.'

'That'd be fine. I'd lie in my cell all day and sleep.'

The camp was hushed when they arrived. The girls who hadn't

been invited to the tea party trooped in, axes over their shoulders. They all looked over at Lorna, and said nothing.

'What's wrong with them?' said Lorna. Then, a flush of guilt. 'Do you think they know about the scones?'

'Just jealous,' said Elspeth. 'They wanted to go have tea at the big house.'

Lorna said, 'Tough luck.' She propped her bike against the hut, and went inside to put the precious scones in her locker.

Duncan Bowman called on Elspeth, beckoned her over with his finger. 'A word.'

For a moment she thought it was the scones. Lady McKenzie had phoned and complained.

Duncan was never very good with words. Delivering bad news was beyond him. He put his hands in his pockets, frowned, looked at Elspeth, looked away, jerked his head in the direction of the hut. 'Your friend's boyfriend's dead.'

Elspeth said, 'Freddie?'

'Yes, him. Tree fell on him.'

'How could that happen?' said Elspeth. 'Surely someone would have called "timber".'

'They did. But the stupid idiot was standing watching the bombers go over, couldn't hear a bloody thing for the noise. Tree crashed down on him, broke half the bones in his body.' He jerked his head towards the truck. 'He's in the back. Taking him down to the morgue at the hospital.' He jerked his head back at the hut. 'You better go tell your friend.'

As Elspeth walked back to the hut, she heard Lorna howl. A scream of anguish. Wood pigeons in trees nearby panicked, took off. The whole camp stopped. Someone had already given her friend the news.

Chapter Twenty-seven
Dirty Secrets

Skimpton had filled up with Americans. They were camped along the riverbanks and on the village green. Children followed them singing 'Got any gum, chum.' They started collections of empty Lucky Strike packets they found in the street. They made money doing the chip run – fetching fish and chips from the shop and taking them back to the camp. Twice the pub ran out of beer. There were fights about that since locals thought the owners of the pub should save the alcohol for them. 'We'll be here long after them Yanks have gone.' When it was overflowing with customers, and the glasses ran out, beer was served in jam jars.

Every day the soldiers in training ran through the village, and beyond, carrying full kit, wearing camouflage pants and vests. Mr and Mrs Brent made a point of watching the show.

'Them Yanks have nice bodies,' said Mrs Brent. 'Fifty years ago, I'd have allowed them a few cuddles.'

'Fifty years ago I'd have fought them for you,' said Mr Brent.

'Fifty years ago I'd have been worth fighting for,' said Mrs Brent.

'Yer worth fighting for now,' said Mr Brent. 'But fifty years ago you were a bit of a lass.'

She took his arm and said, 'Happy days.'

When Izzy skimmed by on her bike, going home, soldiers hooted, whistled and clapped. She was usually too tired to notice or care.

'There won't be a virgin left in the village,' Julia said.

Diane said she doubted there had been many left before they arrived.

Morning and they were in the mess waiting for Edith to bustle in telling them the chits were up.

Izzy was, as usual, spread out over two chairs and in a semi-snooze while watching Dolores, back after two days' leave, hold up her left hand, fingers spread.

'Hey, you guys, I'm married.'

Julia snorted. 'I knew she was after Alfie.'

Diane said, 'Well, good for her.'

'I'll be Lady Meyers,' said Dolores. 'But you can still call me Dolores.'

'We plan to,' said Julia.

'We did it yesterday. Just me and Alfie and Mr and Mrs Ramsay.'

Diane asked, 'Who are they – friends of yours?'

Dolores shrugged. 'A couple who were passing by. We asked them to be witnesses. Anyway, we just snuck off and married. Big celebrations on Saturday night.' She held her arms out wide, indicating the bigness of the celebrations. 'Party at our place, everyone's invited.'

'Our place,' said Julia. 'Five minutes married and she's calling Alfie's home our place. It's been in his family for centuries. I'm not going to the party.'

Diane called her a sourpuss. She congratulated Dolores and shouted that she'd definitely come to the party. 'I love a party.'

She turned to Julia. 'You're a fool. Alfie throws a wonderful party. And have you seen his wine cellar? It's vast. Stretches for bloody miles, a huge labyrinth. That's where all his money's gone. Wine and the horses. Even counting the amount they swig every night, there's bound to be lots left for us.' She leaned forwards, face close to Julia's. 'When did you last have a decent glass of Margaux?'

Julia thought about this. 'I can't remember. Actually, Walter might like to go. I could introduce you.'

'Excellent,' said Diane. 'Introducing your young man to your friends, this must be getting serious.'

Julia shrugged. 'A little. Anyway, he's not young. He's even older than you.'

Diane smiled and said, 'Pour soul.' She turned to Izzy and asked, 'Going to the party?'

Izzy said she was working on Saturday. 'I'll be tired.'

'Nonsense. You can come with me. We'll sweep in together and take the place by storm. Then we'll get filthy drunk and tell each other our dirty secrets.'

'I don't have any dirty secrets.'

'Well, get some by Saturday. I want to hear them.'

Edith stuck her head round the door, said, 'Chits are up,' then disappeared. There was the usual scramble, elbowing and jostling and Edith shouting for order.

Julia was duty pilot today, flying the taxi Anson. She dropped Izzy and Diane off at Preston, where they were to pick up Spitfires to deliver to Elvington. Izzy said she'd see Wanda.

'Good-oh,' said Diane. 'I'd like to meet Wanda.'

'He's actually Jean-Louis, but he's stuck in my mind as Wanda.'

'Well, as long as he doesn't mind,' said Diane.

'He only became Wanda so he could fly. Anything to fly, I suppose.'

'The things people do for a thrill,' said Diane.

The planes were ready. Izzy climbed in, did her cockpit check and thanked the ground crewman who helped her into her harness. She put on her helmet, taxied to the end of the runway and, when she got a green light, took off. Diane followed, five minutes behind her.

By now, Izzy knew the countryside into Yorkshire well, and barely had to look at her map as she headed towards York. Cows in fields didn't look up, but sheep, she noticed, still scudded in all directions, tiny hurtling white bodies, as she skimmed overhead.

She was in the air so much these days, she even flew in her dreams. Not the lovely flying dreams she had when she was a little girl. This dream was full of the thrum and throb of being in an aeroplane. She'd wake up surprised to find she was in bed. No matter what she did, what perfume she might put on or how many baths she took, she still felt she smelled of petrol and hot metal.

She landed, taxied to the delivery bay, went through the ground routine – tail wheel unlocked, gills open, gauges check, flaps up. She powdered her nose, fixed her lipstick, ran her fingers through her hair and climbed out. Diane was now coming in. She went through the same routine. Together they went to get their chits signed. Then, in the mess, they looked for Wanda.

'He's small,' said Izzy scanning the faces in the mess. 'Smokes all the time.'

'Well, that could be anybody,' said Diane.

Izzy remarked on how quiet it was.

'Indeed,' said Diane. She knew that kind of quiet when she heard it. And she'd often heard it. It was the stunned hush that fell on a squadron when they'd suffered heavy losses. She went to the counter to fetch their tea. She thought Izzy might need a cup, she doubted Wanda was going to be around today.

She turned, saw Izzy sitting at a table, hand over her mouth. She'd been told about her friend.

'Over France,' said Izzy. 'Two nights ago. Nobody saw him bale out.'

Diane put her hand over Izzy's. For a while neither of them spoke. Then Izzy said, 'He was a frightful lech. All he thought about was flying and sex.'

Diane said she'd met the type. 'But you liked him?'

'Oh, enormously. He was fun. Julia would say he's been bumped orff.'

'It's only her way of dealing with things. We all have our own way of coping. I've decided to wait till the war's over, then I'm going to lock myself in my bedroom and cry for days and days. I've lost a lot of people.' She caught Izzy's look. 'Starting with my husband. He went down in the Battle of Britain somewhere over the English Channel. I'm not over it. I just try not to think about it. Not for now, anyway.' She held up her cup. 'Tea today, tears tomorrow.'

That night, Izzy went to bed early. Outside she could hear American soldiers walking by the river whistling at local girls who were also walking by the river.

She lay in the dark, and, as Mrs Brent would say, made friends with her sadness. She'd found Wanda again, and now she'd lost him. Her father had always told her she wasn't alone, whatever happened to her happened to others. So probably, right now, in homes all over the world people were grieving for friends, lovers, husbands, sons and daughters they'd never see again. Her father told her thinking of others sharing her grief or loneliness would be a comfort. But, lying there, staring into the gloom, she discovered it wasn't.

She heard Claire slip out of the front door, going wherever it was she went these nights. Izzy didn't know, but she suspected to a lover. Later Julia and Walter came in. They'd gone for dinner at the Golden Mallard. She listened to their voices bubble up from the kitchen where they were making tea, but couldn't make out what they were saying. But when they moved from the kitchen to the living room, Izzy heard Julia say, 'I don't want a big do, darling. Just us at the registry office, then a few days together somewhere quiet. Long walks, lovely dinners a lot of time in bed. Then back to work for us both.'

Walter said, 'Suits me.'

Then they went into the living room, shut the door and Izzy couldn't hear anything more. But she thought, Gosh. Julia's getting married. She sighed, and acknowledged a pang of jealousy. She didn't want to get married, but it would be nice to be asked.

Her love affair was made up of snatched moments. She and Jimmy walked together by the river, they had meals at the Golden Mallard, they drank warm beer at the pub. But most of their time together was spent in bed. He told her he loved her body, her hair, her voice. But he never told her he loved her. She sat up and punched her pillow, and cursed. 'Bloody life,' she said. She considered saying 'fuck', but couldn't. It was too rude. Besides, that was the word Jimmy had encouraged her to say. Not saying it pleased her. She wasn't sure that she and Jimmy were speaking right now.

He'd phoned earlier in the evening. 'How are you?' he'd asked.

She'd told him she was fine. 'Well, not so fine. I found out that my friend died.'

She'd told him about Wanda. He was sorry to hear that, told her to take care of herself.

'Are you free tomorrow night?' Izzy had asked. 'Only one of the pilots got married and she's having a party. She's American. It's in this big house.' Thinking these two things would swing it.

'Izzy,' he'd said. 'I've had three hours' sleep and I'm going on duty. All I want to do tomorrow is sleep some more. I'm not in a party mood. Actually –' But, they were cut off.

Izzy had stared at the receiver, tried to phone him back but the operator told her there were no lines available. In bed now, after listening to the world outside, feeling jealous of Julia and punching her pillow, she settled down to worry about that 'actually'. What had it meant? What was about to come after it? Actually, I don't want to see you again? Actually, I've met some-one else? Actually, I've been posted abroad? 'Damn,' said Izzy. 'Damn blast and bugger the phones. Bugger the war. Bugger everything. And bugger saying fuck, I'm not going to do it.'

Next day was warm. The air was soft, the sky cloudless. This was perfection, cycling to work, shirtsleeves rolled up, jacket draped over the handlebars of her bike. Izzy sped in front of Julia and Claire. Today was a flying day for sure. She forgot her worries, because nothing mattered more than joining the sky.

She and Diane were given a plum job, flying back and forth, taking four Spitfires to a unit down the coast where they'd be packed for sending abroad. Izzy took the Spitfires, Diane followed in a Fairfax, a small plane used for ferrying one or two passengers. 'Lovely work,' she said.

On the way back from the first delivery, Diane said they might get off early. 'Give us plenty of time to get tiddled up for the party. Is your young man coming?'

'No,' said Izzy. 'He's awfully tired. He's hardly getting any sleep.'

'Pour soul,' said Diane. 'You're going, though?'

Izzy said she was. 'I want to meet Alfie.'

Diane told her she'd love him. 'He's a sweetie.' Then, she added, 'I hope you've got your dirty secrets ready. You promised me you'd divulge them.'

'I don't have any dirty secrets,' said Izzy. 'Do you?'

Diane said of course she did. 'Very juicy they are, too.'

By now they were circling Skimpton airfield, Diane was too busy landing the plane to say more.

It wasn't till the second trip back to base, over an hour and a half later, after the second plane had been delivered and signed for, that Izzy got the chance to ask Diane about her secret.

'I'll tell you one, if you tell me one. It has to be good, though.'

Izzy said, 'OK. You first.'

'My daughter is not my husband's child.' She turned to Izzy, smiled and raised her eyebrows. 'Beat that.'

Izzy said, 'Really. Did your husband know?'

'Of course he did. I was very young, very alone and very afraid. Henry was my only friend and when I told him, he offered to marry me.'

Izzy asked, 'What about the real father?'

'Oh, he was in the army and buggered off to India as soon as he found out I was in the pudding club. Henry stepped forwards, saved me from scandal. Didn't even flinch when my father called him a scoundrel.'

'You must miss him,' said Izzy.

'Every minute of every day. Except for when I'm flying, and when I'm being naughty with my lover.'

'You have a lover!' said Izzy. 'Who?'

'That's a whole new dirty secret. And one I am never going to divulge.'

'Do I know him?'

'Not telling,' said Diane.

By now they were back at Skimpton, Diane was waiting for a green landing light and was preoccupied. 'It's your turn, Izzy. Next trip, you confess.'

The next trip, the third of the day, was in the afternoon. The sun was high. Izzy leaned against the window of the plane, watching its shadow skim over the fields below. This always fascinated her.

'So,' said Diane. 'What's your dirty secret? I won't tell.'

'My boyfriend thinks I'm too withdrawn. I should embrace life more. Laugh and swear and let go.'

'Yes,' said Diane. 'He's right. You should. But that's not a secret, that's more of a moan. You're looking for sympathy and you're not going to get it from me. I agree with him. Secrets, please, Izzy. That's the game we're playing.'

Izzy didn't take her eyes off the speeding shadow below. 'My father doesn't know what I'm doing. I let him think I'm an ops officer. An assistant ops officer, actually.'

'Why on earth did you do that?'

'He thinks a woman's place is in the home, in the kitchen. Preferably making puddings.'

'You can't beat a pudding-making woman,' said Diane. 'I do like my puddings.'

'So do I,' said Izzy. 'Maybe one day I'll take up pudding-making. But right now I'd rather be a pilot. Only my father thinks it's a man's job. He's sure no man would want me because of that. And he hates to see women in trousers. It really upsets him.'

'That's his problem, not yours. You have to tell him what you do. You should be proud to be a pilot.'

'I am.'

'So tell him.'

'It isn't that easy,' said Izzy. 'You don't know what he's like. He's right about everything. He has a loud voice that drowns you out. He's a man. He's full of manness.'

'Oh, I know what he's like. I had to tell my own father when I was but a slip of an unmarried girl that I was pregnant. I know about that rightness and the utter, controlling manness.'

Izzy said, 'Well, you'll understand why I haven't told him.'

'I understand. But I don't condone it. You can't be one Izzy – the Izzy we all know and love here at the base – and another Izzy back at home. You can't live by another person's rules. You have to be you, the complete Izzy, wherever you are.' She looked over at Izzy to see what her reaction was. But Izzy wasn't looking at her; she was staring down at the shadow. 'Look,' said Diane. 'I'll come with you and we'll confront your father together. Or, even better, invite him down here to visit us. Me, Julia, Claire and Dolores will win him over with our womanly wiles; he won't be able to resist. He'll be so proud that you're one of us, a lady pilot.'

'I don't think I am one of you,' said Izzy. 'I'm just me.'

Diane asked what the hell she meant by that.

Izzy said that the other pilots were all rich. 'You're all poised and confident and you've all got posh accents. I'm just ordinary.'

'Oh, Izzy, that's nonsense. You're not ordinary. Nobody's ordinary. Ordinary's a myth dreamed up by people with no self-confidence. You think Julia and Claire and the others don't doubt themselves? Of course they do. You went to proper school, learned about poetry and grammar and multiplication. We got taught by governesses. We learned what fork to use at dinner parties, how to walk with our heads up, how to keep silent when men were talking, how to shoot and ride. We were groomed for marriage. This working for a living is a revelation to us. We all think that you know so much more than we do about life, proper life. God, I envy you working for Betty Stokes Flying Show. Izzy? Are you listening to me? Can I ask what the hell you're looking at?'

'I'm watching our shadow,' said Izzy. 'We're being followed by a cloud.'

Diane looked down. 'That's not a cloud. That's smoke.'

Izzy looked harder. 'It is smoke. Bloody hell.'

They were coming into Skimpton and could see the base.

'Damn fuel tank's leaking,' said Diane. She was calm, composed. 'We'll just shoot over the base. Let them see what's up. Perhaps you should jump out.'

'At this height,' said Izzy. 'I'll hit the ground before my parachute opens. Besides, I don't want to jump out. I've always dreaded doing that. And I won't leave you.'

'Oh, for God's sake, Izzy, it's only a little fire. We're just about home. I'll be fine.'

'So, I'll be fine, too.'

By the time they were skimming over the base, flames were sparking out, caught in the slipstream, flashing behind them. People on the ground saw them and started running. Hooters sounded. The ambulance and fire engines, bells clanging, raced up the runway.

Diane brought the plane low. 'Bloody hell, Izzy. I'm not liking this at all.'

Flames licked up the side of the cockpit. Shot past Izzy's face. 'Fuck!' she shouted.

'That's the ticket,' said Diane. 'Bit of cursing helps.'

They bumped down, rushed along the runway. Flames curled round the plane. Smoke curdled round them, thick billows. Izzy wrestled with Diane's harness. She couldn't see what she was doing.

The fire engine was clanging alongside them. Izzy was aware of people outside. The plane slowed, stopped. The roar of the blaze drowned her shouts. 'I can't see anything!'

There were people on the wing outside, yanking at the door. Hands were reaching for her, grabbing her, hauling at her. She was pulled out. Dragged clear.

The noise was awful. Hooters – the airfield alarm – an ambulance and fire engine bells rattling, people shouting. There was a woman screaming.

Several men were holding Izzy. One had her in a headlock. She struggled, bit and kicked. The heat was searing and she was being heaved back from it. She realised that she was the woman screaming. She was flailing her arms, shouting, 'Diane's still in there! Diane's still in there!'

Chapter Twenty-eight
There's no Such Thing as Fair

Nothing stopped work in the forest, not even death. The morning after Freddie Tait died, Elspeth rose at her usual time, dressed and went to the stables. She shovelled out the dung, swept the floor, rubbed down, fed and watered her horse in silence. Nobody spoke, nobody sang. Frazer said he didn't like this gloom. 'It does nobody no good.'

Elspeth said she supposed this was true, but she couldn't help it.

Work done, she walked back to camp, thinking she'd have to persuade Lorna to get up. But no, she was sitting at the table in the dining hut, sipping tea but ignoring her porridge. 'They don't give you a day off for having a broken heart,' she said.

'No,' Elspeth agreed, 'they don't.'

'They should, though. They should let you just lie and stare for a few days. Let you get used to your grief.'

Elspeth said she should eat. 'It's hard work out there loading trucks. You need to keep your strength up.'

'Tell that to my stomach,' said Lorna. 'It's working hard dealing with the tea. It'd just send the porridge back up the way it came.'

They walked together up the track to where they were working in the forest. Elspeth led the horse. Not that it was necessary. It would have followed her, anyway.

It was a good day, warm, cloudless. A couple of buzzards cruised the thermals high above them, birds hopped about in the branches of trees nearby and the ground beneath Lorna and Elspeth's feet was dry. It didn't get much better than this.

'I woke up this morning, saw the sun and felt happy,' said Lorna. 'Then I remembered I was miserable and I wondered for a moment why that was. Then it came to me. Freddie's dead.'

Elspeth took Lorna's hand and squeezed it.

At first, when dealing with her sixty-logs-a-day quota, Elspeth had tried to divide it into thirty logs in the morning and thirty in the afternoon. But that left her struggling at the end of the day when her legs ached. Now, she did forty in the morning, fifteen after lunch and five after the afternoon break. But still she felt breathless and her joints were sore by the time the workday ended. She was getting too old for this.

Today the only sounds were of people working, saws and axes. The atmosphere was raw. It was a relief when two of the girls, unable to stand the silence, started singing 'Mairzy Doats and Dozy Doats'. Everyone joined in, the chorus bellowing through the trees, getting louder and louder till everyone, even Lorna, heaving logs onto the back of a truck, was singing till her throat hurt.

Lunch was a treat – cheese sandwiches and strong tea. Elspeth sat with Lorna and asked how she was coping.

'I'm bloody tired out and hoarse,' said Lorna. 'But now I know what to do when something bad happens. I'll chop down a tree and drag it about. Being bloody tired out really helps.'

Elspeth looked up, saw Duncan approaching, 'Uh-oh, here comes the boss.'

'Moon,' he said. 'You're to give a recital at the big house next Thursday night.'

'Am I?' said Elspeth.

'Yes.'

'May I point out that evenings are my own free time and nobody can just tell me what to do.'

'Lady McKenzie is offering a five-pound fee to entertain her friends.'

Elspeth didn't hesitate. 'OK, then.'

'I'll drive you in the truck. Don't want you falling off your bike on the way there.'

When he'd gone, Elspeth nudged Lorna. 'Five whole pounds. The fish and chips and a drink in the pub are on me.'

Lorna said, 'You'll be alone with him in the truck. He'll make a grab for you. I think he's in love with you.'

Elspeth told her not to be daft. The whistle went. They drained their mugs, got up and went back to work.

The week passed slowly. On Sunday afternoon the local minister came to the camp and held a service for Freddie in the dining hut. They sang the twenty-third psalm, listened as Tyler spoke of his friend, but it was only when everyone stood up and sang 'You'd Be so Nice to Come Home to', Freddie's favourite song, that Lorna cried.

When it was over, she went with Elspeth and Tyler to their spot by the river, filled their mugs with whisky, and talked till stars came out. They shared memories, dreams, plans and ambitions. When Tyler spoke of returning to Newfoundland, and, once again, asked Elspeth to marry him and come home with him, Elspeth kicked him on the shins.

'You bloody tactless fool,' she hissed, as they walked back to the camp. 'Lorna was planning to go back with Freddie. You didn't have to remind her that she can't do that now.'

He shrugged and shuffled down the track to his hut. 'Offer's still open,' he said. 'Always will be.'

On Thursday evening she put on her uniform and went with Duncan to the recital. He was wearing a tweed suit, shiny with wear at the elbows and cuffs, a white shirt, blue tie and shoes polished to a mirrored gleam. His hair was sculpted into a skull-clinging gloss, thick with Brylcreem. The smell of it lingered in Elspeth's nostrils all evening. He hardly spoke on the drive to the big house.

The recital was held in a huge drawing room, lit by a giant crystal chandelier. At the far end was a baby grand, complete with gold candlesticks, a candle aglow in each one. There were chairs – gold-leaf arms and red velvet cushions – lined up in neat rows. Elspeth felt sick with nerves.

There was a large buffet set out on a table, and several waiters, all wearing white gloves, wandered about with trays bearing glasses of champagne. Elspeth wasn't offered one, but Duncan took a glass, sipped and coughed. It wasn't to his liking.

Elspeth took off her jacket and beret, sat at the piano and ran through some scales to warm up since she hadn't played in some time. But, eventually, at half past seven, the evening got underway. Elspeth discovered that being rusty didn't matter at all. Hardly anybody noticed her mistakes. At the end of each piece, they clapped enthusiastically.

Halfway through the proceedings, there was an interval. Champagne for me, thought Elspeth. But no, she was dispatched to the kitchen, where the cook might have prepared a little something for her.

This turned out to be a good thing. Cook, an ample woman, red of cheek, kind of heart, gave Elspeth a sandwich with a slab of warm roast beef spread with mustard, a slice of fruit cake and a plate of small almond pastries.

'Where did you get all this?' said Elspeth. 'Don't they ration the upper classes?'

Cook said that there was them as has and gets and them as don't and that's how it is and how it always has been. And made Elspeth a second sandwich. The kitchen was large and warm, heated by a cooking range. Cook bustled, asked after Elspeth's health, said it must be cold up in them forests in winter and if ever Elspeth needed a little something extra to eat, just to come to her. 'Use the tradesmen's door, of course.'

Sustained by the rush of sudden protein, Elspeth played well in the second part of the recital. Bach, Mozart and Schubert poured into the room, and she hit only a few wrong notes. Nobody noticed.

When she'd finished, people exclaimed in wonder at her talent. A few wished they'd stuck in at their piano lessons and some thought it such a waste that someone so musically gifted should work all day chopping down trees. 'Surely there must be other things she could do. Entertain the troops, for example.'

But Elspeth said she loved the outdoor life. Which wasn't true.

At ten o'clock, Lady McKenzie thanked Elspeth and led her to the front door. Duncan followed. As they stood on the front step, Lady McKenzie shook Elspeth's hand and said they must do it all again sometime soon. Elspeth didn't think so, and wondered when she would get her five pounds.

'Duncan,' said Lady McKenzie, shaking his hand. 'We are all

deeply grateful to you for allowing Elspeth to play and for bringing her along.' She took two envelopes from the pocket of her silk jacket. 'One for the musician. And the other is what's due for the fertiliser.'

They drove home, Elspeth still wondering when she was going to get her money. Duncan stopped the truck at the end of the track leading to the camp. He turned off the engine, turned to Elspeth, put his hand on her knee and told her she was a lovely-looking woman. 'And gifted, too.'

Elspeth thanked him, removed the hand and said, 'Can I have my money now?'

'What money?'

'My money. I was told I'd get five pounds for playing at the recital.'

He tapped his pocket. 'It's here.'

She held out her hand.

'Well,' he said. 'I arranged it. I drove you there.'

'I played the piano,' said Elspeth.

He admitted that was true. Took out one of the envelopes and gave Elspeth two pounds.

'I was told I'd get five.'

'Who told you that?' asked Duncan.

'You.'

'I said there was a five-pound fee. I didn't say that was what you'd get. I've got my cut, you've got yours.'

Elspeth called him a bastard. 'You've cheated me.'

Climbing out of the truck in a fury, she remembered the fertiliser fee. 'Is that for the dung?'

'It could be.'

'I trundle dung for miles every Friday night and you sell it?'

He said nothing, scratched his cheek.

'Don't you think you could slip the stable people a pound now and then? We do all the graft, shovelling and such.'

He said, 'And the horses do all the shitting and I don't pay them, either.' That was the way of things. He was head forester, he took the decisions, he had all the responsibilities and when a little something extra came his way it was only what he deserved.

Elspeth slammed the truck door and stumped up the track, cursing.

In the morning, she was still furious. She stamped about the stable, raged as she heaved muck outside. 'He cheated me. He bloody stole my money.' She was standing, one hand on her shovel, the other on her hip.

'He's awful fond of you,' said Frazer.

'What's that got to do with it?' said Elspeth. 'I'd hate to see how he treats people he's not awful fond of.'

Frazer said, 'Duncan's getting old.'

Elspeth said, 'So?'

'So he'll have to retire. He'll lose his house, everything. He'll need all the money he can get.'

'Including my money. I need all the money I can get, too. And I'm getting old. So are you, come to think of it.'

'Yes, but the cottage where I live has been in the family for generations. My grandfather and great-grandfather lived there. When Duncan retires, he'll have nowhere to go.'

'That's still no reason for taking other people's money. It's just not fair.'

Frazer asked where she'd got the notion that anything was fair. 'Nothing's fair. If it was, you'd be spending time getting pampered at that big house, and bloody Lady McKenzie would be here shovelling shit. He wagged his finger at her. 'Get fair out of your head. It doesn't exist.'

'So Duncan gets away with cheating me. Taking my money.'

'Ah now,' said Frazer. 'I may not believe in fair, but I do believe in justice. We all get what we deserve in the end. What Duncan really wants is you. You sitting by his fireside, you cooking his tea, you in his bed.'

Elspeth said, 'Yuck.'

'See, he's never going to get what he wants.'

'Too bloody right he's not,' said Elspeth. 'Bloody bastard. I bloody hate him and I'll bloody get even with him.'

Without even turning to look at her, he said, 'No you won't. Just leave him alone to dig his own grave. He'll get what's coming to him. One way or another, we all get what we deserve.'

Chapter Twenty-nine
Tears Later

Hiddlington Hall surprised Izzy. The drive was long, tree-lined, rutted. The car juddered and jolted over it. The house was huge and shabby, outside and in. The rugs were threadbare, the leather sofa in the drawing room was leaking horsehair, paint peeled from the doors. A huge dresser by the main door was draped in coats, newspapers and unopened mail. Portraits were askew. At the far end of the drawing room a large, worryingly shaky heap of logs smouldered in an ornate fireplace.

People were standing around in quiet groups, sipping drinks and speaking about Diane. 'Great lady, wonderful pilot. Can't believe she's gone.' Some told horror stories about gruesome things that had happened to them when a thousand feet up, instead. Things people had seen, things that had happened to them – filled the room. There were stories about windscreens covered with oil, undercarriages that wouldn't come down, leaking fuel pipes. Someone remembered brakes failing as she scudded along a runway at over a hundred miles per hour, someone else told of having to fly for miles and miles after the bottom of their plane fell off. Another said she'd once sheared off the wing of her plane when she'd hit the wire of a barrage balloon. 'Fell out of the sky, plane completely broken, and I walked away with hardly a bruise.'

'Let's not line shoot,' said Julia. 'Not today.'

'It was a beautiful service,' said Claire.

They'd sung 'For Those in Peril in the Air'. The CO had delivered a moving eulogy. The church had been alive with flowers.

'Who sent the roses?' asked Claire. 'So lovely. There wasn't a note with them.'

'Do you suppose Diane had a secret admirer?' asked Julia.

'Gal like Diane?' said Dolores. 'You bet she had.' She had offered to let the mourners from the funeral gather at her house after the service. It was close to the base, and most of the people who'd come to say goodbye to Diane worked there.

Dolores was touring the room with a tray of drinks. But most people opted for tea. They'd been given a couple of hours off to attend the funeral and soon would have to go back to work. And, the CO was standing in the corner – watching. This didn't bother Dolores. She continued her tour, thrusting the tray at her guests.

Izzy was on the sofa. She sipped tea, surveyed the room over the rim of her cup. Everyone was here – Julia, Claire, Edith, Fiona the adjutant.

She noticed Jacob on the edge of the crowd. He'd driven Edith and Fiona here and was meant to wait outside. But he hadn't. He took a glass of sherry and leaned against the wall, watching the goings-on.

Dolores put down her tray and lit up a Lucky Strike. She'd been given several packets at an American base for helping to cool the beer. She'd packed several cases into the plane she was picking up, done several circuits at fifteen hundred feet and come down again. 'Cold up there.'

Alfie was by her side. Izzy hadn't met him before. She'd

313

imagined an overweight county-type, tweed jacket, waistcoat, cravat and thick walrus moustache. But he was thin, elegant, Brylcreemed and had only a sliver of hair on his upper lip.

People flitted from group to group. Every time anyone walked past the giant fireplace, clouds of smoke wafted out. Izzy's eyes nipped and her cup shook, rattled in its saucer.

And all the while, images from that afternoon were stuck in her head. She kept seeing the wrecked plane, the heap of metal and wood, the huge scar it had left as it ploughed across the airfield, tangled, scorched metal scattered. After she'd be hauled free, and after she'd stopped fighting to get back to help Diane get free, she'd been transfixed staring at the plane, thinking, Diane's still in there. Diane crushed and burned. There, in her mind, was a young ground engineer holding up the bag, knitting intact, which had been thrown clear. She could see the fire engine and the ambulance – the blood tub, Diane called it. The noise, the smell, everything was imprinted behind Izzy's eyes. It was a vision that kept visiting her, unwanted, uninvited and unwelcome. She could be at the cottage in her bath, making her porridge, listening to the radio, sitting at the kitchen table writing to her mother or Elspeth, and there it would be – that vision. The roar and heat of a plane consumed with flames and Diane inside it.

Ever since the accident, Izzy had felt numb. She was in a tunnel. It was as if the entire world was carrying on, everyone going through normal routines, but she had stopped. She was on the brink of screaming, but couldn't quite let go and do it. Tears were always a breath away.

She put her cup on the table and went outside to sit on the steps, heaving in air and shivering. She wanted to go home. Not home to the cottage, but all the way home to the manse. She wanted her mother to tuck her up in bed with a hot-water bottle, stroke her brow and say the magic words of comfort, 'There, there.'

She had been on the step for about half an hour, numb and staring at the pitted driveway and the neglected lawns, when she became aware of someone by her side.

Carlton Willoughby, the CO, was next to her, head bowed, quizzical expression. 'How are you doing, Izzy?'

'Fine,' she said.

'You're coping?'

'Yes, of course I am.'

'Jolly good.' He put his hand on her shoulder. 'Take your time.'

Izzy asked what he meant.

'Take your time to get better. Don't come back to work till you're ready. We don't want to see you till your up to flying again.'

'I'm up to flying now,' said Izzy. 'I'm always up to it.'

'Give it a week, then we'll see.'

Izzy sighed.

'It'll take a while before the pictures in your head fade away. Truth is, they'll never go completely. They'll just fade a bit.'

'You know about that?'

'Oh, yes. I flew in the first war. Saw some horrors. You can't go through life without some horror happening to you.' Then he smiled. 'You'll miss Diane.'

'I already do. Can't believe she's gone.'

He asked what she'd been like 'at the end'.

'Cool, calm. Making jokes. I swore and she said, "That's the ticket. Swear." The whole time it was happening, she hardly turned a hair. She kept flying. She was wonderful.'

He said that indeed she was.

His agreement seemed mild to Izzy. Heated, she said, 'Diane was the most wonderful, wise woman I've ever met. I loved her.'

He stood up, shoved his hands in his pockets. 'I know. So did I.'

Izzy stared up at him. 'It was you, she wouldn't say.'

'Wouldn't say what?'

'We were telling each other our secrets. She said she had a lover but wouldn't tell me who it was.'

'And now *you* won't tell anyone who it was. Don't want my wife finding out about it.' He leaned down, took her arm. 'C'mon. I'll get Jacob to drive you home.'

Ten minutes later, Izzy was in her kitchen, sitting as the watching Jacob put on the kettle. 'Tea, I think. Then bed.'

'I don't need to go to bed. I'm fine.'

'You need to sleep. You're in shock,' he said.

Izzy didn't reply. He said he'd fill a hot-water bottle. 'Where is it?'

She pointed to the cupboard. He fetched it. Filled it.

'So when the accident comes to mind you chase it away. You think about good things. Bring happy memories into your head. I have seen many, many bad things. I have seen children being shot. When that comes to me, I think about my wife lying beside me in bed, or my wife laughing. Or, I think about when I was a child staying with my grandparents and we walked over the fields to collect honey from their beehives. I make the sun shine in my mind. You must do that.' Then, he said, 'Drink your tea. I'll put this hot-water bottle in your bed.' He asked which room was hers.

She told him it was the second on the left upstairs.

It was a good room, he thought. Small, sloping ceiling and a window that looked out across the fields. Izzy's dressing gown hung behind the door. There was a framed photograph on the dresser – a woman in a straw hat standing beside a wind-up gramophone in a garden. Jacob wondered who it was. She looked nothing like Izzy, so not a relative. A friend, he decided.

He put the hot-water bottle in the bed, then looked round. In the top left-hand drawer of the dresser, under Izzy's knickers and bras, he found a thick pile of notes. Several hundred pounds, he guessed. Silly girl, she should use a bank. He didn't take anything, but it was handy to know where there was a stash of cash should he ever need some in a hurry.

Downstairs again, he told Izzy to go to bed. 'Sleep is what you need. Sleep and happy thoughts.'

He waited while she climbed the stairs and went into her room and, a few moments later, heard the creak of her bedsprings as she slipped under the blankets. He stood a moment, surveying the room.

He didn't want to take anything that would be missed. The pen, he now thought, had been a mistake. Izzy was bound to have missed it, and she'd have guessed he took it.

He looked in drawers, found a watch he was sure belonged to Julia. It was too precious, she wore it often at work. She'd make a fuss if she couldn't find it. There were a few coins on the mantelpiece. He took a shilling. He pocketed a packet of needles from Claire's sewing box along with a reel of black thread. He went through to the kitchen and helped himself to a packet of tea and a tin of Spam from the cupboard. He thought a small vegetable knife might come in handy. On the window-sill, behind the sink, he found a cameo brooch that he put in his pocket. It looked neglected, as if it had been lying there for a while and had been forgotten. That was enough for now.

He let himself out and walked up the path to the car. He had to get back to the funeral gathering to collect the people he'd driven there and take them back to the base. Work went on. But he was pleased with his little haul. Small things were what he wanted. Easy to carry, and good to barter for food and transport when he was making his way back to Poland, and home.

Chapter Thirty
Twenty to two

Izzy was off work for a week. She spent a lot of that time in bed. Julia and Claire put their heads round the door every morning before they left and again in the evening when they got back, asked how she was doing and if she wanted anything. They brought her magazines. But Izzy didn't read them. She slept.

One morning Julia said, 'Your boyfriend phoned when you were sleeping, and I told him you had almost been bumped orff. Nearly burned to a crisp.' She was orff to London for a few days, darling. 'See you when I get back.'

Dolores cruised in one evening and told her she'd missed one hell of a party. The original celebration had been cancelled after Diane's death. But last Saturday it had gone ahead. 'Well, actually, it wasn't much of a party. We were all a bit shocked and drunk. Very drunk. I passed out and didn't do the consummating I'd planned. Still, made up for it soon enough.'

Izzy said, 'That's the ticket.' Remembered Diane, and felt a rush of grief.

Someone sent flowers. 'My,' said Mrs Brent, 'you're popular. A secret admirer, no less.' She gave Izzy the card. 'Get well soon and keep thinking happy thoughts.'

'Any idea who they're from?'

Izzy said she hadn't a clue. She examined the note, suspected it had been written with her tortoiseshell pen. Bloody Jacob.

She allowed Mrs Brent to make a fuss of her, covering her knees with a blanket when she sat on the sofa in the afternoon, plumping her pillows and bringing her beef tea – 'Cures everything.' Izzy moved into the realms of pleasantness. Listening to the world outside – children going to school, the postman coming up the path, the milk lady calling, 'Milko!'

In the mornings, she was content to lie in bed and hear comforting kitchen sounds drifting up from downstairs. Mrs Brent preparing food. Mrs Brent bustling. She'd bring up a tray heavy with toast or scones and tea. She'd pat Izzy's arm. 'Eat up, get your strength back. Can't have you feeling poorly.'

Izzy said she wasn't poorly, 'just shocked'.

On Friday morning Izzy was well enough to feel a little bored. She'd eaten breakfast, bathed and was now back in bed staring out the window at the sky. She was contemplating getting up and going for a walk. 'Bit of fresh air wouldn't go amiss,' Mrs Brent had said. 'Good for you, fresh air.'

She heard footsteps walking up the front path, someone banged on the front door. Mrs Brent opened it. Voices. Then Mrs Brent called, 'You've got a visitor.' More footsteps climbing the stairs, then Jimmy stood leaning on the door frame, smiling. 'Julia phoned and told me you'd almost been bumped off.' He came over to the bed, stooped to kiss her.

'I'm fine,' said Izzy. 'The plane I was in caught fire. I got out. Diane didn't. Now I have to wait till I'm passed fit enough to fly.'

Mrs Brent stood watching this small embrace, then picked up a chair and placed it several feet from the bed, indicating that's where Jimmy should sit. Not on the bed, not a man on the bed of a woman he wasn't married to, that wasn't right. She busied away. Noisily made the bed in Julia's room, then Claire's room, going back and forth past the open door of Izzy's room. Izzy and Jimmy waited till she went back to the kitchen before they kissed properly. But then Mrs Brent came back with tea and ginger cake. 'Made it myself.' She hovered while they ate.

All morning, Mrs Brent cleaned and polished and sang and clattered, reminding the pair in the bedroom that she was there, and no nonsense was allowed. But, eventually, she left. She was due at the Golden Mallard, where she worked washing up.

Izzy held back the blankets, inviting Jimmy into her bed.

'You're sick,' he said.

'No, I'm not. Besides if I am sick, it's in my mind. Not in any of my interesting bits.'

He stripped off and climbed in beside her. They lay awhile, chatting. Conversation was easier now Mrs Brent had gone, and they were lying down, side by side and undressed.

He asked if she was all right.

'Of course I am. I wouldn't have invited you in beside me if I wasn't.'

He told her Julia had been worried about her. 'She said you'd been traumatised by your friend's dying.'

'I was upset. I *am* upset. I got a little depressed and sometimes the picture of it comes into my mind, vividly and I can't get rid of it.'

He said he saw a lot of that.

'My friend Wanda died, then Diane died. People die and you'll never see them again. There's a hole in your life.' She propped herself on her elbow, kissed him. 'I'll miss them both.'

'You never stop missing them,' he said. 'I've lost friends. I've lost guys who were carried into the hospital screaming and there was nothing I could do for them. When this is over, I won't forget them. I'll put a little bit of every day aside to think about them. Just a few quiet moments.' He looked at his watch. 'Twenty to two. That'll be your remembrance time.'

Later, they went to the Golden Mallard and had a late lunch outside on the terrace. The day was warm, the air smelled of newly mown lawns, but Izzy shivered. 'I'm a bit shaky. Haven't been out much. I must stop lying about.'

He agreed. 'Doesn't do to get maudlin.'

She told him she had an interview with the CO on Monday. 'To see if I'm fit to fly. Probably a psychological test, too. I'll tell them about setting aside time to remember Diane. Organised grief, they'll like that.' Then she said, 'Actually . . . ?'

'Actually, what?' he asked.

'Last time we spoke on the phone and I asked you to go to Dolores' party, you said you couldn't. Then you said "actually", and we were cut off.'

'Oh, yes. I was going to say that I have some leave due in August. We could go to Scotland then.'

They spent the rest of their time planning their trip north. Izzy reminded him they wouldn't be able to sleep together.

He said they could have a couple of nights in Edinburgh on the way back. 'To make up for lost pleasures.'

'Another actually, would you mind not talking about my work. My father doesn't know I'm a pilot.'

'He doesn't?'

'I just haven't told him what he doesn't want to hear.' Izzy looked away, watched a couple of wood pigeons strut across the lawn. 'Don't,' she said.

'Don't what?'

'Don't tell me I'm stupid for not telling my folks what I do.'

'I wasn't going to. I didn't tell my folks I'd joined up till a couple of days before I had to report. Couldn't face the fuss.'

'That's it. I can't face the fuss. I'll probably tell my father when I see him. And in that case we might find ourselves leaving early and having more than a couple of nights in Edinburgh.'

She caught him looking at her, scrutinising her. She knew he wanted to ask her again if she was all right. And she knew he wouldn't. Because she'd only tell him once more that she was fine.

When they got back to the cottage, he got into his car. He had to get back, he was on duty that night. They smooched on the doorstep and promised to see one another again soon. Before he drove away, he leaned out of the car and said, 'Twenty to two. That's your time.'

Izzy agreed. 'Twenty to two.' She waved goodbye.

Inside, Julia was sitting by the fire. 'You're up,' she said.

'Out of bed and walking about,' said Izzy. 'Did you have a good time on leave?'

'Oh, yes,' said Julia. 'Guess what I did.'

'You went out dancing? You ate at the Savoy?'

'Yes,' said Julia. 'And I got married.'

Chapter Thirty-one
A Grand Night Out

Saturday night and Elspeth and Lorna resisted the dance. Lorna said that the whirl and the sweat of it would make her feel sick. 'And there's all that eyeing up the boys and them eyeing you up back. I'm not in the mood.'

Elspeth put her arm round her and said that dances would be fine if they were just about dancing. 'But they're not. They're about who you're going to kiss tonight and who's going to take you home.' She thought about this. 'Not that anybody would take us home. Not to where we live.'

'I just want to go somewhere quiet and be sad,' said Lorna.

So Elspeth suggested they squander her recital earnings on a meal at the local hotel. 'There will be carpets and waitresses and cakes.'

'That's what we need,' said Lorna. 'Something to remind us we're human beings.'

The White Cockade Hotel in the centre of the village square was where Elspeth stayed with Izzy on her visits. Tartan carpets stretched from the foyer to the dining room and on up the stairs. Lorna and Elspeth were led to a small table by the window, beyond was a view of the river and mountains and forest in the distance. 'If I didn't work in that bloody forest,

I'd think this view lovely. But trees will never be the same to me now.'

Elspeth agreed. She looked across the dining room at the table where she and Izzy normally sat. Bloody Izzy, she thought. Where are you? No visits for months and no letters for weeks. Too caught up with your love life and your glamorous job to think about me. She felt ignored, rejected, left behind and sorry for herself. She missed Izzy.

So instead she became hearty, clapped her hands and said, 'Let's stuff ourselves.'

A waitress in a black dress and white apron brought them menus. They considered their options. Elspeth chose roast beef, Lorna fish and chips.

'I know, fish and chips, I could have that across the road at the chippy for half the price.'

'But,' said Elspeth, 'this time your fish and chips will be on a posh plate, you get to pour your own tea from a silver teapot and the cutlery will be splendid.'

'Can we have pudding? Pudding's important when you're out for a treat.'

'Pudding's a must. We have to eat pudding. Life without pudding is a dull affair.'

'You can say that again,' said Lorna.

Elspeth suggested they start with a glass of sherry. 'Since we're being posh.'

The waitress brought them two small, ornate glasses filled to the brim. Lorna drank, made a face. 'It's horrible.'

Elspeth agreed. 'Tastes like it's been under the kitchen sink for a year or two. Still, we have to finish it. We're on a spree. Look on the bright side, the fish and chips will put the taste away.'

So, they sipped some more. 'Doesn't taste so bad once your throat knows what's coming. And it warms you up a treat,' said Lorna.

'Does it help with the sadness?'

'A little.'

'How are you coping? Do you miss Freddie awfully?'

'Yes,' said Lorna. 'I save up my sadness for when I'm in bed at night. I pull the covers over my head and I'm alone so I can cry.' Then she asked what Elspeth thought about when she pulled the bedclothes over her head.

'My little cottage. I used to dream about running away to it. I'd light the fire to heat the boiler for a bath, then I'd make tea and just sit.'

Lorna said that just sitting sounded good. 'Freddie and me will never just sit by the fire in the evening listening to the wireless. We'll never have kids. We never even made love. I should have done that. I shouldn't have kept telling him no. I said I was a good girl and good girls saved themselves for marriage. I was a fool. I wish I was a modern girl, like you.'

Elspeth told her not to be silly. 'You were true to yourself. That's what Freddie loved. If you'd been like me, he'd never have looked at you.'

They ate in silence. Food was too serious for conversation. Afterwards, Lorna said food did taste better when it was on a nice plate and the tea in a china cup and your feet were on a carpet. 'It spoils you, proper china. I'll know what I'm missing when I get back to my tin mug.' They had trifle for pudding, drained the last of the tea from the pot and declared themselves stuffed to bursting.

Lorna patted her stomach and said the meal had been grand. 'I feel a lot better. Food always cheers me up.'

Elspeth paid. Outside, the evening was warm, the sun still shining. Newfies were crowding into the pub. They called on Elspeth and Lorna to join them, but they refused. 'I don't fancy all their rude jokes and showing off tonight,' said Lorna.

'The camp will be empty,' said Elspeth. 'We could go down to the spot by the river and swim. Nobody would see us, they're all here, drinking.'

'Are you sure?' said Lorna. 'I don't want hundreds of blokes looking at me in the buff. I've never seen myself naked. We're not naked people in my family. My grandmother used to keep her vest on in the bath.'

Elspeth laughed. 'I don't believe you.'

'She did, too. She thought it a sin to be in the nude. She'd keep her vest on, and wash her bits under it without pulling it up.'

They propped their bikes against their hut, went inside and gathered a towel each, some chocolate Izzy had sent and Elspeth's accordion.

The path down to the river was overgrown, thick with brambles and bracken; nobody had been down it for weeks. But Elspeth's spot was as lovely as ever – lush grass and willows trailing in the water. The night was still warm, the sun fading and a slip of a moon rising. Elspeth stripped off, and waded into the river. She called on Lorna to join her.

'Nah,' said Lorna. 'I can't stop thinking that there's someone watching.'

'There's nobody,' said Elspeth. 'All the men are drinking in the village. Then they'll be at the dance, eyeing up the girls, hoping for a cuddle.'

She spread herself into the coolness, let water lap round her and swam. Up and down she went, rolled on her back and watched the sky. The first stars were coming out, the moon getting brighter. 'Night comes fast!' she called.

She climbed up the bank, dried herself, dressed and shared out the chocolate. 'I'll play some music. Just for us. What would you like?'

'You know that stuff, that classical music that I didn't used to like before I came here and heard you play it. What's that bloke's name?'

'Bach?'

'That's the chap. Play him. It makes me sad. But I don't mind being sad when it's him I'm listening to.'

As Elspeth played the 'Goldberg Variations', Lorna lay back. 'That's how I feel,' she said. 'That music says everything.' She sighed. 'I wish I'd learned to play something. The violin, I'd like to play that.'

'Still could learn,' said Elspeth. 'It's never too late.'

'Nah,' said Lorna. 'Better to dream about it. In my dreams I can make wonderful music, people clap and cheer. I'm a star.'

'You don't have to be a star. You could just learn to play for your own pleasure.'

'I couldn't play the violin in real life as well as I can in my dreams. I like the me I am when I daydream. I can do wonderful things in my dreams. I can play the violin and I haven't had the bother of going to lessons.' She leaned forwards. 'That's the point, you can be what you want to be. I wouldn't daydream about playing the violin badly, would I?'

Elspeth supposed not.

'See, it's better just to imagine things. What do you dream about?'

Elspeth looked momentarily vacant. 'I don't know. I don't daydream any more. I've lost the knack.'

'Oh, you should take it up. It's a good hobby, cheap and fun. Could you play some more? It's lovely being with someone who makes actual music. Especially out here. The notes mix with the leaves and the water. It's calming.'

Duncan Bowman thought the music perfect. This must be the best evening of his life. He'd been walking with his dog when he'd heard the girls' voices, and had slipped into the trees to watch them.

Elspeth swimming, how his heart thundered. He made sure the sinking sun was behind him so there would be no reflection on his binoculars. He held his breath as she slipped into the water, seen, to his delight, her floating on her back, arms rippling by her sides, feet waving slightly. Now she was playing his favourite music, he could hardly contain his joy. 'Oh, my,' he said.

He sat down and listened. Bach drifted up to him, filled his heart. He was utterly happy.

When Elspeth stopped, put her accordion back in its case and said it was time to get back to the hut, he wanted to shout out, 'Don't stop! Play on. Play all night.' He wanted to tell her he'd give her the money she'd earned at the recital, and more if she wanted. But he kept quiet. She'd be furious at him if she knew he'd been spying.

He climbed back up through the trees to the path that led to his cottage. Progress was slow. He'd been sitting too long and was stiff. He stopped, rubbed some warmth into his aching knees. Swore at the pain he was in. As he straightened up, another pain shifted through his chest, heavy, squeezing his heart and shooting down his arm. He fell, could hardly breathe. He slumped to the ground. This is it, he thought, this is the end of me. He lay, sweating, taking shallow breaths, looking up at the stars, feeling helpless. The dog sat quietly looking at him, waiting.

It passed. The pain eased. He struggled to his feet. He started to slowly, slowly head home. Just as well he hadn't given Elspeth that money. Bloody arthritis, bloody heart. His bloody body was letting him down. He'd need every bloody penny he could get his bloody hands on when the time came. He'd have to pay the doctor.

Chapter Thirty-two
Everything I Need

Izzy was happy. She'd been passed as fit to fly. At her interview, she'd mentioned setting time aside to remember Diane. 'It means I am in control of my feelings,' she'd said. 'Work now, tears later. That's what Diane told me.'

The CO had smiled and asked Izzy if she had nightmares.

'Just a couple of bad dreams,' said Izzy. She didn't tell him she'd woken up screaming. But she knew he was smart enough to know she must be suffering. 'I mean,' she added, 'I can't help having a dream or two. You don't walk away from something like that whistling.'

He'd smiled again.

'I'm fine,' Izzy said. 'Really. I want to get back to work.'

He'd said, 'All right, Izzy.'

In the end Izzy thought it was all a matter of priorities. He couldn't afford to lose a pilot. She wanted to get back into the air. She'd told him what he wanted to hear. And he'd known she was telling him what he wanted to hear.

'That's the way of it,' Julia had said that night. 'He figures if you're sane enough to tell him you're sane enough to fly, then, damn it, you're sane enough.'

At half past eight in the morning Izzy, Claire and Julia cycled to work through the village, past the long queue of women behind the notice outside the local shop – TINNED SALMON AT NINE O'CLOCK TODAY. ONE TIN PER CUSTOMER.

Further up the road there was turmoil. Overnight, the American troops had gone. Before they left, soldiers had given villagers blankets, Hershey bars, chewing gum and nylons. Now, the police were trying to confiscate everything.

The three stopped to watch. Policemen, along with military police, were banging on doors, going into each house, searching and coming out again, empty-handed. Meantime, it was mayhem in all the back gardens. As officers entered at the front of houses, goodies were being thrown out of back windows into neighbours' arms and taken into homes that had already been searched.

'Jeepers,' said Izzy. 'What's all this about?'

'People want to keep their goodies,' said Julia. 'Can't blame them.'

'But why are the police taking the stuff?'

'The military must be covering up every sign that the GIs have been here. It must have been a secret.'

'Some secret. They've been drinking and shouting and keeping us all awake at night, *and*, probably half the women in the village are pregnant,' said Izzy.

Julia told her not to exaggerate. 'It's probably only a quarter.' They climbed back on their bikes and started towards the base. Izzy asked Julia if she was enjoying married life.

'So far. Though it's much the same as single life. Only, the sex is legal.'

Last night, Julia had gone to her favourite club in Blackpool with a couple of pilots and Dolores and Alfie, the night before she'd eaten at the Golden Mallard with friends. Married though she was, life was still a whirl. She didn't think that being someone's wife should stop her putting on her glad rags and stepping out to have a good time. Tonight, though, Walter was coming for a few days.

'You'll be able to practise married life. You can warm his slippers by the fire, cook his supper and go to bed early.'

'I don't think so,' said Julia. 'He doesn't own any slippers. We're going out to eat. But we might go to bed early.'

Claire came along behind. She was worrying as usual about her children, but, from time to time, Simon would come to mind. His face was what she imagined. Just that, a good face that made her smile every time she saw it. She wanted to wake up in the morning and see that face. She wanted one night when she didn't have to get out of bed and go home.

Soon, she'd get her wish. They were going to London for a couple of days. They wouldn't stay in her house at Hampstead. That would be taking her unfaithfulness too far. They'd booked a hotel. They'd laze in bed in the morning, eat breakfast together, walk hand in hand, kiss when the need grabbed them. For a while, they'd openly do all the things lovers did.

It was warm. Izzy wore her flying overalls without a jacket. The Spitfire she was delivering had been sitting in the sun and was hot inside. While in the air, she saw several huge convoys – trucks, ambulances and tanks, heading south. Several American bombers were also flying south, and, at the base, there was another. The CO had flown it in earlier, bringing the giant thing easily over the hedge and landing it as if it was light as a butterfly. All these bombers, all the GIs suddenly disappearing, Izzy thought, Something's up.

Walter was at the cottage when she arrived home. His case was in the hall. He was in the kitchen making tea. Julia was with him. 'Walter's staying for a few days,' she said. 'We can play at being an old married couple.' She turned to Walter. 'Izzy was asking me this morning if I warmed your slippers by the fire.'

'I don't own a pair of slippers,' Walter said. 'But, soon as this war's over, I'll get a pair. I'll settle down, get a dog, start smoking a pipe and live a quiet life.'

Julia told him he'd find that impossible. 'You love what you do. You're hooked on it. You love talking to your colleagues about war and you love danger. You get high on it.'

He didn't deny this. Admitted that he'd found the desk-bound months since he'd come back from Africa boring. 'Met some fascinating people. But I miss being where the action is.' This put him off drinking tea, and he reached for the whisky he'd brought. He held it towards Izzy. Did she want a glass? She shook her head, lifted the lid of the pot Mrs Brent had left on the cooker and peered in. Sighed. 'Some kind of sausage thing with bits of apple and onions.'

Julia said Izzy could have her portion. 'We're off out in a while.' She took a glass of whisky and said she'd drink it in the bath.

Walter leaned against the sink. 'Well, Izzy, had a good day?'

'Excellent.' Though, the heat in the Spitfire had made her feel nauseous. And, she was beginning to wonder if the daily drone of engines thrumming in her ears meant she would be deaf before she was thirty. All that, and she ached from sitting all day, every day, in cramped cockpits. More than all that, she'd been terrified. She'd constantly checked her gauges, watching for a sudden drop in the fuel tank. She'd been plagued by images of the burning plane. Her hands had been clammy, sweat oozed from her brow. As soon as she was back on the ground, she'd gone to the ladies' loo, locked herself in, leaned on the wall, breathing, clenching her fists, trying to stop shaking.

'What did you do?'

'Flew a couple of aeroplanes. You know I can't say more. You?' She grinned. Mustn't admit to the fear. Mustn't let it show.

'I had a very good day. A splendid day. Can't say more.'

'You seem very jolly,' said Izzy. 'Well, you would be. You don't have to eat Mrs Brent's sausage thing.'

'Come eat with Julia and me if you don't want your sausage thing.'

Izzy shook her head. 'It's important not to incur Mrs Brent's wrath by spurning her food.'

Julia came in, dressed in a simple red dress, high collar, tight at the waist. Walter whistled.

'Ready?' she asked.

He drained his glass and told her, 'Yes.'

This was the routine for the next few days. Julia and Walter went out to the hotel to eat and, once, to Blackpool to Bertram's, to dance, eat atrocious food and listen to jazz – Louis Armstrong, Duke Ellington and Billie Holiday.

The place was smoky and noisy, but Walter liked it. 'This is much better than the stuffy, tinkling, genteel atmosphere at that hotel you frequent,' he told Julia. 'Though the food's ghastly.'

'Just eat it,' she said. 'It'll do you good to taste the sort of thing ordinary folk have to put up with instead of the perks you enjoy as a war correspondent.' At that, she shoved her own plate away, almost untouched.

She asked what he was going to do when the war was over. 'Find a new war, somewhere?'

He said there would always be some skirmish or other somewhere across the globe. 'But, I'm rather taken with the pipe and slippers we were discussing earlier.'

'I have difficulty imagining it,' she said. 'How would you earn a living?'

'I'd write. I've seen enough to fill a book or two. I could do a jazz column for some magazine. I'd enjoy that.'

'Reviews?'

'Yes.' He leaned over, touched her cheek, ran his thumb over her lips. 'I could write a review of your mouth, and a lavish review of your body.'

She sighed. 'Flattery will get you everywhere.' She took his hand and suggested they dance. A slightly crackling record of 'Muskrat Ramble' by Louis Armstrong and his Hot Five was playing on the gramophone. Walter's feet were tapping.

He swirled her round the floor, gripped her waist, leaned into her, kissed her neck and whispered, 'For God's sake, just once, could you let me lead?'

She said she'd try, but it was hard. She was naturally bossy.

They stayed in on Friday night. Walter said they should have a trial run at domesticity. They sat on the sofa, shoeless feet sharing a footstool placed close to the fire. They held hands, listened to the wireless, drank too much whisky and agreed they could get used to this. They went to bed early.

In the morning Julia woke, yawned, stretched and reached for Walter. He wasn't there, had left a note on the pillow.

My darling,

I just hate to leave you. But things are happening that I can't resist seeing and reporting. It's in my blood, I think. Will be back to be with you very soon. Then I will make an effort at the pipe and slippers life, I promise.

W x

PS I love you very much. Did I ever tell you that?

On Tuesday the sky was black with bombers, hundreds of them roaring south. Izzy and Julia stood at the window of the mess, watching, listening to John Snagge read a special bulletin –

'D-Day has come. Early this morning . . .'

'This is it,' said Izzy.

Julia nodded. 'Walter's there.'

Everyone was grounded that day. Julia stayed in the mess, listening to reports on the wireless, drinking hot orangeade. When, eventually, Julia did go home, there was a letter for her on the small table in the hall, propped up beside the telephone.

My darling,

I suppose by now, you'll have guessed what I'm up to. Soon I will board the Lance Empire *and join the Northumbrian Division I travelled with for a while in North Africa. I won't be able to contact you once I'm aboard. The ship will be sealed, as everyone will know when we will attack, and where and how.*

I am watching troops scramble up the rope ladders onto the ship and I can hear music playing on a minesweeper not far away, and I am thinking about you.

I will be safe – at least six miles offshore, watching events

*from a distance. But this was too good to miss. I have my steel
helmet and a bottle of whisky, I have everything I need. Don't
worry about me.*

I love you.

W x

Chapter Thirty-three
Mrs Middleton

At first, Claire and Simon planned to travel to London separately. They didn't want to be seen together at the railway station. It would look suspicious. But there was a war on, trains were unreliable – noisy, busy, dirty, unpunctual, prone to breaking down, too. They met on the platform of the railway station instead.

The place was a haze of brown and blue uniforms, couples saying goodbye and porters, all of them women, bustling past them.

They sat next to one another on the train, didn't hold hands, though they wanted to. Claire looked out of the window, watched the world she knew so well from above go by. Simon read. From time to time, they'd smile at each other. Right now, they were too filled with anticipation about their two days, and two nights, together to feel any guilt.

In London, they got a taxi to the hotel near Hyde Park that Simon had booked. Wanting to savour Simon's company on the last small part of their journey, Claire asked the driver to drop them at the end of the street, they'd walk the rest of the way. It was away from the main drag of traffic. Now, they held hands.

Their bliss didn't last long. The hotel wasn't there. Instead, there was a huge heap of rubble where it, and a neighbouring building, had been. 'Buzz bomb,' said a passer-by who saw the two gazing in dismay at the ruined building. 'Couple of nights ago. Everyone was killed.'

Claire said, 'How awful.' There was still the acrid smell of cordite in the air. 'Awful, awful,' she said. She wasn't just lamenting the people who'd died in the hotel. She was lamenting her ruined weekend. 'That's it now. It's over.'

'No, it isn't. We can find another hotel. There are lots of them. We could go to the Savoy.'

They started to walk towards Hyde Park.

'We'll get a taxi to Oxford Street,' said Simon.

'Not the Savoy,' said Claire. 'I'm known there. So is Richard.'

She hadn't been there since she'd been based in Skimpton and doubted if anyone would remember her. Indeed most of the staff who'd known her then would probably have been called up, replaced by new faces. But, no doubt, there would be some old friends there – people who knew Richard. 'No definitely not the Savoy.'

'Well, we'll find somewhere,' said Simon.

'It's not the same now,' said Claire. They'd decided to book in as Mr and Mrs Middleton, and Claire had for the last few hours been enjoying her new identity. It had been quite a thrill to be someone else for a while. But this, the rubble that had once been a hotel, was an omen, she thought. The affair was doomed.

'Have you ever seen a buzz bomb?' asked Simon.

Claire shook her head.

'I have. I was flying up the coast, saw this thing buzzing along. Thought it was a plane, at first. A plane, one of ours, came after it, shot it down. The blast was enormous, shook the plane I was in, huge shock waves.'

'Horrible things,' said Claire. 'Come on. I'll take you home. Haven't been there in months and months, time I had a look at it.'

*

The house was musty. Claire swept the covers from the furniture in the living room, opened the curtains to reveal windows with taped-up panes, looked out into the garden. 'It's neglected.'

She took bedlinen from a cupboard in the hall and went upstairs to make up the bed in the spare room. She couldn't face sleeping with Simon in the bed she'd shared with Richard.

They went out for a meal since there was no food in the house. 'Not even a tin of Spam,' said Claire. Afterwards, on the way back to the house, they kept their distance, walking slowly, chatting, not touching. Claire hoped they wouldn't run into anyone she knew. Here she was, Mrs Alton, wife of Richard, mother of two, church-goer, hostess of tea parties and dinner parties, keen gardener and a respectable member of the community.

She preferred Mrs Middleton. She was impulsive, rather wild, danced a lot, never, ever, went to tea parties and was passionately in love with Mr Middleton. Claire liked her a lot.

Mrs Middleton knew all about love. Mrs Alton didn't. The feelings she had now were new to her. The only word of affection she could say with honesty was 'fond'. She was fond of Richard. He was kind, handsome (in his way), humorous and generous. What was there not to be fond of?

Mrs Middleton's passion surprised Claire. She hadn't known she had it in her. The way she unbuttoned Mr Middleton's shirt, pressed her naked self against him, explored him with her tongue, thought about him all the time, felt a strange tremor within when their eyes met, by accident, in the mess. Mrs Middleton was unashamed in lust.

Claire had married Richard to get away from her parents and their bleak, cold, ghastly house. Also, because it had seemed impolite not to say yes when Richard had asked her. 'Marry me,' he'd said. 'Please.' Claire was never very good at saying no.

Mrs Middleton would be. She'd have said no to Richard, and then left home. Mrs Middleton was a woman who knew what she wanted, and got it. She would have waited for love.

Claire did have one wish come true. She woke up next to Simon. After they'd made love, she put on her robe and went downstairs. 'I may be able to find some tea.'

She found some coffee. Oh joy. Brewed a pot and was about to take it upstairs when Simon appeared. He sat at the table, smiled at her and asked if she'd mind listening to the news.

'. . . troops are moving inland in a front broad enough to be more than a bridgehead . . .'

'It will be over soon,' said Claire.

'But not yet. They won't give up without a fight. We've still got time together.' He said he liked her house. 'Bigger than mine.' Then, he said, 'That was the spare room we slept in, wasn't it?'

She said it was. 'Couldn't quite allow myself to sleep with you in the bed I share with Richard. Sorry, I shouldn't have brought you here.'

'Oh no. I like it. I'm glad I've seen where you live. Where you'll be when the war is over. When I think of you, I'll imagine you here.'

He'd meant it kindly. He'd wanted her to know he'd never forget her. But he'd told her what she already knew, and hadn't faced up to. When the war was over, they'd part. Claire felt Mrs Middleton slip away.

Chapter Thirty-four
Useless, Useless

Elspeth decided it was time for a holiday. She was allowed one week off a year. She'd no money for a trip. And, even if she had, it would take so long to get anywhere, she'd have had to turn round and return almost as soon as she arrived. So, she stayed put.

On Monday, she filled a bottle with cold tea, took a sandwich from the kitchen and cycled down past the stables, past Duncan's cottage and on – out of the forest into the hills beyond.

The road was narrow, neglected, gravel gathered at the edges, grass pushing through the tired tarmac. She left it, followed a track that led into the hills. Pedalling was hard work, now. The track was bumpy; there were dips, holes and boulders to avoid. Eventually, she dumped her bike.

Clutching clumps of heather, she climbed, till she found a spot where constant winds had kept the grass short. It had grown into a dense soft carpet, not unlike Lady McKenzie's Wilton. Elspeth sat down, leaned against a stunted pine tree, bent by gales, gnarled and lonely, defying the elements. She took her bottle of tea and sandwich from the deep pocket of her dungarees and surveyed the world about her. The view was splendid. Miles and miles of nothing but heather, hills and sky.

This was the perfect place for a woman to contemplate her

stupid life. Elspeth was never kind to herself when she considered her past. She thought she was a fool, an impulsive fool. Being prone to notions was all right, she supposed. Acting on them was madness.

Once, years ago, in another lifetime, when she was a different person, Elspeth had stood in the hallway of her home in London, eavesdropping on the conversation her parents were having in the living room. Her mother had told her father that Elspeth was the most gifted musician she'd come across in all her years of teaching.

Now, swigging tea, Elspeth wondered why she hadn't just been pleased to hear such a compliment. Young and rebellious at the time, she'd thought that her mother shouldn't tell her father about her gifts. She'd clenched her fists and been enraged that this valuable information hadn't been handed to her.

Only now did it occur to her that neither her mother nor her father had ever encouraged her or praised her talents. It wasn't their way. In fact, now she thought about it, they had barely said a kind word to each other. Elspeth had never seen them kiss or put their arms round one another.

'Didn't want me to get above myself,' Elspeth said aloud. She sighed, bit into her sandwich and added, 'But in this world, above yourself is where you have to be. Otherwise, you'll get trampled.'

Two weeks after Elspeth had stood listening to her parents discussing her, her father dropped dead in Hammersmith underground station – a heart attack. Four months after he was buried, her mother – bent and grey with grief – had announced she was going to Scotland to live in the small Perthshire village where she'd been born. 'Going to Fortham, back to my roots. I want the peace of the countryside around me. And this house is too full of memories. It breaks my heart to live in it.'

It was only now that it crossed Elspeth's mind that perhaps the memories weren't good. Perhaps that house had been filled with disappointments, lost ambitions, a life-long wishing for tenderness. 'Gosh,' she said. 'Never thought of that.'

Elspeth had refused to go with her mother to Scotland. 'I'm not giving up my job. There are women who'd die to work on the perfume counter at Selfridges. Mr Selfridge himself stopped by once and said, "How're you today, Miss Moon?" He knows my name, a man as famous and rich as that.'

It was agreed that Elspeth would stay in London. She would lodge with Sylvia Hatton-Smythe, an old friend of her mother's. The house was in Chelsea; Elspeth's room was on the third floor. It was small, and was rented at a reduced rate as she had agreed to entertain Mrs Hatton-Smythe's friends in her lushly patterned lounge – thick velvet drapes, Persian rugs hung on ornately papered walls – on candlelit Thursday evenings, playing Mozart, Chopin and Brahms on the pianoforte, as Mrs Hatton-Smythe called it.

Sometimes, people would notice her playing and clap. But mostly they stood in small groups sipping champagne or cocktails, discussing the work of Augustus John, George Orwell and that simply outrageous book *The Laughing Torso*, by that bohemian woman Nina Hamnett.

Sitting on her stool, fingers (at that time, long, slender and perfectly manicured) flying over the keys, it was plain to Elspeth that very few people talking about the book had actually read it. Then, she'd thought that darling and very clever. Now, she'd changed her mind.

Still, it was in that house that she met her first love. Gregor Fox was an artist. He rented a room along from Elspeth's on the third floor, only his was large and faced north. 'North light is vital,' he said.

For some time, she had been aware of him watching her come and go. In the morning, when she left for work, he'd be standing at the window, looking down at her tripping along the street in her red coat with matching hat and gloves.

They shared a bathroom that was opposite Elspeth's room. One night, as Elspeth slipped across the hall with only a towel wrapped round her, Gregor swung open his door and said, 'Drop it.'

Elspeth stopped, clutched the towel closer and said, 'Drop what?'

'That towel you are hiding behind. Drop it, I want to see you.'

Elspeth said she'd do no such thing. 'I'm not that sort of girl.'

He said, 'Of course you are. All girls are that sort of girl, you're just afraid to admit it. Drop the towel, I want to see you. I'm an artist, I will look at you professionally.' He stepped forwards, grabbed the towel and whipped it away. He stood, hands on hips, scrutinising her. 'Perfect, absolutely perfect. In fact, exquisite. I will paint you.'

It had taken him days to persuade Elspeth. He'd banged on her door demanding to be allowed in, he had to explain his art to her. 'It's not anything in the least sexual. It's art. Of course you will be without clothes, but I don't see the nudity. I see the woman.'

So, Elspeth agreed. He told her to look defiant. 'Being unclothed is natural. It's how we come into the world. Be proud. Laugh at anyone who might be shocked.'

It wasn't long before Elspeth began to enjoy their sessions together. She loved being naked, loved the feel of air on her skin.

She loved that he told her she was perfect, exquisite, beautiful. And she loved that she was doing something that would horrify her mother.

Now, chewing her sandwich, she thought that was the real reason she'd done it. She'd been at an age when horrifying her mother was a good reason for doing anything.

Gregor took her to the Fitzroy Tavern, pointed out Augustus John. Once they stood at the bar next to Dylan Thomas. Another time they'd spotted George Orwell sitting alone at a table. Elspeth was impressed. Fancy that, she thought, me mingling with intellectuals and artists.

After an evening at the Wheatsheaf, giddy from a surfeit of gin, Elspeth let Gregor take her to his bed. The affair lasted for six months. Elspeth was proud of herself. She worked at the perfume counter in Selfridges, she was an artist's model, she'd rubbed shoulders with famous people. She had a lover. She was a woman of the world.

Soon, though, she was just another abandoned girlfriend. One evening, returning from work, clicking along the street, anticipating the fabulous things she and Gregor would get up to that night, she met him. He was carrying a large suitcase and a portfolio. 'Off to Paris,' he said. 'Montparnasse, that's the place for an artist to be.'

Elspeth asked when he was coming back.

He told her, 'Never. I may move on to Provence, or Greece. But this country is too dull and cold. I need light and warmth.'

Elspeth sniffed. Uninvited tears welled, and slipped down her cheeks.

'Oh for God's sake,' said Gregor. 'Don't cry, that won't do. When someone wants to up and go, you smile and say goodbye.

You're not bloody falling in love with me, are you? I wouldn't recommend that.' He hurried past her, disappeared round the corner, didn't look back. Elspeth never saw him again.

It took months for her heart to recover, but, in time, she met Michael Harding. He was kind, considerate, moderately handsome and quite well off.

'And I let him go because I wanted to learn the accordion.' Elspeth finished her bottle of tea, dusted crumbs from her dungarees and declared herself a fool. 'A bloody idiot, flitting from notion to notion. Not just a butterfly, a stupid butterfly.'

She considered the view. Now, it was no longer splendid. It was bleak. An unwelcome wind whipped round her, shoved through her hair. She shivered. Looked down at her muddied boots and dungarees and told herself she hated her life. 'I have plummeted from exotic to ordinary. Not like bloody Izzy. She has risen from shy little dumpling of a girl to flying ace. Bloody Izzy with her bloody American boyfriend going to bloody dances, eating at bloody posh hotels, living the bloody high life. And it's all down to me. I'm the one who brought her out of her shell. I taught her about love and life and art and music. I encouraged her to learn to fly. And what does she do? She ignores me. She used to visit every few weeks, then it was every month or so. Now it's never. And not a letter in ages. Bloody Izzy has forgotten all about me.'

In a rage she stood up, sniffed, wiped her self-pitying eyes. It was time to head back to bloody, bloody camp to eat bloody Spam and bloody boiled cabbage.

She slid on her bum down the heathered slope, climbed onto her bike and started the long cycle home. She didn't have a watch, but could make a rough estimate of the time by the sun. It was about six o'clock, she reckoned. Puffing as she pedalled home-wards, she vowed that the minute peace was declared, she'd go back to London, and she would be outrageous.

She'd come further than she'd thought. It took her two hours to get to Duncan's cottage, a few miles from the camp. She decided to take the short cut through the woods. She'd have to walk, pushing the bike, but it would take a couple of miles off the journey.

Dark, that moment when the air turns granular, bats were coming out, and the forest was full of noises. Such things no longer scared Elspeth. Rustlings would be deer, foxes or, perhaps, a badger. She was hungry. Had missed the evening meal and hoped Lorna had saved her something.

For a fleeting moment, when a hand gripped her shoulder, Elspeth thought it was Tyler. She turned. Duncan held her close, pressed his lips onto hers. Hot whiskied breath in her face. She tried to push him away. He held on, moved his lips to her neck, saying, 'Please.'

She struggled, pushed, twisted her face from side to side, avoiding his lips. He said, 'Please,' again. Then pushed her to a tree, slamming her against the trunk, knocking the breath from her.

He tore at the top of her dungarees, grabbed her breasts, rubbed himself against her, shoved his hand between her legs. Told her he wanted her. 'I just want you.'

She kicked his shins.

He slapped her and told her he knew she wanted him, knew she wanted any man. He'd seen her with that Newfie. He yanked down the straps of her dungarees and tore at her shirt.

It was a silent, desperate scuffle. He tried to hold her by the wrists to stop her slapping him. Then his hand gripped her breast. Hard, calloused against her skin. He pulled her to the ground, pressing against her as he wrestled with his belt, unbuttoned his trousers. He yanked her dungarees down past her knees.

She bit his lip, scratched his face, screamed and shoved him away. He punched her. The blow landed on her cheek. She slapped him. He grabbed her wrists, held them above her head, looked down at her. Then the writhing and wrestling stopped. He hated her. Punched her again and again. 'What kind of woman are you? You've done this to me. This never happens to me.'

She pushed him from her, struggled to her feet and kicked him. Caught him on the knee – the troubled, aching, withering knee. She was shouting and sobbing.

'You're not even a man. You can't manage, can you? Can't get it up? Useless, useless.'

He howled. Bent to grip his leg and she kicked him again, caught him on the face, and sent him reeling. He was on the ground, clutching his knee. 'Please.'

She kicked him again. Said he couldn't have her. 'Please, you say please when you're doing that?'

He said, 'Please,' one more time. 'I just couldn't take all that wanting any more.'

'Useless, useless,' Elspeth repeated. 'You don't just take a woman because you want her.' She picked up her bike and ran down the path to the road.

She cycled to camp, and only stopped once she'd passed the stables, to straighten her clothes and run her fingers through her hair. She was shaking, and only now realised she was hoarse. Her throat hurt. She'd been screaming much more than she realised.

Once in the camp, she propped her bike outside the ablutions hut and went inside to wash. Her face hurt where his blows had landed. She touched it softly, felt the swelling. There would be bruises tomorrow. Her shirt was torn at the shoulder, and she was bleeding. He'd bitten her. 'Bastard.'

When she'd finished, she went outside, stood awhile breathing, collecting herself. Then she went into the hut where the girls were getting ready for bed. The stove was on, lamps were lit, Lorna was waving. 'Here you are. I was getting worried.' Then, shocked, she said, 'My God, Elspeth, what's happened?'

Elspeth said, 'I fell off my bike.'

Chapter Thirty-five
Just Round the Corner

Julia had thought that Walter would travel to France, watch the first stages of the invasion and come home again. But he hadn't. She'd heard nothing from him in two weeks. Nights, she stayed home listening to the news, imagining Walter making his way across Normandy, crossing fields, taking cover behind hedges.

Every time she turned into the lane leading to the cottage, she expected to see him standing by the gate, waiting for her. And, when he wasn't, she'd think he'd have taken the key from under the stone by the front door and he'd be inside, sitting at the kitchen table, drinking whisky and brimming with tales to tell her. She'd go inside, run down the hall looking for him. She was always disappointed.

She asked Izzy how things were at Jimmy's hospital. 'Are there a lot of casualties?'

'Goodness, yes,' said Izzy. 'It's overflowing with patients. So many, they've put tents between the Nissan huts. Big sheets of black canvas, and people in beds under them. Jimmy's working round the clock; I hardly saw him last time I went over there. Nurses running about, people all bandaged up and Jimmy looked awful. He'd hardly slept for days.' Then, forgetting to be tactful, she said, 'It was carnage on Omaha Beach.' Seeing Julia's expression, she added, 'But Walter was at Gold Beach. That wasn't so bad. He'll be fine. Anyway, he wouldn't have gone ashore till the beach was taken.'

Julia said she supposed so. 'But I haven't heard from him.'

'I don't think he'll be anywhere he could sit down and write a letter,' said Izzy. 'But he'll be thinking about you.'

Julia sighed. 'I hate this. I hate looking out for the postman, hoping for a letter, and I hate waiting for the phone to ring. I hate being in love. I always said it was something to be avoided.'

'My friend Elspeth said it was the most wonderful misery you could ever experience.'

'True,' said Julia. 'I think I'd like Elspeth. You must introduce us one day.'

Izzy said she would.

'What else did Elspeth say?'

'Oh,' said Izzy. 'She said flying was better than sex.'

'Do you agree with that?'

'Depends on which one I'm doing when I think about it. I don't know what Elspeth thinks now she's chopping down trees in the far north of Scotland. I don't expect there's a lot of opportunity for sex.'

'Aren't there any men working near her?'

'Oh, yes. Hundreds and only forty or so women.'

There was a long silence.

Julia said, 'Izzy, you're a goose.' She slapped her hands on the table. 'You've cheered me up. C'mon, let's go out. I can't sit here feeling glum any more. It's not good for me. We'll have supper at the hotel. My treat.'

The Golden Mallard was packed, but they got a table – Julia always got a table – and ordered roast chicken.

'Do you think it's real roast chicken? Or some mocked-up chickeny thing?' asked Izzy.

'Of course it's real,' said Julia. 'But it will be scrawny. Chickens are on rationing just like the rest of us.'

They tried not to speak about the war. Julia didn't want to be reminded of it at the moment. She asked Izzy about her trip to Scotland in August.

'We're going to visit my folks. It will be good, relaxing.'

'Yes,' said Julia. 'We could all do with a bit of relaxation these days. Shall we go through to the bar? I feel like a drink.'

The bar was even more packed than the dining room. Julia pushed through the crowd, saying hello as she did so. She knew a lot of people. She ordered a whisky for herself and bought Izzy a shandy and said they should take their drinks outside to the terrace. 'It's too smoky in here. And there are too many people I know, I don't feel like chatting tonight.'

The sun was dipping low, the sky red. Some swans flew over. Izzy said, 'I love swans. They're so serene. Not like me.'

'You'd like to be serene?' asked Julia.

'Yes, sort of quietly knowing. Sophisticated.'

'You'd have to drink something a little more daring than shandy,' said Julia.

'I like shandy. It's the only alcoholic thing I can drink. Whisky makes me sleepy and that's not sophisticated at all.'

Julia asked if Elspeth was sophisticated.

'Yes. She once posed nude for an artist in Chelsea. She went to fashionable bars and she listens to Mahler. But she jumps from notion to notion. That's how she ended up working in the forest. She thought it would be wonderful to commune with nature, and she thought she'd get a plaid shirt.'

'And she didn't,' said Julia.

'No. She says it's bitterly cold in winter, it's so cold it hurts to breathe. And the food's atrocious. There's no electricity and no plumbing. She dreams of hot baths.'

'I have problems committing,' said Julia, 'I wouldn't even buy furniture for my flat. I thought, what's the point? I might die. Walter insisted I get a sofa at least. Something to sit on.'

'Something to sit on's good,' said Izzy.

'He said I should commit to being alive, and I should commit to him. So I did.'

'You bought a sofa.'

'I got married,' said Julia. 'No sofa, yet.' She looked at her watch. It was almost nine o'clock, normally the start of an evening out for her. 'We should get back.' Walter might be there. She might have missed a call. Or, he might call later. She needed to be at home when the phone rang.

Just before they turned the corner at the end of the lane, Julia's hopes rose. Walter would be standing, leaning on the gate, waiting for her. When he saw her coming towards him, he'd take his hands out of his pocket and wave.

He wasn't there. The phone wasn't ringing. As she passed it in the hall, Julia lifted the receiver, listened, checking the dialling tone. It was still working.

This was her routine for the next two weeks. Coming home from work, she'd freewheel down the hill, thinking that surely Walter would be there at the gate or at the front door watching out for her to arrive. When he wasn't there, she'd run inside hoping he'd be there. When he wasn't, she'd go into the hall, lift the phone receiver, checking the line.

When the package arrived, Julia turned it over in her hands, then took it upstairs to her bedroom. She wanted to be alone when she opened it.

It was from the news magazine Walter worked for and contained several of his notebooks, a couple of letters he'd written to her and a letter from the editor. He was sorry to inform her that Walter had been killed on 18 June, as he crossed a field in Normandy. 'He was,' the editor wrote, 'an outstanding war correspondent and a wonderful man. He would be sorely missed not just as a gifted colleague, but as a remarkable raconteur, drinking companion and friend.' He was deeply sorry for Julia's loss. 'I am enclosing two letters he wrote to you while covering the Normandy landings, along with his notebooks. Walter was buried by his companions in the field in a cemetery outside Caen.'

Julia sat on her bed, holding Walter's letters. She didn't cry. Not yet, she told herself. She sighed and admitted she'd known for some time that Walter was dead. In fact, on that morning when she'd reached across the bed to touch him, and found an empty space, a rumpled pillow and his blankets thrown back, she'd known he wouldn't come back to her.

She went downstairs and gave the others her news. 'I think I'll go for a walk,' she said. 'I need to think.' Izzy offered to go with her. Julia shook her head, 'I'd rather be on my own.'

She walked by the river, hands in pockets, kicking the occasional stone. If anyone else was on the path, she wasn't aware of them. She passed the little tearoom and the hotel, walked till the path ended in a tumble of fallen trees, branches and brambles. She stopped, picked up a stone and tossed it into the water, watched the ripples spread where it landed and sank to the bottom. That's it, she thought. I'm on my own and I better get used to it. She'd been married for three weeks.

Back at the cottage, she went upstairs, switched on the light and lay on the bed to read Walter's letters. The first had been written when he was still aboard the ship. He described the landings at Omaha Beach – planes strafed the beach first, then the whole place was lit by chandelier lights, men poured off their ships . . . the men aboard the ship would do the same in half an hour at Gold Beach.

I will follow later. The mood here is tense. Men who know they might die soon have slipped into silence, thinking, I suppose, of their wives and lovers back home. Can't resist one last battle. Then, I promise, I'll settle down. I have a notion for a rose-covered cottage somewhere. I will get a Labrador, stroll the lanes, grow vegetables in the garden and write thrillers. You can learn to bake scones. We will be happy in our little cliché of contentment.

I love you and very soon I'll be with you again.

The second letter was written in a tent somewhere outside Caen. He described the onslaught.

They are flattening the place. The mood is of elation, triumph, fear (a lot of that), bravado (we don't admit to being afraid) and a certain amount of anger that we need to be here at all. The war is definitely coming to an end. Perhaps even by Christmas. This will be our first Christmas together. I propose we spend it alone. We shall have a tree surrounded by glorious presents, we shall eat and drink ourselves silly and make love by the fire.

I think we should be in Paris next month. After that, I'll

357

come home. I just want to see it liberated. I'll bring you some Camembert and, since I am in Normandy, a bottle of Calvados, if I can find it.

I love you. You are constantly in my thoughts. I will keep myself safe for you. Keep yourself safe for me. There is so much for us to do together, I would make a list but it would stretch for pages.

Love

W x

In the morning Julia got up, dressed and went to work. She flew a Spitfire to a base not far away in Lancashire. And every time she thought of Walter, when tears threatened, she'd swallow, take a deep breath and say, 'Steady, steady.' The words her nanny said if she tripped running down the stairs, hurt her knee and started to howl.

In the evening she cycled home. Approaching the corner to turn into the lane, she thought, Walter will be there. For months and months, that was her thought, Walter is just round the corner, waiting for me.

Chapter Thirty-six
What Have I Done?

Elspeth rose early, packed her case in the grey light while the other girls slept. She stepped out into the morning, cool air on her aching face, and went into Duncan's hut.

'Look at me.'

He was behind his desk, filling in a report, and put down his pen, lifted his scratched and bruised face. 'I'm not looking so good myself.'

'You think I care about that? Look what you've done to me.'

He turned away and muttered he was sorry.

'Don't say sorry. Sorry is nothing to me. I need to get away. I can't let anybody see me like this.'

'Didn't the girls see you last night?'

'The hut was dark. They only saw me in the half-light. I said I'd fallen off my bike.'

He nodded. 'What do you want?'

'I want to go to my cottage till the bruising fades. I want you to give me the money for the fare. And I want you to drive me to the bus stop.'

'What if I say no?'

'But you won't say no, will you? I won't just tell everyone what you did to me, punching me, biting me. I'll tell them that in the end you couldn't manage. You couldn't get it up. You're useless. So give me the money.'

'You'd humiliate me?'

'Just as you tried to humiliate me. Yes, of course I would.'

He reached into his back pocket, pulled out his wallet and threw two pounds onto his desk. Elspeth looked at it, shook her head and stared at him. He put another three pounds on top of the two already there. 'Blackmail,' he said.

'You bet,' said Elspeth. 'What are you going to do about it? Tell the police? Now drive me to the bus stop. I'm going to my cottage. I'll be back when my bruises have gone down.'

He reached into a drawer and threw a letter on to the desk beside the small pile of notes. 'Arrived for you yesterday.'

They drove in thick, vile silence to the village. Red flares of morning flickered through passing trees. Elspeth looked out the side window; Duncan stared ahead at the road. At the bus stop, Elspeth climbed out.

'The bus isn't due till nine,' said Duncan.

'The wait might calm me down,' Elspeth told him.

He put the van into gear, turned to her and said, 'It was the drink.'

'Oh, that's all right, then. It was the drink. You're not to blame at all. There's not one iota of shame in you, is there?' She slammed the door.

Duncan drove off. Yes, he was ashamed. He was ill with shame. He'd just long forgotten how to show it.

The bus got into Fortham at noon. Elspeth walked, collar turned up, head down, watching her feet move over the pavement –

familiar ground, same old cracks. She didn't meet anyone, but curtains moved. Her return had been noted.

She walked up the path to her front door, noted the scrambling weeds in her front garden and the overgrown hedge. The lock was stiff; she had to bang the door with her hip to open in. But, at last, she was inside, alone and safe.

She walked down the hall, put her case in the bedroom and, in the living room, sat on her sofa and wept. When she stopped, when she'd no tears left, she wiped her eyes with the back of her hands, sniffed and looked round. God, the place was dusty. It smelled of stale air and damp. The curtains were drawn. It was gloomy.

She got up, pulled back the curtains and opened the windows. In the kitchen, she filled the kettle to boil water for a pot of tea. She fetched coal from the cellar and lit a fire in the living-room hearth. She fetched sheets from the linen cupboard and made up her bed. She dusted, wiped, polished and swept the kitchen floor. The activity made her feel better, hungry even.

Her cupboard, however, was bare, save for a packet of tea. 'Shop or starve,' she said. 'Better shop.' She combed her hair, powdered her nose, put on her jacket and stepped out. The shops were only a few minutes' walk from the cottage. If she walked quickly, she might manage to avoid meeting anyone and having to explain her bruises.

She had her story ready, and had to use it in every shop she visited. She had the same conversation in every shop. 'Miss Moon,' said the butcher, the woman in the fruit shop and Jean at the grocer's, 'you're back. Long time no see.' They'd peer at her and declare, 'What's happened to you? You've been in the wars.'

Elspeth always answered that she'd fallen off her bike. 'It was dark, couldn't see the road properly. I took a bit of a tumble.'

The shopkeepers told her she'd have to be more careful in future. Elspeth headed for home with a basket of treasures – a lamb chop, two ounces of bacon, potatoes, bread, onions and an egg. 'Treats,' she said.

As she walked home, she planned her days ahead. She'd laze in bed, read by the fire, bathe in hot water, she wouldn't go out much – she'd pamper herself. She hurried up the hill to her house, eager to get home, lock the door and shut out the world. She wanted to be alone.

'Elspeth,' came a voice behind her. 'Good heavens, Elspeth.'

She turned. Izzy's father was striding towards her. Her heart sank. She had never liked this man.

'How's our little lumberjill? How is life in the forest?' he asked.

She stopped, smiled a thin smile and told him she was fine and life in the forest was hard, 'but healthy'.

'That's the spirit,' he said. 'Doing your bit for the country.'

Elspeth said, 'Yes.'

'It's man's work, though.'

'I manage,' said Elspeth. 'All the girls manage.'

He asked how long she was home for.

'Just a few days.'

'But we can expect to see you in church on Sunday?'

'If I'm still here.'

'That's the spirit,' he said and put an enthusiastic hand on her shoulder. She flinched. Pretending not to notice, he asked if she'd heard from Izzy recently.

'No, not for a while. I expect she's busy.'

Elspeth remembered the letter Duncan had given her that

morning. She'd recognised the writing on the envelope. It was from Izzy – bloody Izzy leading her bloody glamorous life.

'We haven't had a letter in a while, either,' said Hamish. 'She usually writes once a week. Keeps in touch.'

Elspeth said, 'Yes.'

He looked at her, putting his face close to hers. 'Are you all right? You're looking a bit bruised. Accident in the forest? I expect it's dangerous work.'

'It can be,' said Elspeth. 'But this wasn't a forestry accident. I fell off my bike.'

He said, 'Ah, can't be too careful.'

It wasn't a good moment for her. She was tired. She hurt. She longed to get inside her cottage, to be safe and on her own. Here she was talking to a man she disliked, at a time when she wasn't feeling kindly to men, all men.

This man standing before her, hands in pockets, talking too loudly, seemed arrogant, overly buoyant.

'Of course,' he said, 'Izzy's bound to be busy right now with all that's going on. It's a big responsibility being an ops officer, directing planes all over the place, checking the weather, keeping in touch with other bases. Hard work, but at least she's desk-bound. Thank goodness we don't have to worry about her having any nasty accidents.'

Elspeth snapped. 'Don't you?'

'No. It's not as if she's flying the damn planes.'

'Isn't she?' said Elspeth. 'Well, that's just fine. Everything in the world is rosy. God's in his heaven and Izzy isn't flying planes. That'll be right.'

'What do you mean by that?' asked Hamish.

'You work out what I mean by that,' said Elspeth. 'You think what you want to think. Or at least, you think what Izzy wants you to think.' She walked away.

At home, she dumped her shopping in the kitchen. She took off her jacket, draped it over the back of a chair, reached down and pulled Izzy's letter from her pocket. She opened it and sat at the table to read it.

> *Dear Elspeth,*
>
> *I'm so sorry I haven't written in ages. I've been in the most awful accident. A plane I was in burst into flames. I got out. Well, I was dragged out. But my friend Diane was burned to death.*

Elspeth said, 'Oh, God.'

> *The smell, I'll never forget the smell. I was off work for a while. But now I've been passed fit to fly. But, Elspeth, I get horrible nightmares. And sometimes, I can't stop shaking.*

Elspeth said, 'Oh, God. Oh, God.'

> *I think of you all the time. I wish you were here. I wish I could talk to you. You were always such a friend to me.*

Elspeth put down the letter. She put her hand over her mouth. She was a terrible person. A few moments ago, she had betrayed her best friend. 'Oh, God,' she said again, 'what have I done?'

Chapter Thirty-seven
Mary Queen of Scots' Teaspoon

Five o'clock, Izzy and Jimmy got out of the bus at Fortham and looked round.

'It hasn't changed. Never does,' said Izzy.

'You thought it might have changed?' said Jimmy.

'I just hoped it hadn't.'

She looked up and down the street as the bus rumbled away. 'There's Mary's sweet shop where I used to spend my pocket money. Digby's the newsagent, the butcher's and Macgregor's the draper where I used to get my school uniform. And, there's the pub.'

'Where you had your first drink,' said Jimmy.

'Hell, no. I've never been in there. My father would disapprove.'

'Your father disapproves of pubs?'

'No,' said Izzy. 'He loves pubs. He's a regular in that one. He just doesn't like his daughter drinking in them. In fact, he disapproves of any woman going into a pub. He's very old-fashioned.' She shrugged.

They walked up the hill to the manse, passed the cobbled square where there was a small hotel, a teashop and an antiques shop. Jimmy said they must go there. 'I might find something to take back to America. Something old and Scottish.'

'Like my dad,' said Izzy. 'Don't tell him I said that.'

He put his arm round her and said he wouldn't.

It was warm, the sun casting their shadows before them as they walked, trees spread up the hillsides beyond the village, the first slight glimmer of autumn in among the haze of green. There was nobody about.

'Where is everybody?' asked Jimmy. 'The place is empty.'

'It's five o'clock,' Izzy told him. 'Teatime. Everybody's at home having their tea.'

She stopped walking, sniffed deeply. 'Lovely. You can smell life here. New-mown grass, somebody's just cut their lawn. Pine from the trees, and coal fires and cooking fat. I love that. It makes me homesick every time I smell it.' She was a little disappointed that the street was so quiet. She'd wanted to show off her American boyfriend.

At the manse, Izzy banged the knocker, burst in through the front door and announced, 'I'm home.'

Her father appeared at the door of his study, smiling. Her mother bustled from the kitchen wiping her hands on her apron. Then she held out her arms ready to embrace her daughter. 'Here you are.' She held Izzy close, then stood back looking at her. 'Still not in uniform.'

'I'm on my holidays,' said Izzy. She introduced Jimmy.

'Pleased to meet you, sir, ma'am.' He shook hands with them both.

Izzy's father said, 'I always like good manners in a person. But none of this sir and ma'am business, we're Hamish and Joan.'

Joan headed back to the kitchen. 'I'll put the kettle on. Tea will be along in a minute. I got a lovely bit of boiled ham at the butcher's. Been saving my coupons.' She turned to Hamish.

'Show Jimmy his room. Bathroom's upstairs. I expect you'll want to freshen up. Trains are filthy these days.'

Jimmy's room was on the ground floor, Izzy's upstairs. They exchanged a small look of resignation, but said nothing. They were both tired. It had been a long journey. Izzy had caught the first train of the morning from Blackpool at six o'clock. She'd met Jimmy at York and they'd travelled north together, sleeping most of the way. At Edinburgh, they'd boarded the train to Perth, after that, a bus to Fortham.

Jimmy said he could do with a wash.

The first sign of discord came when they were gathered at the dining-room table. Hamish asked Jimmy how he and Izzy had met. Izzy kicked Jimmy under the table. He looked surprised, leaned down to rub his shin and said it was at a dance. 'We hold them at the base most Saturdays. Izzy came along with Claire.'

'Her parents live near the base,' said Izzy. 'She's a pilot.'

'So,' Hamish asked Jimmy, 'what do you think of this business of women flying?'

Jimmy said from what he'd seen, they seemed to be very good at it.

'I doubt that,' said Hamish. 'Women don't have the logic or the reactions for flying. They don't anticipate danger like men. Women are made to nurture.'

Izzy said, 'That's rubbish.'

Hamish said he knew what he was talking about. 'Women weep easily. Not good in an emergency. Have any of the women you work with had an accident?'

Izzy said that her friend Diane had been killed. She prodded her food with her fork. She didn't want to think about this. 'Some of the men seek out danger. They take risks – do rolls and loops in the air. They fly under bridges rather than over them. They hedge hop.'

Her mother drew in her breath. 'A woman dying in a plane crash, that's horrible.'

'It wasn't her fault,' said Izzy. 'The plane was wrecked so the results of the enquiry weren't conclusive. But they think she'd had a leaking fuel pipe.'

'See,' said Hamish, prodding the air with his fork, 'that's what I mean. A woman just doesn't have a mechanical brain. A man would have spotted that right away and would have had it fixed before he took off.'

Izzy said that wasn't true. She didn't like the way this conversation was heading.

Hamish said, 'I hate to think of a woman in danger. I hate to think of something awful happening to one of them. They are gentle souls. A man's job is to take care of them. How would a man live if he knew a woman he loved died a horrible, violent death?'

Joan ended the dispute in the way she dealt with all fraught situations. She brought out her fruit cake and scones. 'Have a scone. Try a slice of fruit cake, made it myself.' She spoke slightly too loudly. Shot her husband a swift and searing look. Enough, it said.

Jimmy asked Hamish if there was any chance of a game of golf. 'I'm in Scotland. I have to play a round while I'm here.'

'Golf,' said Hamish. 'Of course. We have a splendid course here. I'll phone the captain of the club in the morning and arrange something. Always delighted to accommodate our American friends.'

*

Next morning, the discord started up again. Hamish arranged for Izzy and Jimmy to play a round of golf and lent Jimmy his clubs. Izzy, who was finishing her breakfast, said, 'Excellent, I'll get changed.'

Ten minutes later she appeared in the kitchen wearing a pair of pale-coloured slacks and a blue shirt, with a red jumper draped round her shoulders.

'And where do you think you're going dressed like that?' said Hamish.

'To play golf,' said Izzy.

'You are wearing trousers.' He pronounced each word slowly, emphasising his disapproval.

Izzy said she knew that. 'I just put them on.'

'Take them off. No daughter of mine is going about wearing trousers. I hate to see women in trousers. It isn't right.'

'Lots of women wear trousers these days,' said Izzy. 'Katharine Hepburn dresses like this.'

'You are not Katharine Hepburn,' said Hamish. 'Put on a skirt.'

Izzy said, 'No. This is comfortable.'

Hamish sighed and asked Jimmy what could he do with a daughter like Izzy. 'Always does exactly what she wants. A son, I could understand, but a daughter puzzles me.'

Jimmy said he never did understand women. 'But then my wife always used to say she didn't understand men. She thought we were too matter-of-fact.'

'You're married?' asked Hamish.

'I was.'

'Divorced?'

'My wife died,' said Jimmy.

Hamish said he hadn't known that. 'I'm very sorry.' Then, telling Jimmy to enjoy his game, headed for his study.

Izzy and Jimmy had an enjoyable round. He played well, she didn't. This suited him. They joked about how often she missed the ball and she pointed out that Mark Twain had said golf was a waste of a walk. 'I may be rotten at the golfing bit. But I'm enjoying the walk.'

He said he'd grant her that. He showed her how to hold the club and keep her eye on the ball. He said, 'Wiggle your hips.'

'Is that necessary?'

'I don't know. I just like to see you do it.'

They deliberately didn't mention Izzy's father. It would have spoiled their fun.

Afterwards, they went back to the clubhouse. Jimmy wanted a beer. But Izzy wasn't allowed into the bar. 'Sorry,' said the steward. 'It's men only.' When they headed for the lounge, the steward blocked the way and told them there was a dress code. 'We don't allow women in trousers to enter the lounge.' Izzy snorted, wheeled round and walked out. Jimmy followed. They walked home, enjoying a friendly bicker about Izzy's gender and dress sense.

'If you weren't a woman wearing trousers, I'd be enjoying a beer right now,' said Jimmy.

'I could have waited outside. Watched you swig your beer through the window and looked sad. You'd have felt guilty.'

'Ah, playing the guilt card. Trousers or not, you're a woman.'

She said she'd thought he already knew that.

When they got back, Joan took Izzy aside. She wanted a word in the kitchen. She shut the door. 'That man you're with has been married.'

'I know,' said Izzy. 'But he isn't now, so it's all right.'

'How old is he?'

'Thirty-four or thirty-five.'

'That's quite a bit older than you.'

'Ten years,' said Izzy.

Joan picked up a cup that was already clean and started to wash it. She never was good at awkward conversations. Needed something to do with her hands while she was involved in them. 'An older man, a man who has been married, will expect certain things from a woman.' She finished washing the cup and started to vigorously dry it.

'Like what?' asked Izzy.

'Things,' said Joan. 'Relationship things.'

Izzy stared at her blankly, what on earth was the woman talking about? Then she realised. 'Oh, you mean sex?'

'Yes, if you must put it that way.' It wasn't a word Joan ever said.

'I do,' said Izzy. 'But sex, don't worry about that.'

She meant that she and Jimmy made sure she didn't get pregnant. Her mother took it to mean their relationship was chaste. 'Good,' she said.

On Sunday they went to church. It wasn't as full as it had been when Izzy was last there. A few of the pews were empty. Hamish's sermon was quieter than the ones she'd heard as a child. He spoke about people in peril, lives being wasted and the yearning everyone had to know their loved ones were safe.

Outside, Hamish introduced Jimmy to his parishioners. 'Izzy's American doctor friend,' he said. People nodded and said they were pleased to meet him. Izzy noted that one or two people went on their way without shaking Hamish's hand. This was odd.

Later, they enjoyed some quiet banter over lunch and, as pudding was brought to the table, Izzy was asked to do her custard prayer.

'Aw, Dad,' she said.

'Did it when she was a lass,' said Hamish. 'Lovely thought, thanking God for the custard. Thanking God for the simple pleasures in life is important.'

Jimmy said it surely was.

They played cards in the evening, they chatted and avoided talking about the business of women flying.

In the days that followed, Jimmy and Izzy took long walks through the woods, stopping regularly to kiss, to hold one another. She showed him the village school she'd attended, and Elspeth's cottage. 'I had my happiest times in there. You'd love Elspeth.'

They explored the local antique shop and Jimmy bought a pewter tankard to take home to his dad. 'It's very old,' the shopkeeper said, 'used to belong to Bonnie Prince Charlie.'

'Really?' said Jimmy. 'No kidding.'

Izzy snorted. 'And I'm Mary Queen of Scots.'

'Talking of Mary Queen of Scots,' the shopkeeper enthused, 'I have one of her teaspoons on display here.' He pointed to a spoon with a crest on the handle. Izzy snorted again and left the shop.

They held hands walking to the manse. Jimmy said, 'You're happy.'

Izzy said, 'Yes. I am really happy. Don't spoil it by talking about it. If you do that, it slips away.'

She was right. They were hardly in the door when Hamish

came out of his study. 'Izzy, a moment.' He jerked his head to the interior of his dusty, cluttered room. When Jimmy moved with her, Hamish said, 'Alone, if you don't mind.'

Izzy sat down, folded her hands in her lap. This was familiar – the two of them in the study, the door closed, her father looking grim. A lecture was in the offing. 'What do you want?' Izzy said.

Hamish folded his hands on the top of his desk. 'The truth.'

Izzy said, 'Ah.'

'You lied to me, you lied to your mother. You're flying, aren't you?'

'I am,' said Izzy. 'How did you find out?'

'The truth will always out. It's a small world. I hear things. Why didn't you tell us?'

'Couldn't face the fuss,' said Izzy. 'It was easier not to tell you.'

'It was easier to lie?'

Izzy shrugged, and said she hadn't really thought of it as lying. 'More not telling the whole truth. I thought you'd worry. You'd try to stop me.'

'A lie is a lie. And I hate lies. You know that. You didn't just lie to your mother and me, you lied to yourself. You let yourself down. You were off living the high life, doing what you wanted to do. What if you'd crashed and died? What if you met an enemy plane and were shot down?'

'Oddly enough,' said Izzy, 'there are very few incidents of our pilots seeing enemy planes. Anyway, I'm fine. I am a pilot third class and proud.'

'You are a silly girl trying to do a man's job.'

'No,' said Izzy. 'I'm not trying to do it. I *am* doing it. And the people who employ me must be happy with what we women do. We get the same pay as the men.'

'You get equal pay?'

Izzy told him yes. 'Why shouldn't I? I do the same job as the men.'

He shook his head and wondered what the world was coming to.

'And now you are seeing a man who is considerably older than you and who has been married. A man like that will expect a lot from a relationship. He'll want more than a girl like you should be prepared to give.'

Izzy asked what he meant by that. He told her she knew exactly what he meant.

Izzy said that he knew about Allan. 'You know what we did.' To mention the act by name wasn't possible. Not here, in this study – scene of many lectures and scoldings.

'What you did with Allan was an act of compassion, a gift to a man who was off to fight for his country. Lust is a different matter. I want you to stop,' he said. 'Stop flying and stop seeing that man.'

Izzy said, 'No. I won't do either of those things. There's nothing wrong with a bit of lust. It's good for the circulation and it keeps you warm at a time when it's cold what with coal being rationed.'

She crossed her legs, folded her arms and stared at him. He stared back. There was no shouting, no flashes of temper. Just two people glaring at one another, jaws clenched and unrelenting. In the hall the grandfather clock ticked, beyond the window, a blackbird hopped across the lawn, and, from the kitchen, the sounds of a meal being prepared. But the silence in the room was awful. Two people were falling out of love. Or, at least, they were realising that the adored one was not the person they thought.

Izzy was no longer Hamish's little tomboy girl who'd hung on his every word. She was a woman who lived her own life. Hamish was no longer the kindly, joking father whose only wish had been that his family be good and be seen to be good. He was an authoritarian who was demanding too much of his daughter. So, they stared.

At last, Hamish said, 'Please God, you are not turning into one of those ghastly modern women.'

'I may well be,' said Izzy. 'You haven't turned into anything. You're still an old-fashioned man.'

'Don't be rude.'

Izzy said, 'I'm not being rude. You'll note I didn't say ghastly.'

He told her he blamed Elspeth for all this. 'She filled your head with nonsense.'

'She only taught me that it wasn't wrong to pursue happiness.'

He laughed. 'Happiness, Izzy, only the foolish pursue that. You were brought up to respect your parents, yourself and your God.'

Izzy squirmed. She was ten years old again. She hated that. She told him he was treating her like a child. That, he told her, was because she was behaving like one. 'You know nothing about responsibility. I suspect you know nothing about being a woman, either.'

Izzy gasped.

'Make no mistake, I love women.' Hamish launched himself into his lecture. 'They give you all they have. They love you and they give you their life. They are soft vulnerable creatures. Men keep a little bit of themselves back from love. It's the burden of responsibility. They have to be strong for their families.'

'The burden of responsibility,' Izzy scoffed. 'That's just an excuse for not helping with the washing-up.'

She wanted this lecture to be over. She wanted to be in the kitchen with Jimmy, drinking tea and eating scones.

Hamish told her she was being childish. 'You're a silly woman living a man's life, doing a man's job and behaving like a slut.' He wondered if, perhaps, she'd abandoned her religious beliefs.

Izzy said she had. 'I don't believe in God. But I'm not a slut. That's a terrible thing to say. To your own daughter, too. To anybody, in fact.' She sat, fists clenched on her lap, face pink with defiance. She watched her father carefully, waiting for his fury.

It didn't come. He scratched his chin. He agreed with her. He'd said a terrible thing. He just wasn't going to admit it. It had been a heat-of-the-moment thing. He wanted her to be safe, to know she wasn't going to get hurt. It would be one less worry in worrying times. If Izzy did as she was told – stopped flying, stopped seeing that man – he could stop fretting about her and concentrate all his anxiety on the absurd rumours about his German sympathies that were still being whispered throughout the village. People were avoiding him.

Still, he thought, the girl is a fool – a stubborn fool. He would put her in her place. He raised his eyebrows and smiled. He smiled harder, then laughed, flapped his hand, waved her from the room. 'I'm not going to have a theological discussion with you.' He laughed some more. 'Izzy the pilot, loose woman and atheist. Come back when you've grown up.'

Izzy said she'd come back when he stopped being so narrow-minded. 'And I am grown-up.' She pointed to her eyes. 'Look, I've just had a fight with you, and I'm not crying. That's a first.' She headed for the door.

'I'll pray for you,' her father said.

'Don't bother.' Izzy walked out.

Hamish wasn't around for supper. He excused himself, saying he had a meeting with the church elders. Everybody in the house was sleeping when he returned. Next morning, Izzy and Jimmy left for Edinburgh. Hamish had gone out early to visit the cottage hospital.

'He's in a huff,' said Izzy. 'He hates it when I don't do what he says. And he thinks I'm childish.'

Joan walked to the gate with them. 'He has his problems.'

Izzy asked, 'What problems?'

Joan said, 'Oh, nothing. Nothing he can't deal with. Nothing for you to bother about. I wish you would pretend you agree with him. Just for the peace of it. That's what I've always done.'

'He's asking too much,' said Izzy

Joan took her hand. 'I know. But, it's only because he loves you. He wants to be proud of you.' She took Izzy's hand. 'I'm proud of you. And so envious. I'd love to do what you're doing.'

Izzy put her arms round her mother. 'I'll write.'

She and Jimmy walked down the road, caught the bus to Perth, then the train to Edinburgh, where they booked into the North British Hotel. They hardly spoke on the journey. In the hotel they climbed to their room on the first floor, undressed, climbed into bed and made love.

Afterwards, Izzy said, 'Sorry.'

'For what?' he asked.

'For all that. For my father. For having a fight with him when you were there.'

He told her to forget it. 'I fought with my folks all the time. They didn't like me smoking, said I drank too much, said I had no respect for them, all the usual things.'

'Do you still fight with them?'

'Hell, no. That was over years ago. You're just having the fight you should have had when you were sixteen. He'll get over it and so will you.'

Izzy said she supposed so. 'It was the worse kind of argument. No bawling or shouting, no sobbing. It's the hardest kind of fight. If one person cries, then the other can put their arms round them and tell them to stop. You can make up after that. One good thing, though, I didn't tell him about my motorbike. He'd really hate that.'

'Izzy, I love that you fly. I think it's great. But that bike is an embarrassment.'

'You think?'

'I know.'

She laughed, rolled on top of him, kissed him. Outside, a train rumbled out of Waverley Station. He shut his eyes.

He'd bought her the spoon that the shopkeeper had said once belonged to Mary Queen of Scots, Izzy would laugh when she saw it. He thought he might give it to her on their last night here, after they'd eaten, and when they were in bed together. He'd tell her to think of him every time she used it to put sugar on her porridge. It was something to remind her of him. 'When I'm in France,' he would tell her. He had it all planned, he would assure her he hadn't asked for the posting. They needed experienced doctors in the field hospitals. He'd hold her and tell her he would come back to her.

Chapter Thirty-eight
Someone To Watch Over You

When Elspeth had returned to work after her holiday, the swelling on her cheek where Duncan had punched her had developed into a splendid bruise – purple at the centre turning to brown then yellow round the edges. There had been jokes and comments, but she stuck with her story. She'd fallen off her bike. She had enjoyed elaborating on her mishap. She had, she said, been cycling in the dark, hadn't seen a pothole in the road, hit it and had been sent sailing over her handlebars. 'A beautiful short flight through the gloaming', before landing on her face.

On her first morning back Duncan had given her a small nod. He assumed that having given Elspeth money for her fare home and a ride to the bus stop, he'd been forgiven for his outburst. Elspeth had ignored him. She hadn't forgiven him. She wanted revenge, dreamed of it. But so far hadn't worked out what form her vengeance would take. Nothing as awful as causing him pain – just a little humiliation, she decided. Making him blush publicly would be very satisfying.

'You've gone all quiet,' Lorna said. 'You're not the same.'

Elspeth said, 'I'm just a bit down. I shouldn't have gone home. I got a taste of normal life. I forgot what living here was like. Now I'm back and I've remembered. It's been a shock.' She was sitting on her bed replying to the letter from Izzy that she'd read at her cottage. In it Izzy had confessed to a new fear of flying after the accident that killed Diane.

Lorna said, 'I don't think it's that. You've gone into yourself. Not speaking much. You're all stiff and wary. You've been like that since you fell off your bike.'

'Have I?' said Elspeth.

'I know getting back in the air after such a dreadful accident must be hard,' Elspeth wrote, 'but you must try not to be wary.'

'You know what you have to do,' said Lorna. 'You have to get back on your bike and peddle like mad till you're not scared any more. That's what they do with people who have almost drowned. They throw them back into the water.'

Elspeth said she didn't think that was true. 'You must fly through your fear,' she wrote to Izzy. 'You know how it was when you fell off your bike when you were little. You had to get right back on it again and peddle like mad till you weren't scared any more.'

Ten days later Izzy's reply arrived. 'You were right. The more I fly, the less afraid I am. But now, my life is in another turmoil. Firstly, Jimmy's gone to France. I miss him and I worry about him. He said he would come back, but I don't know if he will. He'll probably go back to America from there. I don't think I'll ever see him again. And, I've had a dreadful row with my father. He found out that I was flying . . .'

Izzy described the fight with Hamish. 'Thing is, how did he find out about me? Who could have told him? Whoever it was, I hate them. Also, I'm feeling really queasy these days.'

Elspeth told her to take Milk of Magnesia to settle her stomach. 'It's just stress,' she wrote. 'Jimmy will come back to you, I'm sure of it. As for who told your father about your job, well, it could have been anybody. It's a small world.'

She was awash with guilt as she wrote this, so quickly went on to describe the weather. 'Autumn now, I can smell cold days coming. It's funny how during summer, I forget about winter. Now I remember how it is – blinding rain in my face, snow trickling down the back of my neck and oozing over the top of my boots, cold winds slicing through me – and I'm dreading it.' She didn't mention her own troubles.

The first hard frosts came in November, and with them, mist – thick, freezing mist. A shroud that clung to trees, made moving about the forest difficult. Disembodied voices called, 'Timber.' Trees crashed through the swirl of white and landed on the hard ground. Sudden figures, black shapes, loomed out of the weather, only becoming familiar when they were feet away.

Working with the horse had its advantages. Elspeth could warm her hands on the horse's belly, press her frozen fingers on the soft flesh where her legs met her body. And, running back and forth meant she didn't get as cold as she had when she was standing still snedding. Back then, there had been that moment when, stepping into the warmth of the hut, her blood had started to thaw and to move more freely through her veins, feeling returned to her numbed fingers and toes. The pain, when that happened, had been excruciating.

The workers had moved to a new part of the forest. They were felling trees on the other side of the road several miles beyond Duncan's cottage. She and the horse turned left at the end of the track instead of right. It had taken the horse over a week to get used to this.

Lorna was not the only person to notice the change in Elspeth.

Tyler also thought her distant, but didn't think it had anything to do with falling off a bike. He'd known women who'd become strangely hardened overnight. One day they'd been laughing and flirting. Next, they'd be removed, withdrawn, buttoned up to the neck. Not a glimpse of tit, he thought. Well, Elspeth wasn't as bad as that. But she'd definitely changed.

He'd seen Elspeth's bruises and thought them familiar. They hadn't been caused by any beautiful flight through the gloaming. He knew the after-effects of a punch when he saw them. The bruising on her arms and breasts had been caused by some man mauling at her, he'd seen that sort of thing before. He also noticed the scratches on Duncan's cheeks. Well, he'd been scratched like that in his life. Long deep red scars like that were the work of a furious woman. He put two and two together, and decided Duncan had raped Elspeth. His lovely Elspeth violated by an ancient, moody, foul bastard. Tyler resolved to get even.

He would wait until the war was over. The night before he took the train south to board the ship home, he'd strike.

Meantime, he kept watch over his woman, as he liked to call Elspeth. Though not to her face – he'd a notion she wouldn't like that. He rose early every morning, followed her as she walked to the stables holding her tilley lamp aloft to light her way. He thought he was being discreet, was sure she didn't know he was behind her. But she called out, 'I know you're there, Bute. Why are you following me?'

'Just out for a morning stroll.' As soon as he'd seen her arrive safely, he'd go back to his hut. On Fridays, dung nights, he trundled her barrow to Duncan's cottage, dumped the load at the foot of the garden, and wheeled Elspeth back to the stables.

Every night he did a tour of Elspeth's hut, walking round it, making sure nobody was lurking in the dark. He often came across Duncan, who'd be standing in the darkness at the side of the hut, hoping to hear Elspeth play.

Tyler would lean against the hut, hands in pockets and stare. Duncan would stare back, but he always lost the battle. He'd sigh, toss his cigarette to the ground, stamp on it and start walking to his cottage. Tyler would follow. Once, Duncan had turned. 'Are you threatening me?' he asked.

Tyler said, 'Why would I be threatening you? Have you done anything that would make me do that?'

When Duncan didn't reply, Tyler said, 'I guess you must be guilty about something.'

By now, Elspeth had resumed her winter routine. She wore her long johns, a woolly hat and socks in bed, and, in the evenings, sat by the stove in the hut, joking with the girls and playing her accordion. Girls put off going to the loo, trips across the duck-boards meant stepping out into the chill. They'd sit cross-legged, jiggling till nature's demands had to be answered. Then, cursing, they'd shove on their coats and hurtle into the night.

The weather got worse. Hail, sleet, gales beat down on them as they worked. 'We'll soon be out of all this,' Elspeth told Lorna. She'd been following the news on her Saturday trips to the cinema. Paris had been liberated in August, Brussels a month later. 'Soon it will be over and we can all go home.'

'Can't wait,' said Lorna. 'Imagine sleeping in a room on your own. No lying awake listening to people snoring and dreaming. No stumping across to a hut to get your breakfast. A bath to yourself alone. Luxury.'

On the last Friday of the month, Elspeth gave a recital in the village hall. 'You won't get paid,' Duncan told her. 'Lady

McKenzie is holding it to raise money for the village Spitfire fund.'

Elspeth shrugged and said she could hardly refuse. 'I suppose there will be tea and cakes, though.'

'There's always tea and cakes,' said Duncan.

He drove fifteen of the forest workers to the village on the night. They all climbed into the back, nobody wanted to ride in the cab with him. Elspeth squeezed herself against Tyler, tucking her hands under her armpits. 'Can't play if they're cold.'

He opened his coat, said, 'Come in here. There's room for two.'

Lorna said, 'Take him up on it. Two in a coat's cosy. Besides, it's lovely to have someone watching over you. Makes you feel safe.'

Elspeth supposed it did. She hated to admit it, but she rather liked the way Tyler kept an eye on her. And, yes, it did make her feel safe.

They trundled and bumped along the road, wind biting their cheeks. At the door of the village hall, they bundled out, stood swinging their arms against their bodies trying to warm up. The poster by the door said, 'Concert Recital by the Renowned Elspeth Moon in Aid of the Spitfire Fund. Entrance Sixpence.'

'I don't have sixpence,' said Lorna. 'I don't have any money. I thought we'd get in free 'cos we came with the band.' She pointed at Elspeth.

'It's all right,' said Elspeth. 'It's my treat. Duncan will pay for you all from my share of the dung money. Won't you, Duncan?'

There were four men in the group, some even bigger than Tyler. They stood, hands in pockets, waiting for Duncan to refuse. He didn't dare. He reached into the back of his good trousers, saved for special occasions like this, brought out his wallet and gave the woman on the door a pound.

Elspeth took the change. Dropped it into Lorna's hands. 'That's more of my treat, for tea and cakes at the end. Tea and cakes on me.' She got a round of applause and a scowl from Duncan. It wasn't quite the dire humiliation she wanted, but, Elspeth thought, it was a start.

The concert went well. Elspeth played her favourites – Brahms, Chopin, Beethoven and Mozart. At the end of each piece, her companions cheered and stamped. Tricia, as ever, surprised everyone by putting her fingers to her mouth and whistling. Lorna gazed at her in awe. She had a new heroine. 'Teach me,' she whispered.

The recital ended with a selection of popular tunes – 'We'll Meet Again', 'As Time Goes By', 'Red Sails in the Sunset', 'I'll be Seeing You', 'The Very Thought of You', and more. Everyone sang.

Then they stampeded to the buffet and ate fairy cakes, malt loaf, gingerbread and jam sponge. All of the foresters nodded their appreciation to one another. Their mouths were too full to speak.

Elspeth and Lorna stood to one side watching the display. 'You can't say us foresters let anyone down when it comes to bad manners,' said Elspeth.

'Yes,' said Lorna, 'I'm proud.'

'You're smiling,' said Elspeth, touching Lorna's cheek. 'Haven't seen you do that for a while.'

'I know,' said Lorna. 'Most of the time I'm bloody freezin' and bloody hungry and the only man I ever loved was killed by a falling tree. But I'm smiling. God knows why. But you're smilin' yourself. You haven't done much of that recently, either.'

Elspeth said that a grand night out with free tea and cakes could sometimes do that.

'Nah,' said Lorna. 'It was seeing you get one over on Duncan after what he did to you.'

'What did he do to me?'

'He attacked you. Come on, Elspeth, everybody knows what happened. You never fell of your bike. He jumped on you. He attacked you. We all saw him in the morning, covered in scratches. And you were bruised all over. I saw when you were getting undressed. Tyler thinks he raped you. But I don't. Dungarees are awful hard to get into. He didn't, did he?'

Elspeth shook her head. For a moment she contemplated disclosing Duncan's failings, but didn't. Blackmailer's honour, she thought. He paid a fiver for my silence.

'Now you've got him back. Hit him where he hurts – in the wallet. Got him to stump up a whole pound. Makes me smile,' said Lorna

Elspeth smiled, too. But she thought that a pound and that earlier five pounds were not nearly enough.

Chapter Thirty-nine
You Goose, Izzy

Izzy was pregnant. Mornings, she would wake, experience a small moment of peace, then she'd realise she was in hell. Her boyfriend was in France. She was expecting his child. She'd lose her job. It was the end of everything.

She was four months gone. But the truth of her condition had only dawned three weeks ago. Pregnancy hadn't been something her mother had willingly discussed. When Izzy had asked what it was like to be expecting a baby, her mother had said, 'Oh, you'll find out one day.' They never talked about anything intimate.

Apart from her mother and Mrs Brent, the only women she knew who'd had babies were Claire and Diane. Neither of them talked about the business of being pregnant – it wasn't a topic that came up in the mess. And now, Diane was no longer around. Izzy vaguely recalled Claire saying she'd been sick for the whole nine months while she was carrying Nell, but she hadn't paid much attention. Izzy had found pregnancy rather frightening, and had no intention of ever letting such a thing happen to her.

The dawning had come when she was sitting on the bathroom floor having thrown up her porridge for the third morning running. A damp clammy sweat glistened on her face. She wondered what on earth could be wrong with her, explored dire possibilities – an ulcer? A wave of realisation prickled over her scalp, buzzed down through her, shifting across her stomach. Oh my God, she thought, I'm bloody pregnant. Up the spout, in the pudding club, having a baby. She was sick again.

She flushed the lavatory, splashed cold water on her face, cleaned her teeth, vowed not to tell anyone. She would keep this a secret for as long as possible. She would keep flying.

Her feelings bewildered her. She was filled with dread – what would happen when people found out? She'd be without a job, that was certain. But would there be whisperings behind her back? A scandal? Shame? Definitely, she thought. There was something relentlessly inevitable about pregnancy. The thing inside would have to come out one day. This terrified her. As did the idea of looking after a baby. The only things Izzy knew about babies were that they cried a lot, were sick a lot, didn't seem to sleep when you wanted them to and needed their nappies changed a lot. And yet, despite the resentment and dread, she rather loved the thing. For a while she called the baby 'It'. Now it was Buster. A word she'd picked up from Jimmy. 'OK, Buster,' he'd said. 'Let's see you hit that ball clean up the fairway to the green.'

At night, in the cottage and alone – Julia had resumed her social life, and Claire was always slipping off somewhere or other – Izzy would chat to Buster. 'Shall we listen to *I.T.M.A.*?' 'Looks like it's corned beef for supper.' In the air she'd give a running commentary on events while flying. 'We're at one thousand feet and the weather's fine, visibility perfect.' She said that even if it wasn't true. She didn't want to worry Buster, since these days, she worried herself. Always, when lying in bed, just before she fell asleep, she'd say, 'Nightie night, Buster. See ya in the morning, when you make me throw up again.'

Of course, it was all her fault. On that night of passion in the Edinburgh hotel with the sounds of night trains rattling in and out of Waverley Station and traffic on Princes Street, she had persuaded Jimmy to make love to her without a condom. He'd given her a teaspoon, such a silly a gift – a private joke between them. 'That tankard belonged to Bonnie Prince Charlie,' she'd said in the antique shop, 'and I'm Mary Queen of Scots.'

That night he'd brought it out. 'Your teaspoon, ma'am,' he'd said. They'd laughed.

When they made love, she had pleaded that just once, just tonight, 'I want to feel you inside me. Just you, just me and not that bit of rubber in the way.' He'd obliged. Perhaps he'd drunk too much whisky in the bar, or perhaps he wanted that freedom, too. Maybe he'd thought it would be his last act of love. He was going to France. He might die there.

This pregnancy was her comeuppance, Izzy thought. It was what her father had always preached about – dire things happened to sinners. She was a sinner, addicted to thrills – flight, sex and – on that night – whisky. She'd had two glasses, and, after she'd got over the shock of how it burned after swallowing, had thought it quite nice. 'Sweet and malty,' she'd said. It had gone to her head, unleashed her deepest passion. The lovemaking had been wonderful. She had given herself over to it. Their passion, deep, intense, filled the room.

When Izzy had said she wanted to feel him inside her, it had been the whisky speaking. But when, after he'd fallen asleep, she'd told Jimmy she loved him, it wasn't.

Three days before Christmas, Izzy had her first letter from Jimmy from the field hospital at Namur. He apologised for not writing sooner, explaining, 'I'm working twelve or fourteen hours a day. When I'm not working, I'm sleeping.' He told her he wasn't going to describe what it was like in the field hospital only that he'd seen things he never wanted to see again. 'God, it's cold here. Snow, snow and more snow. It's about three feet deep. Supplies are brought in by road, the Red Ball Express. They have cut down on winter clothing to make more room for ammo, gas and food. I am treating a lot of trench foot and frostbite. And it's snowing. I did I mention that? Snowing so hard you can't see what's going on outside.'

He told her he dreamed of Montana. 'I smell it in my sleep, grass, clean air coming off the mountains, everything fresh and pure. I hope, when this is over, that I can persuade you to come visit me there.'

Izzy replied, saying that she'd love to go to Montana one day and that life with her was pretty much business as usual and she hoped that, despite everything, he had a good Christmas. She didn't mention Buster. She thought he had enough to worry about. It never crossed her mind that hearing he was about to become a father might delight him.

On Christmas Day Izzy and Julia were working. Claire had said she was going to visit her parents. On Christmas Eve she'd made a big show of going out the front door carrying her overnight bag. She'd shouted goodbye, and 'Happy Christmas when it comes!' Then she'd walked down the lane and slipped across the bridge to Simon's cottage. The pair planned to spend the day holed up together, doors locked, curtains drawn, fire blazing in the hearth. They'd toast each other with whisky, eat the chicken Simon had bought and spend as much time as possible in bed.

Izzy had a pleasant day. A familiar flight into Yorkshire, passing over rooftops, gardens, copses and country roads she'd come to know well. She chased clouds, passing through one, moving on to another. Always a pleasing thing to do. She was home by five o'clock, met Jacob coming out of the cottage.

'What the hell are you doing?' she asked. She wasn't in a good mood. The only thing she'd eaten since she'd thrown up her porridge that morning was a bar of chocolate for lunch. It had given her heartburn. Now, she – and Buster, she presumed – were hungry.

Jacob said Mrs Brent had sent him to deliver some turkey for supper. 'Left it on the kitchen table. It's good.'

'You haven't taken anything, have you?' said Izzy. 'I know you take things, don't deny it.'

He said he hadn't.

'You haven't taken my teaspoon,' said Izzy. 'It's important to me.'

He shook his head. Tried to look hurt at her suspicion. In fact, he'd seen the spoon, turned it over and over, examining it, decided it was worthless and abandoned it. After that he'd slipped upstairs to Izzy's room to check that her stash of money was still tucked beneath her underwear. 'I haven't touched your spoon,' he said. He walked away, arms stiff by his side. He had Izzy's bicycle pump up the sleeve of his jacket.

By the time Julia arrived home, Izzy had heated the roast potatoes, gravy, bread sauce and Brussels sprouts. She asked Julia if she was eating out tonight. 'It being Christmas.'

Julia shook her head. 'Nope. Staying in. Got invites to a couple of parties, but I'm not in the mood.'

They listened to the wireless as they ate. The news was of the battle in the Ardennes. Izzy switched it off. 'Can't bear to listen.'

After they'd eaten, they sat by the fire. Julia poured them both a whisky, held up her glass. 'Happy Christmas.'

'You, too,' said Izzy. She held her glass to her lips, made a show of sipping, but nothing passed her lips. She'd gone off whisky.

Julia asked how the weather was tasting these days.

'Snow coming,' said Izzy. 'The air has a grey, gritty and damp feel on the tongue when that's happening.'

Julia sighed, 'I do like snow at Christmas. So did Walter. This would have been out first time together at this time of year. We were looking forward to it. We planned to have a tree and everything.'

'You really miss him,' said Izzy.

'I surely do. He was my best friend. He slipped into my heart while I wasn't looking.' She took another drink. 'At first I didn't believe he was dead. I kept thinking I'd come home, swish round the corner on my bike and he'd be there, waiting for me. Actually, I still do think that.'

'I suppose it's hard to accept that someone you loved is gone. That you won't see him again,' said Izzy.

Julia nodded. 'It's really hard. I got to thinking that he'd been mean to me going off and not saying goodbye properly, just leaving a note. So I hated him a bit. Then I decided I'd imagined it all. I wasn't really in love with him. He wasn't wonderful. The times we'd had together weren't wonderful. You know, when he made me laugh in bed, when we danced – those things. But that strategy didn't work. Now I think I was lucky to have known him. He helped me. He honoured me by letting me into his life, and I sort of had my own honour restored by that. I've changed my ways. I no longer think you should always have two lovers, and I don't think love is something to be avoided.'

'Well, that's good,' said Izzy.

'We wanted to have babies,' said Julia. She gave Izzy a sharp look.

'Did you?' Izzy fought to sound innocent on the subject of babies.

'Yes,' said Julia. She refilled her glass. 'Ever flown a Warwick?'

Izzy shook her head. 'Ugly things, aren't they?'

'Ugly and horrible to fly. I had one today. And I thought about you.'

'Thank you very much,' said Izzy, offended.

'No, listen,' said Julia. 'It has all these petrol cocks that you have to check pre-flight. I had to laugh, because written in the handling notes in huge letters, it's got – All cocks should be checked before flight.' She snorted. 'Everybody has a little laugh when the see that.'

Izzy smirked.

'I don't mean to be filthy but, you didn't do that, did you, Izzy?' said Julia. 'Check the cock before you took off.'

Izzy blushed. 'What do you mean?'

'You didn't take precautions. You're pregnant, aren't you?' said Julia.

Izzy couldn't look at her. Stared into her glass. 'Yes. How did you know?'

'You're not very silent when you're throwing up in the morning.'

'You won't tell anyone, will you?' said Izzy.

Julia said, 'No, I won't tell. I promise on my newly found honour.' She reached over, took Izzy's hand, squeezed it. 'You goose, Izzy.'

Chapter Forty
Eating for Two

By the end of February, Izzy was wearing her flying suit most of the time at work, even in the mess. It was voluminous, big enough to take two of her, ideal for concealing her condition. She knew, however, that the day of reckoning was coming. She couldn't hide Buster for ever.

She was alone in the cottage most evenings. Claire was always out. Julia, too, since she had taken up her social life again. 'No lovers, though,' she told Izzy. 'I just like being with friends. It stops me brooding.'

Izzy sympathised. She was doing quite a lot of brooding herself.

She wrote to Elspeth, to Jimmy and to her mother and told none of them about Buster.

'One day it will all come out,' Julia said. She was on her way out to go with some airmen friends to her favourite club in Blackpool. She planned a lot of dancing. 'Going to a sweaty, smoky dive. Such places remind me of Walter.'

Izzy said that one day Buster would come out, and that would be it. 'No hiding him.'

'Buster?' said Julia. 'You're not going to call the baby Buster, surely. That's a dog's name.'

Izzy said she knew that. 'I have no idea what I'll call the baby, but for now it's Buster.'

Julia said, 'Whatever.'

A car tooted outside.

'I'm off. Look after yourself, darling. Go to bed early. You and Buster need your rest.'

Izzy waved goodbye. She still envied Julia. Grief had not diminished her beauty. If anything, it had enhanced it. There was a deep and remote sadness in her eyes. Something that said, keep away from me, which had a magnetic effect of men. Julia's beauty filled every room she entered; people stared. That beauty had filled this small living room, made Izzy feel lumpen, dowdy. But then, that could have been the hideous dressing gown she was wearing.

There was Julia, off to a nightclub, to drink, dance and flirt, no doubt, in her blue dress. Lips and nails painted scarlet. And here was she, bundled into an enormous and unflattering garment her mother had chosen, suffering dreadful heartburn. Life wasn't fair.

Julia was rich, beautiful and had a brand-new handbag. She'd got one of the pilots to bring it back from Brussels, where leather goods weren't rationed. She had asked Izzy if she wanted one. 'Shoes, too, if you can trust a man to bring you something you'd actually wear.'

Izzy had refused. 'I need all my money for when the baby comes.'

Still, Izzy, Claire, Julia and all the others were busy. Izzy figured as long as she kept out of the way, slipping into the operations room and the mapping room when they were too busy for anyone to notice her, her secret was safe.

*

Of course, Mrs Brent had noticed Izzy's condition. She had scrutinised her, noticing the glow in Izzy's cheeks. 'She's in the family way,' she told Mr Brent. 'I know when someone's expecting. I've seen it too many times.'

'It's not right,' said Mr Brent. 'Flying about and her in the puddin' club. Little baby won't know what's happening to it, whooshing about way up high.'

'It'll be snug as a bug where it is,' said Mrs Brent.

They were at the kitchen table, spread before them was a selection of chutneys, jams, scones, cheese and an apple pie.

Today had been a good day for Mr Brent. He'd traded a dozen eggs for two bottles of cider at the pub, a rabbit – skinned and ready for the pot – handed in to the doctor's surgery had bought him ointment for his bunions, a hen, too old to lay, had been slipped over the counter at the chemist's shop and three bars of soap, some toothpaste and a jar of cold cream slipped back at him. Soon, it would be warm enough to open the beehives. He'd planted this year's potatoes, carrots and cabbages in the garden. The strawberries, blackcurrants and gooseberries had survived the winter. Rationing didn't really touch the Brents' lives.

He reached over for a third slice of pie, just a sliver to go with the last of his cider. Mrs Brent slapped his wrist. 'Greedy guts. That's for Izzy. We've got to keep her fed, she's eating for two.'

Mr Brent drew back his hand, sighed and wondered who was the father of Izzy's baby.

'That Yank she's been seeing. When she was ill that time, he came to see her. I was there, but I had to go to do the washing-up at the hotel. But I slipped back later to see she was all right.

Well, the pair of them were in bed, curled up together, sound asleep, stark naked. Didn't see me. I left them to it.'

Mr Brent tutted and said, 'Young people these days.'

Mrs Brent folded her arms, leaned back in her seat and told him that Izzy and her Yank doctor weren't doing anything they hadn't done. She turned heftily in her chair and shouted, 'Jacob, I know you're out there in the hall eavesdropping. There's some apple pie and cheese here for you to drop off at Izzy's on your way to the pub.'

Hearing about Izzy's pregnancy upset Jacob. He had his moves planned. As soon as peace was declared he'd start his journey back to Poland. He hoped to get a flight to Berlin with one of the pilots. He assumed they'd be taking supplies over there. All he had to do was find someone corrupt enough to take a bribe. He had his eye on Gerald Harper, a pilot who'd been court-martialled out of the RAF for hedge-hopping and had a fondness for women, whisky and gambling. Jacob reckoned Gerald might be tempted by fifty pounds in cash. The fifty pounds, Jacob had in mind was, right now, in Izzy's knicker drawer. It was Jacob's wish that it stayed there. If Izzy moved away, his plan would be scuppered.

He put the apple pie on Izzy's kitchen table – he'd eaten the cheese on the way – and told her it was a present from Mrs Brent. 'She says you'll need it now you're eating for two.'

Izzy picked at the pie, popped a sliver of pastry into her mouth and asked how she'd known that.

'She knows everything,' said Jacob. 'She looked at you and knew.'

Izzy said, 'Yes, I'm pregnant.' Then, she pleaded, 'You won't tell anyone, will you?'

'Your secret is safe with me.' Of course it was. He needed Izzy to stay put. If her pregnancy was discovered, she'd be sacked, and she might leave the village.

She thanked him and offered him some pie. 'Or a cup of tea? Some cheese? We have Camembert. It's a bit ripe, we've had it for a few days.'

'How did you get that?'

'Somebody brought it back from France and gave it to Julia. She has her admirers.'

'And how did the pilot get it? Did he buy it?'

Izzy said, 'No. I don't know what use money is over there. People seem to be more interested in getting things that aren't available in the shops.'

'Such as?' said Jacob. For someone who planned to barter his way home, this was interesting.

'Bicycle tyres, apparently,' said Izzy. 'Everyone's keen to get bicycle tyres.'

Jacob helped himself to a piece of runny cheese and said, 'Really.' Bike tyres, in a million years, he'd never have thought of that.

Izzy lasted in her job for another three weeks. She was to remember the exact date of her downfall for the rest of her life. On 24 March 1945, she was standing in the mess listening to a report about airborne troops crossing the Rhine. She'd been thinking about Jimmy. He hadn't been in touch for weeks. She was standing in the doorway, sideways on to the corridor, hands in pockets with the light behind her, highlighting her shape.

Edith bustled past, small steps, shoes squeaking on the lino. 'Hello, Izzy,' she said. Then she stopped, backtracked, 'Izzy? Izzy? Are you . . . ?'

Izzy blushed and said, 'Yes.'

Chapter Forty-one
The Truth About Love from Mrs Brent

Izzy wrote to Elspeth. 'I have goofed. I have truly messed up my life. I'm going to have a baby. I am a fool. Obviously, I've left the ATA. To be honest, I feel so stupid and ashamed, I hate going out. I am going to be that most reviled thing – an unmarried mother.'

Within days, Elspeth replied. 'Oh Izzy, I'm so sorry. I wish I could get away and come to you.' Then, 'By the way, does your father know?'

He did. Izzy had written to her parents, telling them. A pile of crumpled paper had gathered under the kitchen table as she worked out the best way to break the news. Looking back, she decided her approach had been too flippant. She should have been remorseful, begging forgiveness.

'The good news is, I've left the ATA and I am no longer seeing my American doctor. He's gone to France. I haven't heard from him in a while. The bad news is I'm expecting his baby.' She'd asked if she could come home and give birth to their grandchild there.

The reply, from her father, came a week later. 'I worry about you. Your life seems to be a journey from stupidity to more stupidity. I wish you and your child well. Unfortunately, you can't come home. Your condition would make a mockery of all my sermons. I'd be a laughing stock.' But, of course, he would pray for her and the child. In fact, Hamish felt there was scandal enough about him without his daughter being spied, fat with child, trudging up the High Street. He thought it better she kept away, gave birth, then discreetly married someone suitable. She could then come home in triumph. Of course, he did not mention this in his letter.

Izzy read the letter several times, then folded it carefully and put it away in her underwear drawer. She imagined her father sitting in his study, furiously writing to her. She thought he might have ripped up her letter to him. The atmosphere in the manse would be thick, black with disapproval and fury.

When she cried, it wasn't from self-pity. It was sorrow for faded dreams. She had imagined sitting at the kitchen table with her family – mother, grandparents and child. She'd dreamed of her father and Buster walking hand in hand in the garden, him stooping low to point out flowers and bumblebees, the child marvelling at the old man's wisdom. This was not going to happen.

So, Izzy stayed at the cottage. She had nowhere else to go. Once a week she travelled three miles to the next village to attend the clinic at the local cottage hospital. She'd sit in the waiting room ready to be examined, knickers off, utility stockings rolled down, to her ankles, clutching a urine sample in an old ink bottle. She went on her motorbike.

She lay on a long table while the doctor pummelled her stomach, told her the baby was coming along nicely and warned her that there were strange blue flakes in her sample. 'Wash out the bottle properly next time.'

A nurse, who Izzy reckoned could only be about four foot six, stood on a box while she pressed an extremely cold trumpet against Izzy's stomach listening for a heartbeat. 'Ticking away,' she said.

The doctor asked where Izzy planned to give birth. 'Here or at home? It'll cost you one and sixpence to have it in the hospital.' His tone was curt. He didn't look her in the eye. He thought her a disgrace and wanted her to know it.

When Izzy said the hospital, and one and sixpence was fine with her, the doctor checked his admissions book. 'You've left it too late,' he said. 'I doubt there will be a bed available when you go into labour. Home birth it is.' He nodded to the nurse, who said she'd tell the Inspector.

'Inspector?' said Izzy.

'The Health Inspector will visit you at home, a general cleanliness check.'

Izzy said the place was immaculate. 'Mrs Brent would be very hurt at your suggestion it wasn't.'

The doctor said there were rules to be obeyed. 'The Inspector will call in a few days. And,' he added, 'if I see you on that motorbike again, I'll refuse to treat you.'

Chided, Izzy went home.

Mrs Brent was at the cottage when the Inspector came, and accompanied her and Izzy on the cleanliness check that took in the kitchen, the bathroom and Izzy's bedroom. 'This is where you plan to have the baby?'

Izzy nodded.

'Now,' said the Inspector. 'Who is going to tend you?'

'That would be me,' said Mrs Brent.

'You?' said Izzy. 'I thought there would be a midwife and a doctor.'

'Well, naturally, the midwife will see you through the delivery. Dr Grant will come along if there are complications. But I meant afterwards, who will tend you?'

Izzy said she wouldn't need tending. She'd be fine.

'Dear girl,' said the Inspector, 'you seem to know nothing about having a baby. Who is going to bring you meals? Who is going to deal with your bedpans? Who is going to look after baby as you lie in?'

'Lie in?' said Izzy. 'I won't have time to lie in, I'll have a baby.'

Mrs Brent and the Inspector exchanged looks, rolled their eyes.

The Inspector tucked her notebook into her bag and said, 'The standard recommendation is a fortnight's bed rest after giving birth.'

'What? A fortnight?' said Izzy. 'I'm not lying in bed for two bloody weeks.'

'You bloody well are,' said the Inspector. 'Is there a neighbour? A relative we could call on?'

Izzy said she shared the cottage with two pilots. But they were away all day, and she was positive neither of them would empty a bedpan.

'There's me,' said Mrs Brent. 'I'll look after Izzy.'

'You're a relative?'

'I'm the housekeeper.'

'So you live in?' asked the Inspector.

'No,' said Mrs Brent. 'There's things to do at home. William needs his tea. She can have the baby at my house. I like babies. Can't be doing with children these days, but babies are lovely.'

'So plainly,' said the Inspector, 'I am inspecting the wrong house.'

Mrs Brent said that anybody was welcome to inspect her house anytime. 'You'll find it as spotless as this one.'

Izzy's days passed slowly. She hid. She spent her time waiting and hoping. She watched for the postman every morning, thinking today would be the day there'd be a letter from Jimmy. Nothing. She sat in the living room staring at the phone, willing it to ring. It never did.

She heard planes flying overhead, wondered who was in them. She listened to the news. She walked by the river, always at five o'clock when nobody was about – everyone went home for tea – as she didn't want to meet anybody. She couldn't bear 'The Look'. She got it everywhere she went.

The Look was about more than disapproval. It went beyond shock and horror that she was – very obviously – a fallen woman. It told Izzy that the bestower of The Look thought she should know better than to get pregnant. Immaculate behaviour was expected of a lady pilot. The Look told Izzy she had no right to get up to mischief with a man. She was a fool, a strumpet, a disgrace.

The first person to give Izzy The Look was the woman in the fish and chip shop. Her eyes had fixed on Izzy's swollen belly, then moved up to her face. Izzy knew she was no longer a hero. After that came the CO. Izzy squirmed when she entered his office and was greeted by it. He did, however, come from behind his desk and took Izzy by the hand. 'We're sorry to lose you,' he said. 'If ever I can be of help, let me know.' It was kind of him. But The Look was what Izzy remembered.

Now, Izzy got The Look from people in the village. A raw

hush spread through shops when she entered. She no longer dropped in at the chip shop. The Look kept her away. Wherever she went, she heard tuts and whisperings behind her back. 'And her a lady pilot, too,' she overheard someone say. She didn't turn round to find out who the whisperer was.

Julia didn't give her The Look, but she often told Izzy she was a goose. 'You should have got a cap, like me.'

Izzy said she couldn't have gone to the doctor in her home village. 'He'd have told my dad.' And, she hadn't wanted to go to someone here in Skimpton. 'I was embarrassed.'

'A moment of embarrassment, a little bit of discomfort, but look at the trouble it saves you. It's what us modern women do,' said Julia.

Izzy doubted she was a modern woman. 'I don't think I'm poised like them. I just lumber through life making mistakes.'

'We all lumber. We all doubt. Just modern women keep their chins up. They don't let their mistakes show.'

Izzy looked glumly down at her swelling stomach. 'My mistake is really showing.'

At first, Izzy had thought that the look she'd got from Claire was The Look, but then decided it wasn't. It was something else. Izzy puzzled over it, till Julia guessed it must be Claire's fear. 'She thinks none of us know about her affair. But it's hard to miss the lustful way she gazes at Simon in the mess. She sees you, Izzy, and she thinks it could be her. She can't bear to think what her husband would do or say if he came home to find a child that obviously couldn't be his.'

But Claire was good to Izzy. Understood her discomfort, brought her bottles of dandelion and burdock to ease her heartburn. Made her put her feet up in the evenings and gave her news of the doings in the mess. She kept quiet about the shock Izzy's pregnancy had been. One of the men had said, 'That's the big difference between men and women pilots. The men aren't going to leave because they're in the family way.' Dolores had told him to shut up.

But still, The Look bothered Izzy enough to stop her going out. She tucked herself away and tried not to think about how she'd get by after the baby came. As for the actual birth, she dismissed that from her mind. It was too much to contemplate.

One morning, as Izzy sat in the living room, feet up, listening to the Radio Doctor advising the nation, in his own kindly way, to open their bowels once a day, Mrs Brent barged into the room sideways. It was the only way she could get herself and the large box she was carrying into the room. 'There,' she wheezed and dumped the box at Izzy's feet. 'For the baby.'

Izzy raked through a pile of knitted jackets, nappies, bootees, tiny shoes, blankets, a shawl and other baby clothes. 'Goodness. Thank you. Where did you get all this?'

'They've been collecting it in the village. Eddie Hicks put up a notice in the garage. The Izzy Fund.'

'Gosh.'

'The word got round, and everyone knows how hard it is to get baby things, so people gave what they no longer needed. Oh, there's those that disapprove of you. But plenty folk know how it is. A moment's nonsense, a bit of passion and look what happens – a baby on the way. That's life for you. Nothing to be ashamed of.'

Izzy said she wasn't ashamed. 'My only mistake was to fall in love.'

'Ach, love,' said Mrs Brent. 'It's all bluebirds and roses,

sighing and longing at first. Then, you end up in the family way, waddling about and plagued with indigestion. After that there's the chapped hands from washing nappies and swollen ankles from being on your feet all day. And you're tired out from sleepless nights.'

'I don't like the sound of that,' said Izzy.

'Well it's the truth. I fell for Mr Brent and I wound up in that cottage worrying about how to make half a pound of mince feed a family of four for two days.' She led the way to the kitchen. 'After you've peeled the potatoes, you can go and thank Eddie for all the stuff he collected. Stupid man still thinks you saved his life. After that, when you come back, I'll show you how to make soup. Soup's handy. Or are you going to sit staring at the phone all day?'

Izzy said she kept hoping Jimmy or her father might get in touch.

'If they do, you'll hear the phone in the kitchen.'

'I want my father to change his mind and ask me to come home. He's disowned me.'

'I know,' said Mrs Brent. She'd found the letter in Izzy's drawer, and read it. Put it back, shaking her head. 'Ach, the man's a fool.'

Izzy said she wanted him to forgive her.

'Perhaps you should think about forgiving him. He's not being very nice, as I see it.'

She took Izzy's arm, heaved her from her seat. 'You can peel some potatoes.'

'He thinks I'm a fallen woman,' said Izzy.

'And so you are,' said Mrs Brent.

The next day Mrs Brent arrived at the cottage and found Izzy on all fours scrubbing the kitchen floor. Izzy looked up at

407

her and said, 'I don't know what's got into me. I suddenly had to do this.'

'Nest-building,' said Mrs Brent. 'It's a sign. You're going to be a mother soon.'

Chapter Forty-two
Not for You, It's Not

It was a whisper, but it spread. One of the men who'd taken a load of logs down to the railway station had heard that the war was over. It had been announced on the wireless. He'd come back to where the girls were working and told Lorna, who'd told Elspeth, who'd told Dorothy; soon everyone knew. They downed tools and started hugging one another. Duncan blew his whistle and ordered everyone back to work.

Dorothy asked if it was true that a peace treaty had been signed. 'Is the war over?'

Duncan said, 'Not for you, it's not.'

Elspeth asked what that meant.

Duncan said, 'It's over when I say it's over.'

Hoots of derision. 'You'll be phoning Churchill to tell him, then,' said Elspeth. 'Better call the King, too. He likes to be kept informed.'

After that, the heated everyday pace slowed. Elspeth abandoned her quota. Why bother? she thought. I'll be going home soon.

On the way back to the camp, everyone sang. They tramped down the road hollering 'We'll Meet Again' and 'Pack up Your Trouble in Your Old Kit Bag'. The girls skipped, danced, twirled. The men whistled.

Elspeth took the horse to the stables, rubbed her down, fed and watered her. She washed in the ablutions hut and joined the others for supper. They were halfway through their meal, when Duncan came in.

'You'll all know by now, the war's over. Tomorrow's VE Day. You'll not be needing to work, it's a national holiday.' He stumped out.

'To victory, ladies!' shouted Tricia.

'To our boys coming home,' said Lorna.

They raised their mugs and toasted victory in Europe with murky tea.

It wasn't a night for sleeping. They kept the blinds up so the moonlight drifted into the dormitory. They lay in their beds, talked, dreamed and planned.

'How long before we get to go home?' asked Tricia.

'A month, maybe two,' said Lorna.

'Two, I should think,' said Dorothy. 'Time the troops come home, settle in and get back to work.'

'Yes,' said Elspeth. 'Two months for sure.'

Lorna said that she'd never look at another tree again. 'Every time I see one, I'll just think about being cold, eating carrot sandwiches and bleedin' snedding.'

'God, snedding,' said Elspeth. 'I wish I'd never heard of it.'

Tricia said, 'I'm going to wear high heels all the time. And lovely skirts and have my hair done and put perfume on every bit of me.'

'Roast beef,' a voice in the dark. 'Soon as I get home, I'll have roast beef, roast potatoes and no carrots. I'll never eat cabbage again.'

Other voices, more wishes – scrambled eggs with butter, tea

from a real china cup, stockings, proper sheets. 'Just soap,' said
Dorothy. 'A bath with lovely scented soap.'

'Home,' they sang. 'We're going home.'

Lorna started to sing 'Keep the Home Fires Burning' and they
all joined in, soft voices filled with longing.

The next afternoon Elspeth and Lorna cycled into the village.
The place was alive with bunting; tables had been set up the length
of the High Street. It was the children's party – adults serving
sandwiches, cakes, jelly and lemonade. Elspeth and Lorna
watched, but didn't join in. Eventually, they strolled arm in arm by
the river.

'I can't remember ever being so excited,' said Elspeth. 'I'll go
back to my cottage first. I'll sleep in my own bed. I'll sleep and
sleep and sleep.'

'Then what?' said Lorna.

'I'll probably go to London. See if I can get a job there. City
lights for me.'

'I'm going to try to get my old job back. I'm going to walk
the old familiar streets, see all my pals and just be normal again.
Nothing fancy. Just plain ordinary life, coming and going. Being
at home with my folks, listening to the wireless at night, having
the odd hot bath and sleeping. I'll be doing a lot of that, too.'

'I know,' said Elspeth. 'Waking up in your own bedroom
listening to the sounds of the day outside, seeing the same old
familiar faces. You don't know how good it is till it's gone.'

They sat down, watched the water, sighed and dreamed.
'Know what I'm most looking forward to?' said Lorna. 'No
whistles.'

'God, yes,' Elspeth agreed. 'A whistle-free life.'

By seven at night the party in the street had changed. The pub was thronged, people spilled out on to the street, drinking. There was a bonfire, flames curling up, sparking into the sky, though it was still light, couples danced round it. Elspeth managed to get herself and Lorna a glass of beer each, and they sat on chairs left on the pavement after the children's party, sipping and still dreaming. They danced with one another, joined in the singing, toasted the King and drank some more beer.

By half past ten the pub had run dry. But the singing and dancing went on. Elspeth took Lorna's arm and said, 'Have you noticed? There's nobody from the camp here. Let's go back, see what they're up to.'

They cycled back into the forest. It was getting late, but still light. Elspeth stopped, standing in the middle of the road, astride her bike, and wept.

'Don't cry,' said Lorna.

'I'm sorry. I can't help it. It's the relief. I'm so happy.'

'I know,' said Lorna. Tears spilled down her cheeks. 'You've set me off, now. I'm happy, too. We'll see each other again, though. We'll keep in touch, write. I'll want to know what's happened to you.'

'Oh, yes,' said Elspeth. 'I'm not letting you go. Never.'

'We'll get back to the camp, find somewhere quiet,' said Lorna. 'And just sit and be glad that we'll soon be on the train heading home.'

Elspeth said, 'Good idea.'

They heard the party long before they reached the track that led to the huts. Singing, shouting, whooping and someone had brought along the gramophone. The Kitty Vitty Minstrels were blaring.

Whisky was being handed round. They'd long abandoned

their mugs and were swigging from the bottle, passing it on. They waltzed, jitterbugged, jived. It was frenzied.

The men gathered round the girls and clapped, egging them on. Tricia had whipped off her shirt and was cavorting in the light of tilley lamps that were lining the duckboards. Other girls joined her. They linked hands, formed a circle and whirled round shouting, 'We're going home! We're going home!'

The circle became a conga line and they whooped along, kicking their legs out as they went, and the chant got louder. 'We're going ho-ome. We're going ho-ome.'

Elspeth and Lorna put their bikes down and joined the men, looking on. Tyler sidled up beside them. 'You've been missing the party.'

He took Elspeth in his arms and swept her up in a dance. 'Home,' he said. 'Back to Newfoundland. Back to where I belong. Sea and sky and forest and family.'

The conga line was now bobbing and weaving through the crowd of drinking men, girls stripping off their tops, shouting, 'Home! Home! Home!'

At first nobody heard the whistle. When they did, and turned, they saw Duncan standing outside the dining hut, cheeks stretched, face red, blasting and blasting.

He turned on the conga line. 'Home? What's this going home? You're not going anywhere. You're all a bloody disgrace.'

'But the war's over,' said Tricia. 'We can go now.'

'Yer not going nowhere till the Forestry says you can go.'

'When will that be?' asked Tricia.

The girls had all stopped dancing, were staring at Duncan, mouths agape. A few clumsily pulled on their clothes.

'The country needs trees. It'll always need trees. And it'll need you to cut them down. It'll be years before you get signed off. Bloody years,' said Duncan. He was getting a great deal of pleasure from giving them this information.

It took a few seconds for this to sink in. A long and awful silence before they howled, 'You're kidding.'

'I never kid,' said Duncan. 'Get to bed, the lot of you. You've got work tomorrow. And the next day, and the day after and after that. For years, do you hear me?'

He limped away back down the path to his cottage. 'Years and bloody years.'

Elspeth reached out, took Tyler's hand. 'All right. I'll marry you.'

Chapter Forty-three
Bike Tyres and a Lucky Stone

Izzy was coming down the stairs when the first pain struck. It shot across her lower back, stopped her in her tracks. She stood, gripping the banister, wondering what had happened. The pain passed, she carried on down the stairs and into the kitchen, put on the kettle, made tea, drank it, started a letter to Elspeth and a second pain screamed across her back. She put her hand against it, leaned into it and groaned. When the third pain came, slow at first, then getting more and more intense, she thought, Oh hell, this is it.

At her last visit to the clinic, the midwife had crisply told Izzy that the baby would be coming very soon, and when that happened she wasn't to panic. She panicked. First she ran up and down the hall, wondering what to do. Then she phoned the doctor but was told he was on his rounds. 'How far apart are the pains?' asked the woman on the other end.

'About an hour,' said Izzy.

She was told to call back when they were twenty minutes apart. She sat down, waited for the next pain. Got bored and went upstairs to pack her bag, then set out for Mrs Brent's cottage. She got as far as the front gate before another pain took hold. She stood, clinging to it, waiting for the pain to pass. When it did, she decided that walking to Mrs Brent's was out of the question. She'd take the motorbike. She'd be there in minutes.

She strapped her bag on the back, hitched up her skirt and climbed on and kick-started the engine. She was in the throes of a contraction when she arrived and sat, head on the handlebars waiting for it to pass, engine roaring. William came out, saw her, and asked, voice at full stretch over the noise, what was up. Izzy said she thought she was having a baby.

Jacob was in the kitchen when William brought Izzy in. He watched with mild interest as Izzy carefully lowered herself into a chair.

'Put the kettle on,' said William.

Izzy said she didn't think they'd need boiling water yet. 'Why do they boil water when someone is having a baby, anyway?'

Walter said he'd no idea, but this was to make a cup of tea. He turned to Jacob and told him to go fetch Mrs Brent, who was at the Golden Mallard doing the dishes. 'Take Izzy's bike.'

Ten minutes later, Jacob burst through the back door of the hotel and told Mrs Brent the news. She abandoned the dishes, dried her hands and ran out to her bike, cycled off, apron flapping, to find Mrs Gribbon, the midwife.

Jacob was never a man to miss an opportunity. He knew Izzy would have left the cottage door unlocked, and he knew she wasn't likely to return to it for at least a fortnight. Julia and Claire were at work. This was his moment.

He parked the bike outside the cottage, walked up the path and knocked on the door, after all, somebody might be there. Nobody answered, so he went inside, climbed the stairs and, once in Izzy's room, opened the underwear drawer.

The money was where it had always been, underneath a pile of knickers. As he took it out, he noticed a letter tucked underneath, and, unable to resist, read it. Izzy's father didn't want her to come home. 'Fool,' said Jacob.

He put the letter back and stuffed the money into his pocket. Halfway down the stairs, he stopped. 'Damn.' He could hear sounds from outside – a thrush singing, radio playing next door. He was breathing loudly and wanted to get away. But it had occurred to him that he was leaving Izzy destitute. And, damn it, he liked the woman. He'd imagined Izzy would marry her American friend and go off to a new life. She wouldn't actually need her money. But there had been no sign of the American for months. 'Damn,' he said again. He ran back up the stairs, put fifty pounds back in the drawer. He found a notepad in the kitchen, tore off a page and wrote an apology to Izzy. 'You owed me.' Back upstairs, panting now, he put the note in the drawer beside the money, and, as an afterthought, dropped the tortoiseshell Parker pen in, too.

He shut the drawer. This was the right thing to do, he was sure of that. He wanted to go home, needed to go home. The journey would be terrible. He'd sleep in ditches, meet desperate and hungry people – he was used to that. Still, in the end, he'd had a good war. He'd slept in a warm bed, eaten well. His wife wouldn't have. It made him guilty. He wasn't used to that. He'd welcome fear, discomfort and hunger. It was what he deserved. It would ease the guilt.

Outside, he climbed onto the bike and roared off. He stopped at the pub, sat on the bench outside, heart pounding. Stealing things, little things, had always filled him with glee. It had given him a surge of triumph, power. He was in control of his situation, gathering small trophies that might, in time, help him on his journey home.

But that had been no fun at all. Still, he needed to get back to Poland. Damned if he was going to wait for the government to repatriate him. And Izzy did owe him, look at how popular she'd become. Yes, he'd done the right thing.

As he sat, waiting for his heartbeat to return to normal, Mrs Gribbon and Mrs Brent whizzed past him, both sedately overweight and both old enough to be called elderly. Heads up, bells ringing, they pedalled with a purpose and didn't notice him.

He had a couple of pints of beer. By the time he got back to the Brents' cottage, Izzy was in bed in the spare room downstairs talking to the midwife, Mrs Brent was making a pot of tea and Mr Brent was in the garden, keeping out of the way. Nobody noticed Jacob going up to his room to pack.

When he came back down again, Izzy was shouting that she didn't need a shave. The midwife was saying firmly that nobody was going to shave her cheeks, 'Why would we do that? No, lass, we're going to shave you down there. Make sure everything's clean for baby when he arrives.'

As he left, he heard Izzy shout, 'Oh, God!' His heart went out to her.

Jacob took the bike out to the base, waited by Gerald Harper's MG, till, at half past five, the man arrived. Jacob asked when he was next flying across to Europe.

'Got a flight to Berlin tomorrow,' said Gerald.

'Just you?'

'Just me in the Anson with a couple of crates of oranges.'

'Take me,' said Jacob. 'Twenty-five pounds now. Twenty-five when we get there.'

'You don't need to do that. You'll get repatriated. Go see the people in London.'

'How long will that take? Applications, visas, papers, hanging about waiting for someone to rubber-stamp this and rubber-stamp that. I want to go now. I have a wife I haven't seen for years.'

Gerald shrugged. 'You get into that plane early. Before anyone else arrives. And when we get to Berlin, you're on your own.'

Jacob said, 'Fair enough.'

He rode back to the village. He sat in the pub till closing time, waiting for the village to sleep.

It was late when he parked Izzy's motorbike outside the Brents' cottage. The ride back from the village had been precarious. His load was cumbersome. Inside, he stood, sniffing the air, feeling the atmosphere. He could hear Mr Brent's thunderous snoring coming from upstairs, and a fainter higher-pitched snore accompanying it. The old couple were sleeping. The midwife was gone. The air smelled antiseptic. The chaos of birth was over.

He took the Brents' large suitcase from their downstairs cupboard and, with difficulty, stuffed the night's takings into it. He brought his own case down from his bedroom, put them both outside. Then, he tapped on the door of Izzy's room, went in to say goodbye.

Izzy was awake. The bed light was on, she was leaning over, staring into the crib. She smiled when he came in.

'I thought you'd be sleeping,' he said.

'Can't sleep,' said Izzy. She pointed into the crib. 'It's a boy.'

Jacob said, 'My favourite kind of baby.'

'What's wrong with girls?'

'They're good, too.' Jacob peered down at the child. 'He looks a bit like you.'

'He's got my hair. I thought babies were bald. Look, perfect fingers.' She reached over, loosened the tight swaddling, lifted out the baby's hand. 'Amazing fingers. Nails and everything.'

Jacob pulled his St Christopher medal from round his neck. 'For the baby, from Anna and me.'

'I can't take that. It's too precious.'

'It's not up to you to accept or refuse it. It's the baby's. And it's bad luck to meet someone who is new in the world without giving them a gift. What's his name, by the way?'

'Haven't thought of one yet,' said Izzy. 'Mrs Brent is nagging me about that. She thinks it's a disgrace – a baby with no name.'

'So it is,' said Jacob.

Izzy said that it was late. 'Where have you been?'

'Just out, had a bit of business to take care of. I've come to say goodbye. I'm going home tomorrow.'

'To Poland?'

'To Berlin, then I'll make my way to Poland.'

Izzy asked how he was going to get to Berlin. He put his fingers to his lips. 'Don't ask. Better that you don't know.'

'I'll never see you again,' said Izzy. There had been times when Izzy would have thought this a good thing. This man was a thief. But tonight it saddened her.

'Perhaps I'll come back one day. I'll bring you chocolate-covered plums. I'll cook you meatballs with dumplings.'

Izzy said she'd look forward to it.

He told her she looked tired. 'I think giving birth must take it out of you.'

'It does. But I feel happy.'

He kissed her, told her he had to go.

'I have to give you something,' said Izzy. 'It's bad luck to say goodbye without a parting gift.' She reached under the pillow, brought out a blue heart-shaped stone. 'It's lucky. It kept me safe. Now it'll work for you.'

'I can't take this.'

'Yes you can. My friend Elspeth gave it to me. She said that when I'd used up my share of its luck, I had to pass it on to someone who'd need it. That's the lucky thing to do.' She said this with such conviction that she almost believed it herself. 'I definitely have run out of luck.' She smiled. 'It started when that plane went on fire. I should have known then that my days of fortune were over. I am no longer blessed. I fell out with my family. I lost the one I love. I fell from grace.' She jerked her head at the baby. 'Not that I don't love him. But the stone's telling me it's time for us to part. That's the rule with lucky things. Or so Elspeth said. I had my luck – I flew Spitfires, I fell in love. I had such thrills. Now you take it, you'll need all the luck you can get.'

He put it in his pocket, thanked her and kissed her again. 'I wish I'd got to know you better. We should have been friends.'

'Perhaps,' said Izzy. 'But you're a rogue, you steal things.'

'Only when I'm here. Soon as I cross the border into Poland, I'll be a good boy again.' He slipped out the door.

Outside the sky was turning pale, streaks of gold on the horizon. It would be morning soon. He piled his cases onto the back of Izzy's bike. Strapped them tight so they wouldn't fall off. He wheeled the bike onto the road, then started it. Riding to the base, his heart lifted. He'd been waiting for this moment for years. The air was cold, the breeze pressing on his chest and face. He was smiling. God, Izzy was lovely. He wished he hadn't stolen her money. He was awfully glad he hadn't taken it all.

By four o'clock the next day, he had stolen a bike and was slowly cycling east out of Berlin. He had discarded his uniform, wore a shirt, sleeves rolled up, collar open. He looked like a farm hand, he looked ordinary, nobody on the road paid any attention to him.

In the case, strapped to the pannier on the back of his bike he had his bartering goods – pots of Mrs Brent's honey, packets of tea, biscuits, tins of corned beef and, stolen from the good people of Skimpton, twenty bicycle tyres. He had Izzy's lucky stone in his pocket. He knew he'd make it home.

Chapter Forty-four
Mrs Alton

Julia burst into the kitchen. 'Somebody's bloody stolen the tyres orff my bike.'

Claire, sitting at the table, drinking tea, said, 'Well, take mine, then.'

'Your tyres are gone, too. And Izzy's. Who would do a thing like that? I'll kill whoever it was if I get my hands on them,' said Julia.

'How are you going to get to the base?' asked Claire.

'They're sending a car. It's doing the rounds picking people up, apparently a lot of people have had their tyres stolen. There's been a spate of tyre thefts in the village.'

Claire shrugged. She didn't care. She wouldn't need her bike today. She wouldn't need her bike ever again. Last night, she'd handed in her uniform, shaken hands with Edith, the CO and the adjutant, said goodbye to all her colleagues and cycled back to the cottage. She was no longer a lady pilot. Today, she'd take the train back to London, then a taxi to her house in Hampstead. She was Mrs Alton again.

Last night, for a few tender hours, she'd been Mrs Middleton. She and Simon had eaten in his tiny kitchen. He'd roasted a chicken.

'A whole chicken, my goodness,' she'd said. 'You must have pulled some strings.'

'I got it from William Brent. I won't tell you what he charged. You'd faint.'

They drank Chablis.

'Where on earth did you get it?' she asked, sipping in wonderment.

'Two tins of cocoa and a packet of tea in Paris last week.'

She told him it was a bargain.

They hadn't discussed any rules about how their conversation should go; they hadn't said that some subjects were taboo. But, both of them knew that talking about the future would be painful. So, they'd avoided it. They reminisced, gossiped, chatted about how lovely an evening it was and that really they should be outside in the fresh air enjoying it. But they'd stayed where they were.

For a while they'd stopped speaking, sat gazing at one another.

'I want to take in every detail of your face,' said Claire. 'I want it here, inside my head, so I'll always remember it.'

'The way you are to me will never change,' he told her. 'This woman you are tonight is how you'll always be.'

She smiled. 'It's nice to think that there's somewhere, even if it's just in your head, that I'll never age.'

They went to bed, made love. They kept the windows open so they could hear the sound of the river just beyond the cottage garden. She hadn't wanted to sleep. Her wish was that she should stay awake all night, feeling the closeness of him, listening to him breathe. But, she'd slept.

At five in the morning she woke. Kissed him, got out of bed and dressed. She was at the front door when he caught up with her.

'You're going without saying goodbye.'

'I just didn't want to say it,' she said.

She was wearing her ordinary clothes. Today was the day she became a wife and mother again. She had wanted to just slip away.

He told her he didn't want to say goodbye, either. So they didn't.

She didn't want to tell him she loved him. She didn't need to. He knew. And, somehow, at this moment, it seemed overdramatic to mention it.

Claire did what Mrs Alton would do. She reached out, took Simon's hand and shook it. 'It's been lovely knowing you.'

She'd kissed his cheek, walked down the path and not looked back. If she had, she'd have run to him, held him and asked him to run away with her, to start a new life somewhere they weren't known. That was not the sort of thing Mrs Alton did.

At ten o'clock she picked up her bag, left the key to the cottage on the table in the hall, shut the door and walked up to the bus stop. Five hours later, she was home.

She stood at the front door, listening to the house. It still had the same creaks and whispers where the draught shifted under the living-room door. It smelled musty.

She hung her coat on the hook by the front door, and set to. Moving from room to room, she peeled the tape from the windows. 'They'll need a wash,' she said. Then she opened them, letting in fresh air. She took the dust covers from the furniture, folded them and stashed them in the cupboard under the stairs. She swept the kitchen floor, dusted, ran the taps till the water was clear. She gathered some flowers from the garden, arranged them in vases that she placed in the hall, the living room and the kitchen.

After that, she took her basket and went to the shops to see what food she could buy.

On the way, she met neighbours who waved and smiled. 'Lovely to see you back, Mrs Alton.'

'Lovely to be back!' she called.

Two days later, Richard came home. There had been no word that he was coming, he just turned up. Claire had been in the kitchen, heard the front door opening and had come to see who it was.

There was a tiny slice of a moment when she didn't recognise him. He was thin, emaciated. His clothes hung loose, his face was gaunt, yellowed, tense. He said hello.

'Richard,' she said. She rushed to hold him. He leaned into her, head against her. Said he was home.

She led him into the living room, sat him by the fire. Stood holding his hand. She wanted to ask how he was, but, really, that seemed stupid. She could see he wasn't well.

'Was it awful?' she said.

'Not too bad,' which meant it was truly awful. 'How have you been?'

'Missing you,' she said. 'I'll put the kettle on.'

But he held on to her hand. 'Not just yet. I want to look at you.'

He asked what she'd been up to.

'Flying,' she said. 'I got a job delivering planes from the factories to the airbases.'

She thought he'd be appalled. He hated women working.

But he said, 'Doing your bit, eh? Good girl.'

Then he got up, put his arm round her and suggested they put the kettle on together.

They went to bed early. Lay side by side in the dark, hardly moving. 'We've gone all shy with one another,' she said. She reached out, took his hand and kissed it. When they made love, it was tenderly quiet. They fumbled. It reminded Claire of how it had been years ago when they were newly-weds. Afterwards, they barely spoke.

The arguments started two days later. He had been following Claire around the house, standing silently watching her as she prepared supper or dusted the dresser. When he followed her to the loo, she gently put her hand on his chest and said, 'Please, there are some things I prefer to do alone.' He nodded. But when she emerged, he was at the door waiting for her.

She tried to be cheery. Kept smiling, put a lilt into her voice. He told her she was being bossy. 'I don't know what's happened to you, but you're taking charge of everything.'

'What do you mean?' she said.

'You're acting like this is your house and I'm some sort of invalid guest.'

'I'm not.'

'You bloody are.'

She walked from the room.

Later, when a light bulb needed replacing, she fetched a new one from the cupboard. He snatched it from her, said he could do it. But, he'd forgotten how hot the dead bulb could be and dropped it, shouting in pain. She led him to the kitchen and put the burned hand under the cold tap. 'I'm not a child. I don't need mothering,' he said. Claire silently picked up a dustpan and brush and went to sweep up the broken glass.

He spotted her in the garden, mowing the lawn and stormed out. 'That's my job. I can do that.' She handed over the mower.

He worked for ten minutes before sitting down on the garden seat, panting and mopping his brow on his sleeve. 'The grass is too damp for cutting.' But she took over. He shouted at her to leave it. 'I am perfectly capable of cutting the grass without help.' She left him to it.

Two hours later he limped into the kitchen, drenched with sweat. 'Told you I could do it.'

They argued about the food she cooked. 'You know I hate liver.'

'It's all I could get. Besides it's good for you. It'll build you up.'

'I don't need building up. And I've told you before, I don't need mothering.'

They argued about where she put his shirts once they'd been ironed. 'I like them hung up, not folded and put in a drawer.'

He told her to stop singing as she washed the dishes. 'It's annoying me.' He drank too much whisky. He hoarded food.

'You don't need to do that any more,' she said after she found a lump of cheese under his pillow. 'You don't need to save it to barter with the guards. There are no guards.'

He told her to shut up. 'You don't know what it was like.'

'Well, how can I know? You won't talk about it.'

'Bugger off,' he said.

And still they made quietly tender love in bed most nights.

One night, as they lay waiting for sleep, he took her hand. 'We made it,' he said. 'We had a whole day without yelling at one another.'

'So we did,' she said.

He told her he thought they were going to be fine.

In two weeks, Claire would go to Southampton to meet the

boat that two people had boarded in South Africa. Nell and Oliver had been children when they left. They were on their way to being grown up now. Claire knew she'd be confronted by a young woman and a young man she hardly knew. She was pretty sure they wouldn't take to their new life. There would be tantrums, fights, comparisons with their life in South Africa. They'd hate the food. They'd hate the weather.

She wondered how long it would take before they became a family again. Sometimes she thought months, sometimes she thought years. Sometimes she thought that it might never happen. When she thought that, she'd shake her head and scold herself for being so pessimistic. After all, she was Mrs Alton, and if there was one thing that Mrs Alton could do, it was cope.

Chapter Forty-five
To Think, We Used to Be Beautiful

The stillness disturbed Julia. The cottage had become silent. Izzy was living at Mrs Brent's and Claire had gone back to London. There was nobody around when Julia got up in the morning, nobody around when she got home at night. All that, and there was never anything to eat.

Thinking Julia went out every night, and very anxious to get home to see Izzy's baby, Mrs Brent never left any food. Julia ate at the Golden Mallard, sitting on her own at a table by the window, a book open beside her plate. She liked to give the impression that she'd chosen not to have a companion. Of course, she hadn't.

The war was barely over, but already things had changed. People had moved on. They'd left the area, got postings elsewhere, or they'd been demobbed and gone home, back to their old lives. The base was quiet now. A lot of the pilots had left. The mess was half-empty in the morning. Face it, Julia said to herself, it's not the same any more.

Lying in bed at night, Julia considered her situation. Soon, Izzy would be back living here. And, though she didn't really mind babies, she didn't feel enthused about living with one. In the world she came from, babies were removed from society. They might be brought into the drawing room for visitors to examine,

coo over, delight at, but they'd be taken away before they dis-
graced themselves by being sick or doing something even more
disgusting.

Here in the cottage, the baby would be omnipresent. It would
cry, there would be baby things lying about the place, it would keep
her awake at night – and she was a person who liked her beauty
sleep. There would be nappies drying in the kitchen, bibs and
mushy food, toys. And there it would be, a baby, reminding her
every time she saw it that she didn't have a child, and would never
be able to have one with the man she had loved. It was time to go
back to London.

In London she knew too many people to be alone if she didn't
want to be. And, she thought, if she was going to be a solitary
soul, she'd rather it was in her own home. She could cry there.

She handed in her notice the next day and, on the way home,
dropped in to see Izzy. She sat on the end of the bed, asked how
she was feeling.

'I'm being tended,' said Izzy. 'I hate it. I'm not meant to put
my feet on the floor for a fortnight. I've done ten days. It's
boring.'

'You haven't got up?'

'Yes, I have. But don't tell Mrs Brent. I get up when she's out
at work and he's away delivering eggs, chickens and whatever
else he delivers and I wander about taking the baby with me. He
likes it.'

Julia said she was sure he did. She went over to peer into the
crib. What happened shook her. The child was awake, staring up
at her, moving his mouth, waving a tiny fist. Julia's heart turned
over. It was such a strange and urgent feeling – and so unexpected
– she took a step back.

'It's all right,' said Izzy. 'He won't bite you.'

'I know,' said Julia. She put her hand to her stomach to quell the longing that had started there. 'I'm just not used to babies. In fact, up till this very moment, I thought I didn't like them.'

'So did I,' said Izzy. 'I was dreading him coming along. But he seems fine. I think we'll get on. Especially once I'm back at the cottage. Here I'm expected to feed him every four hours on the dot and not pick him up otherwise. Mrs Brent and the midwife say if I do I'll spoil him. But I intend to spoil him. I wasn't spoiled and look what happened to me.'

Julia smiled. 'Actually, that's what I came about – the cottage. I'm leaving. Going back to London. You really will be on your own, darling.' She was secretly pleased to see Izzy's disappointment.

'I'll miss you,' said Izzy.

'I'll miss you. But I won't be that far away. You can come see me any time.'

'I know,' said Izzy.

Julia asked if she'd be all right. 'You know, money and everything. You'll be paying all the rent now.'

Izzy said she'd be fine. She had a load of money saved. 'I'll have to move on myself, sometime. Get a job somewhere. Don't know what I'll do, though.'

Julia said she'd been wondering about that herself. 'I wrote after several jobs, but nobody's hiring women pilots. Absolutely nobody.'

'Doesn't really surprise me,' said Izzy. 'Thing is, flying is the only thing I can do.'

'Me, too,' said Julia. She got up, kissed Izzy, said she had to go. 'So much packing to do.' Then she leaned into the cot, touched the baby, and said, 'You take care of your mother.' At the door she turned. 'By the way, what did you call him?'

'Sam,' said Izzy. 'I don't know anybody called Sam. Haven't slept with anybody called Sam and nobody in my family is called Sam. So, it's a whole new fresh person in my life.'

'Good plan,' said Julia. 'I'll be orff.'

'Well, orff you go,' said Izzy. 'I'll miss not having someone in my life who says "orff" instead of "off". I've come to like it.'

Julia said, 'I'm orff, then.' As she walked to the front door, shouted, 'Orff, now. Taking orff and orff I go.'

She got Eddie Hicks to drive her, and her cases and large trunk, to Blackpool. The women porters there loaded her luggage onto the guard's van. In London, she gave her taxi driver a five-shilling tip to help her get everything up the stairs to her flat. Both of them were bent double, sweating and complaining.

Then she was on her own. She dragged the trunk inside, shut the door and sat on it, looking round. Walter had been right, she needed furniture.

She opened a couple of windows, put the kettle on and walked through to the bedroom. She touched the pillow where Walter had put his head, opened the wardrobe, stroked his jackets. She held one of his shirts to her face, breathed him in. The scent of him – cologne, tobacco – she'd forgotten that. She went back to the trunk, sat on it. Now was the time to cry. But she couldn't. She thought she'd forgotten how.

Over the next few weeks she visited salerooms, and eventually found a sofa and a chair that she liked enough to buy. She furnished her kitchen, put rugs on her floors, bought cups and plates. In the evenings she wrote to everybody she knew asking for a job. There was nothing. There was no chance of anybody employing a woman pilot. She gave up. Celebrated her defeat by putting on her favourite evening dress and going out to the 400 Club to drink champagne and dance.

In late July, the heat lay outside, a huge tangible thing. All the windows of the flat were open. Julia lay on her sofa, reading. She wore a silk robe, sipped the iced tea she'd made.

When the doorbell rang, she considered not answering it. She really wasn't feeling sociable. But it rang and rang. Whoever was out there was keeping a stubborn heavy finger on the bell. Sighing, she got up and opened the front door. Almost wept with relief.

'Charles.' She opened her arms, took him to her, hugged him.

He held her with one hand, the other was gripping a black-lacquered stick that was keeping him upright.

She stood back, considering him. He was thin. He looked older, tired. 'You look absolutely awful,' she said.

'Thank you,' he said. 'Shot in the knee.'

'How absolutely awful for you.'

'I'm just lucky it wasn't higher up.'

She laughed, a small snort, for she didn't really think it funny.

'It's not without advantages,' he said. 'A limp, a stick and a uniform have some perks. I get offered a seat on the train, cars let me cross the road in front of them, people step aside with deference on the pavement. I'm enjoying it.'

'You would,' she said.

He limped through to the living room. 'My God, furniture. Very grown up of you.'

'Yes,' she said. 'I thought it time.'

He sat on the sofa, wounded leg stretched, unbending, in front of him. Walking stick propped against the arm. She sat next to him and asked what happened.

'We were under fire. I was on one side of a track, dug in. The enemy not far beyond us. Chaps on the other side of the track, but about half a mile away from me, were making breakfast. I tried to run back to get some. Got hit in the knee.'

'Trust you,' she said. 'Wounded in pursuit of a fry-up.'

He put his arm round her. 'That's right.' Then, he said, 'Met some of your cronies at the Savoy last night. They told me you were in town, and about your husband.'

She said, 'Walter.'

'Yes.'

'Not long after D-Day, in France. Silly bugger had to see the action.'

'You're a widow. I'm going to limp into my dotage. Not so good, is it?' He sighed. 'To think, we used to be beautiful.'

'I still am,' said Julia.

He kissed the top of her head and said, 'Of course you are.'

Chapter Forty-six
Should've, Should've, Should've

Sunday lunch at the manse was no longer lavish. Of course, rationing meant large joints of beef were no longer available, but Hamish had also lost his appetite. 'Just don't feel like eating these days,' he said. 'Haven't been feeling quite myself for weeks.'

He toyed with the small slices of brisket on his plate. Joan told him he should keep his strength up. Then, she said, 'That was a lovely service this morning.'

He'd spoken, with passion, about the evils of gossip. He'd told his parishioners to cast rumours aside. 'Listen to your heart,' he'd said. 'Judge the man, the person you see before you, by what you know and not what others say about him.' There had been coughs and the sound of people shifting in their seats, tweed sliding over old wood.

Joan fetched the pudding, apple crumble and custard, and put it on the table.

'I noticed you biting your tongue when you were at the door saying your goodbyes and thanks for coming. That was good. You didn't boom.'

After the service, several people who'd been avoiding Hamish had shaken his hand, but didn't look him in the eye. He'd been tempted to boom, 'You were all wrong. Gossiping is wrong.' But hadn't. Joan had shot him a scathing look.

'I'm prone to booming,' Hamish said. 'Must stop.'

Joan served two portions and handed Hamish the jug of custard. He gazed into it.

'Custard makes me sad. Reminds me of Izzy. How is she, do you know?'

Joan said she'd tried to get in touch last week. 'She wasn't answering the phone. It rang and rang. I phoned the local cottage hospital to find out if she was there. She wasn't. I have no idea where she is. She hasn't written, either. I haven't had a letter for a few weeks.'

'Izzy,' said Hamish. 'I should've let her come home. I should've welcomed her and her baby. I should've been more understanding.' He pushed his plate away. 'Should've, should've, should've, my life is full of should'ves – things I ought to have done.' He got up, said he was going for a walk. 'It was all about me. I didn't let Izzy come home because I was worried about me, my reputation.' He jabbed himself in the chest.

Izzy was back in her cottage. The move had been a grand affair. Lacking a car, and not wanting to see the new mother walk for several miles, William had borrowed a horse and cart.

Mrs Brent, holding the baby, sat up front with William. Izzy was in the cart with the crib and a box of baby clothes. It had been an enjoyable trip that had involved a lot of waving as they trundled through the village. As a means of transport, Izzy rated horse and cart second to flying. For a few days, she'd toyed with the idea of trading in her motorbike for a pony and trap.

Mrs Brent had scoffed at the notion. 'Where would you keep a pony? And how would you feed it and groom it when you've a baby to look after. You've no sense, girl.'

'It was just a thought,' said Izzy. 'That ride on the horse and cart was the most fun I've had since . . . since . . .'

'Since you got yourself in the family way.'

Izzy thought that might be true, but didn't admit it.

Mrs Brent said, 'The fun's over for you, my lass. You've a baby to look after, responsibilities. Mark my words, once you've had a baby, it's downhill all the way.'

The child had been crying at the time and Izzy was walking up and down the kitchen, making soothing sounds, trying to calm him. 'I think he's bored,' she said. 'It must be boring being a baby. All they do is sleep and eat. It'll be easier for him once he can read and chat.'

'It gets worse as children get older,' said Mrs Brent. 'First, they're not where you put them down. They crawl away. I don't know about reading, mine never did that. But talking. You'll rue the day you taught your boy to speak. First, it's questions, questions, questions. Then they start to answer you back. Like I said it's downhill all the way from now on.'

With Julia and Claire gone, Izzy had told Mrs Brent she no longer needed to come and clean the cottage. 'I don't think I can afford you. Not with having to pay all the rent on my own.'

Mrs Brent understood. But she still visited everyday. If there were dishes to do, she did them. If the floor needed swept, she swept it. She bustled. It was a habit. She brought food, couldn't help it. She was sure Izzy would neglect herself.

'Just a bit of pie I had left over, couldn't see it go to waste,' she'd say, laying a large portion of rabbit and mushroom pie on the table. 'I expect you don't have time to cook, what with the baby and all.'

Izzy was grateful. Cooking bewildered her.

Her life had changed. Izzy had thought she'd miss flying, but she hadn't the time. She lived in a whirl of washing clothes, feeding the baby, picking the baby up, walking about with him, beseeching him to sleep. She had imagined a quiet, contemplative life – reading, sitting by the fire listening to the wireless, writing long letters to Elspeth. But none of this happened. She was too busy.

She had visitors. As well as Mrs Brent, Eddie Hicks and his wife sometimes stopped by, and Dolores was a regular.

'Left the ATA,' she said. 'Soon they'll close the whole thing down.'

'Pity,' said Izzy. She sighed. 'I don't know what I'm going to do. The time will come when I need to earn some money. I've got a bit saved. But it won't last.'

'Well,' said Dolores. 'Alfie and me are going to get busy on the house. If we don't do some repairs soon, the goddam place will fall down. Then we've got to get the estate going. I fancy cattle, I know something about that.'

'Won't all that take a lot of money? I thought . . .' She stopped. It didn't do to discuss money.

'Oh, you thought Alfie didn't have any. You're right, he doesn't. But I do. My family own half of Texas. I think that had something to do with him marrying me.'

'Oh, surely not,' said Izzy.

Dolores flapped her hand. 'Get real.' She looked down at the baby, smiled. 'Cute,' she said. 'Can I pick him up?'

'Of course,' said Izzy.

Dolores reached into the crib, took Sam up in her arms, rocked him, kissed his head. 'I love babies. That's the next job I've got lined up for Alfie. I want one of them.'

After Dolores left, Izzy went upstairs to check her savings. She had a plan. She had enough to put down a deposit on a house. She'd take in lodgers to pay her mortgage. Then, when Sam was old enough to attend school, she'd get a job – any job.

At first, she couldn't believe what she saw. She stood holding a small bundle of notes. I had more than that, she thought. She raked in the drawer, pulled out her knickers and found Jacob's note: 'You owed me.'

'Bastard!' she cried.

She sat on the bed, staring across at the open drawer. 'Bastard.' Jacob had come into her room, rummaged through her personal things and stolen her money. 'Bastard.' And given her back her bloody pen. 'Bastard.'

She imagined him striding towards Poland, smoking a cigar, laughing at her. She went downstairs, slumped into a chair, gave in to despair. Across the room, the child started to cry, then bawl, then scream. Izzy ignored him. She sat, head in hands, mourning her lost cash. 'I should've put it in a bank. I should've taken it with me when I was having the baby.'

The baby's shrill screaming heightened Izzy's turmoil. She rounded furiously on him. 'It's your fault. You did this. It's you made me lose my job. And it's your fault I wasn't here so Jacob could come in and take my money. You're to bloody blame for everything.'

She rushed at the crib in a fury, stared down, saw her son, sweat-drenched, fists flailing, face red, lips blue, tearful and her heart turned over. The guilt. She scooped him up, pressed his rigid body against her, rocked him, hushed him. Loathed herself for her foul accusations. Then, she calmed. Comforting the infant, she momentarily comforted herself.

She couldn't stop the rage, though. It was there when she woke every morning. Sometimes, she'd be walking back from the shops, or preparing supper, or sitting in the kitchen feeding the baby, and it would come to her. *That bastard has stolen my money.* She imagined herself destitute, living on the streets, clutching a hungry child – homeless.

It was Thursday, rent day. Izzy had just returned from the landlord's office when the phone rang.

'Izzy?' A voice shrill with anxiety. It was her mother. 'Where have you been? I've been trying to get in touch.'

'Having a baby,' said Izzy. 'A boy.'

'But I phoned and there was no reply.'

'I went to Mrs Brent's,' said Izzy. 'So there would be some-body to tend me, as they say.'

'You should've been here. I should've looked after you.'

'Dad didn't want me there,' said Izzy.

'That's why I'm phoning. Your father's dead. He had a heart attack a week ago.'

'Last week, why didn't you tell me?'

'Well, I tried, but nobody answered the phone. He went out for a walk and didn't come back. So, I went looking for him. He was in the garden. Sitting on the bench out there. He'd just died.'

Izzy said nothing.

'I didn't know how you'd feel about it, but I thought you should know. We buried him on Tuesday,' said Joan.

'You should've told me. I would have come for the funeral. I should've been there.'

'It would have been a long journey. And you with a baby.'

'You didn't know about the baby. I would have come.'

'I know.'

Another long silence. Then Izzy said, 'I should have come to see him. I should have told him I was sorry. I should have asked him to forgive me for lying to you both.'

'It was as much his fault as yours. I don't think you should berate yourself too much. He did admit he'd been wrong. It was almost the last thing he said to me.'

Izzy asked her mother what she was going to do now.

'Well, I can't stay at the manse. They will be appointing a new minister soon enough. I've decided to use the money you sent us to buy a small house in the village and stay on here.'

'I thought you were going to move to the seaside.'

'Not now. I don't want to go where I don't know anybody. I have friends here.'

'Can I come and see you?"

'Well,' said her mother, 'in time, when you feel up to it.' She hadn't told anybody about Izzy's baby. She was torn between seeing Izzy and the baby and facing up to a bout of scandal – her unmarried daughter and her child. Oh, the whisperings that would set up. 'How is he?'

'He's fine,' said Izzy. 'He's beautiful. You should come and see him if you're too ashamed to have me up there.'

'One day, I will.'

Izzy said she'd look forward to it. The pips went and they were cut off.

Sometime, long after midnight, the baby woke her. She lifted him from his crib and took him into bed with her. Sitting, leaning on her pillows, she dropped the front of her nightgown and fed him. She stroked his head. She loved that little head, loved the smell of it.

She thought about her father. The way he'd been to her. The games they'd played, the music they'd danced to. She thought, I should have done what he wanted. I should have given up flying. I should have let him know I loved him.

And he was right, she thought. Look at me, an unmarried mother. I've been robbed. I'll be broke soon. I haven't heard from Jimmy in weeks. He's bound to be back in America, he's forgotten about me. And my father is dead. And I didn't make up with him. Dead, and he probably never forgave me.

She started to cry. The infant lost his grip on her breast, grappled to find it again and started to cry. Together, in the dark, they both howled. Izzy reached over for her watch to check the time. Twenty to bloody two, mourning time. She clutched her yowling child and wept some more.

Chapter Forty-seven
Time to Let Go

Early August, ten o'clock at night, light fading, bats skimming round the eaves of Duncan's cottage and Tyler leaned against a tree waiting for the old man to come home from his nightly stroll. Tonight was getting-even night. Tomorrow he was leaving the forest.

In fact, this was his stag night. He'd left the party early, saying he wanted one last stroll along the paths that had become so familiar. Friends and fellow drinkers in his hut had mocked, saying that this was his last night of freedom and it shouldn't be wasted going for a walk. 'You'll be under the wife's thumb tomorrow.'

Tyler said that if there was one place he wanted to be it was under Elspeth's thumb. 'She's got lovely thumbs.'

He waited half an hour before Duncan turned up. Tyler heard him first. The old man was shuffling along, swearing at every step. 'Bloody, bloody, bloody . . .'

When he did at come into view, his pace was achingly slow, his head down as he examined the ground watching where he placed his feet. His breath rasped in his throat. From time to time, he'd stop, breathe deeply and reach down to rub his knees and hips. 'Bloody, bloody, bloody . . .'

The sight shocked Tyler. He hadn't known the old man was so ill. He almost felt sorry for him.

'I know you're there, Tyler Bute!' Duncan called. 'I know you're waitin' for me. I can feel you there. I can smell you. There's not a thing goes on this forest that I don't know about. Not a single thing.'

Tyler stepped out onto the path, stood a few feet in front of Duncan.

'Come to get your revenge for what I did to your girlfriend?' Duncan asked. 'Come to beat me up? Do what you will. You can't make me sorrier than I already am.'

Tyler said nothing.

'Just lost control for a minute, that's all. I wanted her.'

Tyler said, 'I know.' He clenched his fists, walked towards Duncan, brushed against him as he passed and carried on up the path. He walked for a few yards before turning.

Duncan had his back to him, making his slow way to his cottage. His head still bent, still carefully considering the ground, choosing where to place his feet. Tyler shrugged, what could he do to Duncan that would make his life worse than it already was? The man was old before his time, in pain, lonely and bitter. Years spent working outdoors in foul weather had taken its toll on his lungs, bones and heart. But, Tyler thought, the things that would hurt him most were his regrets. Duncan had the rest of his life to turn them over in his head, sitting alone in his cottage cursing himself. Punishment enough, Tyler decided.

Elspeth rose early next morning. She put on a green tweed skirt with matching jacket, and a white blouse. It was her wedding outfit. Not what she would have chosen if she'd had the opportunity to shop, but it was smart. It would do. It was all she had. It was, also, too big for her. She'd lost weight working in the forest.

She left her uniform in Duncan's office, and walked to the stables. Time to say goodbye to Frazer and Harry.

Frazer was grooming the horse when she arrived. 'We don't have nobody to take your place, yet.'

Elspeth felt a pang run through her. She didn't want anyone else to take over the horse. Harry was hers. 'Well, make sure whoever gets the job is good to her. She likes her food slightly warm and she's fond of a song, especially a bit of Mozart. And a carrot, I pinch carrots for her. And . . .'

'Time to let go,' said Frazer. He came over, took her hand. 'I may just miss you. And I don't say that to many people.' He swept his arms round her, kissed her. 'There, a kiss for the bride. It's lucky.'

'Who for?'

'For me,' said Frazer. 'I don't kiss many brides these days, and I need a bit of luck.'

'What about me,' said Elspeth, 'don't I get any luck?'

'A lass like you? You make your own.' He kissed her again. 'There, double luck for me.'

It surprised Elspeth how upset she felt. This was the moment she'd been waiting for, longing for. She should be jumping for joy. But she wasn't.

On her way back to camp, she stopped and leaned against a tree. She touched her lips, still wet from Frazer's clumsy kisses, and gave herself a talking to. This is an adventure, she told herself. Today I marry, I'll be Elspeth Bute. She didn't know if she liked the name. Tomorrow I set off on the journey of a lifetime. A train to Southampton, a ship to Halifax, a train – a big Canadian train with mournful whistle – to Nova Scotia, then a boat across the Gulf of St Lawrence to Port-aux-Basque and another train to Goobies, where I'll live for the rest of my life. Elspeth and Tyler Bute – good living, kindly folks of Goobies, that'll be us. She felt a little downhearted. Then clenched her fists, thinking, It will be wonderful. We'll light fires to heat our house when gales and snow whip round the walls. I'll play my accordion. We'll dance round the kitchen, sing songs, eat cod's roe and fresh salmon. I'll learn to make heavy fruitcake, laden with blueberries and cherries, and bake apple pie. We'll fry trout by the river, we'll have four or five children, all apple-cheeked, sunny natured and full of joy. 'Order to self,' she said out loud, 'I will be happy.'

As soon as she entered the dining hut, all the girls started singing, 'Here comes the bride, fifty inches wide . . . la la la la . . .'

Elspeth told them to shut up. She took her place beside Lorna, who asked if that was what she was getting married in. 'This jacket and skirt?'

'Yes,' said Elspeth. 'It's all I've got.'

'But it's green,' said Lorna. 'That's unlucky.'

'I don't believe in superstitions,' said Elspeth. 'Besides, the wedding doesn't matter. It's the marriage that counts. I intend to be very happy.'

'OK,' said Lorna. 'Guess what happened to me.'

'I can't,' said Elspeth.

'Duncan called me to his office and said that there were openings for girls who wanted to go to Germany. Work in the sawmills. So I said yes. I mean, it can't be worse than here, can it? I'll be measuring German wood.'

Elspeth asked if she was sure she wanted to do that. 'I mean the country's been flattened by our bombs. There's not a lot of food. You don't know what you're letting yourself in for.'

'I'll be fine,' said Lorna. 'It's either that or stay here for years. Besides, I don't want to be here with you gone. I'll miss you. There'll be nobody to have a laugh with. It'll be an adventure. You're always saying folk should have adventures.'

'So I am,' said Elspeth. She put her arm round her friend. 'That's both of us off adventuring.'

At eight o'clock the taxi that Tyler had ordered arrived. He and Elspeth packed it with their two small cases and the accordion, climbed in, and drove away. The girls gathered round cheering and waving. Elspeth turned and watched them till the car turned the corner, and she could see them no more.

They took the bus to Inverness, and were married at the registry office. A swift ceremony that took ten minutes, a couple booked to be married after them witnessed the occasion. Outside Tyler took Elspeth in his arms, kissed her and said, 'Mrs Bute. My Mrs Bute.'

Elspeth looked down at her hands, rough, calloused – a lot older than she was. She never could get used to these hands and now there was a thin gold ring on the finger of her left one. She linked her arm in his, and said, 'Mrs Bute, and proud of it.'

They dined at the Station Hotel, where they'd booked to stay the night. Tyler leaned over the table and hissed, 'Let's get this over as soon as possible and get upstairs to bed. We've some serious consummating to do.'

Elspeth said she was having pudding first.

But they did make it to the bedroom. Tyler peeled off his shirt, picked Elspeth up and said, 'First time in a bed, Mrs Bute.'

This was true, so it shouldn't have irritated Elspeth, but it did. It was hardly romantic.

'We'll go outside if you prefer it in the open air,' she said. 'It's warm enough.'

He laughed threw her onto the bed, lay beside her and pulled her on top of him. 'Oh, no. I've been looking forward to this.'

She hadn't noticed how loudly he spoke before this. His voice filled the room. She lifted her finger to her lips. 'Sssh, they'll hear you next door.'

'I don't care. I'm happy.' He pulled her to him and kissed her. Elspeth thought that the people next door could hear that, too.

Afterwards, he lay back, sighed and said, 'Now we really are Mr and Mrs Bute and nothing can come between us.'

They boarded the train for London early the next morning. Tyler put their cases and the accordion on the rack and took a seat next to Elspeth. She asked if he wouldn't prefer to sit across the aisle where there was a window seat available.

'No, I would not like to sit there. I'm sitting here. I want to feel you next to me all the way to London.'

A woman sitting in the corner of the carriage looked over at them.

'Just married,' said Tyler. 'This is my wife, Mrs Bute. We're on our way to Newfoundland. I'm going home, taking my new wife with me.'

The woman said, 'How lovely.'

'Thousands of miles we'll travel,' said Tyler. 'But this time next week we'll be in my house, sitting at my table, eating good Newfie food, cods' tongues or a tasty salt beef dinner.'

Elspeth thought the woman looked awfully glad it wasn't her going all that way. She hadn't realised Tyler was so hearty. She

supposed he was an open-air sort of man. He lived his life with
gusto. She would have to teach him new ways, or get used to him.

By the time they reached Perth, Tyler had told his story to
every new passenger that came into the carriage. Elspeth looked
out of the window at the familiar station, resisting the urge to get
off the train and travel the few miles to her cottage. She thought
it would be wonderful to see it again. But no, she was a different
woman now, a new life ahead of her. As soon as she arrived in
Newfoundland, she'd write to her solicitor and tell him to sell the
cottage. Probably, she and Tyler would need the money, especially
once the children came along.

When they reached Edinburgh, the train emptied and a fresh
set of passengers got on – a new audience for Tyler. He introduced
his new wife. He described his house. 'Built it myself, with these
hands.' He held them out for examination. 'That house will
withstand all the weather God throws at it. It has stood through
hundred mile an hour gales, wind so fierce it'd blow yer face away.
Drifts of snow high as the roof and temperatures low as forty
below.'

A ripple of 'Goodness,' spread through the carriage. Elspeth
was thinking about Izzy. She wondered what Izzy was doing now
her baby was born. A boy, Izzy had told her. 'Looks a bit like me,'
she'd said in her letter. Elspeth wondered how Izzy was managing
motherhood. It pained her to think she hadn't seen the baby. It
pained her even more to think she might never see Izzy again.

By the time the train reached York, Elspeth and Tyler had been
travelling for eight hours. The platform was busy, porters rushing
up and down, heaving cases and trunks on board. A man trundled
a wooden trolley past the carriage window. He was selling cups of
tea, sweets and magazines. Passengers could buy tea, and hand

over the cup to a similar trolley-man at the next station. Elspeth stood up and said that since there was a ten-minute stop here, she thought she'd stretch her legs and go buy a magazine. Tyler, deep in conversation about fishing with a man on the other side of him, gave her a smile and said he'd see her soon.

Elspeth walked up the platform, bought a *Woman's Own* and stood thumbing through it. She wondered if Tyler would like a cup of tea, but she didn't buy one. She stood looking at the train. The guards were moving up the platform shouting, 'All aboard!' Slamming doors shut. The train was shuddering, heaving, steam gushing from the engine.

Elspeth would always wonder if she'd planned this, or if it was just another of her notions. A moment in her life when an unexpected decision came to her. The guard blew his whistle, waved his flag and the train chuntered slowly away. Elspeth watched it.

Everything from her forest life was on that train – her long johns, her beloved blue eiderdown, her accordion. But she stood clutching her *Woman's Own*, and said goodbye to it all. Time to let go, she thought.

Chapter Forty-eight
A Stranger in a Green Suit

Mr Hudson, the local solicitor who managed the lease on the cottage, folded his hands on his desk, peered over the rim of his specs and asked Izzy how she was.

'Fine,' said Izzy. 'Actually, I was wondering if there was anywhere smaller I could rent. I'm on my own now. I don't need all these rooms.'

He told her there was a cottage across the river from hers. 'Very small. One of your pilots had it. He left not long ago. It's a bit run-down. Cheap.'

Izzy said, 'I'll take it.'

She moved across the river into the tiny cottage that had, not so long ago, been the scene of Claire and Simon's grand passion.

She settled in. Moved into what she called her 'Babytimes'. She rose early, fed the child, ate porridge, did the washing in the kitchen sink, shoved it through the old green mangle that stood at the back door, watching it crumple gracefully into a tin tub. This, she found very satisfying. She felt a glow of achievement seeing her washing flapping on the line in the garden. She mastered a small culinary repertoire, she made the bed; she told herself she was happy. 'Well,' she said to the infant as she loomed over him – she felt that lately she did a lot of looming – 'I am breathing. I can walk without holding on to the wall. I can keep food down. This is as good as it gets, right now.'

Afternoons, she strolled with the baby, trundling her ancient, third- or fourth-hand pram along the path by the river, or up through the village. She was returning from one of her strolls, shoving the pram ahead of her, letting go, running to catch it, when she saw a stranger – a woman in a green tweed suit – knocking at her door. She looked familiar, but Izzy couldn't quite place her.

The woman turned, peered at her. 'Izzy?'

Izzy peered back. 'Elspeth?'

She abandoned the pram, ran to her friend. They hugged, held one another at arm's length, each drinking the other in and hugged again. They went inside, both talking at once. 'It's been so long.' And, 'How did you get here?' And, 'You look so well.'

Izzy stood in the hall. Her arms felt oddly empty. 'God, the baby.' She ran to get him.

Elspeth looked at him, said hello and told Izzy he was her double. 'Your hair and everything. Look at you, a mother.'

Izzy said, 'Who'd have thought it.'

'Not me,' said Elspeth.

They went into the kitchen. Izzy put on the kettle.

Elspeth asked, 'What about his father? Have you heard from him?'

Izzy shook her head. 'He'll be in Montana, I guess.'

'Does he know about the baby?'

Izzy said, 'Nope.'

'Does he know where you are?'

'He could find me if he wanted to. You found me.'

Elspeth had gone to Izzy's old address, knocked on the door

– nobody answered. She'd peered through the windows, the place looked unlived in. She'd walked about the village asking for Miss Macleod. People had scratched their heads, looked puzzled. 'Macleod? No, don't know anybody of that name.' Eventually, she'd given up and asked at the local garage when the bus for Blackpool left. Eddie had told her it would be a while. 'Couple of hours.' Then, because he was nosy, he'd asked, 'Are you on holiday?'

She'd told him no. 'My friend lived here. She was a pilot at the base, Izzy.'

'Izzy,' he'd said. 'I know Izzy. Everybody knows Izzy.' He'd taken her outside, pointed the way to the cottage. Elspeth had run all the way.

'Such a lot of catching up to do. A whole war has happened to us,' she said.

The catching up took days – a meandering conversation filled with laughter and memories. They spoke when they first got up in the morning, carried on through lunch, through the baby's feeds, when they took him for an afternoon stroll, at his bath time and on till it was dark and the radio stations had stopped broadcasting and it was time for bed. Then, they'd speak some more. Elspeth, sleeping on the sofa, curled under a pile of blankets, would shout to Izzy in the bedroom, 'Hey, Izzy, remember . . .' And off they'd sail on a tide of memories.

Elspeth had been staying for days before Izzy asked, 'Did you mean it? Did you just marry Tyler to get out of the forest?'

Elspeth said she did. 'It was an impulse. I'd just heard we wouldn't be able to leave, perhaps for years and I said, "I'll marry you."'

'Just like that,' said Izzy.

'Just like that,' said Elspeth. 'But I did think at the time I'd go with him to Newfoundland. I didn't plan to get off the train, it just happened. I realised I couldn't go there. I would have been miserable. I'd have made him miserable. I stood there watching the train pull away, and I felt numb. It was an awful thing to do.'

They were sitting outside on a travelling rug spread out on the small, weedy lawn. The baby was between them, lying kicking his legs, staring with fascination at his fist, held up against the sky. A plane buzzed past.

'I'll never get the picture of that train moving off, the whistle, the steam and me standing there with my *Woman's Own* out of my head. And I'll always have my images of Tyler looking about, wondering where I was, going out into the corridor, walking up and down calling my name. I guess he hates me now. I deserve that.' She sighed.

'He won't hate you,' said Izzy. 'Maybe one day he'll be grateful. He might meet someone else and be glad he's free.'

'But he won't be free. He'll be married to me. Unless I manage, somehow, to get a divorce.'

They both stared down at the baby. Elspeth put her finger in his hand, he pulled it to his mouth, sucked it.

'So what happened to your accordion?' asked Izzy.

'It's on its way to a land I'll never visit to have adventures I'll never have.'

Next day it rained. Elspeth and Izzy stayed in, sat by the fire and talked.

'You owe it all to me, you know. Everything that's happened to you is all down to me.'

'So, it's your fault I had a baby. Elspeth, you had nothing to do with that.'

'I got you flying. If I hadn't, you'd never have come here, you wouldn't have been in that plane you had to land at Jimmy's base so you wouldn't have met him. You've me to thank.'

'Well, thanks,' said Izzy. 'It's your fault I got robbed of my money. Your fault I had a baby.' She sighed. 'I'd like to know who it was told my father I was a pilot. That's what started my downfall.'

Elspeth looked down at her shoe, took a breath and said, 'That was me.'

'You? *You* did that.'

'Me. I blurted it out. I've always been a blurter.'

'That was one hell of a piece of blurting,' said Izzy.

'I was at home. I met him in the street and I told him. He was being so patronising, crowing about you having a desk job while I was slaving in the forest doing a man's job. I was jealous of you. You with the wonderful job and me trudging about the forest, exhausted. And you hadn't been in touch for ages. And I wanted to hurt him. I wasn't enthused about men at the time. There had been a hiccup in my life. I hated men.'

Izzy asked why.

'One of the men in the forest tried to rape me. I'd gone home to recover. When I met your father, I was covered in bruises. I said I'd fallen off my bike.'

'You were raped?' said Izzy. 'Elspeth, that's more than a hiccup. Who?'

She told him it was her boss. 'But he didn't actually manage to do the deed. I think he got a little overexcited too soon. In the end, when it came to the bit, he wasn't up to it.'

'Oh, Elspeth.'

'He sort of knocked me about. But I gave a good account of

myself. He didn't come away unscathed.' She made scratching movements in the air.

'Oh, Elspeth.'

'So, in a way,' said Elspeth, 'I *am* responsible for everything that's happened. Except for Jacob stealing your money. That's your own fault, keeping your cash in your knicker drawer.'

All Izzy could say was, 'Oh, Elspeth.'

Elspeth said, 'I'm sorry. I rather think I buggered up your life.'

Chapter Forty-nine
All the Way from America

Mrs Brent knocked on the cottage door and walked in, shouting, 'Only me!'

Izzy was making soup; Elspeth was at the table, watching. They both turned.

Mrs Brent handed three letters to Izzy. 'For you, all the way from America.'

Izzy wiped her hands on her apron, and took them.

'They've been delivered to your old cottage. I was in there doing a bit of tidying up and there they were on the doormat.'

Izzy looked at the letters, turned them over, read the sender's address.

'They'll be from your young man,' said Mrs Brent. She waited for Izzy to open them and tell her what they said. But Izzy told Elspeth, to mind the baby and went outside to be alone while she read them.

Mrs Brent hovered, looked out the window at Izzy, looked at Elspeth who was saying nothing. As no gossip was forthcoming, she left, saying she'd keep an eye out for any more letters and hand them in.

When Izzy returned, she put the letters down on the table and went back to making soup.

'Well?' said Elspeth.

'He's back in Montana, working at a local hospital. He's building a house near to where his parents live. He's living with them at the moment.'

'And?' said Elspeth.

'He wants me to go there.'

'Go,' said Elspeth. 'You must go.'

'I have a baby. I can't just get up and go halfway across the world at the drop of a hat.'

'Take him with you. He might like to meet his son.'

'He doesn't know he has a son.'

'Well, write and tell him,' said Elspeth. 'He should know he's a father.'

Izzy said that indeed he should. She'd write and tell him.

'Go and see him, take Sam with you. It'd be an adventure,' said Elspeth.

'I have no desire for an adventure,' Izzy told her. 'I've had enough of adventures.'

'Go,' said Elspeth. 'America, Izzy, how can you resist? You might meet Clark Gable.'

Izzy told her not to be silly. 'Besides I'd rather meet James Stewart. I prefer him.' She sighed. 'Why doesn't Jimmy come to me?'

'Because his life is there, he wants you to see it. Maybe he wants you to share it.'

'He hasn't said he loves me,' said Izzy.

'Do you love him?'

Izzy was silent for a long time before saying, 'Yes.'

'So go and find out if he loves you back.'

'I've not got the money.'

'So, get the money,' said Elspeth. 'Beg, borrow or steal it. But get it.'

At night, when Elspeth slept, Izzy sat in bed reading Jimmy's letters. He said he'd wanted to come to her but had been shipped to America. He told her he wanted her to see this place where he lived. 'You'll love it.' In his next letter, he pleaded her to get in touch. 'Why haven't you answered my letter? Is there something wrong? Is there someone else?' In the third letter, he was desperate. 'I have phoned your cottage – no reply. I'm hoping that if you no longer live there, someone will post this on to you. I also phoned the manse to speak to your parents. I was told your father had died and your mother was living somewhere in the village, I wasn't told where.' He begged her to write to him.

Izzy took up her tortoiseshell pen and wrote, 'Dear Jimmy, You have a son . . .'

When that was done, she started a second letter – 'Dear Julia, I have a huge favour to ask of you . . .'

Chapter Fifty
Do You Miss It?

Julia swept into the cottage and did what she always did, filled the place with her beauty and her scent. She looked round, pursed her scarlet lips and said, 'God, Izzy. This is the smallest cottage I've ever been in.'

'Small,' said Izzy, 'but perfect. You don't have to walk far to get to anything. Three steps and you're in the bedroom, another three and you're in the loo. That's what I call handy.'

Julia turned to Charles, who'd come with her. 'Izzy's ever the optimist.'

'I'd call it pragmatic,' said Charles.

There were four of them in the room, and really that was two more than it could comfortably accommodate. Julia suggested Charles and Elspeth went for a walk. 'You could show him around. And he could buy you tea somewhere.'

Elspeth said, 'Why not. It's stuffy in here.'

'No, it isn't,' said Izzy. She didn't like anyone to make derogatory remarks about her cottage.

'Well, it's going to get stuffy,' said Elspeth. 'Besides, it's quite nice to be bossed about. I'm tired of being the bossy one.' On the way to the front door, she asked Charles what happened to his leg.

'Stupid bugger got shot trying to get some breakfast in

Burma,' said Julia. In a space this small, it was hard for innocent questions and remarks to go unheard by everyone.

'I've done some pretty stupid things myself,' said Elspeth.

As they walked up the garden, Charles said she'd have to tell him about them.

Julia sat down and heaved some papers from her handbag. 'I've got your passport application form and everything else. I thought you might like to fly to New York, then a train to Chicago and another train out to Great Falls in Montana. Jimmy can meet you there.'

'You've got it all worked out,' said Izzy.

'Darling, I've discovered that I love organising people. I think I've stumbled upon a great skill I didn't know I had.'

'Maybe you should become a politician,' said Izzy.

Julia gave her a withering look, 'I don't think so. Too much skulduggery and back-stabbing. No, I'll just look about for a career where I can sit back and tell people what to do.'

Izzy said, 'Thank you.'

'Thank *you*,' said Julia. 'I have loved doing this. I feel useful. I'm touched that you asked for my help. You made me feel like a friend. It's the nicest thing that ever happened to me.' She thought about that. 'Well, the second nicest thing that ever happened to me. Or maybe the third or fourth. But nice, anyway.'

They sat quietly for a while, then Julia asked, 'Do you miss it?'

'Yes,' said Izzy. 'Every single day. There are still one or two planes going over, but fewer and fewer, soon the base will be closed. It will all be over.'

'Great times,' said Julia. 'God, I'm going to miss the war, happiest days of my life.'

'I know,' said Izzy.

They sat some more, let memories flow. Izzy asked if Julia would like a cup of tea. She said, 'Why not?'

But Izzy didn't move. She was enjoying the memories, moments in the air, alone in the sky, singing to herself, watching the world below skim past – rooftops, hedges, fields, roads like black ribbons, sleek rivers. She sighed. 'It's over, isn't it? There's nothing for us now. Nobody wants a lady pilot.'

'No, they don't,' said Julia. 'We'll have to find another thrill.' She reached once more into her handbag, brought out a fat envelope. 'For you.'

Izzy opened it, peered inside. 'Gosh. This is a lot of money.'

'It's mostly dollars, darling. I changed some money yesterday. But there's enough for a first-class ticket to London and a little for extras on the way. I'll buy your flight tickets and give you them when you come to London. I'll take you to the airport. The ticket will be one-way, you understand.'

'One-way? What about coming back?'

'Oh, I don't think you'll be coming back, darling.' She smiled at her. 'Travel in hope. And if you do want to come back, your lovely American can pay. After all, he did lure you out there.'

Izzy said, 'I'll pay you back.'

'Naturally,' said Julia. 'But take your time. Well, it will take you some time, won't it?'

'I rather think it will,' said Izzy.

'You should have told me sooner,' said Julia. 'You should have let me know as soon as you found out Jacob had stolen your money. I'd have helped. You didn't need to come and live in this hovel.'

Izzy protested, 'It isn't a hovel. It's a cottage that has a simple rustic charm.'

Julia said, 'You goose, Izzy.'

*

Charles and Elspeth strolled along the path by the river. They picked up stones, tossed them into the water, speculated about the love lives of the ducks that drifted past, told one another their lives. When they came to the Golden Mallard, they went through the gate, walked up the long lawns and went in to order tea.

They sat on the terrace. Elspeth poured. 'I won't make any remarks about being mother,' she said. 'I hate that. Actually, I don't think I ever want to be a mother. I don't think I'm the type.'

He said, 'Probably you aren't. It's not a thing to be done on impulse. And you are a creature of impulse.'

She nodded. 'I left that train on impulse. Though I'm sure it was a good impulse. I joined the Forestry Commission on impulse. I bought an accordion on impulse.'

'You wanted to form an all-girl accordion band.'

'Yes,' she said. 'I imagined us all on a brightly painted bus, travelling the country. Playing hearty, stomping music at village halls.'

'Do you actually know any other women who play the accordion?' Charles asked.

'No,' she said. 'Now you mention it, I don't.'

'So how would you have formed a band?'

'I'd have advertised,' she said. 'Oh, I don't know. Don't ask sensible questions.'

Charles said, 'Sorry.' He thought he'd stumbled upon the perfect woman. She could play the piano, was impulsive and, best of all, she was married. She wouldn't expect him to make an honest woman of her.

'So what now?' he asked.

'I was planning to go to London, get a job and be outrageous.

But I think I may put that off for the moment. I'll go back to my cottage and live there for a while. Then Edinburgh, I think. I'll teach the piano to reluctant children while I ponder what to do with the rest of my life.'

He said he liked Scotland. 'Might take a trip up there. Do a bit of fishing. Is there a river near you?'

'Yes,' said Elspeth. 'There are rivers all over Scotland.'

'Would you mind if I paid you a visit?'

'Not at all. I have a spare room.'

He raised his teacup and said, 'Excellent. See you there.' He didn't tell her he'd no intention of using the spare room.

In the evening, after Julia and Charles had left, Elspeth told Izzy she thought it time she went home. 'I want to see my cottage again. I need to sleep in my own bed. Make peace with myself. Also, I've been wearing this damn suit since I got married. I want to put it away and never see it again.'

Izzy said she understood.

'I don't suppose you could lend me the money for the train fare. I have nothing.'

'Of course. I have a huge pile Julia lent me. I'm sure I could spare twenty pounds. That should see you with some left over.'

Elspeth said she had a small amount in the bank at Fortham. I'll pay you back so you can pay Julia back.'

Elspeth left the next morning. 'No tearful goodbyes. I will be seeing you again, even if I have to come to Montana to find you. Just lots of letters, please.'

Elspeth climbed aboard the country bus, took a seat by the window, waved as it pulled away. Izzy watched it go, watched till it disappeared down the High Street and stood watching long after it was gone. She sighed, pushed the pram back to the cottage, head down, looking at her feet moving over the pavement. Soon she would be leaving this place, and she liked it here, felt safe here. She loved her little hovel with its rustic charm, its tiny rooms, snug now the first September winds were rattling at the windows. In fact, the more she thought about the journey she was about to take, travelling across a strange land with a child, the more she felt she didn't want to go.

Chapter Fifty-one
You Used Me

Nine o'clock at night, Elspeth walked up the path to her front door. The windows were lit, smoke drifted from the chimney and she thought she heard the wireless playing. How lovely, she thought, Izzy had phoned her mother and asked her to light a fire to warm the cottage for her. There would be hot water for a bath, and she did like her baths.

Inside, she walked down the hall, sniffing. Fish, she thought. How odd. Into the living room – a soft fire flickered in the grate, someone was in her favourite armchair, feet up on the stool in front of it, socks off, snoring.

'Hello, Tyler,' said Elspeth.

He woke, rubbed his eyes, stared at her blankly as he came to. Then, he said, 'There you are. Where have you been?'

Elspeth took off her jacket, flung it over the arm of the sofa. 'Izzy's,' she said. 'Visiting my friend and her new baby.'

'You just went without telling me?'

Elspeth shrugged. She didn't know what to say. Yes, she had gone to see Izzy without telling him. She knew that if they stayed married, she'd do it again. She hated herself for that. And rather disliked him for putting up with it. Well, she imagined he would put up with it.

'You got off the train and went to see your friend and didn't say anything. That's the sort of wife you are?'

'So it seems,' said Elspeth. She told him she needed a cup of tea. He followed her to the kitchen. 'You just got off the train and disappeared.'

'I know,' said Elspeth. 'It wasn't planned. I just did it. I was on the platform, the guard blew his whistle and the train moved off and I watched it. I couldn't move. I just stood.'

'I looked for you on that train. I went up and down the corridor looking for you. Then I got off and took the train back to York. Looked for you everywhere in the station. Called your name. Asked the porters if they'd seen you.'

'You shouldn't have done that,' said Elspeth. 'I'm really sorry.' She filled the kettle.

'Then I thought I'd missed you. You'd got the next train to London. So I got the one after that. By then it was late. So I slept in the station and got the first train to Southampton. I was sure you'd be there. But you weren't.'

Elspeth warmed the teapot, put in two scoops of tea and filled it with boiling water. 'Do we have any milk?'

He shook his head.

She sniffed the air. 'Have you been cooking fish?'

He told her he had.

'Where did you get it?'

He pointed to the world beyond the window. 'There's a river out there.'

'Tyler, that's poaching. You could get into serious trouble for that.'

'We took fish from the river in the forest.'

'That was different,' she said. 'There weren't gamekeepers there. There are here.'

He shrugged and continued with his story. 'By the time I got to Southampton, the ship had sailed. When I checked the passenger list, you weren't on it. So I came here. I went to the post office and told the woman there I was your husband and she told me where to come.'

Elspeth poured two cups of tea and handed one to Tyler. 'How did you get into the house?'

He told her the back door hadn't been locked. She took her tea back to the living room. He followed, telling her as he went that there was another boat leaving in a couple of days. 'I've booked us on it.'

She sat on the chair he'd been sitting on and waved him into the smaller one opposite it. 'Tyler, I'm not going to Newfoundland.'

She hated that he meekly sat on the small chair without complaint. He should have claimed the comfy one she'd taken.

'Why not?' he asked. 'You said you'd come with me. I had it planned.'

'I know. At the time, it sounded wonderful. But on the train you started to talk about gales and huge snowdrifts and cold. Tyler, I've had enough of the cold. I want comfort. I want lights. I want to live in a city.'

'I'll live in a city with you, then.'

She shook her head. 'You'd be miserable. You'd hate all the concrete. The roads are covered with tarmac. The trees are mostly in parks. There's very little wildlife. You'd feel hemmed in. You'd go mad.'

'But I'd have you.'

Elspeth shook her head again. 'It wouldn't work. I'd want to go to concerts, the theatre, the cinema. I'd be teaching the piano and what would you do? Where would you work?'

He said he'd find something. 'I don't care as long as we can be together.'

Elspeth shook her head. 'You'd hate it. You'd end up hating me.'

They sat. Logs shifted in the hearth. Outside some people walked past, voices carrying in the night air. Elspeth couldn't make out what they were saying. The silence in the room was awful. She wished Tyler would shout. Yell at her, call her foul names. Threaten to hit her. She could deal with that. She could yell back. His sudden meekness was unnerving.

Eventually he said, 'You used me.'

She didn't reply.

'You used me,' he said again.

'I didn't mean to. I didn't plan it. I just heard that I'd have to stay in that forest for years and reacted. I didn't think it through. I wanted to go home. Actually, I didn't even know I was going to say I'd marry you till I'd said it.'

He got up. Fetched his boots from where he'd left them beside the chair Elspeth was sitting on and shoved his feet into them. He brought his case from the hall, opened it, went to the kitchen and brought the shirt and socks he'd washed and shoved them in beside his clothes. 'I didn't unpack. I thought we'd be leaving soon as you got here. Your accordion is on its way to Newfoundland with your other things.'

She shrugged. 'Doesn't matter. I don't want it any more. My accordion-playing days are over.'

He got his coat from the stand, hauled it on.

'You're not going now,' said Elspeth. 'It's late. There are no buses and no trains.'

'I'll hitch a lift. Don't want to stay.'

'You can go in the morning.'

He buttoned his coat, shook his head. 'No.'

'I'll get a divorce,' said Elspeth. 'I'll say it was me. I'll say I slept with someone else.'

He shook his head. 'No divorce. I'm not going to let you off so easily. You married me, you'll stay married to me. You won't be able to marry anyone else. Ever. That's my deal.'

He picked up his case and headed for the front door. Elspeth followed him. 'You're being silly, walking out this time of night.'

'I'm getting away from you. If I can't have you, I don't want to see you.' He opened the door, walked out. As he stumped up the path, he called, 'You used me!'

Elspeth shut the door. She went back to sit by the fire, hands clasped in her lap, head hung. The shame she felt was unbearable. He was right. She'd used him.

Chapter Fifty-two
I Don't Want to Go, I Just Want to Be There

Izzy wrote to Jimmy to tell him she was coming to see him. 'It's a long journey. I'll be on the train for days and days, I hope Sam will be all right.' She was going to write that she was longing to see him again, but didn't. Instead she said she was looking forward to meeting his family, and she'd let him know when she'd be arriving as soon as she knew herself.

He replied that everyone was really excited to be meeting her at last. He'd told them all about his lady pilot and her passion for pork chops. 'I'll be at Great Falls when your train comes in.'

It took weeks for Izzy's passport to come. After it arrived, she phoned Julia, who booked her on a flight. 'Next week,' she said. 'I'll pick you up at the station and take you to Heathrow.'

Izzy asked if Charles would come along, too.

'He's gone to Scotland. I think he is rather taken with your friend Elspeth.'

'Really' said Izzy. 'She didn't mention anything about that to me.'

'She must be taken with him, then,' said Julia. 'Women are always secretive about someone they rather fancy, don't you think?'

Izzy said she supposed they were.

That night, Izzy fished out her tortoiseshell pen, sat at the kitchen table and wrote to her mother. 'I am going to America to see Jimmy. Don't worry about me, I'll be fine. I don't know when I'll be back. But I'll write to you and tell you all about it. I was going to ask your forgiveness for what I've done. But, really, I don't think there's anything to be forgiven for. I am not married, and I had a child. But now there is someone in my life I love more than I thought possible.'

She posted her letter the next morning. On her way back to the cottage, she counted the number of times she said hello. Six. She thought it a shame to leave a place filled with so many familiar faces. Soon she'd be a stranger in a strange place. Dread of stepping into the unknown seeped through her.

She was due to leave on Monday morning. On Saturday, she dropped in at the garage and asked Eddie Hicks to pick up her motorbike and sell it. He asked what he should do with the money he might get. 'It isn't worth much.'

'That's not what you said when you sold it to me,' she said.

'True,' said Eddie. 'But I lied.'

'Give it to Mrs Brent. I owe her a lot more than the bike's worth. But that's all I have to give her.'

They were standing in the oil-smeared garage forecourt, chatting, idly watching the two o'clock bus rumble in. Passengers spilled out. Izzy stopped talking, drew her breath, peered at the people milling at the bus stop. 'Sorry,' she said to Eddie, 'got a bit of a shock. I thought I saw my mother.' She looked again at a woman in a neat blue coat, red hat snug on her head. 'Oh God, it *is* my mother.' She took off, thrusting the pram in front of her, running, shouting, 'Mum!'

Joan stopped, turned and waited for Izzy to reach her. They stood a moment, staring at one another. Izzy's mother threw her arms round Izzy. 'Look at you, a mother and off to America.' Izzy disentangled herself, held her mother at arm's length and gazed at her. That face, so familiar, so beloved, had grown old, tired and marked with grief.

But once inside the cottage, she looked round and was her old disapproving self. 'I can't believe you've been living here. It's a hovel.'

'It's snug,' said Izzy. 'I like it.'

'Where am I to sleep?'

'In the bed. I'll take the sofa. Elspeth says it's very comfortable.' She sat on it, and it wheezed and creaked in protest.

Joan was in the armchair, holding her grandson. She'd been holding him since she arrived and it looked like she wasn't going to let him go. Every now and then she leaned over and peered into the kitchen. At last, she could stand it no longer. 'Let me in there, there are dishes to do. Can't sit here looking at them.'

A few seconds later she appeared at the kitchen door. 'Izzy, what is there to eat?'

'Soup,' said Izzy. 'Mostly I eat soup. It's all I can make except for fried eggs.'

'There's no food here.'

Izzy shrugged. She didn't much care about eating these days.

'You're as thin as a pin,' her mother said. 'That's not right. You need feeding up.'

At five o'clock Mrs Brent stopped by. 'Heard you'd come,' she said to Joan. 'Eddie told his wife, who told Jack Harman, the postman, who told my William when he was in at the Duck's Foot, and he told me. Well, I said, that Izzy won't have a bite to eat. She never does. So I brought you a ham and egg pie and a bit of brisket for roasting tomorrow.'

Joan thought about asking how Mrs Brent had come by so much food, but decided against it. There were Mrs Brents in the village where she lived, there were Mrs Brents everywhere.

They spent Sunday packing. Or rather, arguing about packing. Joan thought Izzy should take two cases, one filled with clothes for her, one with clothes for the baby.

Izzy said, 'I'm not lugging two cases and a baby all the way to Montana.' She won.

'You're just like your father, stubborn,' said Joan.

Izzy didn't answer this.

'He thought you did something very wrong,' said Joan.

'I didn't do anything hundreds of other women did.'

Joan said she knew that. 'But surely you could have taken precautions.'

'I did. We did, Jimmy and me. It was just the one time we didn't.'

'One time is all it takes,' said Joan.

'Well,' said Izzy, 'I'm not sorry. I refuse to be sorry. Dad should have been sorry for being so unforgiving.'

'He was,' said Joan. 'I told you that . . .'

'Did he ever talk about me?'

'All the time,' said Joan. 'Right before he died, he was talking about you.' She thought Izzy had broken his heart, but didn't mention it. Too much pain, too much sorrow, too much to regret, she thought.

They caught the eight o'clock bus to Blackpool.

'You don't have to come with me to the airport,' said Izzy. 'You could just head home once we get to London. There is a direct train.'

Joan insisted she was coming to see her daughter off. 'It isn't lucky to go on huge journeys without someone to wave you goodbye. Besides, I don't know when I'll see you again.'

'I'll be back,' said Izzy.

'If not, I'll be out there to visit. I fancy an adventure. I'd love to see America. I've been there often in the movies, I'd like to go for real.'

At Blackpool, they boarded the train for London, took their seats in the carriage. Joan held the baby. 'I don't want to let him go.'

Julia was waiting at the station when they arrived, she ran forwards waving, shouting, 'Yoo-hoo, darling!' Something that embarrassed Izzy. By now she was getting nervous. She was thinking about changing her mind. She was very quiet on the journey to the airport, and was struck dumb on entering the departure tent.

'My,' said Joan, 'isn't this lovely. Like a sultan's tent. Sofas and everything.'

'I phoned ahead and ordered drinks,' said Julia. 'But I didn't know you were coming.' She apologised to Joan.

'Oh, don't mind me.'

'She can have mine,' said Izzy. 'I don't feel like anything.' Her stomach wasn't taking kindly to the idea of the journey ahead. She had butterflies.

'You're nervous,' said Julia.

'Just a little,' Izzy agreed.

'Don't you want to fly to New York? Aren't you excited?'

'No,' said Izzy.

'Oh,' said Joan. 'I'd be excited. Now I see this place, carpets, people milling about, drinks, I want to go on an aeroplane. I never thought it would be so luxurious.' She sipped the sherry that was meant to be Izzy's. 'I don't know why you're so reluctant,' she said to Izzy. 'Anyone would think you didn't want to go.'

'Well,' said Izzy, 'I want to be in Montana, I want to see Jimmy and his family. I just don't want to go there. I am dreading the journey.'

'The journey is everything,' said Julia. 'You should enjoy it. Flight to New York, taxi to Grand Central Station, train to Chicago . . .'

'I don't know what platform the train leaves from,' said Izzy.

'Track three,' Julia told her.

'How will I find it?'

'There will be notices. When they built Grand Central, they knew you'd be passing through one day and thought they'd better put up signs for you. You'll find it.'

When the flight was announced, Julia linked arms with Izzy and led her out. They kissed. Izzy kissed her mother. Then hugged Julia once more. 'Thanks for everything.' She turned, hesitated.

Julia pushed her. 'Go.' She stood with Joan, watching the plane take off, waving till it was out of sight. Then she said, 'Well, time for tea, I think. We'll go to the Savoy. Then we'll see about getting you on a train back to Scotland.'

Joan said she was worried. 'I don't think Izzy has any money. I mean American money.'

'She has five hundred dollars; I went to the exchange for her. I will phone Jimmy and tell him she'll be arriving at Great Falls on Friday.'

'You're very organised,' said Joan.

'I know. It's a gift. I have discovered I have a knack for bossing people about. Tea, then we'll get you on a train to Scotland.'

It would be a long haul home, Joan thought. Miles and miles.

And thinking about Izzy all the way. Oh, Joan thought, my Izzy, my lovely daughter, flying planes, now travelling across to the other side of the world. I should have done things like that. I should have been fearless. I've always been afraid.

All the way home, travelling north for miles and miles, she'd wonder what on earth it was she was afraid of.

Chapter Fifty-three
Nobody There

Izzy had worried that Sam would cry all the way to New York, but no, he looked about, he smiled and he charmed the air hostesses. Later, thirty thousand feet above the Atlantic, he slept. Izzy supposed he must be used to flying, he'd done enough of it when she'd been expecting him. She sank back in her seat and slept herself.

In New York, she discovered the trick of travelling. She followed the crowd. She passed through immigration, stepped out into the New York afternoon and took a cab to the station, all by walking purposefully behind a man who'd been on the same plane she'd been on.

The cab driver carried her case down the huge stairway into the station, showed her where to buy a ticket to Chicago and called her 'ma'am'. She liked that and tipped him five dollars, wondering if it was too much or too little. The man at the ticket desk called also called her 'ma'am' and pointed the way to track three.

Aboard the train, Izzy took a seat by the window. 'So we'll get to see the scenery,' she told Sam.

A middle-aged woman took a seat beside her. 'Going to see my daughter,' she said. 'She just had my first grandchild.' She was enthused about Sam. Smiled at him, touched his fingers. 'How old?'

'Five months,' Izzy told her.

'You're not from New York,' the woman said. 'Is that a Boston accent?'

'No,' said Izzy. 'Scottish.'

The woman froze. 'You're not one of them damn war brides, are you? Only, we're not too keen on them.'

Izzy said, 'No. I'm just here to visit a friend. Someone I met during the war. I'm not a war bride.' She was about to add that she wasn't married, but stopped. After all, she had a child with her; not being married didn't look good.

'There have been protests, you know,' said the woman. 'I'm Ida, by the way. Not long ago a whole boatload of war brides came over and there were protests at the docks. The women had to be locked in their buses to keep them safe. Women over here were angry about these Brits stealing their men.'

Izzy said, 'Well, back in Britain some people were angry about Americans stealing their women.'

Ida said, 'I guess there's always two sides to every argument.'

The train swayed and bumped, rattled. Scenery hurtled past. Ida asked Izzy if she wanted to go to the dining car. 'I hate eating alone.'

Izzy ordered a hamburger. Ida had chicken. She did most of the talking. In fact, apart from when she slept, Ida spoke all the way to Chicago. Izzy was glad about that, it stopped her worrying about catching her train to Great Falls.

In Chicago, Ida led the way to the ticket office, where Izzy paid for a roomette on the train. 'It'll be easier to look after Sam,' she said. 'I won't have to slip off to the loo to feed and change him.'

Ida agreed and showed her to the train. She shook Izzy's hand and told her it had been a pleasure to meet a real Scottish gal, then slipped off into the crowd.

The roomette was to Izzy's taste – small. It had a seat by the window that folded into a bed, a long seat and a table. When Sam slept, she wrote to Elspeth.

I'm on my way. The world flickers past, little stations gone in a whoosh before I can really see them, before I can even read the name on the platform. There are miles and miles of rolling green beyond the window of the train, and mountains. They look blue, snow-capped.

Elspeth, everything is big here. You'd love the sandwiches, they're huge. They have food here that we haven't seen for years. I can't tell you how many cups of coffee I've had. Everyone is friendly. I think it's because the country is so big, they keep talking to one another so they don't get lost. I'll be on this train for two days, and I've just done two days on a train to Chicago. Imagine, two days on a train!

This train is orange and green and the engine is immense, bigger than your house. The dining car is all lit with tables with actual tablecloths on them. It's all shiny at night. The coffee cups rattle as we sway along. The people serving call me 'ma'am', can you imagine? I get called 'ma'am' everywhere I go.

I love the sound of these trains, it's like a sad song, it actually makes you want to travel somewhere. It's mournful. Lying in my little bed, in this roomette, I hear it and I can even feel homesick for somewhere I've never been. No wonder people write songs about it.

All in all, though, I think I will like it here.

At two o'clock on Friday afternoon, Izzy stepped off the train at

Great Falls and looked about. It was cold. She searched the crowd. Jimmy wasn't there. People shoved past her, met up with other people, hugged, kissed, gathered their luggage and disappeared into the world beyond the station. Izzy stood alone.

Soon the platform was empty. The train shoved out of the station, hooting its mournful call. A slow wind curled round her. Izzy sat on a bench, considered the empty platform, hugged her child. Worried and wept.

Chapter Fifty-four
Grand

Three o'clock in the morning, Elspeth woke, sat up in bed, eyes wide open, put her hands on her face and gasped. She'd had a horrible thought. A what-if scenario that had led to more what-ifs and set her mind in a spin. What if Tyler told the authorities that she hadn't gone to Newfoundland, and those authorities – whoever they were, she didn't know – decided that she was still fit to work in the forest, came to get her and dragged her back. 'Oh, my God.'

Charles had planted the seeds of the worry. He'd told her she was very easy to find. 'I just phoned the local post office and asked for your address.'

'And they gave it to you?' Elspeth said.

He nodded.

Charles had turned up two days ago. He'd limped down the garden path, banged on the door and grinned at her when she opened it. 'Surprise,' he'd said. 'Thought I'd drop by and say hello.'

She'd told him he'd come an awfully long way just to drop in and say hello.

'Not a lot to do these days now I've been demobbed. I need to be somewhere quiet where I can review my life and decide what to do next.'

Now, he was sleeping in the spare room. He'd hinted that he'd rather sleep in Elspeth's room, in her bed, but she'd told him not to be rude. 'I don't sleep with men I barely know. In fact, the trouble sleeping with men has got me into, I may never sleep with one again.'

Charles had said he doubted that. 'A woman like you is unlikely to resist her passions.' Still, he'd limped off to the spare room without a backwards glance. All in all, though, Elspeth found him an ideal companion. He could talk about history, the relevance of Darwin's theories, the intricacies of Bach's music and the importance of popular music in times of trouble. He liked jazz and tapped his toes or did a shuffling dance to the catchy tunes that were played on *Music While You Work*. Elspeth liked him. And was pleased to note that he liked her. More than liking she did not want.

Next morning, before Charles was up, Elspeth went to see her solicitor and told him she was putting her house on the market. 'I want you to handle the sale.'

When he asked where she was going, she told him Edinburgh. 'I'll find work there. And I need to start making some money.' Then, she added, 'I don't want you handing out my new address to anybody. I am starting a new life and I don't want to be easily found.'

On the way back to the cottage, she was aware of the stir she was causing. People stared at her, nudged one another as she passed by. There were whisperings – not loud enough for her to make out what was being said, but loud enough for her to know that what was being said wasn't very flattering.

Oh, she could understand it. First, a huge lumbering man carrying a battered suitcase and speaking in a song of an accent had turned up in the village and announced himself to be her husband. Then, he'd disappeared. Now, a second stranger, this time with a plummy accent, had turned up, and he was staying with her. Elspeth wanted to stand in the High Street and shout that Charles was just a friend and furthermore was sleeping in the spare room. What good would that do? Her neighbours and fellow villagers had decided she was a loose woman. She doubted they'd allow their children to step over her threshold for piano lessons. It was time to move on.

When she got home, Elspeth phoned the letting agency her solicitor had recommended and arranged to view a three-bedroomed flat in Edinburgh's New Town. 'Just a step from Princes Street,' she said. 'Just the thing – shops, lights, theatres only minutes away.'

'Do you have to sell this place?' said Charles. 'I rather like it.'

'I'm selling,' Elspeth told him. 'I'm getting out of here, doing a bunk.'

'A bunk? You? Why?'

'I need to disappear before the police come for me.'

He stared at her, baffled. 'What have you done? Robbed a bank?'

'No. I married to get out of the forest. I was expected to go to Newfoundland. But I didn't. If they find out, they might send the police to take me back up there.'

'They?' said Charles. 'Who are they?'

Elspeth didn't know. She imagined some faceless but ruthless authority that dealt harshly with people who jumped off trains and refused to go to Newfoundland. 'I don't know who they are. I'm just getting away from them.'

'There has been a war. Troops are coming home. Thousands

of people are being repatriated. Government departments will be flooded with bits of paper, phones will be ringing, people will be queuing in corridors, do you really think anyone is going to notice one woman who got off a train and didn't sail to Newfoundland?'

'Oh, it's all very well for you to sound reasonable, it's not you who'd be shipped off to the middle of nowhere to chop trees and sleep in a hut. I'm not taking chances. I'm doing a bunk.' Elspeth was adamant.

'To Edinburgh?'

'Yes, to a city. To walk along busy pavements. To be where nobody knows who I am.'

He said he could see the appeal of that.

Next day, he went with her to view the flat. It was in Abercrombie Place, on the ground floor of a large Georgian building. Elspeth fell in love with it before she went in. 'Look at this street, so wide, and look, there are gardens on one side. I could stroll in them, sit reading and I wouldn't have to mow the lawn or weed. It's perfect.'

The landlord, Mr Parker, met them at the door. He sized them both up, glancing from one to the other. He grinned. 'Mr and Mrs Moon. Oh, I'm so glad.' He turned to Elspeth, 'Only, when you phoned, I got the impression you were single. You didn't mention Mr Moon.'

Elspeth opened her mouth to explain. Charles put his arm round her, gripped her shoulder. 'I'm afraid my Elspeth is a very independent-minded young woman.'

There was a huge living room with bay windows. It was partially furnished with a dark-blue velvet sofa in front of the fire and two matching chairs, one by the window, the other beside the sofa. There was one huge bedroom with a four-poster bed and two

smaller ones along with a large kitchen that led out into a courtyard. The ceilings were high – there was light, there was air, there
was room for a piano. Elspeth thought it perfect. She loved this
flat. She wanted this flat.

Mr Parker smiled at Charles. Charles grinned at him. 'I'm not
too happy about letting out to a single woman. They have a
tendency to run off and get married, leaving me without a tenant.
And, you never know these days, I don't want the wrong sort of
person, if you know what I mean.'

Charles said he surely did. 'Can't be too careful,' he said. He
took Elspeth's hand, lifted it to his lips, kissed it. 'Be assured, Mr
Parker, Elspeth is well and truly married.'

Mr Parker beamed. He asked what they did.

'I was in the Royal Artillery. Saw action in Burma. Going to
finish my PhD, then I'll be looking for a teaching post – history.
Elspeth, here, is a musician.'

It was plain that Mr Parker thought them the perfect couple.

'We'll take the flat,' said Charles. 'Elspeth loves it.'

Outside, Elspeth sprinted along the pavement. At the corner,
she stopped and waited for Charles to catch up with her. 'What do
you think you are doing?'

'Getting us a place to live.'

'I'm not going to live with you. I just wanted somewhere to
take my piano. Teach music and reflect on my stupid past. I didn't
factor you into my future life.'

'Well, do some factoring now. Think about it. I'm all for reflect-
ing on your stupid past, by the way. We all should do a bit of that.'

'You told that man we were married,' said Elspeth. 'What if he
finds out we're not? He wouldn't approve of our living in sin.
Besides, I hardly know you. I want to live alone.'

'You wouldn't have got the flat if you hadn't had me, Mr Moon, to vouch for you. I'm going to love being Mr Moon. A new beginning for me. Meet Charles Moon.'

He said she could live alone. Only, he'd be living alone with her. 'In the same flat sort of thing. Or, we could get married.'

'You know I can't. I'm already married. My husband won't divorce me, a punishment for using him. I deserve that, I suppose. I was married for a whole day. God, I'm stupid.'

'No,' he said. 'Not stupid, just impulsive. I like that.' She could play the piano. She had modelled in Chelsea. She'd once seen George Orwell sitting alone in a bar, and she was married, which left her free to not marry him. 'You're perfect.'

He linked arms with her. 'What do you think, Mrs Moon? Are you going to let me do a bunk with you? I think it'll be grand.'

Elspeth thought, Here I go again, another stupid step in my life. But she said, 'Where shall we put the piano?'

Mrs Brent took a second chocolate plum and popped it into her mouth. 'These are good.'

William took one, too. 'They're Izzy's.'

'I know,' said Mrs Brent. 'But Izzy's not here, is she? We might as well have them. Can't let them go to waste.'

'I don't think it right you opened her package.'

'Well, neither do I, really. But what would have happened? The plums would have sat there and gone off.'

'True,' said William. 'Village is quiet these days.'

'I know,' said Mrs Brent. 'They've all gone away. All the pilots. All the Americans. Everybody. I miss them.'

'Yes,' said William. 'It was a grand war.'

'It was,' said Mrs Brent. 'I miss Izzy. She was my favourite. Bit stupid in the end, though. You'd think a girl like that would know to use a you-know?'

'Rubber Johnny?'

'Yes. Lovely baby, though.'

'Lovely baby,' William agreed. 'Wonder what Jacob meant when he said he owed her.'

'Dunno,' said Mrs Brent.

'Do you think they were – you know?'

'Having a bit on the side? Sleeping together? No. Not Izzy, she just had her American.' She took another plum. Slurped at it, brandy running down her chin. 'Grand.'

'Well, what could he owe her?'

'Money,' said Mrs Brent. 'I think she gave him all her money so he could get home to his love. She was soft-hearted.'

'She was that,' said William. 'And here's us eating her plums all the way from Poland.'

'She wouldn't mind. She was grand.'

Chapter Fifty-five
Come in

There was a slice of a moment when Izzy didn't recognise Jimmy. She stared up at him and thought, Who the hell are you?

He smiled and said, 'Izzy.'

She sniffed, wiped her nose and told him he was late. 'I've been sitting here thinking I'd have to find a hotel. I was imagining I was alone in a strange country, knowing nobody and I thought I'd missed you, that you'd gone off without me.'

He wondered why she thought he'd do that.

'I don't know. I was imagining all sorts of things. I didn't reason it out. I thought perhaps you'd been here and I hadn't recognised you.'

'Of course you'd recognise me.'

'I might not.' She waved her hand at his jeans, boots and blue-checked shirt. 'I've never seen you in ordinary clothes. I've only seen you in uniform and in your underpants and naked.'

'When you put it like that, I can see your point.' He took Sam. 'Is this him? My boy?'

'Of course it's him.'

Jimmy took him, held him up. 'He's beautiful. He looks like you.' He pulled Izzy from her bench, kissed her. 'God, it's good to see you.'

He kissed Izzy again, kissed his son. He took Izzy's case and, still carrying his child, led the way out to where his car was parked. 'I got held up. Got stuck behind a truck for miles, couldn't pass. Crawling along at thirty miles per hour, pumping my horn, panicking.'

Outside walking up the street, Izzy said, 'Gosh, that's a big car.'

'A Chevrolet. We got big cars here, we got big roads here. It's a big country.'

'Everything's big,' said Izzy.

He said she'd get used to it.

She sat, Sam on her knee, in the front. He told her they had a ways to go and asked if she wanted a cup of coffee or anything.

She said mostly what she wanted was a bath.

As they bowled along, Izzy said, 'It's shiny here. All that sky.'

'Yeah.' Then, he asked, 'How did Sam take to travelling?'

'He was fine. He looked about and took everything in. I thought he'd cry and cry, but no. He just looked interested. Babies just accept things, I suppose, as long as they're with someone they know.'

'He's a Newman,' said Jimmy. 'We're adaptable.'

'He's a Macleod,' said Izzy. She put her head against the window, and cried, 'I'm tired. I am so tired.'

He reached over, stroked her hair. 'I know. You've come a long way.'

'You were late. You were late and I thought you weren't coming and I was sitting alone and people were looking at me.' She punched him.

'Jesus, Izzy, I told you I got held up. I couldn't help it.' He pulled over, stopped the car. 'Did you punch me? Was that a punch? Listen, if you're going to punch someone in this country, you got to do better than that. That was like a fly landing.' He put his arms round her. He held her, told her she was exhausted and nervous. 'Nothing to worry about. My folks are dying to meet you and Sam. They're so excited. My mother is cooking pork chops.'

Izzy said, 'Actually, I quite like pork chops. But not as much as you think. I only ate so many of them that time because I hadn't had them for ages, they kind of reminded me of home. Also, I was hungry.'

He said he guessed that. 'Only my mother asked what you liked and that's all I could think of.'

He started up the car again.

After another while, Izzy said, 'Do you play much golf here?'

'No, I'm not that much of a golfer. I only wanted to play it when I was in Scotland.'

Izzy said, 'Oh.'

Jimmy turned to Izzy and said, 'We hardly know each other. We spoke about our childhoods and our dreams. Well, my dreams. I don't think you had any plans for after the war.'

'Now you mention it, no.'

'Mostly when we met, we f–' He stopped himself.

'Fucked,' said Izzy. She put her hands over the baby's ears. 'Don't want him to hear that language.'

'Yes, that's what we did. Now we've got to get to know one another. You have got to get to know my family, and I have got to get to know Sam. It'll take time. But I think we'll be fine. I just know we'll be fine.'

Izzy said she hoped so.

'Come to think about it,' he said, 'I've never seen you angry.

We've never had a fight. I've never really seen you cry. I think we should get acquainted, then we'll get married.'

Izzy said that seemed like a decent enough plan. 'And if we don't like one another after we get acquainted, we won't get married.'

He smiled. 'Something like that.' Then, he asked, 'So, how do you like America?'

'I love it. Though sometimes I can't make out what people are saying. I haven't got the hang of the accents.'

He said, 'Snap. I had the same problem in Scotland.'

She said she still had the Mary Queen of Scots teaspoon. He smiled.

'I've got a horse picked out for you,' he told her. 'I'll teach you to ride. Sam will grow up round horses, he'll be riding almost before he can walk.'

'What makes you think that?' said Izzy. 'I might not stay.'

'Izzy, you'll stay. I know how to make you stay. You know you'll stay.' Then knowing how to tempt her, he said, 'We've got a plane. It's a way of covering the ground, seeing for miles when you're looking for stray cattle.'

Izzy said, 'Well, you do have a lot of sky in Montana.'

Later she said, 'I've been trying to work out how America smells. It smells of coffee and food in the streets, petrol and something else. I can't decided what it is.'

'Home smells of coffee and wood burning and usually there's some food on the go.'

'I can smell snow,' said Izzy. 'It's going to snow. Snow smells the same everywhere.'

He guessed it did, asked how it was when she had the baby.

'I had him at Mrs Brent's house. She was there and the

midwife. I swore a lot. But people were mostly kind. They gave me clothes for Sam.'

'My mother has been buying toys and clothes. You should see the stuff. God, she's excited. Her first grandchild. She can't wait to meet him.'

Izzy said that was good. 'Can't say my family were enthused. My mother came round in the end. I think my father did, too. But he never did think much of unmarried mothers. We were sinners who'd given in to our passion.'

'I loved the passion,' he said.

Izzy snorted, a slightly embarrassed laugh. 'My father's dead.'

Jimmy said he knew.

'I never made friends with him after that fight. I never said sorry. He said he'd pray for me and I said, "Don't bother." These were the last words I said to him.'

'I'm sure he would have forgiven you. I'm sure he'd have loved his grandchild.'

'I like to think that, too,' said Izzy. 'Sometimes I try to remember his face. I shut my eyes and try to conjure it up. Mostly I manage. But his eyes, I can't get his eyes. I can't remember what colour they were.'

Jimmy said, 'They were blue.'

It was dark when they arrived. They turned into a long bumpy drive, fenced on either side and after miles drew up at a ranch house. It was a long, two-storeyed building, a veranda outside. All the lights were on. Izzy climbed out of the car, stretched and looked about. She breathed in, let the air slip over her tongue. 'Snow,' she said. 'I was right, snow's coming.'

'Sometimes it comes early,' he said. 'Sometimes the temperature slips to minus thirty overnight. It gets cold. It snows.'

He took her case, lifted Sam from her arms and strode inside. He left the door open, thinking she'd follow. But she hesitated, suddenly shy, overwhelmed, the old reticent Izzy. Alone, in the dark, in a new place and fearful of the new faces she had to meet.

She heard the cries of welcome as Jimmy stepped across the threshold. 'Look who I've brought.'

She saw figures, a man and a woman, dark against the bright light, step up to meet her son, arms stretched. And still she hung back.

Voices. 'Oh, isn't he gorgeous. Oh, my baby. Oh, my boy.'

There was laughter.

And Izzy hung back.

A woman appeared in the doorway, tall, slender, wearing a skirt and a white shirt, she stepped onto the veranda, the house was warm and bright behind her. She smiled, held out her arms and said, 'Izzy, what're you doin' standing out there in the cold? Come in.'

Epilogue
A Very Good War

They talked. And they talked. And they talked. Jimmy said he'd never seen anything like it. 'Well, heard, actually. How can two people have so much to say without repeating themselves?'

But Izzy and Elspeth could. Their conversations rambled through reminiscences, anecdotes, favourite old stories and the five-year catching up they had to do. The pair started at breakfast, carried on till lunch, chatted through supper and, in the evening, sat on the swing on the veranda of the house Izzy and Jimmy had built, looking out across the garden to the world beyond – a huge green landscape, the river, trees, then mountains bluing into more mountains – talking. It had been going on for three weeks.

In the morning, as Izzy clattered in the kitchen, making coffee, pancakes and scrambled eggs, Elspeth said, 'Time was the only thing you could make was porridge.'

'Needs must,' said Izzy. 'People have to eat. Jimmy's mum, Maggie, taught me.'

'You get along with Jimmy's folks?' asked Elspeth.

Izzy nodded. 'Yes. It was easy. That night when I first arrived, Maggie called to me, "Come in," she said. In I went and they were so lovely, so welcoming, I knew everything was going to be fine. I belonged. And so did Sam.'

The school bus arrived to pick up Sam, Jimmy hauled on his jacket, said he had to go. He was doing what he'd said he would do – working at the local hospital and, in his spare time, breeding horses. There were five Appaloosas in the stables behind the house. He kissed Izzy, picked up Amelia, kissed her and told her to be a good girl and left. Amelia, Izzy's newest arrival, four years old, with tumbling curls and huge eyes, was a wilful child and stubborn, like her mother.

'That's it,' Izzy had told Elspeth. 'No more babies.'

'That's what you said after Sam.' Elspeth reminded her.

'Yes, but this time I mean it. Also, after Sam I forgot what giving birth was like. The memory of it melted away. First pain with Amelia, I remembered. And, I'm still remembering. Definitely, no more.'

At first, when Elspeth had said she was finally coming, Izzy had wanted to go to New York to meet her and accompany her on the journey to Montana. But Elspeth had written to say that wasn't necessary. 'I just have to get on a train and sit,' she'd written. 'I want to do that. I want to travel the route you travelled and see it for myself.'

As she went, she wrote long letters to Charles. They spoke about endless unfenced landscapes, mountains, the dining car and how she'd bonded with her fellow travellers. Though she'd hardly spoken to them – 'They have become familiar faces,' she'd said. She'd told him about the long mournful whistle. 'It adds to the allure of this journey. It's romantic, it tells a story, everyone's story. Sometimes when I hear it, I think I could go on travelling forever. I'd just sit here, staring, dreaming, thinking about my past and never arriving anywhere.'

*

This letter had been addressed to Mr Moon. Seeing it on the envelope had made Charles laugh. He read her thoughts on endlessly travelling and thought, That's my Elspeth. Throws herself into whatever she's doing. Right now, she'd be living on Izzy's ranch and imagining herself living the cowboy life, riding the range, sleeping in the bunkhouse, rounding up cattle. She'd come back to him. He knew that. She'd told him she loved him.

'I seem to have fallen in love with you, Charles Moon,' she'd said. 'Despite myself, I don't know what's come over me. I've never had much control over my heart. But love, it's damnable. It stops the flow of logical thought.'

He'd said he didn't know she had logical thoughts.

'From time to time,' she'd told him. 'However, I find that I am thinking of you when I should be thinking of sensible things. I watch the clock, waiting for you to come home. It's awful. But, there you are. I love you.'

He'd told her he loved her back. He thought he'd loved her from the moment he first saw her in that dreadful cottage Izzy had lived in with her baby.

'I hope that loving me won't stop you from stopping me doing stupid impulsive things,' she'd said.

He'd frowned, working this out. Then he told her he loved that she did impulsive things. 'I love your stupid past life. It makes me smile.'

Her letter made him smile. He folded it. Put it in his pocket. Then, taking his walking stick, he left the house and started his long morning walk to the university where he wasn't Charles Moon. He was Charles Marriot, lecturer in history. He smiled all the way. Soon his Elspeth would come back to him. She'd enjoy the journey.

*

'Of course,' Elspeth told Izzy. 'It didn't last long. His being Mr Moon, I mean. Somehow, Charles got the landlord to think he'd made a terrible gaffe and we became Mr and Mrs Marriot. You can't just live together. People call it living in sin. You'd think that would make more people do it. Living in sin sounds so juicy.'

Izzy shrugged. 'When you put it like that, I suppose it does.'

'Anyway,' said Elspeth, 'he thinks life would be easier if I changed my name by deed poll. I'd be Elspeth Marriot.'

Izzy made a face.

'I know,' said Elspeth. 'I wouldn't feel like me any more. Still, we are living as man and wife and if we want to buy the flat, it might make things easier.'

'It might,' Izzy agreed. 'Did you start living as man and wife straight away. Soon as you moved in together?'

Elspeth shook her head. 'I made him wait.'

'How long?' asked Izzy. 'Twenty minutes?'

Elspeth snorted. 'Three weeks. I went to bed one night and he was in it. He said his bed in the spare room was uncomfortable and cold, and, since he was paying more of the rent than me, he thought he should have the best bed. I just got in beside him. And that was that.'

On Elspeth's first night with Izzy, she'd spent some time looking at the wedding photographs. She wished she'd been there.

'Oh, it was a small do. Just me Jimmy and Sam and Jimmy's folks.'

Six weeks after Izzy's arrival, she and Jimmy had married. 'Had to do it,' Izzy said. 'His mum and dad wouldn't let us sleep together. We were sneaking to secret places for a cuddle. Like teenagers, now I think about it.'

As they poured over the photos, Amelia asked where she was. 'Why didn't you take a picture of me?'

'You weren't there,' said Izzy. 'You weren't born yet.'

'Yes, I was,' said Amelia. 'I was there. You just didn't see me. I was there. I sang a song.' She started to sing 'If I'd Known You Were Coming, I'd Have Baked a Cake', her favourite. The rendition was to Elspeth's liking. It was in perfect tune. The girl had a good voice, unlike her mother.

Hearing the song sung loudly and without a trace of embarrassment from the singer, and marvelling at Amelia's firm belief that she was at a gathering she couldn't possibly have attended on account of not being born at the time, Elspeth realised that Amelia was Hamish all over again. Resolute in her beliefs and fearless in letting other people know about them.

'That one's going to be a handful,' Elspeth said. 'She's like her grandfather.'

'Yes . . . I already figured that,' said Izzy.

Afternoons, Izzy worked in her garden. Elspeth sat on the lawn, watching. Amelia helped. She drenched plants with her toy yellow watering can, bossily wagging her finger at them, telling them to be good boys and girls and, 'Grow.'

God, she's *so* like Hamish, Elspeth thought. Looking round, she realised that this small part of Montana was an exact replica of the garden at the manse in Scotland.

'It's my homage to my father,' Izzy said. 'I'm thinking that if he can see it from wherever he is, he'd approve. I'm apologising to him for telling him not to bother praying for me. The time came when I needed a prayer.'

Elspeth said Hamish would love this place and asked after Izzy's mother.

'She's well. I'm going over to see her next year. Dropping in on you and Mr Moon, by the way. Then when I come home, she's coming with me. We're trying to persuade her to live here with us. There's room. I think she might. She's always saying it's time she had an adventure.'

Elspeth smiled.

'My mother says she wants to be like me. She thinks I'm fearless. I make rash decisions and follow them through with no thought of the consequences.'

Elspeth picked a daisy, twirled it between her fingers and asked if Izzy thought that was true.

'Nah,' said Izzy. 'I just don't think about things properly. I decide to do something, do it, then think about it. I just never factor in failure. It doesn't occur to me. So, I bumble through life bumping into things, making mistakes, getting into trouble, following my nose, really. I really ought to consider the consequences more. But if I did, I wouldn't have had Sam, I wouldn't have joined the ATA and I'd never have flown.'

'You'd have missed your true calling,' said Elspeth.

'Yeah,' Izzy agreed.

She still flew. From time to time, Jimmy's father asked her to take up his plane to survey the ranch, looking for stray cattle.

It still brought rapture into Izzy's life, a thrill so wild, so deep, it took her breath away. Brushing shoulder to shoulder with mountains, cruising high over pastures, gullies and the river that wound through Jimmy's father's land. She'd spot strays and radio their position to the hands on the ground. It was heaven. She was always alone in the sky. But not lonely, never that. Lonely was scary. Lonesome, she thought. Yes, lonesome.

Lonesome was the stuff of country songs and old legends. It was romantic.

From time to time, Izzy and Elspeth went for a ride. They took it slowly. Elspeth was keen to help with the horses. She groomed and fed them. She sang to them. Getting into the saddle was something else. She never did get onto the back of the horse she'd worked with in the forest. They ambled along, not chatting all that much, just enjoying the air and the view.

Sometimes, Izzy would burst ahead, spurring the horse into a gallop, yelling back to Elspeth, 'Come on. Give it a go. You'd love a gallop.'

Elspeth always refused. She didn't want to fall off.

Julia had fallen off her horse. She'd fractured her skull. That had been over four years ago. Izzy hadn't been able to go to the funeral, she'd just given birth to Amelia. She imagined Julia thundering towards a jump, whooping with joy, jacket flapping, scarlet silk lining flashing. She always did love a bit of scarlet silk. Julia had died instantly.

'Never seen so many flowers,' Elspeth had told her. 'The church was full of them. The scent was overpowering. I met Claire, too. Charles knows her. Do you keep in touch with her?'

'We send Christmas cards. We write, but not that often.'

'Claire's like an Englishwoman from a Hollywood film,' said Elspeth. 'Perfect skin, friendly and slightly aloof. When she was speaking to me, I got the impression she was thinking about something else.'

'Did you meet her family?' asked Izzy.

Elspeth said she hadn't. 'Charles said her husband took months and months to recover from the POW camp. But now he's something important in the city. Her daughter got a place at Oxford. Her son rebelled. He never settled after they brought him home from South Africa. He dropped out of school and ran away back there. He works on his uncle's farm.'

Izzy almost said that Claire had once slept with Charles, but held her tongue. Instead she said there was a lot more to Claire than met the eye. 'A smouldering passion.'

'Talking of smouldering passion, you should have seen the young men at Julia's funeral. Masses of them.'

'Julia had a few more boyfriends than she told us about,' Izzy said.

'But nobody after Walter. Charles was sure of that.'

Izzy smiled, 'Beaux, darling. That's what Julia would have called them. I can't say that. I could never call a boyfriend my "beau". I guess I'm not posh enough. And, she called everyone "darling". Sometimes, I used to think it was because she forgot people's names. But now, I think she was just friendly. And, she could get away with it.'

'You never saw her after you left for America?'

Izzy shook her head. 'We wrote. I paid her back the money I owed. And, she was right, I didn't need a return ticket. She was lovely.'

'You miss her,' said Elspeth.

'I miss them all – Diane, my father, Julia. I have my quiet time when I think of them – twenty to two. Jimmy told me to do that. Put aside a little bit of every day to remember the people who have gone from you. It helps.'

Elspeth supposed it would.

Their best conversations were in the evening, after they'd eaten supper and the children were in bed. The two would sit outside on the swing, gazing out at the gathering dark, remembering distant moments, speculating about the future. They'd drink coffee and speak aloud their meandering thoughts.

'Now I think about Jimmy and me, we did it all the wrong way round,' said Izzy. 'People are supposed to meet, fall in love, find somewhere to live, get married, do it, you know, in bed, then have children.'

'That's the myth of love stories and songs,' said Elspeth.

'But I met Jimmy, slept with him, had a baby, married him, built a house with him, then we fell in love and had another baby. It's all jumbled up.'

Elspeth said that the war jumbled up a lot of peoples' lives. 'Look at me. I met Charles, moved in with Charles, shared a bed with him, then fell for him. And for a while, he took my name. In the scheme of things, I'm meant to take his.'

Izzy agreed.

'It was the war,' said Elspeth. 'It stopped us in our tracks. Took us places we never imagined we'd be, introduced us to people we'd never normally have met. If Hitler hadn't invaded Poland, I'd never have married Tyler. I'd never have met Lorna. I'd know nothing about trees. The things I saw in that forest. It'd take years to tell you it all. I was hungry for four years. I've done things I'm ashamed of.'

'Everybody's done things they're ashamed of,' said Izzy.

'Not all that many married to get out of a forest, and ditched their husband after one day. I still can't go past York on the train without feeling awful. Tyler's out there somewhere trudging through a dense wood, cursing me.'

'Don't be silly,' said Izzy. 'He'll have moved on. He'll be happy. It's his nature. And if he is in some dense wood, he won't be trudging. He'll be striding. He'll be where he loves to be in the country he longed to go back to.'

'Well, thanks for that, I feel a little less guilty.'

Izzy said, 'Don't talk to me about guilt.'

Elspeth looked at her, eyebrows raised, shocked. 'What have you got to be guilty about?'

'Everything,' said Izzy. 'It was a war, Elspeth, a bloody war. Men trudged through France and Belgium. People died, thousands and thousands of them. People went missing. People lost limbs. What did I do? I saw a woman burned to death and that was awful. I lost people I knew. But I made a lot of new friends. I met my husband. I had a baby. I flew. I loved it. I lived for it. It was a thrill. I saw marvellous things from where I was in the sky.'

'What's to be guilty about?'

Izzy sighed. 'All in all, in spite of everything, I had a very good war.'